Catherine

Bestselling Author of *Shadower* and

Shadow
Crossing

LOVE
SPELL

$5.99 US
$7.99 CAN
£5.99 UK
$14.95 AUS

A BURNING QUESTION

"Is that why you asked me to kiss you yesterday? To see what it's like without actually having personal contact with a man?"

He had cut to the heart of the matter with unerring accuracy. She realized how ridiculous she must look to him. A woman haunted by demons from her past, coming on to an android to appease her sordid curiosity. "Pretty pathetic, isn't it?"

"No, Celie." He stepped closer. "It's not pathetic at all."

She was acutely aware of his body almost touching hers, of the compassion warming his eyes to a molten gold. "Your actions are understandable," he said, his deep voice resonating through her, soothing and stimulating at the same time. "I'm sorry you've had bad experiences with men. But I'm not the one to chase your ghosts away. I'm . . ." He paused, and she found her attention riveted to his sensuous mouth. What would that mouth feel like, pressed against her lips? Against her body?

Other *Love Spell* books by Catherine Spangler:

SHAMARA
SHADOWER
SHIELDER

Shadow Crossing

Catherine Spangler

LOVE SPELL NEW YORK CITY

LOVE SPELL®

April 2003

Published by

Dorchester Publishing Co., Inc.
276 Fifth Avenue
New York, NY 10001

ISBN 0-505-52524-0

Printed in the United States of America.

Visit us on the web at www.dorchesterpub.com.

To David Gray, for sharing his vast stores of technical knowledge, creativity, and ideas, as well as his friendship and encouragement.

To Rosemarie (Rose) Brungard and Giselle McKenzie (aka Byrony), good friends and readers extraordinaire, for helping me to whip Celie into shape and demanding I save the Tobal.

And to my coworkers Angelica Blocker, Robyn Delozier, and Beth Gonzales, for reading my stories as I create them and listening to my ideas with unlimited patience.

Thank you all.

ACKNOWLEDGMENTS

Special thanks to Susan Grant for generously sharing her knowledge on landing aircraft. Any errors are my own.

Thanks to my professional mentors: Roberta Brown for her hard work in the agenting arena and for her friendship; and editor Chris Keeslar for believing in me and taking a stand on my behalf.

As always, thanks to my support network, the Musketeers (Jennifer, Linda, and Vickie), and to my wonderful husband, James.

Shadow Crossing

Chapter One

She was outnumbered, two to one. The flashing lights on her console warned that the encroaching ships had activated their weapons banks. She welcomed the familiar adrenaline rush as she would an old friend, an intoxicating drug she'd come to crave. It honed her concentration and sharpened her reflexes.

She always expected trouble when she traversed Shadow Crossing. This was the deadliest sector in the quadrant, a desolate stretch of space frequented by smugglers, pirates, bounty hunters, and Controller agents, and not a place to be stopped by Anteks—especially since she was carrying illegal goods. Capture meant an automatic death sentence, which was why she refused their orders to surrender.

Better to fight and possibly die than be taken to a Controller prison. Her ship was lighter and faster than their heavily armored craft. And her will to survive was strong.

The alarm clanged: a laser discharge. She nosed her ship at a perpendicular angle to the Antek craft, and at the last possible moment pulled back the throttle to hurtle out of danger. The laser flashed harmlessly past through space. Celie knew what to expect next. There it was: the powering of a torpedo. Anteks were entirely too predictable.

She primed her laser banks, waiting for the missile to be discharged. Bringing her ship around, she locked her laser on the torpedo rocketing toward her and exploded it into debris. She let out a victory whoop and prepared to launch her counterattack. There was no doubt who would win this skirmish, and it wouldn't be the brutish Anteks. . . .

Celie Cameron shook herself out of her daydream. That memory was from another life in another time and place. With a sigh, she executed a textfile landing on the pad, shut down her hoverlifts, and cut the engines. She unhooked her harness and swung around. Another cycle, another delivery. She had performed hundreds such over the past six seasons—some of them illegal and highly dangerous, others very legal and as bland as kerani milk.

Unfortunately, the deliveries of the past two seasons fell in the latter group: uneventful, dull. She'd grown up under the terrible, destructive reign of the Controllers. Back then she'd smuggled contraband all over the quadrant, surviving solely by her wits and bravado. Now she found existence in this new, relatively unknown quadrant of the Verante constellation almost too benign. It was downright boring, as a matter of fact.

She knew she should be grateful to live in a universe where myriad planets and cultures were united under interstellar laws that afforded justice and a peaceful existence to all its inhabitants. In this quadrant, every being was treated with fairness and equality. She'd seen

2

no evidence of any sort of caste system, an amazing accomplishment that had been engineered by the Interstellar Council, a massive contingent composed of representatives from every planet in the quadrant and headed by a powerful High Council. Their achievement was even more impressive when considering that this quadrant was far vaster and more heavily populated than either Celie or the Shielders had initially realized.

She should be glad to be free of the evil veil of terror perpetuated by the Controllers and their Antek minions in the other quadrant, from which the majority of the Shielder people had fled two seasons ago, along with a small group of non-Shielders, including Celie.

But . . . there were no longer any challenges. There was no longer the thrill of evading Antek forces, or flying an illegal shipment onto a planet under the cover of darkness and jammed transmission frequencies. No rush of adrenaline when her ship was stopped and searched, when she faced possible discovery and imprisonment. Celie tried to tell herself it was a good thing she no longer faced such dangers. Yet the truth was that she was bored. Totally, utterly bored.

She pushed to her feet. Best to get the shipment unloaded, although she couldn't drum up any sense of urgency. She'd complete this delivery only to go on to the next one, and the next, each running into the other in an endless flow of unmemorable cycles. As she had numerous times before, she cursed her restless spirit, cursed the inner drive that sent her traveling through the stars time and again in search of adventure—in search of something more.

She pulled on her meroni-skin gloves, then checked the charge on two laser guns and strapped them to her utility belt, a holdover habit from the past. She'd never once needed weapons since she migrated to this new life. Standard laser and pulse weapons were legal, but

3

with the virtual lack of serious criminal elements or activities, weapons were rarely needed or employed by interstellar security forces. But those old habits died hard for Celie, and she continued to carry her weapons.

Striding to the hatch, she wondered idly what the Joba settlement was like. She hadn't checked her reference files for information on Joba, or its host planet, Mangon, as she normally did. In the past two seasons, she'd found nothing remarkable or surprising about any of the settlements she visited. Most of them were relatively small and scattered throughout the twelve sectors of the immense quadrant, although there were a few very heavily populated planets such as the giant Jartan.

When she stepped outside, though, she realized instantly that something was very different here. The landing bay was unusually dim, illuminated only by solar torches affixed along the walls. No bright halogen lights glared overhead, and the few ships scattered through the bay cast eerie shadows. Nor was the bay well ventilated; noxious exhaust fumes choked Celie's lungs, sending her into a coughing fit.

Great.

Cupping her hand over her mouth and nose, she hurried toward the exit, almost tripping over the crumbling, uneven surface—most definitely not the standard granite mined on Roi. Stumbling through, she inhaled the night air and almost gagged. An awful stench, an apparent combination of raw sewage, rotting food, and Spirit knew what else, assailed her. She hadn't smelled anything so foul since a brief incarceration in a Controller prison eight seasons back. What *was* this place?

Baffled, she looked for a viewboard to direct her to the commerce center. She saw nothing but a winding pathway, illuminated only by the twin moons above.

Stranger and stranger. Everyplace she'd visited since relocating had sported well-lit pathways, laid out in an

4

orderly fashion, with ample viewboards to direct visitors. The Interstellar Council provided specific guide-
lines on the development of settlements in the quadrant.

Unsnapping an emergency flare from her belt, Celie
flipped it on and started up a dim pathway flanked by
scrawny trees. She saw no one else, although the odious
fumes remained strong. A shuffling noise from behind
had her whirling, automatically reaching for her weapons. But there was nothing there, only the murky shadows cast by the overgrown foliage along the path.

Blowing out her breath, Celie shook away her unusual edginess and continued on. She walked about half
a kilometer before she saw any buildings. They loomed
alongside the path, most of them boarded up, a few with
faint rays of light emanating from within. An ominous
silence, broken only by the squeaking of krats, enhanced the bizarreness.

With a jolt, she realized this place reminded her of
Calt; a hellhole planet in the old quadrant. The potential
challenge of navigating this pit sent adrenaline sizzling
through her. Placing a hand on her weapon, she strode
on. The path widened into a main thoroughfare with
more buildings, these unboarded. She heard voices
now, saw indistinct beings lurking in the shadows
against the walls. She knew how places like this oper-
ated. If she could find the main bar, she'd be able to get
information on the whereabouts of her contact to make
her delivery.

Realizing it was foolhardy to draw attention to herself
in this questionable environment, she snapped off her
light but kept it in her left hand. She continued along
the thoroughfare, keenly aware of the forms in the shadows and their guttural mutterings. Light drifted from a
building ahead on her right, and she heard loud voices
and raucous laughter. That would be the place to start.

As she crossed a side alley, intent on her destination,

a startling cry commandeered her attention. A baby? Here, in this Spiritless place? Surely not.

The pitiful, mewling cry came again, from the dark alley. Celie whirled, snapping on her light.

The glaring circle caught three forms huddled inside the alleyway: a woman, with two small children burrowing against her. She clutched a baby in her arms, her hand over its mouth to muffle its sobs. All were filthy, dressed in tattered rags. Their eyes were huge with fear; they looked like helpless animals trapped in a snare.

Shock dulling her thoughts, Celie took a step toward them. "What are—"

"Hey there, pretty thing. Here to have some fun?" A rough hand grasped her arm, jerking her around. She faced a man with tangled, greasy hair and rotten teeth who reeked of liquor.

"I can be lots of fun," he leered, groping at her breast.

"I'll just bet," Celie muttered with a chop to his arm.

He yelped, falling back. She slammed her knee into his groin. Squealing like a baby lanrax, he doubled over. She landed a high kick on the side of his head. He crumpled like a crashing starship.

"I can be lots of fun, too," she assured the moaning man. Whirling back toward the alley, she scooped up the flare she'd dropped. The alley was empty. Scurrying sounds drew her attention, and she looked around to see the ragged figures darting down a path leading away from the landing bay.

"Wait!" she called. "Let me help you."

But they vanished into the darkness like vapor. Troubled, Celie turned back toward the main building. Something was terribly wrong here. In all her travels in this quadrant, she'd never seen any poverty, nor had she come across any rundown settlements. The Council's dictates contained provisions to ensure no one

6

went hungry, and that the various colonies were laid out with both practicality and aesthetic beauty.

She kept her hand on her weapon and a wary lookout as she approached what appeared to be the central building in the colony. Hearing another scuffling noise behind her, this time she palmed a laser in one hand and steadied the flare in the other before she spun. A figure shrouded in a dark cape and hood stood ten meters back, frozen in the flare's light.

"Halt right there," Celie ordered, "unless you want to be incinerated."

The figure extended its arms sideways in a gesture of surrender. "Don't fire, Celie. It's me."

The familiar voice sent shock barreling through her. "Raven?" Celie angled her flare toward the hood, but she couldn't see past the shadows cast by the fabric. "Show yourself."

Delicate hands raised to lower the hood. Ebony hair tumbled free, cascading around an oval face dominated by huge dark eyes. Raven—Chase and Nessa McKnight's oldest child—stared at her.

"What the blazing—" Celie caught herself before she could mutter something too indecent for an innocent to hear. She slid her laser gun back into its holster, wondering how many more nasty surprises she would encounter this cycle. "What on Shamara are you doing here?"

Raven's chin lifted as Celie approached. "I want to help you make deliveries."

"What?" Celie halted, staring down at Raven. She was a lot taller than the diminutive girl. Yet something about Raven's defiant stance, the challenge in her caroba eyes, reminded Celie of herself six or seven seasons back, when she'd had a major I-can-take-care-of-myself attitude and the burning desire to strike out on her own and prove herself.

"I want to travel with you," Raven declared. "I'm tired of living on Shamara. It's boring. Nothing exciting ever happens any more. I'm nineteen now and—"

"You're nineteen?" Celie couldn't believe it. She remembered quite clearly when she'd first met Raven. A shy, battered young girl who had been sold into slavery after her Shielder family was brutally murdered by Anteks, Raven had been rescued and later adopted by Nessa and Chase. She'd been so small, so vulnerable, only twelve seasons of age. Now she was nineteen?

"I turned nineteen a full lunar cycle ago," Raven declared smugly. "I decided it was time to see some of the universe. So I hid on your ship and here I am."

Celie mentally kicked herself. She'd grown too soft. She should have checked every part of her ship before she left port—especially after Eirene had done this exact thing. Of course, Celie could relate to Raven's restlessness—but she was six seasons older than Raven physically, and light years ahead in experience in the real universe! She sighed. "Did it occur to you to ask me if you could come along?"

Raven's chin notched higher. "Would you have let me?"

"Maybe." Celie glanced around the littered path. "But then I didn't know a place like this existed in the quadrant. I don't like being here, and I certainly don't think you should be. Do your parents know where you are?"

Raven tossed her hair back, rebellion in every inch of her posture. "I'm an adult now. I don't need their permission to leave Shamara."

Celie resisted the urge to grab the girl's slender arms and shake some sense into her. How could she pass judgment when she was looking at herself a few short seasons ago?

"Common courtesy has nothing to do with whether or not you're an adult, Raven. Your parents deserve to

8

know where you are, so they won't be sick with worry."

Guilt flashed through the girl's eyes. "I left them a holocording," she admitted. "I didn't want them to worry. But I also didn't want to argue with them. They're too protective, treat me like I'm still a child. I'm not. I can take care of myself."

Celie couldn't argue either way. She knew all Shielders still went through basic combat training, learned how to handle weapons. There had never been any real need for such defenses in the new quadrant, but they never forgot how the Controllers had nearly destroyed them. Yet nothing prepared a person like real-life experience, and Raven had been pretty sheltered since Nessa rescued her from slavery six seasons ago. Celie supposed none of these considerations made any difference, anyway, because right now Raven was on Joba.

"All right," she conceded. "You're here, and that's that. As soon as I get this delivery made we'll take off, you can contact your parents, and we'll decide what to do from there."

"As soon as *we* get this delivery made," Raven corrected.

Celie thought of the lowlife who'd just tried to molest her, of the ragged family in the alley. "I don't know if that's such a good idea. As I said, Joba isn't like the rest of the quadrant. I don't think it's safe. You'd be better off waiting on the ship."

"You can't make me go back," Raven said, stepping around her. "Besides, it's farther to the landing bay than it is to the settlement. It makes more sense for me to come ahead with the delivery." She made for the building Celie supposed was the settlement's tavern.

Celie's mouth fell open in shock, but she quickly recovered. Snapping her mouth closed, she strode after Raven. "Whoa." She grabbed the girl's arm and spun her around. "You may think you're an adult and don't

9

have to listen to me, but I'm the one with experience here. I'm responsible for you, and I happen to take my responsibilities very seriously. Maybe I can't make you obey me, but I can stun you and take you back to Shamara faster than light speed. I suggest you work with me here."

"Fine." Raven rolled her eyes. "Strong-arm me. Threaten me. I'll let you make the decisions if you're going to be *that* way about it."

Celie clenched her fists. "Now, listen—"

Raven held up a hand. "You're right, of course. I'll do whatever you say."

Celie wasn't sure she believed that. She blew out her breath, counted to ten. "You have to admit I have more experience in this business. And I do have your welfare at heart."

"Just don't treat me like a child! I'm not. I'm as old as many Shielders were when they had to fight the Controllers."

And most of those young Shielders had died, blown to bits by ruthless agents, never getting the chance to experience life. But this wasn't a battleground, Celie told herself, and Raven only wanted to stretch her wings. Joba might have some unsavory elements, but the buildings *were* much closer than the landing bay, and it might just be simpler to complete the deal and then get the Hades out of here. At least she'd have Raven in sight the entire time.

"All right," she conceded. "And I'll try to treat you as an adult, but please give me the benefit of my experience. Stay close and follow my lead. Do you know how to use a laser gun?"

Raven presented an angelic smile. "Of course. I've got one right here." She opened her robe, revealing a utility belt with a very sizable weapon.

"But do you know how to use it?"

10

"Yes," Raven said with exaggerated patience. "Don't worry so much, Celie. I can take care of myself."

Little Raven packing a weapon the size of a small fusion cannon, along with an I-know-everything attitude. Great. Celie turned back up the path, willing this cycle over. She was ready for a hot shower, some wine, and to work on her latest painting. Somehow she suspected it might be a while before that happened.

Raven moved alongside her. "This place is creepy. The landing bay was awful, and the smell. Ugh." She glanced toward the figures huddled against the darkened structures. "Those guys look . . . scary."

"If they make a move, shoot first and ask questions later," Celie advised. "You're right. Something is very wrong here. I saw a pitiful family in an alley a short while ago. They looked like they hadn't had enough to eat in days."

Raven stopped, surprised. "That can't be right. I thought the Council made sure everyone has food."

Celie took her arm, urged her on. "What we hear is not always the truth, sweetness. This place shows that."

"But why would Joba be any different from the other settlements in the quadrant?"

"I don't know." Celie slowed as they reached their destination. "I suggest you put your hood back up. Stay close to me and keep a low profile." She saw the rebelliousness flare in Raven's eyes and moved to stave it off. "Please. Do this for me."

"All right." Grudgingly, Raven raised her hood and drew her robe closed over her weapon.

Celie had been right; the large central building indeed housed a bar, dreary and rank-smelling. Hazy lighting and narcotic-ridden smoke created a nightmarish ambiance. "Try not to breathe in too deeply," Celie said as they entered. It was eerily similar to Giza's, the bar on

11

Calt in the old quadrant. It appeared lowlifes were the same everywhere in the universe.

The bartender, however, was a different story. Celie's memories of Giza's had her halfway expecting another Thorne, a small gnomelike man with an oversized head. Instead, she saw a bulky, furry beast with a snout and two tusks. Its bulging eyes settled on her; its snout tipped upward as if scenting first her, then Raven. Although it bore a slight similarity to an Antek, Celie had never seen a creature exactly like this. She couldn't help but stare.

It snarled a string of sounds, definitely not the universal language spoken by virtually all inhabitants of the quadrant. Fortunately, the neural translator implanted in Celie's ear was up to the task of deciphering the guttural speech.

"What's it saying?" Raven whispered, sidling closer.

" 'Either buy a drink or get out,' " Celie whispered back. She made direct eye contact and raised her voice. "I'm looking for Max. Is he here?"

More growling. "State your business."

"My business is with Max, not you."

"All here is my business."

A standard power-play for a hellhole like this. Celie gritted her teeth. "All right, then. I have a delivery for Max. Where is he?"

The creature drew back its lips, giving her a show of teeth. "I don't know a Max."

She drew a gold coin from the pouch on her belt and slapped it on the counter. "Does that help your memory?"

A low growl was the reply.

Raven turned her face close to Celie's ear. "Want me to threaten it with my laser?" she asked hopefully.

"Absolutely not. Let me handle this." Celie pulled another coin from her pouch and added it to the first.

12

Six coins and a lot of frustration later, she and Raven followed the bartender down a narrow, dingy hallway that opened off the rear of the bar, both coughing from the smoke. Celie drew her weapon, trying to watch both behind and ahead of them. The bartender stopped before a panel, which slid open. Celie tried unsuccessfully to peer around the creature's massive hairy form, determined to know what she and Raven were walking into.

"What is it, Yarsef?" came a man's voice.

"The person is here to deliver the shipment."

"It's about time. Show him in."

Yarsef stepped to the side. He snuffled both Celie and Raven, who squeezed past into the chamber, trying their best not to come in contact with him. Celie kept Raven behind her. A man sat behind a scarred table, his booted feet crossed and resting on its surface. He lowered the scanner he held, his impassive gaze moving to Celie.

His eyes widened, fixing on her face. The blazing intensity and unusual color of those eyes stole her breath away. She'd never seen anything quite like them. They were golden, but a far different hue than the deep color of her sister Moriah's eyes. These were paler, the color of a muted sun, of the sands of Calt. They were striking, powerful, like the unblinking gaze of the huge birds of prey common on planets with forests.

His boots thudded to the floor, and he rose in a single, graceful movement. "You're a woman." He glanced at Raven. "Both of you."

He strode around the table and halted before Celie. He was tall, almost a head taller than her own impressive height, and solidly built, with broad shoulders and a muscular body. She noted the luxurious mane of hair that flowed over his shoulders. It was dark brown, streaked with lighter shades, as if bleached by the sun.

13

Some of the strands were golden, like his eyes.

"You're female," he repeated, his tone implying he found the fact incredible.

She shook off her odd reaction to him. His reaction sparked her ire. Would she be forever proving herself in a male-dominated occupation? "Very astute of you to notice," she retorted. "I'm Captain Celie Cameron, and you must be—"

She froze, surprise spearing through her as he held out his hand. Silver triton banded his arm, from his wrist to about ten centimeters along his forearm. A small control panel was inset in the band, with blinking indicators.

"You're an . . ." She stammered, then drew a deep breath. What in Hades was wrong with her?

"An android," he finished for her. Amusement flashed in his golden eyes. "Am I your first?"

"An android," Raven breathed in awe. "Wow."

Celie ignored what sounded to her like a sexual innuendo, as well as the android's outstretched hand. "I take it you're Max?"

"No. *I* am Max," came a masculine voice from the left corner of the room.

She turned as another figure stepped forward, her fingers tensing around her weapon. She hadn't even seen him. She'd been so engrossed with the android, she hadn't taken the time to scan the chamber—another alarming sign that she was losing her edge. Such laxness could be deadly in the wrong situation. Especially when at least one of the beings she was dealing with was an android, and thus not easily stopped.

More surprise skittered through her when she realized Max looked so similar to the android that they could almost pass for clones—almost, but not quite. Max was the same height and build, with gold eyes and brown hair, but his eyes were emotionless, cold. They

14

didn't radiate the intensity of the android's, didn't have the same odd effect on her. And his facial features appeared slightly different, harder somehow. Even so, the similarities between the two were amazing, especially considering she didn't see any triton control panels on Max's body to indicate he was another replicant.

She lowered her weapon but kept it activated, unwilling to holster it yet or let her guard down in any way. "Can I assume *you're* not an android?" she asked.

Max smiled, revealing even white teeth. "Only one android here," he confirmed. He gestured toward the golden-eyed figure. "That is Rurick, my pilot. I think you will find him a technological wonder."

No doubt that he was, but Celie's only concern was making her delivery and getting Raven and herself safely off this planet. "I'm not here to discuss technology," she said tersely, "so let's get down to business. Credits first, if you don't mind."

"As you wish." Max unsnapped a compact currency unit from his belt and activated it.

Rurick stepped closer, drawing Celie's attention. She could feel warmth radiating from his body, an odd sensation when one considered he was artificial and shouldn't have body heat. But she'd never seen an android in the flesh before—so to speak—and now could only assume their electronic systems generated a certain amount of residual warmth.

"May I?" he asked, reaching past her and taking the unit from Max. His voice was deep and resonant, laced with calm assurance. "By the way, you don't need that weapon here."

"After seeing Joba and meeting some of its inhabitants, I'm not so sure about that."

"I can't fault your logic. I merely meant to offer reassurance that you're safe with us." He entered a lengthy code and a credit amount, then extended the unit to Celie. "That is the amount you were expecting?"

Surprised that Max would allow his pilot—and an android at that—access to his personal credit codes, she took the device. Raven pressed against her other side.

"Stars!" she exclaimed. "That's a lot."

Celie shot her an exasperated look. "We don't need to discuss it here." She nodded at Max, determined to deal with him rather than his android. "That's the correct amount, and the availability code is valid. We'll transfer after you inspect the supplies." She held out the compact to Max.

"Fair enough." Rurick intercepted the unit and snapped it onto his own belt. He blandly met Celie's surprised stare. "Max prefers for me to handle all his financial transactions. I have a better memory capacity."

She couldn't get over his eyes—like the golden hues of an Elysian sunset. They'd be an interesting challenge to paint. She shook her head, annoyed with herself. She needed to deal with the transaction at hand. "Doesn't matter to me who handles the credits. That's your business. I'll take you to my ship now. I presume your craft is in the terminal's main landing bay?"

"There's only one bay on Joba, but whether or not it qualifies as an interstellar terminal is highly debatable," Rurick replied. He gestured toward the entry. "Shall we?"

Taking Raven's arm, Celie started out of the chamber, but Max cut in front of her. "Let me go first," he said, then led the way.

Celie followed with Raven in tow, acutely aware of Rurick behind them. She almost gagged when they stepped back into the smoke-filled main room, and wondered how much opiate she and Raven would have in their bloodstreams before they got clear.

Max and Rurick moved them through and quickly outside. Although still foul with the stench of waste and unwashed bodies, the night air was significantly better.

They headed for the landing area at a brisk pace, and the men immediately took up flank positions, Max on the right by Raven and Rurick on the other side of Celie. They also drew blasters from their belts and activated them. Celie knew her protective male friends would have done the same thing, but she was surprised that these virtual strangers took such an action, and did so with no discussion. She didn't bother to tell them she could take care of herself and Raven because she wasn't foolish enough to turn down any protection—especially in such an unsettling place as this.

On the narrow pathway back they could only go two at a time, so Max took Raven's arm and held her as Celie and Rurick went first. Celie didn't protest his action, having decided these men weren't a threat. She had thoroughly checked out Maximilian Rior's references before taking the delivery contract, and they'd been solid enough. The thing that baffled her was why he'd pick a place like Joba for a delivery of food and medicine—unless he was going to black market it here.

Exhaust fumes assailed them as they entered the landing bay, sending Raven into wracking coughs. "Blazing hells," Celie muttered. "Let's hurry up and get her on my ship. Over there."

"Colorful language," Rurick commented as they strode toward Celie's craft. "Where did you learn that expression?"

"Another world, a long while ago." Odd, but the skirmishes with the Controllers, and life in the other quadrant, did seem a lifetime away. Celie looked back and saw Max had swung Raven into his arms and was carrying her without a hitch in his stride. Still coughing, the girl turned her face against his chest.

Celie was relieved when they reached her ship. She decoded and opened the hatch, and they all hustled

17

aboard. "Put her there." Celie indicated the co-pilot's chair in the cockpit, then pressed a button beneath the console. "We have several oxygen lines in here."

"I'm all right," Raven gasped, waving away the mask that had dropped from the console. "Really." She drew a deep breath, coughed a little. "It was that bad air in the bar and then in the bay." She took another breath, then shot a blinding smile at Max. "Max just picked me up and carried me. He's so strong."

Celie didn't like the way Raven was looking at Max. It sparked a sudden memory flash of when she herself was sixteen and enamored with the handsome Shielder commander Jarek san Ranul. It had been the childish crush of a teenager. Raven, at nineteen, seemed highly susceptible to the same emotions. No matter—as soon as they transferred their cargo, Max and Rurick would be gone from their lives forever.

"I'll move our ship closer to yours," Rurick said. "We have filtration masks we can use while we make the transfer."

"Stay here and catch your breath," Celie told Raven. "Use the oxygen if you need it. Max, why don't you come with me and inspect the inventory while Rurick moves the ship?"

Very quickly, Rurick maneuvered Max's ship close to Celie's. The three began transferring the crates of goods, using two air carts.

Max's was an incredible craft, Celie thought, admiring its sleek lines. Almost twice as large as her own, it had two levels, with powerful thrusters and mechanical workings, as well as four external loading bays, on the lower level. She estimated the craft could carry at least ten crew members. It was painted a deep royal purple, with some sort of fancy crest in gold on each side— wonderfully rich colors, overall, an extremely nice ship.

They had almost finished the transfer when the beam

18

of a laser rifle exploded a crate less than a meter from Max. Near simultaneously, a chunk exploded out of the air cart between Rurick and Celie. Stunned, Celie leaped back as another burst took out the top half of the cart.

Someone was firing at them. They were under attack!

the

Chapter Two

Celie's combat reactions might be rusty, but that didn't appear the case with Max. He leaped the two meters separating him from Rurick and Celie, knocking them behind the damaged air cart. Just as quickly, he had his blaster out and was returning fire. Celie scrambled to a crouch, drawing her laser. She ducked as another blast hit.

"What is going on?" she asked incredulously, scanning the dim bay for signs of their assailants. "Who's firing at us?"

"I do not know," Max said grimly. "But I estimate there are at least four shooters."

Celie didn't have time to wonder how he could know that as another barrage came at them. The trio returned fire, at the same time edging the damaged air cart closer to Max's ship. The noise was deafening, and metal shards flew around them.

At last they were able to slip behind the crates stacked

between the cart and Max's ship, which afforded somewhat better protection. The attack seemed to intensify, forcing the three of them to return rapid bursts to hopefully prevent their assailants from getting any closer.

Celie didn't have time to wonder at the oddness of an all-out assault in this quadrant, where there was little crime and no warfare; it took all her concentration to duck flying debris and return fire. She forgot about everything, until a peripheral movement caught her attention and she looked around. Raven was standing just outside the hatch of her ship, eyes huge as she took in the battle.

Celie's heart leaped in her chest and panic clawed at her. "Raven!" she screamed, whirling toward the girl. She lunged forward, but a strong arm snagged her from behind, slipping around her waist and dragging her back behind the crates. She struggled fiercely, adrenaline giving her extra strength.

Rurick hauled her closer, his arms pinning her despite her flailing and kicking. "Stop!" he ordered. "You can't go charging into weapon-fire."

"Let me go! Raven—"

"Let Max get her. He's faster and trained for combat. Look."

She watched as, with a burst of seemingly superhuman speed, Max raced to Raven and dragged her behind the sled base of Celie's ship. An explosion followed them, tearing off hunks of alloy. Her pounding heart felt like it would burst. Raven!

"We have to draw their fire," Rurick said, loosening his hold. "Think, Captain Cameron. Calm yourself and *think*. We must distract them and give Max a chance to get Raven to safety."

He was right. If Celie hadn't let herself get so soft the past two seasons, she'd have considered that course of action herself. "All right," she conceded. "You can let go of me."

He gave her a little shake. "You'll stay right here?"

"Yes," she said through gritted teeth. "I know the drill."

"Good." He moved her to the side, then raised his blaster and resumed firing at their attackers.

Celie joined in, discharging her laser in the same direction. Immediately, the hostile fire zinged around them even more fiercely, exploding one crate and setting another on fire. They hastily ducked down. Celie felt embers showering her and smelled singed hair.

She ignored the painful burns as the cinders scorched holes in her uniform and seared her skin. Her sole focus was providing cover for Max and Raven. She glanced over to see the pair edging toward the nose of her ship, then crouching in readiness for a run to Max's.

"Hit them with another burst," Rurick ordered. He and Celie let loose their combined firepower. Then Celie saw something that froze her breath: two hooded assailants slipping through the murky haze, positioning themselves at the far end of her spacecraft.

"Look!" she cried, ramming her right elbow against Rurick's arm. She gestured toward her ship's aft.

"Stars," he muttered. More weapon fire came from the opposite direction.

"They're trying to surround us," Celie said grimly. "You continue firing forward, I'll keep these bastards occupied." She shifted her fire, praying her laser's charge held out.

From the corner of her eye, she saw Max and Raven running for their lives. So did their attackers, who targeted them. Max hurled himself over Raven, driving her to the ground, just as a laser hit his back. He jerked, then collapsed atop her.

Spirit! Celie started in that direction, but Rurick

dragged her back once again. "Stay here and cover me," he ordered, then was gone before she could argue. Taking the second air cart, he used it as a shield, directing it swiftly toward Max and Raven. Celie kept discharging in a semicircle, right then left.

Rurick reached Raven and Max. He heaved his unconscious employer off Raven, then pulled the girl up. They started back toward Max's ship, Rurick dragging Max, while Raven scrambled alongside him in a half crouch. The cart took quite a few hits, disintegrating as they went, but it provided enough cover to get them to the open loading bay.

Rurick shoved Raven inside and gestured to Celie. She took a running leap, landing in a rapid roll—something she'd learned in her smuggling days. She came up into a crouch at the bay entry and fired off another burst while Rurick dragged Max inside.

"Quick, get in!" Rurick hauled her up before she could even think to move, then pounded the keypad to raise the bay ramp and close the entry. A blast hit the ship, rocking it.

Celie stared at a gaping hole beside the entry. It was at least twelve centimeters in diameter. "I don't believe this." The weapon technology being used was very advanced!

"Max!" Raven cried, kneeling by the unconscious man.

"Don't touch him," Rurick ordered sharply.

"But why? I can help him," she tried to explain.

The ship was jolted by another hit. Celie heard an ominous hissing, an indication of a burst pipe.

"We don't have time to do anything for him now." Rurick leaned over Max, heaved him up against the wall. "We have to get out of here."

Celie turned to look out the portal. Her heart stuttered, threatened to stop. "Spirit help us," she gasped.

"They're rolling out some sort of bigger weapon. Looks like a neutron cannon."

"You two go aboveboard," Rurick ordered. "Hurry! Celie, take the co-pilot's seat. Start the engines and prepare to depart. Raven, strap yourself into a crew seat. I'll be there as soon as I secure Max for takeoff."

Celie thought briefly of her ship, but she knew their only chance for survival depended on an immediate departure. She turned and clambered up the metal ladder to the top level, Raven right behind her. Down the corridor she ran, through a passenger section.

"Strap into one of these, Raven," she ordered, dashing into the cockpit, just forward of several seats. Sliding into the co-pilot's chair, she studied the unfamiliar panels.

She found the pad for the start-up sequences and breathed a sigh of relief when the powerful engines roared to life at her keyed command. At least the lockout codes weren't activated. The ship shuddered with another hit. She prayed their assailants' neutron cannon wasn't fully charged yet.

Rurick appeared and slipped into the pilot's seat, shoved the magnetic clasps of his harness together. "Let's get out of here." His expression grim, he grabbed the yoke and gave the lifts a burst of power. They rose from the ground, hovering roughly.

Hades. They could be disintegrated any moment now. Another explosion sent them listing, and the sudden blare of alarms verified that bleak reality. Rurick righted the ship, but they could only move so fast until they got outside the bay. They needed evasive action, and fast. Celie might be rusty, but she remembered the tricks she'd relied on in the old quadrant.

"Computer, estimate the direction of hostilities and do an infrared scan body count," she requested.

"Sixty degrees to port, six humanoids, who are now

within twenty meters of the ship," came a sultry female voice.

"Rurick, steer the ship's nose around until we're aimed one hundred and eighty degrees away from those cretins," Celie ordered. "Where is the control for waste jettison?"

"Why?" he asked, revving the thrusters and putting more distance between them and their attackers.

"We can dump waste matter on them and use the rear thrusters to project it. That should slow them down until we're out of the bay."

"Interstellar Council regulations state that waste cannot be jettisoned except in deep space," the computer intoned, "at least one hundred kilometers—"

"Where in the blazing hells is the jettison control?" Celie snapped. "I'll do it myself!"

"It's done," Rurick said, punching a pad. He revved the thrusters, expelling waste from the rear of the ship. "That's a smart ploy, Captain," he commented. "You'll have to share some other tricks sometime."

"Sure. I'll be glad to. Assuming we get out of here intact."

Rurick's face was set in determined lines. "I have every intention of doing just that."

They concentrated on getting out of the bay, and Celie breathed a sigh of relief when they did so.

The next concern was whether or not the damage to the ship was extensive enough to compromise the hull's integrity, and then seeing if they had enough power to clear Mangon's atmosphere.

"Computer, damage report," Rurick requested.

"Six holes in the outer hull, affecting bays one and two," the computer intoned. "They have been sealed off."

"We won't be able to fly into space with Max down there," Celie said, concerned.

25

"I put him in the airlock at the top of the ladder, in an emergency harness," Rurick replied. "Computer, continue report."

"Widespread external damage. Two holes in the reactor fuel tanks. Self-sealing successfully completed; however, that is a temporary measure. Radar is at forty percent capacity. Infrared sensors are nonfunctional; cameras are off-line."

The computer droned on, giving a lengthy list of damage, including destroyed circuitry and burst pipes in the affected bays. Fortunately, the ship had ultra-advanced control systems that were already dealing with the issues.

When the report was finished, Rurick leaned back and shook his head. "A lot of damage. We'll have to pump out the bays before we can start repairs down there."

"I didn't hear anything that will prevent us from taking off," Celie commented, sending silent thanks to Spirit.

"No, we should be able to get off the planet, as long as the fuel lines from those damaged tanks don't get blocked," Rurick agreed. "But we can't safely travel any distance until our external sensors are repaired. Then there are the holes in the hull, and those circuit panels and burst pipes to be fixed."

Celie thought of her own ship, her heart heavy. That ship was everything to her. It held all her worldly possessions, along with the deepest expressions of her soul—her paints and artwork. It was her haven against the world . . . and against the memories. She couldn't bear to leave it behind. Yet, even as these emotions pounded her, the cool, analytical voice of her intellect told her there was absolutely nothing she could do right now. Her survival, and that of everyone else on Max's ship, depended on them getting out of the landing bay and off of Joba immediately. All she could do was help facilitate their escape. Then, after they got away from the immediate danger and things had time to calm down, she'd ask to be returned to her craft.

She worked with Rurick as they flew over Mangon's barren terrain. The reactors held steady, apparently getting enough fuel. Then Rurick nosed the ship straight up and engaged the thrusters at full throttle, taking them away from the planet. Within moments, they cleared the atmosphere and headed into space.

He sat back in his seat. "That was too close for my liking."

"What were those people after?" Celie asked. "We only had food and medical supplies, and those items are abundant throughout the quadrant."

He turned his head, his golden eyes piercing her. "Are you sure of that?"

"Well, yes, I . . ." She paused, considering what she'd seen on Joba. "I've never seen any shortages or poverty anywhere, at least not before now."

"You can't believe everything you see," he said curtly, unhooking his harness and standing. "I've got to tend Max. The ship is on autopilot, so you take care of Raven."

Celie hoped Rurick's employer had regained consciousness, and that his injuries weren't life threatening. "You should let Raven look at him. She has quite a bit of medical knowledge. If he's seriously injured, you might need to get him to a medical facility."

"I don't think we can plan anything until we get the sensors and the fuel tanks repaired. But Max didn't appear too badly injured, and I'm sure he'll be fine. I'll take him to his cabin and tend to his needs."

"Raven is a gifted healer," Celie persisted. "She might be a great help."

"I've got medical training and can treat Max. You

27

take care of Raven and see if she has any injuries. I'm sure you both have scrapes and cuts. That one on your cheek needs attention, and I saw a burn on your back. Help yourself to our medical supplies, which are in the main supply vault. There are also extra flight suits there that you can use."

Celie realized that, as an android, Rurick probably had more than enough medical software installed in his systems. She had to keep reminding herself that he was an android, because he seemed so real. So alive. "All right," she said, rising from her seat. "I'll check on Raven. Let me know if we can do anything for Max."

"We'll be in cabin one. Use the comm if you need me." Rurick rose and strode away, and Celie was struck by how well he filled out his black flight suit. He was incredibly arresting, even if he was an android. And a fascinating individual—if you could call a machine that. She'd love to study him more closely, but that opportunity wouldn't be forthcoming. She and Raven would be returned to her ship as soon as possible.

Rurick dragged Max into the cabin and dumped him facedown on the bunk. His android had been hit in the upper back, and as Rurick peeled away the charred flight suit and synthetic flesh, he saw exposed wires and circuits. The damage was severe enough that Max had shut down all his systems. *Great.* Now Rurick would have to repair Max as well as work on his damaged ship.

It was going to be difficult to keep Celie and Raven away from Max until he was repaired, though—both seemed genuinely concerned and compassionate individuals. That was commendable, up to a point, but in this case, Rurick needed to keep them at a distance. He had made a vow to his family that he would never disclose his true identity while he was traveling, that Max would present himself as the real Maximilian Rurickko

Riordan. Since Rurick always honored his word, he would have to maintain the charade with Celie and Raven. Tough, but doable.

He also needed to analyze what had happened on Joba. He was stunned by the attack, and further shocked at the caliber of weapons the attackers had at their disposal. A neutron cannon? Such weapons weren't generally used in the quadrant. He and Max carried stunners for personal safety; they had only just started carrying more formidable protection after they'd made their appalling discovery about the ninth sector.

Celie Cameron appeared highly knowledgeable about weapons and how to use them. She seemed familiar with evasive maneuvers as well. Very interesting. He would consider all these things after he got some rest. Right now, fatigue dragged at him.

He was also hungry, so he decided he'd take care of his own minor wounds, check on his guests, then bring food back to this cabin on the pretense of feeding Max. Naturally, his android didn't need sustenance, but Rurick did.

He peeled off his ruined flight suit and tossed it into the disposal. He had some minor burns on his chest and arms and noted gratefully that a flight suit would cover them; so Celie wouldn't notice and wonder why an android had skin burns—and burns that healed. She appeared to be very sharp, and it wouldn't do for her to become suspicious.

The lady was also very attractive—tall and statuesque, an unusual distinction from the petite, dainty females of his own society. Her coloring was also striking: silky blond hair and eyes the rich dark brown of a wishing stone.

Seeing her on Joba today had been a double shock: that a woman was making the delivery and that she was so beautiful. Very professional, though, and all business. She'd proven she could take care of herself, both in her ability to handle weapons and to handle another man's ship. Intriguing.

Too bad he couldn't act on the attraction he felt toward her, especially since it appeared they might be together for a while. He had to maintain the charade, and most people knew androids didn't feel sexual attraction.

Rurick cleaned and treated his burns and cuts. He washed his face and was putting on a clean flight suit when his comm went off. "Yes?"

Celie's husky voice drifted over it. "How is Max?"

"He's going to be all right. I can treat his injuries, but he'll be confined to his cabin for a cycle or so."

"I'm glad. He was so heroic, and I'll always be grateful to him for saving Raven."

Max had been created to do just that—protect and rescue—but Rurick couldn't tell Celie that. He found himself wanting to.

"Raven needs to rest," she continued. "I'd like to put her in one of the other cabins."

"Of course. You two can use cabins three and four. They're clean and ready for occupation."

"Will do. I'll send Raven to one, but I'll remain in the cockpit monitoring the systems until you're ready to take over the auto-pilot or stop us for repairs."

He would have done the same thing himself. She was careful—a necessity when traveling on long space voyages. "Fine. I'll be there shortly."

He did as he said and joined her a few moments later. She sat in the co-pilot's chair, gazing out at the vast array of stars. The steady hum of equipment told him that they were on the set course and so far the moderate pace wasn't straining his damaged ship's limits.

30

"Thanks for keeping an eye on things." He slipped into the pilot's seat. "Is Raven all right?"

"Bruised and scraped. Exhausted." She pivoted toward him, and he was again struck by the beauty of her dark eyes and the perfection of her skin—except for the ugly cut on her cheek.

"Why didn't you take the time to tend to your face?" he demanded. His gaze drifted lower, noticing for the first time two charred gashes in the top of her flight suit, and the red welts beneath. "Or those burns, and the one on your back? I thought you said that girl was a healer."

Celie shrugged, as if her injuries were nothing, though Rurick knew they must be painful. "She is, but she was roughed up pretty badly. I think today's events were overwhelming for her."

"So you took care of her but not of yourself." He felt his anger rising but clamped it down. "Despite the risk of infection and the fact that we may be stranded in space for a while."

"My injuries are minor. I'll worry about them later. I want to talk to you about returning Raven and me to my ship."

"That's not possible," he said, checking the controls, then rising. "Come on. We're going to take care of those burns."

"I can deal with the burns. The issue of retrieving my ship is far more crucial."

This was his ship and he was responsible for the situation that had put her here. He also knew better than she, as evidenced by her inattention to her wounds. His orders would be carried out, as they were back at his palace. "Not if infection sets in and we can't reach medical facilities. Come with me. Now."

She balked, her eyes narrowing and her hands clutching the armrests. "I'm not a crew member on this ship, and I don't intend to take orders from you. You're not

31

the commanding officer. You're not even . . . real."

"I'm real enough, and capable of forcing your compliance." Leaning down, he grasped the sides of the top of her chair, trapping her. He stared into her eyes, determined to establish the fact that he was in charge. "With Max injured and unable to command this vessel, I am the captain of this ship. The full and final authority. Make no mistake about it."

Her chin lifted a defiant notch. "I don't care who's in charge. My key concern is to get back to my ship. My injuries are secondary. Unless my ship is damaged, I assure you I can reach medical help on my own."

Dealing with the lady was going to be a definite challenge. That thought shot a surprising surge of anticipation through Rurick. He wasn't used to anything other than immediate and submissive compliance. He pulled away and stepped back. "We're not going back to Joba."

She stood, facing him squarely. "I must return to my ship."

"The decision has been made. Come." He turned and strode from the cockpit, knowing full well she'd follow, if only to press her case.

"Captain Rurick." Her voice came from directly behind him, but he kept walking. "Captain!" She grabbed his arm and jerked him to a halt with surprising strength.

He turned, keeping his expression stern, although he was more amused than irritated at her tactics. She was staring down at where her hand clutched his forearm, an amazed expression on her face. "You feel so real," she said. "So warm. Incredible."

This was not good. He removed her hand from his arm. "My society's technology is truly amazing," he agreed coolly. "But I was not made to be handled."

"Understood. I want to see Max now. I'll discuss returning to my ship with him."

"No. I repeat, with Max injured and out of commission, I am in charge. You'll discuss the matter with me." He spun sharply on his heel, then strode on.

She followed. "Fine, then. Let's discuss it."

"We'll do that while we take care of your injuries." He stopped by the supply vault, retrieving the basic medical kit. "Which cabin is Raven in?"

"Number four, but—"

"Then we go to number three. Come." He gave her no chance to object, striding to cabin three and entering.

She entered behind him then paused, looking somewhat wary. "Why in here?"

Her sudden change of attitude baffled him. It certainly didn't mesh with earlier. "This is your cabin for the duration of your stay. It's as good a place as any." He gestured toward the bunk. "You can sit there."

"Look, I can take care of my own injuries. Just give me the kit and a few moments."

"You can't treat the burn on your back," he pointed out. "Someone else has to do that."

"Then I'll get Raven and—"

"Captain Cameron—Celie—I have the necessary medical training. Why disturb Raven, when she's had such a rough time of it?"

She nodded reluctantly. "I guess you're right."

But she radiated discomfort as she sat stiffly on the bunk. Pondering her sudden absence of bravado, Rurick sat beside her, noting the increased tension in her body. She *was* leery of him. Why? "I'll try not to hurt you," he said quietly, "but the solution will most likely sting."

33

She nodded, and he opened the kit. "Let's do that cut on your cheek first. Turn this way."

She complied, wincing slightly when he applied the antiseptic to the raw skin. "Now I remember why I didn't ask Raven to do this," she said.

"I didn't peg you for a coward, Captain Cameron," he said lightly. "You should know better than to let this go, even if it stings. I'm going to clean it a little more."

He rewet the cloth and dabbed the wound again. She had great bone structure, with high cheeks and intriguing hollows beneath. Her nose was straight and regal, her mouth suggestively lush. Her skin was like the finest Sarnai satin, smooth and rich with golden undertones. He wondered if she were that smooth all over.

Discomfited by his thoughts, he shook them off and reached for the salve. "This will help prevent infection." He spread it over the cut gently and applied an adhesive bandage. That done, he reached for her flight suit top. "Now for the burns."

She drew back, her hand going protectively to her chest. Great. Not only was he battling an unprecedented attraction to this woman but also her apparent distrust of him and her innate resistance to authority—the latter two something he had never before encountered. Although he hated the deception, he knew it would be the easiest way to do what must be done.

"Look. Being what I am, I'm no threat to you or any woman," he reminded her. That much was true. He usually had the opposite problem; having to turn women away.

"I keep forgetting you're an android." Celie hesitated a moment, then nodded. "You're right." She ran her slender fingers along her flight suit's seam, opening it all the way down. She paused, then shrugged and slid the top completely off.

Totally unprepared for that, Rurick could only stare

34

at her generous breasts, beautifully rounded with rose-tinged nipples. His body reacted immediately and painfully. Swallowing hard, he reached for the medical kit, clumsily knocking it to the floor. Gods!

"Sorry about that," he muttered, sinking down and hastily gathering up the contents. "I must have hit it too hard."

"Well, androids are stronger than humans."

He came upright, the kit in his hands, and found himself at eye level with those lush breasts. "Right." He hoisted himself back onto the bunk, fumbling with the kit. *Get a grip*, he told himself. *This is strictly a professional situation.* It wasn't Celie's fault her bare breasts had turned him into an idiot. She thought he was a machine.

Swallowing again, he forced his attention to the two nasty spots over her left breast, trying to keep his focus there. He wet a clean cloth with antiseptic and, his breath hitching, pressed it against the burns. With a gasp, she jolted upward, bringing that abundant flesh in full contact with his hand. His breath hissed out and he pulled away, feeling scalded himself. Gods, but her skin was every bit as supple and warm as he'd imagined.

"Sorry," she murmured. "Caught me off guard. I guess I didn't realize it would sting so much."

Or how beautiful her body was, and how much he was affected by it. "Understandable." He put more solution on the cloth, then steeled himself. "I need to do it again."

She nodded, her body rigid as he eased his hand back over her breast. They both seemed to be holding their breath. She closed her eyes, her hands clenching the edge of the bunk as Rurick cleaned her burns.

Her nakedness aside, there was something intimate, sensual, about the simple act of touching her, of tending to her. It was just a necessary procedure, he told himself. Yet he was acutely aware of the heat rising off her flesh, of the rapid beat of her heart beneath his hand. He felt sweat beading on his forehead and wiped it away with his free hand before she noticed.

Stars. He was acting like an adolescent lusting after his first crush. It was ridiculous, and not the reaction a grown, sexually experienced male should be having. Forcing himself to relax, he reached for antibiotic salve. "You had concerns you wanted to discuss with me?" he asked, needing to change the direction of his thoughts—and his line of vision.

"Oh. Yes." Celie's eyes opened and she paused, as if composing her thoughts. "Captain, I—"

"Call me Rurick," he urged, smoothing salve as gently as possible over her burns. "I would say the situation warrants a little less formality, wouldn't you?" *Definitely less formality.*

"All right then, Rurick. I'm asking that you return Raven and me to my ship. Please. The ship is everything to me. It contains all my possessions. Some of them are irreplaceable."

"I can't take you back yet." Wiping the salve off his hands, he met her darkened gaze.

"Why not?"

"I'm not sure this ship can handle reentry into a planet's atmosphere, not without us completing the necessary repairs."

"I'm very aware that we have to do the repairs first," she said. "But then you should be able to return us to my ship."

Except he and Max had urgent business on Altair before they could possibly return to Joba. Rurick knew they'd have to tell Celie and Raven something before they reached Altair, but felt it would be prudent to wait as long as possible. "Repairing the ship could require quite a delay," he hedged, "which is probably for the best, because Joba might not be safe right now."

He paused, then added, "I'm sorry."

Her eyes narrowed. "There's no need to say that. How can an android be sorry, or feel anything for that matter?"

Stars, he was going to have to be careful around her. She was far too observant. "Androids are programmed to gauge humanoid emotions, analyze pheromones, and respond appropriately," he explained. "I can tell this situation is upsetting you."

"That's an accurate assessment," Celie retorted, then fell silent until he finished bandaging her. "Why isn't it 'safe to return to Joba'?" she asked. "What's going on there?"

"I need to do your back." He gestured for her to turn around. "And I'm afraid I can't answer those questions."

"Why not?" She pivoted away and flipped her hair onto her chest. She had an elegant, long neck and a beautiful back, sleek, with that smooth, golden skin.

Feeling more relaxed now that she was turned away from him, he focused on the serious issues raised by her questions. As he considered what to tell her, she glanced back over her shoulder. "Why won't you answer my questions? Because you can't, or you won't?"

Why not indeed? Frustration roared through him at his lack of knowledge or control over any of his recent discoveries. Shocking, universe-shaking discoveries that had rocked the foundation of his beliefs about the Interstellar Council and the life quality codes the Council had sworn to uphold. Yet he and Max had seen for themselves that the ninth sector offered no guaranteed quality of life for any of its citizens. Instead, poverty and disease appeared to be rampant. But there were no immediate explanations as to how this had happened, or why.

"Rurick? Are you going to answer me?"

He concentrated on the burn on her right shoulder. "I don't really know the answers."

"Were those people after Max specifically? Or were they just pirates, after anyone who might have something of value?"

Rurick was almost positive the attackers had been after him, in an attempt to stop him from probing the ninth-sector situation more deeply, but he had no idea who had sent them. Unfortunately, traveling in a ship marked with the Riordan royal crest clearly broadcasted his identity. It was also the only way he could move in and out of the ninth sector freely. "I don't know for sure," he stated.

"Well, *what* do you know?" she retorted.

Her fiery annoyance intrigued him. "Not very much, it would seem."

She muttered beneath her breath, something about "poorly programmed androids."

"What was that?" he asked politely.

"Just another question," she said smoothly. "What in Hades is going on in Joba? Why is it so rundown? I saw a pitiful group of people dressed in rags, and they looked like they were starving. I've never seen anything like that, not in this quadrant, anyway. This needs to be reported to the Council."

That addressed one suspicion that had nagged him— whether or not Celie was an active participant in the black market created by such great need. Obviously she wasn't, for which he was grateful. "Yes, it needs to be reported," he agreed.

The problem was, to whom? The horrendous living conditions in the ninth sector were so widespread, and word about those conditions apparently so repressed, that some of the Interstellar Council members had to be behind the cover-up. The question was, who? That question was the one reason he hadn't gone to the High Council yet; he didn't know who could be trusted.

He'd tried to bring up the situation to his father, but Domek had become distraught and insisted that such a thing couldn't possibly exist. Then the king had become extremely ill, and Rurick hadn't said anything further. He'd wondered if the members of the High Council would have the same reaction as his father. Or worse, if those who were behind the situation might try to block him from giving assistance to the sector. So he hadn't yet approached the Council or gone public with his discovery. He felt it imperative he uncover the perpetrators first. For that reason, he had opted to have the supplies delivered to him in an obscure location, and had Max commission Celie to make the delivery to Joba. For the same reason, he didn't dare tell Celie more.

He finished bandaging the burn. "All done."

She rose from the bunk and turned, giving him another tantalizing view of her breasts as she slipped on her top. He felt a great sense of relief when she sealed the seam.

"It's not any of my business what you were doing on Joba," she said, "or what you plan to do with the supplies I delivered. I just want my ship back."

Surprised, he realized she thought *he* was planning to sell the food and medicine he'd purchased, black-marketeering and taking advantage of the needy. Of course, what else would she think, based on so little information? He'd wondered the same about her, so it seemed a fair turnaround.

"It's not what you think," he said. "I wish I could tell you more, but I don't have the answers myself."

"You've told me nothing," she pointed out. "I don't need to know your agenda. I only need my ship. Surely there must be some recourse. I can't just leave it at Joba."

None of this was her fault. Her only crime was doing business with him, and in being in the wrong place at the wrong time.

Yet it was crucial they head directly to Altair. Already, Rurick feared how many might die of starvation or disease before he could get the precious supplies there. Afterward, he could return Celie to her ship. For now, he'd have to dodge her questions.

"I've already explained there's no other recourse. We will return you to your ship," he told her, "after we repair our craft." And went to Altair. He only hoped her ship was still on Joba and intact when they could finally return. He could always buy her a new one.

"Why can't you take us to a checkpoint station? They're scattered throughout the ninth sector, and you wouldn't have to worry about this ship attempting atmosphere re-entry."

He strongly suspected those stations were part of the problem—or at least part of the system repressing word of the sector conditions. He wouldn't leave Celie and Raven at one.

"That's not a good option," he stated. "They don't have many transports going in and out. We'll get you back to Joba. Right now, we have to concentrate on the repairs to the ship so we can resume business as quickly as possible."

She frowned. "How long do you think those will take?"

He shrugged. "I have no idea."

"Son of an Antek," she muttered.

"More colorful language."

"Oh, that's mild compared to some of my vocabulary."

He couldn't help it; he laughed. His ship was badly damaged, Max was incapacitated, and the ninth sector was in dire straits, yet Captain Celie Cameron was lightening his mood. She was as entertaining as any royal performer.

"I didn't know androids had a sense of humor."

Rurick thought of the quirky humor that had been programmed into Max. "Some do."

"So you really have no idea how long the repairs will take?"

She was persistent; he'd give her that. "The external repairs will be the most time consuming. The fuel tanks and the damaged sensors will probably take two or three cycles. We'll have to weld the holes in the hull and replace circuit panels and fuel pipes. Since Max will probably be incapacitated for a few cycles, we won't be able to count on his help."

"I've had quite a bit of mechanical training, and I do my own repairs," she said. "I'll help you. You have been programmed for ship mechanics, haven't you, android?"

Max had extensive software for mechanical repairs, but Rurick had always shown strong mechanical inclinations. He enjoyed working on spacecraft, even if his family thought it was beneath him. He was quite sufficient in that area. "That I do." He nodded.

She rolled her eyes. "Well, finally, a straight answer." She cocked her head and studied him. "It will be interesting seeing what an android can do."

If she only knew, Rurick thought. *If she only knew.*

Chapter Three

While Celie and Raven slept, Rurick spent his time repairing Max. With his cabin computer intoning instructions, he replaced most of the destroyed circuits, enough that he was able to reactivate the android. That done, Max began reprogramming his damaged software and running a self-diagnostic. Once that was complete, he would be able to instruct Rurick in any remaining repairs.

Rurick slept for a few hours, then took a shower in cool water—both to wake himself up and help dissipate the lines of fatigue on his face. Androids never looked tired, and he didn't want to rouse the perceptive Captain Celie's suspicions further.

Max was still in diagnostic mode, so Rurick left him to it and went to see what his guests were doing. He found Raven alone in the galley, sipping a cup of tea. When she saw him she practically leaped from her seat.

"How is Max?" she demanded anxiously. She was

very pretty, with lustrous ebony hair and eyes. And she was tiny. Standing, she only came to the middle of his chest. He saw she had taken advantage of his offer and donned one of the standard-issue gold flight suits he stocked, although it was quite large on her. She tilted her head back, looking up at him expectantly. "Is he all right?"

"Much better. He's moving around, and it appears he'll make full rep . . . er, recovery." Rurick began programming the food replicator for a high-protein meal.

"Did he lose much blood? Is he very weak?"

"No, not much blood loss." Since androids didn't have any blood, that much was true. "He's a little weak but already regaining his strength. As a matter of fact, I'm going to take him a meal." Which Rurick planned to eat himself. He was starving.

"Let me do it," Raven urged. "I can check his injuries. My father is a physician and taught me many healing techniques. I can stay with Max while you and Celie work on the ship. She's already belowdeck, welding the holes in the hull."

"Is she, now?" Rurick glanced at his chronometer. Seven hundred hours. The lady was certainly anxious to return to her own craft. "Thank you for offering, but Max doesn't want either of you in his cabin right now."

Raven's expression was crestfallen. She looked so young, Rurick had to wonder about her being allowed to travel around the quadrant, much less into the ninth sector. Of course, he reminded himself, the terrible conditions of the sector appeared to be a well-kept secret.

"I'm sure Max wouldn't mind seeing me," Raven persisted. "I'd like to thank him. He was so kind to me yesterday. He protected me on the way to the bay and carried me to Celie's ship. Then he saved my life. He's the bravest man I know!"

Her eyes shone and her delicate skin was flushed as

she described Max's amazing accomplishments. Amused, Rurick wondered what the real android would think if he knew this young human girl had a galactic-sized crush on him. Not wanting to hurt her feelings, he fumbled for a gentle refusal.

"Max is a little shy around women," he hedged.

"He didn't seem shy at all yesterday." She smiled dreamily. "He seemed strong and confident."

She was right about that. Max had superhuman strength, and he could be downright obnoxious at times. "Well, perhaps he's not all that shy. But he is a little vain. He hates for anyone to see him when he's sick and not looking his best. He'd be very embarrassed if you went to his cabin right now."

"He would?" Raven's incredibly dark eyes grew even larger. "I'd hate to make him feel worse."

"The best thing to do is give him a cycle or two to recover. Then you two can visit and get to know each other better."

The glow returned to the girl's face. "Oh, I'd like that. Max is really wonderful."

"He's amazing, all right," Rurick said dryly. "A real marvel." He retrieved the meal from the replicator and turned toward the corridor. "I'll tell him you were asking about him. I'm sure he'll be pleased."

Celie concentrated on welding the edges of the patch she'd made for one of six holes in the ship's inner and outer hulls. Max's ship was a wonder, composed of an amazingly lightweight but resilient alloy, the likes of which she'd never seen before. She'd found precut sheets of the alloy in the maintenance bay and been impressed with their lightness and flexibility. She'd expected to have to pump out the bay before she started the repairs, but the ship's computerized systems had automatically funneled away the runoff from the pipes after sealing them.

Shutting down the welder, she moved to the other side of the patch. "Celie?" The voice came through her headset, startling her, but she recognized Rurick's distinctive voice instantly. "Where are you?" he asked.

"I'm in bay one. Still working on the first patch."

"Do you mind if I turn off the grav? It will be easier to move crates and equipment around."

Apparently this android didn't have super-human strength, or he didn't want to exert himself. Zero gravity would certainly facilitate shifting things. "I don't mind at all," she replied. "Just be sure to warn Raven."

"I already told her, and she's gone to her cabin."

"Then do it."

A moment later, she felt an odd sensation in her body, almost like dizziness, as the gravity field shut down. She felt herself drifting and pushed off the bulkhead, which sent her toward what would normally be the bay ceiling. It had been a long time since she'd been in zero gravity—or a spacesuit, for that matter. These suits were another surprise: also ultra thin and lightweight. She hadn't realized how advanced the technology was in this quadrant.

But then she'd never seen an android before, never imagined there were machines that looked so lifelike that they could be mistaken for a human. Rurick's triton control panel was the only thing to indicate he was anything other than human. He looked amazingly real, with those mesmerizing eyes that blazed with seeming passion and intelligence. Of course he was intelligent, Celie told herself. He had a computer brain. But there was something more in his gaze—something biting, intense, compelling. She found him fascinating.

A moment later she had the real thing to look at as he entered the bay. At least she assumed it was him,

45

since Max had been pretty seriously injured and shouldn't be up. The two looked so much alike, it was difficult to tell them apart, which she thought was rather odd. Why would an android be made to look exactly like a human? An ego thing, maybe—or perhaps there was another reason. She'd have to think about that.

Yet Max made no attempt to hide the fact that Rurick was an android. Rurick's armband made the distinction clear. And oddly, his vibrant eyes also set him apart from Max, whose dispassionate eyes seemed dull by comparison. Amazing technology indeed.

"How's it going?" The deep voice surged into her headset, sent her pulse jumping. Definitely the android. His voice was also different from Max's; richer, more resonant.

He moved toward her, navigating zero gravity with ease, muscles flowing beneath the spacesuit that seemed molded to him. Her pulse speeded up even more. Spirit, what was wrong with her? She'd never before found herself attracted to any man, much less an android. It was just the masculine perfection of him, she told herself. He could be considered a mechanical work of art.

"I wouldn't think you'd need a spacesuit," she commented, trying to shift her thoughts to safer ground.

"An android has to protect the circuits and outer covering of its frame against the elements."

That made sense. Celie resolved to do some research on androids at the first opportunity. She knew very little about them. "I'm almost through repairing the first hole in the inner hull," she reported.

He nodded. "Good. After we repair the other five, we'll be able to pressurize the lower level and turn the grav back on. Then we'll have to go outside the ship to seal off the fuel leaks and repair the sensors."

That would take at least another full cycle. Then there

were the circuit panels and the damaged pipes, which could take several more cycles. More time before she could return to her ship. Frustration and concern about her spacecraft surged through her. But Celie knew there was nothing to be done, certainly not until this ship was repaired. Resigned, she powered up the welder to do the next seam. "How's Max doing?"

"Much better. I predict a full recovery. He should be up and about tomorrow."

Then tomorrow Celie would have to find something to occupy Raven while she herself assisted Rurick with repairs. The girl had talked nonstop about the ship's captain since waking up. She was enamored of Max, even though she barely knew him. She was far too innocent for the two to be alone together.

Ugly memories reared their heads, dark remembrances of two men who'd made the lives of Celie and her sister Moriah a living Hades. She shivered, shoving the images away. Those men couldn't hurt her now. They were both dead: another memory Celie shelved. But she refused to take any chances where Raven was concerned.

Rurick propelled some crates away from the second hole. They drifted slowly toward the opposite interior wall. "I saw Raven in the galley. She looked fully recovered from her experience yesterday. How are your injuries?"

A picture flashed through Celie's mind, the image of Rurick's long, lean fingers pressing against her chest, the warmth from his touch as he applied salve to her sensitive skin, the strange sense of intimacy she'd experienced. Heat rushed through her, tingling in her breasts and face.

Enough! She had no idea why this man—no, this *android*—was having such an effect on her, but she was determined to ignore it. She stared at Rurick's intrigu-

47

ing face, slightly blurred behind the plexishield of his helmet. He inclined his head expectantly, and she realized he awaited her answer.

"Much better," she managed to reply, wondering if maybe she did have an actual infection and was running a fever. Surely not. She fumbled for the temperature control of her suit, turned the setting sharply down.

"Something wrong with your suit?"

Celie took a deep, calming breath. She was just off balance from yesterday's events. It had been a while since she'd been in any type of weapon skirmish, plus she was concerned about retrieving her ship. Add to that her minor injuries and the issue of Raven's safety, and it was understandable that her equilibrium was a little off.

"Captain?"

She forced a smile. "Please, just Celie. I thought we dispensed with formalities yesterday."

"So we did. Is everything all right?"

"Yes, just fine. These suits are impressive. I had no idea the technology in this quadrant was so advanced."

"Much of what we have comes from the Enhancers, and I understand a lot of that knowledge was imparted to them by the Shens."

Interesting, but not surprising. No one had ever suspected the true scope of magic, power, and technology the Shens had commanded for hundreds of seasons. Until Jarek and Eirene san Ranul visited the Shens on Aldon before the Shielder exodus, no one had even realized the mysterious race was so advanced. It remained one of the best-kept secrets of the past.

It also explained the remarkable realism of this android. Celie forced her attention back to her welding. She and Rurick concentrated on the repairs, working in silence for the most part. Several hours later, the holes were repaired, and they went aboveboard to take a break.

Celie managed to get her helmet off but struggled with the releases of her spacesuit.

"Here, let me help," Rurick offered. He turned her toward him, his beautiful, firm hands sliding up her arms to tug at the clasps on each shoulder.

Even with the distraction of his touch, she couldn't tear her gaze from him. He was quite possibly the most striking man—real or otherwise—she had ever seen. He had removed his helmet and his hair brushed against his broad shoulders, streaks of gold reflected from the recessed lighting. He leaned closer, his expression intent as he snapped open the suit clasps. Her attention shifted to his mouth. It was full but firm, and oddly appealing. Alluring . . . suggestive, actually.

What would it be like to kiss a man? she wondered. It was something she'd never experienced, at least not in a sexual way. There were men in her life, men married to the women who were part of her extended family. These men were affectionate, hugging and kissing her, but only in a chaste, brotherly mien. No man had ever kissed her in a sexual way. Until now, it was something she'd never particularly cared to sample.

"There you go."

She felt her suit loosen, slide down her chest. Shaken, she jerked her gaze away from Rurick's lips and stepped back to remove it. "Do you need help with yours?" she asked, trying desperately to corral thoughts she'd never before entertained.

What in the universe had kicked her libido into high gear? She was twenty-four seasons of age, well past the time most females experienced hormonal surges and adolescent sexual fantasies. She would never have a relationship with a man and knew the reasons why. The fact didn't bother her; rather, it offered a certain security, and a haven from having to face the memories. She had more than enough in her life to keep her content: family and friends, the freedom to travel space, her art. She didn't need, or want, a relationship with a man.

"I'm not going to remove my suit yet," Rurick answered, drawing her thoughts back to the fact that they were in the sealed airlock entry to the lower levels. "I'm going to check on Max, then get started on the external repairs."

The repairs. That's where her focus needed to be. The sooner Max's ship was repaired and fully operational, the sooner she could return to her own. And to her normal, safe existence. The sooner these unsettling carnal urges would be laid to rest.

"Do you need assistance? I've got some experience with external repairs in space," she offered.

"I appreciate it, but I'd rather have you in the cockpit, maintaining ship stability and monitoring the screens for meteors or debris."

"Of course. I can handle that."

His gaze settled on her, and his golden eyes seemed to glow. "I have no doubt of your capabilities."

The expression in his eyes, the quiet certainty in his voice, sent another wave of warmth through her, along with surprise that the approval of a virtual stranger— an inhuman one, at that—would mean so much to her. Unsettled, not at all pleased with his effect on her, she retorted, "Maybe you should hold the accolades until you're safely inside the ship again." She turned and hung up the suit, then punched the pad to open the panel.

Striding down the corridor, she didn't look to see if he followed. Even though his tread was silent, she knew he was behind her. She could sense him, feel his presence, which seemed to reverberate through the corridor. It appeared she had developed an inexplicable awareness of this android, a startling attraction that both baffled and alarmed her.

It was nothing, she told herself. As soon as she was back on her ship, her libido would return to normal, as would her life. Safe. Routine. And, unfortunately, boring.

Her voice was melodic, sensuous, suggestive of the Sarnai satin sheets on his huge bed at the royal residence; and of steamy, pleasure-filled hours, tangled in those sheets with a palace courtesan. Not that Celie had said anything provocative while he had worked outside the ship for over three hours. Instead she had kept him anchored and focused. She'd given continual reports on space conditions, on equipment readings, and his progress in fixing the damage. She had monitored the readouts from the repair robot, and waited patiently while he made the tedious repairs on the fuel tanks. She was capable, steady, and totally professional.

It wasn't until he was in the airlock, undergoing decontamination, that Rurick allowed himself to think about Celie's sultry voice, and the nonprofessional effect it had on him. Strange as it was, he suspected she had no idea how alluring and provocative her voice was, or her attractiveness as a whole. Despite her poise and competence, she didn't radiate the confident awareness that most beautiful women seemed to innately possess. She appeared innocent—a very unlikely possibility, given her looks and the exposure from her chosen career.

When he emerged from the airlock, she was waiting for him, wearing one of the gold crew flight suits that were kept in readiness on the ship. The color was stunning on her, emphasizing the tawny tones of her skin and her blond hair. She'd put it up in a neat twist, which made her appear older, more sophisticated. She looked cool and poised. He offered a weary smile, hoping his sweaty state wasn't noticeable.

"Thanks for your help," he told her. "I managed to knock out most of the outside repairs."

"How much more is needed?"

"Probably another two hours outside. The tank leaks are sealed, but I still have to weld the hull breach over them. Then we still have the external sensors and the bay repairs to worry about."

"So another cycle to complete everything?"

"Probably two," he said, watching disappointment cloud her lovely features. "I know you want to get back to your ship, and I promise we'll get you to your ship as soon as we can."

He meant what he said, although he wasn't ready to tell her he couldn't take her and Raven directly to Joba. He had to deliver the supplies first. The need was too great, and he feared the delay they suffered had already cost lives. Retrieving Celie's ship was secondary to those.

"I appreciate that." She turned with him, and they started down the corridor. "I'd like to minimize the delay if possible. If anything happened to my ship . . ." She paused, drew a deep breath.

Guilt twinged through him. If her ship was lost, he would make it up to her. He could easily afford to buy her a hundred ships. "It's getting late," he said, changing the subject. "I need to replicate a meal for Max. Have you and Raven eaten?"

"No, and I am hungry."

"Where is Raven?" he asked, wondering what the diminutive girl had done with herself the entire cycle.

"She's in her cabin, researching new healing techniques. She tells me your computer system is superior. Let me get her, and we'll go with you to the galley."

But the girl wasn't in her cabin. "I wonder where she

went." Celie whirled from the panel and headed toward the lounge area. Raven wasn't there, or in the cockpit, or the galley, or Celie's cabin. That left only one place: Max's—actually Rurick's—cabin.

"I told her to leave Max alone." Her face pale, Celie started toward Rurick's cabin. "I don't want her with him."

Somewhat alarmed himself at what Raven might discover, Rurick followed. "There's no need for concern. Raven is perfectly safe with him."

"You don't know that. She's only nineteen. She's an innocent and doesn't know anything about men and their ways."

Surprised at the remark about men, and the underlying panic he sensed from Celie, Rurick caught her arm and pulled her around to face him. "What exactly does that mean?"

She drew a breath as if to calm herself. "I keep forgetting you're an android, that you don't think like a human man."

"Please enlighten me."

"Look, it's a long story. I just want to get Raven out of Max's cabin."

He felt the tension reverberating through her, but her expression was closed, and he sensed she wouldn't give him any more information. "All right." He let her go, and she whirled and strode off.

Celie entered Max's cabin without sounding the tone. Relief poured over her when she saw Raven seated at a small oval table, Max sitting across from her. They appeared to be engaged in an animated conversation. They looked up when Celie entered, and a wide smile spread across Raven's face.

"Oh, Celie, Max has been telling me the most amazing things! He is so fascinating."

53

"Really?" Celie willed her heart to slow its frantic pace. She realized she'd overreacted and panicked unnecessarily over Raven being with Max, but she had no control over these particular fears. They were too deeply ingrained, too indelibly imprinted on her soul to ever be purged, which was why her solitary lifestyle suited her. "You shouldn't be bothering the captain. I'm sure he's still recovering from his injuries."

"It is all right," Max said, rising from his chair. "I am much better, thank you."

"I'm glad to hear it," Rurick said from behind her. "I didn't expect to see you up and about quite so soon."

Celie drew another deep breath, forcing her body to relax. "I want to thank you for saving Raven's life. It was a very heroic thing you did, and I'm forever in your debt."

"It was nothing," Max said. "I have extensive combat training, and I work well under pressure."

"Max knows so many things," Raven said, rising, her adoring gaze fixed on him. "I could listen to him for hours."

It appeared the girl's youthful obsession with the ship's captain had increased and become even more firmly cemented. Celie knew she'd have to keep a close watch on the two of them. She was responsible for Raven and didn't want her to do anything foolish, or for Max to take advantage of her infatuation.

"I'm glad you enjoyed visiting with him," she said neutrally. "But now I'm sure he needs to rest. And you need to eat." She stepped forward to take Raven's arm and urged her toward the entry. She nodded to Max. "Take care of yourself. We want you fully recovered." She pulled Raven through the panel, determined to keep a closer eye on the girl from now on.

*   *   *

"You wouldn't believe the stuff that Max told me," Raven said. She and Celie sat cross-legged on the bunk in Raven's cabin after a quick meal in the galley. "He's very rich. He can afford anything he wants."

Celie looked around the beautifully appointed cabin. It was most likely a guest berth, because she'd seen the crew quarters and they were smaller in size, boasting double bunks. Both Celie and Raven's cabins had lush carpet, pastel-tinted walls adorned with fine artwork, solid wood furniture, and rich satin fabrics. Max's cabin was twice as large and even more opulent. The entire ship, from the cockpit to the lounge and the galley, was furnished with the finest of materials.

Max must be very wealthy. Why then had he been purchasing basic supplies of food and medicine, and in the most desolate—and apparently most destitute—sector of the quadrant? Unless he made his wealth by selling on the black market. The disturbing doubts, which Celie had managed to put to rest, returned.

People taking advantage of the poor and underprivileged was nothing new; it had been a fact of life in the old quadrant. But it bothered her to think that Rurick would be involved in such, and that he would lie to her about it. He was an android, she reminded herself, not a human. He was probably programmed to think and say whatever Max wished.

"Max told me a lot about androids, Rurick in particular." Raven's voice broke into Celie's musings.

"What?" she blinked and looked at the girl, noting her mischievous expression.

Raven scooted closer, grinning like a lanrax that had stolen a choice piece of food off the table. "Max explained about androids and how they're created. They can be programmed to provide any service. Even *sexual* functions."

"Max talked to you about *that?*" Celie demanded,

appalled. "That's not appropriate subject matter for a mature man to discuss with a young girl."

Raven waved a hand dismissively. "It was only in the interest of science. Besides, I'm the one who brought it up."

"You asked Max if androids can perform sexual acts?"

"I was curious about it." Raven leaned forward. "Don't you want to know all the things Rurick can do?"

"No. Absolutely not." Celie felt her face grow warm at the very thought, and at the sudden rush of recent memories of Rurick touching her in intimate—albeit innocent—ways.

"They call it 'pleasure training,' " Raven continued blithely. "The androids in Max's society are programmed to provide sexual pleasure to male or female humans, as well as to a variety of other species. Max said the android on our ship has extensive pleasure training and can do more than a human."

"We don't need to be discussing this," Celie said, although part of her, a part she'd never realized existed, was utterly fascinated. It was merely sordid curiosity—of which she was greatly ashamed, she told herself—and none of her concern.

"Well then, if you don't want to hear anymore . . ." Raven sat back and stretched her slender arms over her head. "I am pretty tired."

Darn Raven. Now she had Celie's interest piqued and she knew it. "Tell me," Celie snapped, more annoyed with her own prurient interest than she was with Raven. "You've shared this much. You might as well tell me the rest."

"Well, if you're sure you want to know . . ."

The little brat. "Just tell me."

Raven leaned forward. "Max says the android is *very* well endowed, if you know what I mean. Any woman

56

would be highly satisfied with his service."

Oh, my. Celie might be completely inexperienced in such matters, but she'd heard other women talking from time to time. She knew that some women put great stock in the size of a man's—No! Why was she even thinking about such things? She would never be intimate with a man, would never give a man that sort of power over her. "I think that's enough for toni—"

"It isn't just his size, either," Raven interjected. "It's his skill. Max claims the android can make a woman scream from the pleasure."

"Listen," Celie said sternly, ignoring her rising body temperature and the sudden erratic beat of her heart. "You don't need to concern yourself with such things. When you're old enough and the time is right, you'll meet the right young man. A man who will want to commit himself to you as much as you want to commit yourself to him. The two of you will be mated, and then you can worry about such things. Not before that!"

Raven rolled her eyes. "You sound just like my parents. You know what your problem is, Celie? You think like an old person. You're all serious and stuffy. But you're not old at all. You're young and beautiful. I'd give anything to be tall like you, and have your figure. Your breasts are great. I see how men stare at them. Even Rurick—and he's an android. So think of the effect you have on *real* men. You need to live a little. Have some fun. Have some *sex*. It might loosen you up."

Celie felt as if she'd been knocked down by a blaster. "I'm not sure we should be having this conversation. In fact, I refuse to discuss this further."

"You know," Raven continued, as if Celie hadn't spoken, "Rurick would be perfect for you. He's handsome and"—she paused, as if looking for the right word—"experienced. Plus he's not real. You wouldn't have to

57

worry about emotional attachments. You could just have sex. Hot, uninhibited sex."

Celie could only stare at her, too stunned to respond. When had Raven become so grown up—and where had she learned such things?

Still, there were situations Raven had never experienced. She knew about the brutality of the Controllers and the Anteks but had no firsthand knowledge of abusive men, or sexual predators. Celie prayed to Spirit that Raven would never be exposed to such.

And she wouldn't. Not if Celie could help it.

Chapter Four

Rurick finished his meal and pushed the tray away. He sat back, exhaustion sweeping over him. "We got most of the structural damage repaired today," he told Max.

Max considered this. "You went outside the ship to do repairs?"

"I did. I didn't want Celie to take the risk. Besides, she thinks I'm an android. Logically, I'm the expendable one."

"You are not expendable," Max declared. "You are the Riordan crown prince, next in line to the throne of Jardonia."

"Tell me something I don't know," Rurick muttered, then held up his hand as Max started to launch into some sort of technical treatise. Max seemed so real that Rurick often forgot he was only a machine, one that took every statement very literally. "Forget what I just said. It was a figure of speech. I'm quite capable of performing those external repairs. There wasn't a single hitch out there today."

"I am the android. I am the one who is supposed to be taking the risks."

"I'd like to see you explain that to Captain Cameron."

"I will." Max started toward the entry.

"No! Don't do that." Rurick shook his head. He was too tired to be dealing with an android.

Max turned, confusion on his face. Rurick was continually amazed at his programmed emotions. "I do not understand. You just told me to—"

"I was just thinking out loud," Rurick interjected. "I intend to honor my father's request to keep my identity secret."

"As well you should."

"So I have to continue playing the android. Which means I might have to take some calculated risks."

"I cannot allow you to take risks. I have been programmed to protect you above all else."

"But I give the orders. We'll continue the charade until we're back on Jardonia." Rurick leaned back and picked up his glass. He swirled the expensive Maran brandy absently. "However, it might be a while before we return home. We must get those supplies to Altair as soon as the ship repairs are complete. Every day we're delayed could mean the loss of more lives."

"A very strong possibility," Max agreed.

Rurick set down the brandy and rose to pace the cabin. "I wish I knew why—and how—these conditions in the ninth sector have come about."

"There is a ninety-nine-point-nine-percent probability that one or more members of the Interstellar High Council is behind the propagation and cover-up of these conditions," Max intoned.

"I know, but that still doesn't answer my questions." Rurick paused before the portal and stared out at the stars. The dark backdrop of space suited his mood. "I intend to have answers, and soon. But first we have to make that delivery."

He turned back and strode to the console, preparing to make his daily entries into the log. "I'm estimating two more cycles before we can be on our way. Have you completed your repairs on yourself?"

"The weapon hit caused several major circuits to short," Max answered. "I had most of them repaired before Raven came to visit me. I will need to shut down for the evening shift to finish diagnostics and corrections."

Rurick spun away from the console. "If you weren't fully operational, you shouldn't have spent the afternoon with the girl." He was concerned that Raven's suspicions might be aroused if Max spouted irrational gibberish, something that could occur if certain circuits were damaged. "I hope you didn't have any glitches during your conversation."

"I was in complete control of my functions," Max insisted. "I merely shared details of Riordan technology with her. She is very bright and asked intelligent questions."

"She might be too astute," Rurick mused. "We need to choose our words carefully around our guests. What did you tell her?"

Max gave the stiff, lopsided grin he employed when he thought himself particularly amusing. "We discussed android specifications."

Rurick felt a sinking feeling. "What does that mean?"

"Mere details that you already know, Your Highness."

Rurick narrowed his eyes. "You're sidestepping the question. What did you and Raven discuss?"

"Many things. I was not the only one conversing. You might be very interested in what I learned from her."

The android was practically humming. He must have garnered some intriguing information. "All right, you have my attention." Rurick returned to his seat at the table. He picked up his glass of brandy. "What did you learn?"

Max took the opposite chair. He could stand indefinitely and never tire, but he liked imitating human mannerisms. "Fascinating information. The girl Raven is a Shielder."

"A Shielder?" Rurick tried to recall what he knew about the Shielder people. "They're the ones who began migrating to this quadrant about two seasons ago, through a wormhole discovered and used by . . . Enhancers? To escape persecution and annihilation by a race called the Controllers, I believe."

"Yes. They have an electromagnetic anomaly that creates a shield of sorts in their brains. They are resistant to the psionic brain waves the Controllers use to subjugate those living in the second quadrant."

"I remember the reports. They've settled nicely into our quadrant, have proven themselves to be self-sufficient and industrious. They already have representatives on the Council. I've met their leader, Captain san Ranul."

Max nodded. "That is correct. They share the planet Candest with the Enhancers."

"Who have refused to participate in the Council," Rurick mused, mulling over the information. "So is Captain Cameron a Shielder as well?"

"No, she is not. But, according to Raven, Captain Cameron's older sister married a Shielder, which forged a relationship between her people and the Shielders. They have lived and worked together since that time." Max's lopsided grin appeared again. "Captain Cameron is most interesting, is she not?"

Rurick often wondered if Max had scanners in the

back of his head, or had somehow been programmed with intuitive abilities. As usual, the android had ferreted out the truth. Of their two guests, Rurick found Celie by far the more intriguing. Raven was still just a girl, balanced on the precipice between youth and adulthood, but Celie was all woman. All beauty and curves and appeal, along with a potent mix of intelligence and humor. She presented an intriguing contrast to the dainty, complacent women of his society.

Then there was the sexual pull she exerted over his libido. Not that he would ever act on it. Casual liaisons with commoners had no place in the life of a crown prince. Palace courtesans were available to meet his needs and prevent him from becoming embroiled in politically incorrect situations. It made life less complicated, and he preferred it that way.

So while he might find himself strongly attracted to Celie Cameron, he would keep his distance. After they made this crucial delivery, he would see her safely to her ship and both of them would get on with their separate lives.

The next cycle, Rurick crouched by a circuit panel and ran a scanner over its blackened surface. "Looks like this will have to be completely replaced. Would you hand me a laserdriver?" He reached behind him, waiting for Celie to press the tool into his palm. He wondered at her silence. She'd appeared subdued all morning. He hoped she wasn't getting an infection from her burns.

A moment later, she finally spoke. "Rurick, can I ask you something?"

He aimed the driver, pressed the activator, and a corner bolt spun out of its slot. "Ask away."

"Do you kiss many women?"

Startled, he dropped the tool, and it skittered a meter

away, coming to rest beneath a dangling pipe. "What sort of question is that?" he demanded, leaning down and stretching to reach for it.

"Actually, that's not what I really intended to ask."

She was just teasing him. Good. He was glad to see some of her spark returning. He touched the driver, wrapped his fingers around it.

"Have you mated with many women?"

He shot straight up, ramming his head into the pipe above him. He fell back on the floor, clenching his teeth to keep from cursing as he rubbed his throbbing scalp. Already a sizable knot was forming. He scrabbled backward until he was clear of the pipe and rolled up to stare at Celie.

She was kneeling by the tool cart, her hands clenched in her lap. Her eyes huge dark orbs, she watched him intently. He couldn't have heard her correctly. "I'm not sure I understood you. Repeat the question."

She lifted her chin, took a deep breath. "Have you mated with many women?"

Shock and amazement and a jumble of other emotions roared through him. Where in the universe had she come up with such an idea? "Why would you ask an android something like that?" he asked, making a great effort to keep his voice level. Not to mention calming his unruly body, which had reacted immediately to her highly suggestive query.

"Because I'm curious about your . . . sexual abilities."

A sense of impending doom sank like a weighted rocket coil in his gut. "Androids aren't known for their sexual prowess," he said, hoping to avert what was bound to be a disaster.

"But Max told Raven you had received pleasure training. He said . . ." She cast her eyes down, took another breath, then flashed her gaze back to Rurick. "He said that you could make women scream from pleasure."

He refrained from throwing the driver across the bay—just barely. "Max has a big mouth. He shouldn't have said such a thing to Raven."

"No, he shouldn't have. I don't know if you have any influence with him, or if you're even allowed to question his actions—"

"I have quite a bit of influence with the captain," Rurick interjected grimly. "He often yields to my superior intellect." Actually, Max had an independent streak, one that some overly presumptuous technician had thought would be great fun to program into him. But Rurick usually managed to gain the upper hand, if only by threatening to power Max down.

"Then you need to tell him that discussing your sexual attributes—or anyone's, for that matter—with Raven is inappropriate and unacceptable."

"Agreed. I'll talk to Max this evening." He gripped the driver, then tackled the matter at hand. "About your question—"

"I don't really want a count of the women you've pleasured," Celie said quickly, her face flushing. "That's none of my business. But I was wondering if you might demonstrate a few . . . things."

"What kind of things?" he asked cautiously, although he already knew where this was headed.

Her blush deepened, but she met his gaze steadily. "You know, kissing, and maybe other . . ." She trailed off and clenched her hands tighter. "Just kissing would do."

Rurick felt surprise and a deep sense of disappointment. He was used to women throwing themselves at him, but it had never occurred in his android role—only when he was in his real role as the Riordan crown prince. Sometimes it was flattering, but for the most part it was irritating and embarrassing.

He would never have thought Celie to be the type of

65

woman to fall into bed with any available male—or android, as the case might be. His high opinion of her sank. As appealing as he found her, he had no intention of appeasing her sexual curiosity about androids.

"I'm sorry," he said brusquely. "Max was wrong to tell you what he did. I can't fulfill your request."

Disappointment and a myriad of other emotions flashed through her eyes. "Not even a simple kiss?"

There would be nothing simple about a kiss between them. He knew if he kissed Celie, he'd want more. His body was already on full alert, just from the mere thought of kissing her. He'd want more, all right. He'd want to strip off the gold flight suit that hugged her luscious curves and lose himself in the satin texture of her skin, in the heat of her body.

He suspected she was hoping for just that. Yet the look on her face—an odd blend of embarrassment and apprehension—along with his reluctance to hurt her, tempered his reply.

"You're a very beautiful woman, Celie," he said gently. "I know many men would be delighted to appease your needs. I'm not able to do that."

Her face took on the shuttered expression he'd seen before. "There won't be any men in my life. Ever."

He stared at her, trying to absorb such a statement. "I find that difficult to believe. A woman like you—"

The comm buzzed, cutting off his words like a laser beam. "Rurick, are you there?" came Raven's anxious voice.

"Raven, what's wrong?" Celie scrambled to her feet, concern chasing all other emotions from her face.

"It's Max. He won't answer the comm to his cabin, or the entry tone, and the panel is secured. I can't get in. I thought he might be asleep, or in the lav, but I've been trying to contact him for over an hour now. I'm afraid something is wrong."

The android was likely still shut down and in repair mode. "He's a very deep sleeper," Rurick said, rising to his feet and facing the comm speaker. "He probably disabled the comm and the panel tone so he could get some rest. I'll check on him."

"But the panel is secured," Raven said, her voice quivering with worry.

"I can get in. I'll be there shortly." Rurick turned to finish the conversation with Celie, but she was already on her way to the ladder. It was just as well, he thought, noting the stiff set to her shoulders and shapely back. It was one of those embarrassing situations best forgotten, never again mentioned.

He glanced down at the telltale bulge in his flight suit, grateful that Celie was already halfway up the ladder. Now if only his body could forget the situation, could stop reacting this way whenever she was around. As soon as he took care of Max, a cold shower would be in order. And a cargo-freighterload of restraint where Celie was concerned.

Rurick paced the cabin, then turned to glare at his impertinent android. " 'Make women scream with pleasure'? Why on Jardonia did you tell Raven such a thing?"

Max practically preened. "Because it is true."

Rurick rolled his eyes. "Spare me."

"It is true," Max insisted. "I am highly trained in giving sexual pleasure. I did not lie to Raven. I used the term 'the android,' not your name, when I itemized my sexual abilities. It is not my fault she assumed I was talking about you."

"*Itemized?* Bragging is more like it," Rurick muttered. "I need to check into some modesty programming when we return home."

"Such programming will not change the facts," Max

retorted. "I can adjust the size of my instrument to the situation, and I leave all females fully pleasured and highly satisfied."

"Your 'instrument'?" Rurick wondered if androdi-cide was illegal. "I don't believe this. You talked to Raven about your *instrument?*"

"It is key to much of the pleasure giving."

"Gods, no wonder Celie came on to me. She thinks I have superhuman mating abilities." Rurick began pacing again. "It wouldn't matter if I did. I am *not* mating with her."

"There is no reason why you should refrain. She is a beautiful woman."

"Since when have you determined my amorous pursuits? I should have you melted down and used for scrap!"

"That will never happen," Max stated confidently. "I am too valuable to you."

"That value is decreasing by the millisecond."

"Indeed," Max continued, undaunted, "I find it highly remarkable that Captain Cameron asked you to service her."

"She didn't ask me to *service* her," Rurick snapped, irritated by Max's offhand terminology. "She asked me to kiss her. And why wouldn't she be interested in me?"

"Because you are a *man*. Or at least a replica of a man, since she believes you to be an android."

That stopped him cold. "*What?*" He stared at Max, unable to entertain the possibility the android was suggesting. "Are you saying the lady doesn't prefer men?"

"I am saying Captain Cameron does not trust men. Raven told me that when she was young, the captain had terrible experiences with men and has never let a male get close to her." Max's lopsided grin appeared. "I calculate a ninety-five-point-seven-percent probability that you could change her opinion of men."

The pieces began to fall into place. Celie's skittishness when Rurick took her to her cabin to treat her injuries, her alarm at Raven being alone with Max, her tentative suggestion that Rurick kiss her, and her statement that there would never be a man in her life.

Seeing it all, he groaned. "So you've decided I should change my profession to that of a spirit healer and sacrifice my dignity in an attempt to heal an emotionally damaged female. That's just great."

"She thinks you are an android," Max pointed out. "Therefore, it would be a logical thought process to consider you a safe experiment. Since you are not a real man, you cannot hurt her—at least not in an emotional sense."

So Celie didn't consider him a real man. She thought he was *safe. An experiment.* Rurick didn't know whether to be insulted or laugh at the irony. Or maybe he should bang his head against the wall or throttle Max. He liked the last option best.

"I don't want you to say another word to Celie or Raven about your sexual prowess, or about mine," he ordered Max.

"I am just attempting to help Captain Cameron," the android said, affecting a hurt expression.

"Not another word. Are we clear on this?"

"Yes, Your Highness."

Rurick chose to ignore Max's condescending tone. "There is to be no demonstration of physical pleasure with Raven. No inappropriate actions or discussions of any sort. She's still young and quite enamored of you, in case you hadn't noticed."

"Of course I noticed. It is quite understandable that young Raven would be impressed by me."

How was it possible for an android to be so irritating? "Don't tempt me to shut you down for the remainder of the trip," Rurick warned, but he didn't really mean it, and unfortunately, Max knew that as well.

The exasperating android wasn't his real problem, however. Captain Celie Cameron was. Tomorrow, he'd have to face her and try to defuse any ideas she might still have about his sexual abilities, and about any possibility that he could enlighten her on the subject of mating. Regardless of what Max and Celie—and Rurick's own rebellious body—seemed to think.

Celie spent another restless night, alternating between trying to fall asleep on her bunk and pacing the cabin. Even though she tried to will her runaway thoughts under control, her efforts were futile. Blazing hells. What was it about that darned android that was so appealing? He wasn't real. His thick lustrous hair, those intense golden eyes, that sensually enticing mouth: none of it was real. *None of it.*

And what about this sudden surge of her hormones, or libido, or whatever it was? What was happening to her? Celie rose and walked to the portal. Actually, she knew what was happening. She just didn't know what to do about it.

The good news, she supposed, was that she appeared to be a normal female, with all the typical urges and desires that entailed. The bad news was that she needed to repress those feelings. It didn't require a spiritual healer to explain the problem. She was well aware that her early experiences with men had created deep craters of pain; had necessitated she build protective emotional walls. Walls that were—and would always remain—inviolate. She didn't want to continually face her fears, or the pain, and had long ago decided that keeping her distance from males was the safest and least disturbing course of action.

Her strategy had worked very well, and she'd lived an uncomplicated and fairly satisfying life, until now.

Until a golden-haired android—an *android,* of all things!—had set her hormones humming and stirred up disconcerting urges she'd never before experienced.

It wasn't denying these newfound physical clamorings that Celie found difficult. She'd lived many seasons with physical hardship, existing on the barest of necessities, before her sister Moriah's smuggling business had become lucrative. Celie knew what it was like to be hungry and cold, with no foreseeable end to miserable living conditions. She was hardy, disciplined, and could readily endure physical discomforts.

What really nagged at her right now was curiosity, pure and simple. She'd always wondered about the attraction between males and females; about the universal appeal of mating between almost every species in existence. But she'd always pushed her curiosity away, closed off her thoughts on the subject. Very successfully—again, until now. For some inexplicable reason, Rurick had triggered her more prurient interests and, in the process, stirred up some highly disconcerting carnal urges. Those urges were just instinct, necessary for the survival of the species, Celie told herself firmly. She could control them. Mind over matter.

And yet . . . A part of her really wanted to know. The mating act was something she'd never attempt to experience, but kissing was another matter. She'd always wondered why it was such a big deal. It looked awkward to her, and the thought of the exchange of saliva was somewhat distasteful, but . . . she still wanted to know. Once she did experience a kiss, she was confident her curiosity would be satisfied. She might even find it totally repulsive, and then she could put the matter to rest.

The more she thought about it, the more she realized Raven's suggestion had merit. Rurick was the perfect solution to her dilemma. She'd never have to approach a real man to experience kissing, placing herself in a position that might create a power play and put her at a disadvantage.

Rurick was safe. He could assuage her curiosity. She had thought about this well into the previous night shift, finally deciding to ask the android to accommodate her and demonstrate a kiss. It would mean nothing to him—or to *it*, if she wanted to be accurate. No one would ever know, and then she'd get on with her life. With her normal, secure existence.

Even so, it had taken several hours to work up enough courage to approach Rurick, which was ridiculous. She'd learned to be aggressive in business dealings and go after what she wanted. But she'd felt foolish asking a lowly android to give her a simple kiss. Finally, angry with herself for such nonsense, she'd asked. And he'd refused her request! Coolly, unemotionally, and probably with some annoying reason why he shouldn't.

"Blazing hells." Celie stopped her pacing and raked her hand through her hair. "Rejected by an android. That's a first."

It certainly hadn't calmed her hormones. Nor had it blunted her curiosity, or her growing determination to experience a nonchaste kiss. She didn't give up easily, and she would try again.

At the next opportunity, she'd ask Rurick why he'd refused her. This time, she'd demand rather than ask that he honor her request. All she wanted was a simple kiss, by the Spirit. Just a kiss. That would surely put her questions to rest, and end this unrest once and for all.

Chapter Five

The next morning, Celie awoke with a start, surprised to see it was later than she'd intended to rise. In the early hours of sleep shift, she'd finally fallen into an exhausted stupor, too deep to hear the wake-up tones. Great. She rolled to her feet and dressed hurriedly, steeling herself for her confrontation with Rurick. She had set her course of action, and now she wanted it over. The sooner, the better, before she lost her nerve. She strode down the corridor, her heart beating an irregular tattoo.

She was disappointed to find Rurick wasn't alone. He and Max and Raven were gathered in the lounge, chatting away as if they'd known each other for many seasons. They all looked up when she entered, and Raven smiled brightly. "Celie! I was about to come looking for you. We've been having the best discussion."

"Sorry I'm late," Celie mumbled.

Rurick rose as his golden gaze scanned her: assessing

and, she could have sworn, concerned. Impossible. Surely an android didn't feel concern. "Are you all right?" he asked.

"Just fine," she answered, even as her breath froze in her chest at the sight of him. He cut a magnificent figure, his gold flight suit setting off his broad shoulders and beautifully delineated chest to perfection. But then he *was* perfect, in a technical sense. They should make all androids ugly, she thought resentfully, trying to control her physical reaction to him.

"You look tired," Raven announced.

"She does look somewhat unsettled, does she not?" Max asked. He looked at Rurick with a peculiar lopsided grin. "As if she needs something."

"That's enough, Max," Rurick said sharply.

"I'm fine," Celie insisted, not sure where this strange conversation was heading. "What's the plan for today? I know we have several repairs to complete."

"I'm going to finish the external repairs," Rurick replied.

"Not a good idea," Max stated. "I am far more qualified to work on the infrared and radar sensors."

"But Rurick is the android," Raven protested, her expression turning fearful. "You don't need to take the risk of going outside the ship."

Celie frowned, unhappy at Raven's obvious concern for Max.

"You're right, he doesn't need to take such a risk." Rurick shot Max an odd glance. "He'll finish the repairs on the circuitry in the bays. He's very qualified to do that."

"If you insist," Max said stiffly, his expression displeased. "I will fix the circuits." He turned sharply and marched toward the entry. Celie sidestepped to let him pass, wondering at the apparent dissension between him and Rurick, and why he was giving in to the android. It seemed to her it should be the other way around.

Rurick strode forward, halting beside her. "I'd appreciate it if you'd monitor the cockpit again while I'm outside." He looked distant and impersonal, as if nothing embarrassing had occurred between them the previous cycle, as if she hadn't asked him to kiss her and he hadn't turned her down flat.

But then, what had she expected? "Of course," she replied, just as coolly. "I'll be with you in a moment." She turned her attention to Raven. "Why don't you join me in there?"

Raven shifted and smoothed her flight suit. "I hope you don't mind, Celie, but I promised Max I'd help him. He's going to explain the different tools to me and let me be his assistant."

"I'm not so sure that's a good idea," Celie protested, both alarmed and protective. Once Rurick was outside, she'd be tied to the cockpit, unable to check on Raven. It might be hours before she was free, hours in which Raven and Max would be alone together. "I want you to stay with me."

"But I want to be with Max." Raven tossed her ebony hair over her shoulder, her dark eyes full of resolve. "You know I enjoy being with you, but Max is so interesting. And he has so much to show me."

Celie was sure Max had a lot of things to show an impressionable young woman, many of them not very wholesome. "I don't think you need to spend so much time with Max. Especially alone with him—"

"It's all right, Celie." Rurick's hand closed over her arm. Startled, she whipped around to stare at him. His gaze was reassuring, as if he could understand her anxiety. "Raven will be completely safe with Max. I personally guarantee it."

How could an android guarantee the actions of his

human captain? "I want her with me. I'm responsible for her." She turned to argue further, but Raven was already gone, a flash of gold whipping into the airlock leading to the lower deck.

"Son of an Antek," she muttered. She started after Raven, but Rurick's grip on her arm stopped her. Whirling, she leveled a furious glare at him. "Let me go."

"She's young, but she is legally an adult," he said quietly. "You have to let her make her own decisions and choices. Besides, I've known Max many seasons. I can vouch for his integrity."

Memories flashed through Celie's mind. Horrifying scenes, still vividly clear all these seasons later: her father, his face red from alcohol and rage, raising his beefy arm to strike; Pax Blacklock, a younger version of her father, just as drunk and just as cruel, dragging off her sister Moriah, to force his sexual lust on her. The blaster discharging, the blood, so much blood . . . She drew a deep breath, forcing the images away. *That was a long time ago,* she reminded herself.

"Celie." Rurick released his hold on her but didn't step back. "What are you so afraid of?"

She turned away, struggling to regain her poise. "I'm worried because Raven is young and inexperienced when it comes to men. They don't always behave honorably."

"Unfortunately, every society has undesirables who do immoral things. But I prefer to believe that most beings in this quadrant are honorable and decent."

"Agreed." And Celie really did agree; however, that didn't negate the facts of the real universe, or rid her of the nightmare memories. "But it only takes one bad man to do irrevocable damage to a woman."

"I take it your observation is based on personal experience."

He was only an android, and in a few cycles she'd be

back on her ship and never see him again. There was no possible harm in her being honest. "You might say that. I've come across a few men who were monsters in disguise, may their souls rot in Hades."

"I'm sorry." He studied her intently. "So, because of your experiences, you've kept your associations with men impersonal?"

He was far too perceptive. She regretted that the conversation had gone this far, wished she hadn't been so honest. But there was nothing to do now but finish it. "It's my choice to avoid personal involvement with any man."

"Is that why you asked me to kiss you yesterday? To see what it was like without actually having personal contact with a man?"

He had cut to the heart of the matter with unerring accuracy. She realized how ridiculous she must look to him. A woman haunted by demons from her past, coming on to an android to appease her sordid curiosity. "Pretty pathetic, isn't it?"

"No, Celie." He stepped closer. "It's not pathetic at all."

She was acutely aware of his body almost touching hers, of the compassion warming his eyes to a molten gold. "Your actions are understandable," he told her, his deep voice resonating through her, soothing and stimulating at the same time. "I'm sorry you've had bad experiences with men. But I'm not the one to chase your ghosts away. I'm—" He paused, and she found her attention riveted to his sensuous mouth. What would that mouth feel like, pressed against her lips? Against her body?

"There are many decent men in the universe who would cherish you and treat you with respect," he continued. "Men who would be all too glad to show you both the spiritual and physical pleasures of mating, how it should be between a man and a wom—"

She didn't give him a chance to finish, hurling herself against him as she grabbed his head between her hands and pressed her lips to his. He stiffened, but allowed her to remain there while she experienced the warmth and texture of his lips.

He didn't resist, but he didn't reciprocate either; didn't return the pressure or open his mouth. He simply stood there, passive and indifferent. After a moment, he took her arms and gently moved her back.

"There. You've been kissed." He said it with no emotion in his voice, as if they were talking about the weather or some other mundane topic. He backed away, his eyes now cool. "I'll be suited up and in the airlock in five minutes." He turned and strode off, his posture ramrod stiff.

Celie stood there, her heart pounding, bitter disappointment washing over her. The kiss had been nothing. Not that she had expected to be greatly affected by it. But how could she know what a true kiss was like when the other party hadn't participated in the least? She wasn't totally ignorant; she'd seen other couples kissing, and she knew most humans employed their tongues in a passionate kiss. But Rurick wasn't human, so maybe he wasn't adept at kissing.

That thought quickly disintegrated as Raven's words came back to her like a taunt. *"Max said the android on our ship has extensive pleasure training, and can do everything a humanoid can do, and more."* She would bet Rurick was more than proficient, not only in kissing but in all aspects of mating.

He just didn't want to kiss her.

Was she so undesirable? Or maybe he was put off by her naïvete, her total lack of experience. Celie knew some considered her attractive. She'd rebuffed her share of overeager males, so she didn't think her appearance had repelled Rurick. It was more likely her inexperience. He obviously didn't want to deal with her fumbling attempt at a kiss. Well, he could rot in Hades with Pax and her father.

She stalked down the corridor and into the cockpit, sliding stiffly into the pilot's chair. She flipped on the comm to Rurick's headset and sat there fuming. A few moments later, his voice came over the speaker, checking with her before he went outside the ship. She answered in curt monosyllables, determined to be professional, no matter how much his rejection stung.

Besides, she had other concerns. As soon as Rurick was set and working on the external sensors, Celie contacted the engineering bay. "Raven, are you there?"

"Right here," came the girl's excited voice. "You should see Max working on the circuit panels. He's really fast. It's amazing."

Max could sneeze and Raven would think it was amazing. "I'm sure he could work better without you in his way. Come join me in the cockpit."

"I don't want to," Raven declared rebelliously. "I want to stay with Max."

Celie took another approach. "Max, please ask Raven to join me. I'm sure you'll get more done if you work alone."

"I like having Raven here," came Max's distinctive, oddly flat voice. "I am instructing her in stardrive mechanics, and she is learning at an impressive rate."

Max might also want to show Raven things that had nothing to do with mechanics. "I could use her assistance here."

"Oh? That is interesting. Rurick has indicated that you are extremely competent in the cockpit. Is that not true?"

Celie gritted her teeth. Of course it was true. "I have everything under control, but—"

"Good. Then young Raven can remain here with me."

Inwardly seething, Celie could do nothing but concede, since she couldn't leave the cockpit with only a small lifeline anchoring Rurick to the ship. "Fine. But I'm leaving the comm line open so I can hear anything that happens down there."

"Celie!" Raven's voice rose indignantly.

"Do not worry about it, little one," Max said. "We can continue our mechanics lesson and—" He lowered his voice to a whisper and said something Celie couldn't hear.

Raven giggled and whispered back.

Celie sat there several moments, listening to a whispered conversation in which she couldn't make out any words. "I can hear everything you're saying," she lied into the comm. "And everything you're doing."

More giggling and muted whispers were her only answer. Throwing up her hands, she stared through the portal into space, brooding. There was a significant advantage to working and traveling alone. She didn't have to be responsible for anyone else, didn't have to endure this worry and concern. She could go where she wanted, when she wanted . . . and be totally bored.

And alone. For the first time, she admitted to her loneliness, at least on a conscious level. She had been terribly lonely these last two seasons. She missed her sister, and the colony on Risa. But she couldn't return to that quadrant, not with the Controllers still in charge. She had not enjoyed living on Shamara, dealing with tedious, day-to-day details. She was a restless spirit, needed to be on the move. She loved space travel and visiting different places. However, making deliveries in this quadrant had been bland and dull, compared to the life-and-death situations she'd faced on a daily basis in the old quadrant.

Her life had been totally boring. Until she'd found

herself thrown into Joba's unsavory environment, with her safety in question—all this while discovering Raven had stowed away on her ship. Until she'd met a mysterious android pilot and his human captain, and engaged in a battle with unknown assailants. In a way, these events had been exhilarating—just like old times.

Now she was stranded on an unfamiliar, damaged ship, unable to reach her own vessel and worried about Raven's attraction to a stranger. Not to mention her own inexplicable attraction to an android. Or worse, her raging hormones and overactive imagination, both demanding that she at least experience a taste of the physical pleasures men and women claimed to enjoy.

Soon enough, she'd return to her ship. She'd take Raven back to Shamara, then set about investigating the strange conditions in the Joba settlement. Most likely the situation was an aberration, and Joba was a colony that had fallen through administrative cracks. Celie would bring it to the attention of the Interstellar Council, then return to her normal existence.

She couldn't say she was looking forward to it.

"Celie, can you read me?" Rurick's voice crackled over the speaker.

She shook away her musings. "I'm here. How's it going?"

"I think I've got the sensors repaired. Would you give me the pressure readouts on the infrared scanners?"

She did, also providing Rurick other information he requested, while she kept part of her attention on the comm connection to engineering, trying futilely to hear the conversation between Raven and Max. At least the two were talking, which she took as a positive sign.

"Celie? Are you there? You didn't answer my last question."

"I was distracted. I'm trying to"—Raven giggled again, and Celie leaned toward the comm, straining to

81

hear more—"monitor Max and Raven while I talk to you."

"Still worried about that, are you?"

She sat back in her seat and sighed. "I do seem to be fixated on certain things, don't I?"

He laughed softly, and her heart skittered. Amazing that an android could display a sense of humor, and that his husky laugh would have such an effect on her. "Yeah, you do," he said. "But it's understandable."

He was handsome, intelligent, sympathetic, humorous—and not real. He was perfect for what she wanted. But he'd refused to cooperate. She'd overcome a lot of obstacles more difficult than this, so why did she feel so stymied? It wasn't in her nature to give up. The more Celie thought about it, the more determined she became. Blazing hells, Rurick was trained to give physical pleasure. He was just a machine. What gave him the right to pick and choose whom he would pleasure? She wasn't asking much—just a kiss. What could be so difficult about that?

She swung her chair around and headed for the airlock. She intended to have her kiss and be done with it. Then her curiosity would be satisfied. And that would be that.

Rurick had found it almost impossible to keep his attention on the tank repairs. Instead, he'd kept thinking about Celie's awkward attempt to kiss him. At the airlock, his body had gone on full alert when she pressed herself against him. Her lips had been warm against his, her lush curves branding both his senses and his body. He'd barely maintained his wits. Fortunately, he'd had the presence of mind not to respond to her kiss, not to crush her to him and ravish her mouth. But he'd sure wanted to.

No other woman had ever had such a strong effect

on him. He'd always prided himself on his discipline and self-control. But Celie, with that striking combination of sunlight hair and dark brown eyes, that tall, toned body and sultry voice, was very alluring. She had a potent affect, like a drug, on his senses. Oddly enough, her innocence made her even more appealing.

Which made it critical for him to keep his distance from her. He knew he had done the right thing by refusing to kiss her back. Celie needed—and deserved—a man who could be there for her. Rurick wasn't in a position to be that man. Not only that, but he'd lied to her by maintaining his android masquerade. She was bound to feel betrayed if she found out the truth. Fortunately, that would never happen.

He pulled off his helmet, then looked up to see Celie striding toward him. Her flight suit hugged her, and he'd never realized he could be so attracted by a woman's legs; the women of his country wore long flowing robes, rarely exposing them. He forced his gaze back to Celie's face, noting her resolute expression. He had a feeling he knew what the topic of the conversation was going to be.

She stopped before him, making direct eye contact. "I want to discuss what happened between us earlier."

She certainly didn't waste time on formalities—a refreshing change from the stilted conversations of Riordan courtiers. "I don't think there's anything to discuss," he answered. "It would be best if we forgot what happened. Let's just say you got what you wanted and let it go at that."

Her chin went up a notch, and he had the distinct impression she was entering battle mode. "What I wanted was a *real* kiss. Since you've been trained to provide much more than that, I don't understand how a simple kiss could be so difficult for you."

Rurick again cursed Max for his big mouth, and his

fondness for flaunting his abilities. "Celie, it's not a matter of sexual training or skills. You need to find a man who will love and appreciate you, and treat you with respect. That man is the one who should be kissing you. Not me. I think it would be best if we didn't pursue this matter any further."

He started to turn away, but she grasped his arm and pulled him back around. "I'm not through yet, Captain."

"I am." He stepped back. She followed, tightening her grip.

"I'm sorry you're put off by my request. I didn't realize my lack of experience would make me so repulsive." She said the words with bravado, but he saw the hurt reflected in her eyes.

He hadn't considered the possibility that she'd assume he found her undesirable. He couldn't let her think that. She might never approach another man if she believed she'd be rejected. Yet he wasn't sure he could convince her of her attractiveness without making the situation worse.

"That's not true." He hesitated, then lifted a hand to touch her face. The feel of her smooth skin and radiant warmth slammed through him, causing a chain reaction in his body. He drew a deep breath, reached for control. "I can't imagine how any man would find you undesirable. You're beautiful, intelligent, and witty. Any man not attracted to you would have to be dead or insane."

"That's hard to believe, especially since you—an android—don't even want to kiss me. I wouldn't expect a machine to be so selective."

"It's not that. I find you incredibly attractive. But we have no business becoming involved. You're human, and I'm—as you said—an . . . android." He stumbled over the last word, hating to lie to her. "You need to find a real man."

Her eyes narrowed and she grabbed the front of his flight suit and jerked him forward. "Kiss me, damn it," she hissed.

He stared at her sensuous mouth, heat and desire spiraling through him. He shouldn't do this. He should back off, refuse as tactfully as possible.

"Kiss me. *Now*," she demanded, leaning closer until her face was mere centimeters from his. "And do it right this time."

Do it right? Good intentions and rational thinking fled beneath an onslaught of angry frustration, fueled by a healthy measure of lust. To Hades with noble self-denial. The lady had issued a challenge, and he was definitely up to it.

"All right," he growled. "Just remember, you asked for it."

He pulled her so tightly against him an atom couldn't wedge itself between them. He lowered his head, taking possession of her mouth. She gasped, and he realized he was being too rough. With a great effort, he forced himself to slow down, to handle her with care. The red haze in his mind and body cleared enough that he could take the time to savor the satiny feel and warmth of her lips as he mapped their shape and firmness.

At first she was tense, then she settled into him, fitting close, as if she'd been made for him. She showed no repulsion, no sign that she wanted to pull away or put a halt to this dangerous sensual exercise. Her lips moved gently beneath his, and suddenly the external contact wasn't enough. He had to have more. He teased the seam of her mouth with his tongue. With a small moan, she yielded to him, and he swept inside.

He told himself that he was doing this to stop her demands. To appease her curiosity. To see if she tasted as good as she looked. And she did . . . oh yeah, she did. By the moons of Jardonia, she was as sweet as nectar.

85

The red haze surged through him again, and every cell of his body responded to the scent and taste of her, to the feel of her. Her tongue touched his tentatively at first, then responded more boldly, in a sensuous duel that imitated what his body very much wanted to do to hers. She was so fresh, so natural in her response. She felt wonderful, her firm back flexing as he stroked his hands downward to her waist, then lightly over her hips.

In a distant part of his mind, he knew he should stop, shouldn't take this any further, but he couldn't seem to help himself. He pulled back slightly and spanned his hand over her flat midriff. She was warm and vibrant, and he desperately wanted to know how the rest of her felt. Almost of its own volition, his hand slid higher, capturing a lush breast. Celie stiffened, but he deepened the kiss, and she again relaxed into his body.

Still kissing her, he explored the exquisite fullness of her breast, brushing his thumb over the taut nipple. She moaned again, pressing against his hand. She was so responsive, so incredibly sexy. He wanted to lay her down right there, strip off her flight suit, and explore every inch of her. Which would lead to initiating her fully into the act of mating . . . which was not a good idea. He groaned, battling for some semblance of control.

"Captain Rurick."

Vaguely, he was aware of someone saying his name. It couldn't be Celie, since her mouth was engaged with his.

"Excuse me, Captain, but I must interrupt this."

Max! Rurick pulled away from Celie and looked up. Raven and Max stood there, staring at Celie and him. He glanced at Celie's flushed face, then realized he was still cupping her breast. He jerked his hand away as if

86

she were a hot brand. He took a hasty step back, dragging air into his constricted chest.

"Captain Rurick! I am shocked at this behavior," Max said primly.

Raven merely grinned and gave a thumbs-up signal to Celie. Shooting Raven a glare, Celie occupied herself with straightening her flight suit.

Rurick resisted the urge to stalk over and beat the smug look off the android's face. "Not another word, Max."

"It is my duty to keep order on this ship," Max intoned. "I must ask you to limit any further displays of passion to private quarters."

"That's enough." Jerking his shoulders forward and pulling his flight suit down, Rurick turned to Celie. "Are you all right?" he asked.

She nodded, then glanced away. "Of course."

He didn't believe that for a millisecond. He wanted to apologize for letting things get so far out of hand. The blame rested solely on him. He was the experienced one, and should have exercised more control. "I . . ." He stopped and turned to stare pointedly at Max and Raven. "Could we have a moment here . . . *alone?*"

"If you insist, but I must remind you that any more erotic encounters will have to be conducted elsewhere," Max said.

"Oh, Max." Raven slipped her arm through his. "It doesn't matter where they do it. I think it's great."

"There's nothing to discuss," Celie interjected. "I'm going to my cabin now." She strode over to Raven and pulled the girl's arm free of Max's. "You, young lady, can come with me."

"But Rurick wants to talk to you," Raven protested as Celie towed her down the corridor. "Don't you want to hear what he has to say?"

Celie glanced his way briefly, her face now pale, her

eyes unreadable. "Our business is finished. Come on."

"See you later, Max!" Raven called, waving madly before she was dragged inside Celie's cabin.

Cursing himself, Rurick ran a hand through his hair. What had happened to the iron-clad control he normally possessed? How could he have treated Celie that way? As innocent as she was, he'd probably shocked her down to her black-booted toes.

"I see you decided after all to change Captain Cameron's opinion of men. I applaud your decision." Max slapped him on the shoulder none too gently, and he stumbled forward. "It appeared you were making great progress at it. With the ninety-five-point-seven percent probability that I have predicted—"

"Shut up, Max," Rurick snapped, "or I'll power you down."

He wanted to kick himself. He'd probably done more harm than good today, and now Celie might give up on men altogether. She was very likely disgusted with his actions, and he couldn't blame her. He should have followed his original instincts and left well enough alone. He should never have kissed her.

One thing was certain: He would not repeat his mistake again. Celie had too potent an effect on him, one he couldn't seem to keep checked. From now on, until they left their two guests at Joba, he'd keep his distance from Celie. No matter how strong the attraction between them.

Chapter Six

Well, that hadn't helped. Not in the least. In fact, the kiss she'd shared with Rurick had only made matters worse. Celie resumed her pacing around her cabin.

Janaye had an expression: *If you take one bite from a caroba pie, you'll never be satisfied until you've eaten the entire pie.* Celie had always interpreted it to mean, *Be careful what you start, or you may find yourself wanting what you can't have.* It went hand in hand with another piece of advice Janaye offered: *Be careful what you wish for. You might get it.*

The astute, psychic old lady had been like a mother to Moriah and Celie, and had often shared gems of wisdom with them. Time and again, circumstances had proven the truth and insight of Janaye's words.

Today had certainly been a case in point. Celie fingered her tender lips, remembering the thrilling way Rurick had kissed. Her body still tingled from his intimate touch on her breast. Nothing in her life had prepared her for the impact their encounter had had on her senses, and most notably on her body.

She'd never imagined such sensations, or the ensuing intense *craving*—there was no other word for it—for more. A craving for Rurick's touch elsewhere, everywhere, on her body. No, she told herself. Not for Rurick's touch, but rather for any man's touch. Rurick was just a machine. Her response to him was biological, nothing else. But, oh, what a response!

At least she knew she was normal, for what it was worth. However, awakening her natural sexual urges had obviously not been a good idea, because now she wanted to experience those shattering sensations again. They were as thrilling as the adrenaline rush from eluding Anteks or making a dangerous delivery. Plus she now had to consider the possibility that the mating act itself might be even more of a rush.

But dark memories and relentless guilt continued to haunt her, and she knew she could never succumb to her newfound sensuality. She could never place herself in a position of submission to a man, never again be powerless and vulnerable.

Rurick's words right before he gave in to her impetuous demand came back to her: *Just remember, you asked for it.* She'd asked for it, all right. And he'd given it to her. But it had only made matters worse. She was more aware than ever of her aloneness . . . and the knowledge that she would remain that way her entire life.

Celie had a horrible night. The nightmare, which had been absent for almost half a season, had returned with a vengeance. As always, she relived that awful event on Elysia with horrifying clarity: the blaster discharge, the open, shocked eyes, the blood. Oh Spirit, so much blood . . .

She leaped from her bunk, rubbing her arms. Her activated libido was most likely responsible for the nightmare's return. She'd acknowledged the sexual side of her nature, had allowed a man—or at least a facsimile of a man—to kiss and touch her in a very intimate way. She had only herself to blame.

Not that she'd expected the nightmare to ever leave her entirely. For the rest of her days, she'd be paying for her crime. The dream was just a vivid reminder of her foolishness in yearning for something she could never have.

The comm buzzed, and she turned toward it, grateful for a reprieve from the grim memories. Max's flat voice came over the speaker. "Captain Cameron, are you there?"

"Yes, Captain. What is it?"

"The repairs on the ship have been completed. We will meet in the lounge in one hour to discuss our next destination. We request that you and Raven join us."

"Of course, Captain. Raven and I will meet you then."

She steeled herself to face Rurick, then reminded herself there was no need to be embarrassed. He was an android. A machine. He probably hadn't given their encounter a second thought.

When they met in the lounge, his cool, impersonal greeting proved her right. She was just as cool, nodding politely. She pushed aside thoughts of the nightmare as she seated herself to his left. Raven sat to her left, and Max was across from her.

"As you know," Max began, "all repairs have been completed, and diagnostics have been run. All systems are operating fully, so we have set the course for our next destination."

Celie breathed a sigh of relief. Now she and Raven could get back to her ship and get on with their lives. "How long will it take to reach Joba?"

Rurick and Max exchanged a glance. "We're not headed to Joba," Max answered. "We're headed to Altair."

Uneasiness slithered through Celie. "What are you talking about? Why aren't we going to Joba?"

Rurick nodded to Max. "Perhaps you should explain."

"There will be a further delay in your return to Joba," Max said. "It is crucial that we reach Altair as soon as possible."

Celie couldn't believe what she was hearing. "I was to understand you would return me to my ship as soon as we made the repairs on yours."

"I am sorry," Max said. "We must go to Altair first."

Blazing hells. Celie considered her options. "Then Raven and I will catch a transport from Altair and get to Joba on our own."

"Altair does not have any public transports. In fact, the settlement is virtually destitute."

"Then why are we headed there?"

"The conditions on Altair are far worse than those on Joba," Max said. "They are so critical, we must go there now."

"I don't understand," Celie said, her heart taking on an erratic beat. She *had* to retrieve her ship. "What is going on?"

Rurick leaned forward. "You may find this difficult to believe, but it appears that all the settlements in the ninth sector, at least all the ones we've seen, are poverty stricken, and some are crime-ridden as well."

"That's not possible," Celie argued. "The Interstellar Council regulates the quality of life for everyone in the quadrant. They—"

"Don't appear to know about the conditions of the ninth sector," Rurick broke in. "Max and I discovered the situation by accident."

Celie considered this, still mystified. "Then why hasn't someone brought this to the attention of the

Council? People travel in and out of the sector on a regular basis. Surely someone would report it."

"We believe it is not being reported because of a deliberate cover-up," Max replied. "The information about these conditions is not being allowed out of the sector."

"Oh, come on!" Celie argued. "How could anyone keep widespread conditions like this a secret?"

"We don't know for sure," Rurick said. "But we suspect that at least one highly ranked official on the Council knows about this sector and has gone to great lengths to keep it hidden. And we believe that the checkpoint stations ringing this sector are the means of suppressing the information."

"How are they doing that?"

"Our guess is that they're erasing the memories of visitors. It's mandatory for all ships to stop at the stations, and all beings must actually disembark and go through checkpoints."

Celie couldn't accept such a possibility. Checkpoints ringed each of the twelve sectors in the quadrant. Their purpose was to enforce tariffs on transported goods, safeguard against parasites or diseases being spread between sectors, and to ensure that all spacecraft passed regular inspections. Extending that purpose to mind tampering was beyond comprehension.

"If what you say is true, as soon as we go through a checkpoint, we won't remember what we've seen. How many times have you been in this sector? Are you telling me you have no memories of previous visits?"

Rurick shook his head. "We've been in this sector quite a few times, and we've been documenting the widespread poverty. We don't have to worry about memory erasure. We're exempt from passing through the stations."

More and more unbelievable. "Why are you exempt?" Celie demanded.

Max and Rurick looked at each other again. "You tell her," Rurick said.

"Very well." Max leaned forward. "I am a member of the Riordan royal family. Because of my imperial status, I do not have to endure the indignity of checkpoints. It is a concession granted to all heads of state."

"You're royalty?" Celie didn't try to mask her incredulity.

"You're royalty?" Raven repeated, her eyes lighting up. "Wow. That is so cool."

"I find this impossible to believe," Celie contended. "You've given no indication of royal status this entire time. What game are you playing?"

"This is no game," Rurick answered. "There was no reason to disclose Max's identity. Did you notice the gold crest on the outside of the ship? That's the Riordan royal insignia."

"This is the ship of the crown prince of Jardonia," Max announced proudly. "The one who is next in line to ascend the Riordan throne."

"You're really a prince?" breathed Raven, looking at Max with total awe. "Do I have to address you as 'Your Highness' or some other title?"

"How can we be certain you're telling the truth?" Celie demanded before Max could answer. "You've avoided disclosing any real information up to now, and suddenly you're giving us this crazy story about royalty and widespread poverty and disease and a quadrant-wide cover-up. You could be black market smugglers, for all I know."

"That is a reasonable assumption," Max said. "But it is incorrect. I believe the truth of our statements about the destitution in sector nine will be verified when we reach Altair. Also, you might consider the attack on our ship at Joba. The royal crest on the ship, while allowing us unrestricted passage in and out of this sector, also clearly marks our presence. I believe our assailants were sent to silence us permanently."

"With conditions so bad on Joba, perhaps they were just after our supplies," Celie pointed out. "It might not have had anything to do with the crest on your ship. It certainly doesn't prove your claim of royalty."

"No, it does not." Max gave his lopsided smile. "You can always research Jardonia and the Riordan royal family."

"You can be sure I'll do that at the first opportunity," she replied grimly.

Rurick scowled at Max, and she wondered at the advisability of openly challenging their allegations. If these two were somehow involved in illegal activities, they might now consider Raven and her a threat to their plans.

"Oh, Max," Raven said, her eyes shining with obvious adoration. "You're really royalty? Do you live in a palace?"

Celie didn't like the direction this was going. First off, the story was too incredible. She had spent many seasons in a world in which walking the line between truth and deception was a way of life, so she knew better than to believe everything she heard. She had no way of verifying whether or not Max and Rurick were telling the truth about the widespread destitution of the ninth sector, but she could do a computer search on the Riordan dynasty and see if Max was actually the heir to the throne.

To make matters worse, Raven now regarded Max as if he were some sort of god, starstruck with the idea that he might be a prince. It would be more difficult to keep the two apart, and far too easy for Max to take advantage of Raven's infatuation.

She sat back in her chair, turning over the information in her mind, while Raven inundated Max with questions about Jardonia and Riordan royalty. Rurick remained silent, but Celie was aware of his watchful gaze. It occurred to her that she could test the men's desire to help the colonists on Altair, and bring aid for Raven and herself, should it be needed.

"Max," she said, interrupting a long-winded spiel about the wonders of Jardonia, "you say there is both starvation and disease on Altair?"

"Yes. Our contact there has informed us that disease is epidemic, and a large number of people have already died, although how many from starvation and how many from illness is not known. You will be able to assess the conditions yourself."

"Then you wouldn't mind if I contacted someone who can offer assistance."

Rurick leaned forward, his eyes narrowed and tension radiating from his body. How could an android be tense? she wondered. "There are few we would trust until we have further information on who is behind this," he said.

She found his reaction interesting—and damning. "I'd like to contact Chase McKnight. He's Raven's father and a highly skilled physician. If you're telling the truth about conditions on Altair, he could be very useful there. He can be trusted implicitly with confidential information. I can—and have—trusted him with my life."

"Oh, yes," Raven seconded. "My father is a great healer. He can help." She clasped Max's arm, her gaze earnest. "Really."

Max looked at Rurick. "I see no reason why we would refuse Dr. McKnight's assistance, if he is willing to come to Altair."

Rurick considered, then nodded. "I agree. We need all the help we can get." His golden gaze speared Celie. "But he'll have to go through the checkpoints. When he leaves this quadrant, he'll lose all memory of Altair."

"Maybe not," she replied. "Chase managed to withstand Controller psionic brain waves when he went through indoctrination in the other quadrant. He might be able to slip through the system."

"Fascinating," Max murmured. "Is Dr. McKnight a Shielder?"

Startled, Celie realized Raven must have revealed her own heritage.

"My father is not a Shielder, even though my mother and I are," the girl explained. "But he once used drugs and hypnosis to avoid Controller indoctrination. If we warn him about the checkpoints, he might be able to do the same thing again."

"Very interesting," Rurick mused. "Dr. McKnight was able to create an artificial immunity to psionics. And Shielders have a natural immunity to them. I wonder if Shielders might also be resistant to memory erasure."

"That is a consideration," Max said, obviously intrigued by the theory. "Depending on the process used at the checkpoints, that could be a real possibility. Since there are limited methods of safely removing memories and implanting false ones in their place, I would estimate an eighty-five-point-seven-percent probability that—"

"Max," Rurick said sharply.

"I was just explaining—"

"I don't think we need to explain further. I believe our course of action is set." Rurick rose to his feet. "Raven and Celie, if you'll come with me, we'll contact Dr. McKnight."

Raven, seemingly anxious to talk to her father, moved quickly to the corridor. Rurick stood back to let her pass, and she headed for the cockpit. Celie followed, but he turned to block her path. "A word with you, please."

There were limited topics for them to discuss, and she had a sinking feeling she knew what this conversation would entail. She had started it, she reminded herself; she would see it through. She drew a deep breath. "About what?"

"I want to apologize for what happened at the airlock earlier."

Her chest tightened as embarrassment rushed through her. "It was no big deal," she managed to answer.

His assessing gaze swept her flushed face. "Really?"

"Really," she said firmly.

"Even so, I was out of line and things progressed to an unacceptable level."

He thought kissing and touching her was *unacceptable?* Anger chased away the embarrassment. "Nothing to worry about, is it?" she snapped. "Since it certainly won't happen again." No matter how much her body yearned for another taste of passion.

His eyes cooled, and he stepped back. "No, it won't."

She knew he meant it, which stung her pride, although she was as determined as he to avoid a repeat performance.

"Then let's contact Chase McKnight so we can see this business finished. I'm ready to get out of this sector." Not to mention away from Rurick and from her physical reactions to him.

"Fine. If he agrees to meet us at Altair, we'll transmit the coordinates." His steady gaze remained on her. "Our own course is already locked in for the settlement. After we deal with the situation there, we'll do our best to get you back to your ship."

She wished she could believe that. The problem was, she didn't know what to believe anymore—not even about herself.

* * *

98

Altair was every bit as bad as Max and Rurick had told them, and worse. Before they disembarked, the two men donned protective suits and scanned the colony to determine which diseases were manifesting. Unbelievably, they were common illnesses for which immunizations were abundant and available to every citizen in most of the quadrant. Why hadn't these people been provided with such basic medicines?

Max insisted that Raven and Celie receive booster immunizations before they left the ship. As they stepped from the craft, a bitter wind swept around them, carrying with it the overwhelming stench of the settlement, reminiscent of that on Joba. Halting, Celie took in the scene before her.

Altair was hardly more than a jumble of crude huts and a scattering of outbuildings. The land was barren, with the exception of a few scraggly patches of crops. There were a fair number of settlers, most of them hunched around the primitive oil fires that burned in front of every hut. The scents of sewage and unwashed bodies mingled with that of the fires. Underlying the smell of putrefaction was something Celie remembered well from her forays in the other quadrant: the reek of apathy and despair.

Many Shielder settlements in the old quadrant had been at least as impoverished as Altair. But this was a quadrant regulated by the benevolent—and magnasteel—vise of the Interstellar Council. Conditions such as those on Altair simply weren't allowed to exist. Or were they?

Just as staggering as the situation on Altair was the fact that Max and Rurick had apparently been right on all counts. The conditions here were truly deplorable, as they had been on Joba. Since Celie had verified that Max was indeed the heir to the Riordan throne, via computer research and a holo of the royal family, she could only assume he and Rurick weren't lying about these circumstances being widespread throughout this ninth sector.

The leader of the pitiful settlement, a man named Taman Rader, came to meet them. Even though he was thin and his clothing was hardly more than rags, and deep lines of worry and fatigue lined his face, Taman had a presence of authority, that of a man who put his people before all else. Celie had seen that same presence in the Shielder leaders, most notably Jarek san Ranul, who had single-handedly discovered the wormhole into this quadrant and led his people to freedom.

"I never dared to hope you would return," Taman rasped. "The few travelers who have stopped here have always offered to bring aid but never did."

"We told you that we would be back," Max replied. "The Riordans always stand behind their word. We have brought food, medicine, and other supplies."

"The gods be praised," Taman said. "Our need is great. We have lost nine people in the past few cycles."

"That's horrible," Celie said, appalled. "We'll try to unload the medicines quickly." Turning, she noticed Rurick was already removing crates of goods from the ship. She started to assist him, but Max stopped her. "I will help Rurick with the supplies. Would you and Raven look over the settlement and determine where we should start?"

Nodding in agreement, Celie saw that Raven had already gone to work. The girl was across the compound, crouching next to a woman holding an infant. Trust Raven to head for the babies, since she adored children. Raven spoke with the woman, then took the baby. She cradled the infant against her, cooing softly. As Celie approached, she looked up, her face etched with concern. "This baby is burning up with fever. We must help him."

Celie noted the child's pallor and listlessness and

glazed eyes, and her heart felt wrenched. "We need to start an infirmary for the sickest settlers," she decided. "An area where we can dispense medicine, and where Chase can tend to them when he arrives." She only hoped that was soon enough, before more lives were extinguished.

Since there was no structure large enough to act as an infirmary, they emptied out the largest storage bay of Max's ship and moved the sickest people to makeshift pallets inside it. Raven moved among the patients, soothing them with her sweet voice and calming touch, dispensing medicine for those conditions she was able to diagnose and treat.

Food and blankets were distributed, as were tools and materials to help repair the dilapidated buildings. That done, Rurick and Taman went to work on the repairs. In light of the emergency medical situation, Celie assisted Raven and Max with the sick. Max possessed an amazing amount of medical knowledge—at least as much as Raven—and Celie worked under their direction.

The hours of the cycle blurred into one another as they all struggled through, driven by a sense of urgency. There wasn't a millisecond to be wasted, with these people in such dire straits. Some of the settlers joined their efforts, but they were weak from illness and lack of food and so weren't much help.

Late into the cycle, Max called a halt to their activity. "We are tired and cannot work efficiently at this point. We will rest now and continue our efforts tomorrow."

Exhausted and disheartened, Celie wiped at the grime on her face. Three people, including the baby Raven had first held, had passed on to Spirit during the cycle. Celie was adamantly determined they had gone to be with Spirit, because Hades was right here on Altair. Hot tears pricked at her eyelids as she thought of those people, how emaciated they had been, of the utter lack of hope in the adults' eyes as they lay dying. And that poor baby . . . Raven had been inconsolable. Celie suspected the desperate needs of those still living had been the sole motivation for the girl to keep going.

"I can't leave the sick," Raven said now, although she was swaying on her feet.

"I will stay in the infirmary during sleep shift," Max told her. "I will call you if the need arises."

"But I'm the one with healing skills—"

"Max has a lot of training as well. He can handle it," Rurick interjected, patting Raven's shoulder. "You're too tired to deal with anything else right now."

"He's right, sweetness," Celie said, grateful for the android's intervention. Raven couldn't take much more this cycle.

"I can't leave them," the girl insisted.

"Allow yourself a few hours' rest before you return," Max suggested. "I will remain active—that is, awake—until you return. I will rest then." He paused then added, "I command it."

If it had been anyone else, Raven probably would have refused. But her adoration of Max, coupled with his clever reminder of his royal status, appeared to win out. "All right," she agreed. "But I'll be back in two hours."

She trudged back inside the ship's bay and headed toward the ladder, her slender shoulders slumping with weariness. She was far too young to be exposed to this, Celie thought. But she'd shown great strength and compassion, had demonstrated that she possessed the Shielder hardiness.

Rurick turned to the settlement leader, who was standing nearby. "We're expecting another ship within the next cycle. Chase McKnight is a physician and will be bringing more supplies."

Gratitude swept across Taman's weary face. "Praise the gods. I can't thank you enough."

"After Dr. McKnight arrives, we would like you to tell him and Captain Cameron everything you told us on our last visit," Max requested.

"I will." Taman shook his head sadly. "But I have little hope it will do any good."

"We'll help you all we can," Rurick promised.

Celie shivered, feeling the temperature drop as the night descended fully over Altair's unyielding barrenness. "If I'm not needed right now, I'm going in." She turned, stumbling from exhaustion, and almost fell. Rurick's strong hand beneath her elbow steadied her. She raised her eyes to his concerned gaze.

"Rest well," he said softly. "And thank you for all you did today."

She thought of the eyes, sightless in death, staring up at her, of the baby. "It wasn't nearly enough."

She made her way through the bay to the ladder. The halogen bay lights were muted, so the room was dim. The shifting and coughing of the ill added to the gloomy atmosphere. It seemed so hopeless. Yet she couldn't think that way, Celie told herself. She had to believe something could be done for these people. And she had to rest so she could do more tomorrow.

Like all the airlocks on the ship, the one at the top of the ladder was designed with a second purpose, acting as a decontamination unit. A very good thing, Celie thought, as she activated the decon rays and slumped wearily against the plexishield. Chase, with his obsession about bacteria, would be pleased about that. She almost smiled at the thought, but the weight of the past cycle was too oppressive.

The rays shut off and the panel slid open. She trudged to her cabin, thankful for the numbness total exhaustion brought. Hopefully, she'd be able to sleep. She peeled off her flight suit and threw it in the waste bin. It might be sterile now, but it was tattered and, worse, stained with the blood and vomit of the ill and the dead.

Stepping into the cleansing stall in her lav, Celie ordered the water on and very hot. She scrubbed thoroughly and stood beneath the cascade a long time, wishing it could wash away the memories of this cycle along with the dirt. Next, she stood under the dryer until her hair was nearly dry, then left the lav.

She didn't have another flight suit; she'd have to get one in the morning. But she did have a robe, also compliments of Max's well-stocked supply vaults. She slipped it on, smoothing the simple beige fabric and belting it at her waist, then went to check on Raven. She found the girl deep in an exhausted slumber. The day's events had taken too great a toll for her to remain awake.

Grateful that Raven had drifted off, Celie returned to her cabin, removed her robe, and climbed into her bunk. But sleep eluded her. The blessed numbness she'd felt earlier was gone, and she couldn't slow the whirlwind of thoughts assailing her. Max and Rurick's claims, images of today, images of the old quadrant, merged and tumbled in her mind. Dominating it all was the image of death, of sightless eyes in wasted bodies.

Throwing back the covers, she rose and donned her robe. She paced a long time, hoping exhaustion would allow her to shut down the disturbing images. When that failed, she knew she had a long night ahead of her. Maybe a drink would help. No, better make that a bottle. She headed for the lounge, hoping there was enough alcohol there to provide oblivion.

Chapter Seven

Rurick sat in the dim lounge, a glass of Maran brandy in his hand. He wanted to gulp it, in the hope it would ease the concerns tormenting him, but he needed to be clearheaded in the morning. He propped his feet on the table and leaned back. His chair was made of the softest, most expensive meroni leather available. He'd never given it much thought until tonight.

Guilt surged through him. He had always lived with the finest of luxuries, taking them for granted, while the people of Altair had been deprived of even the most basic necessities of food and medicine. And others like them across the ninth sector were suffering just as much.

It was unconscionable, both for his country and the members of the Council, to allow such conditions to exist. Yet until he knew who was behind the atrocities, and how they were covering it up, he had to move carefully or his efforts might be halted. During this political maneuvering, more people would surely die.

He raised the glass to his mouth just as the entry panel slid open. Celie stood there, her figure silhouetted by the light behind her, shining through the thin robe she wore. He'd never seen her bare legs and admired them a moment before realizing his precarious position. If she saw him with the drink, his charade would be blown. He sat up and slid his feet off the table, nearly sloshing the brandy on himself. His motion drew her gaze.

"Oh. I didn't realize anyone was here." Her husky voice seemed to drift on the air. "I'm sorry to disturb you."

He stood, hastily sweeping the glass behind his back. "It's all right. Come in."

"I will, if you don't mind." She took a step forward. "I really need a drink."

"I'll get you one." He turned his back to her, deftly bringing the glass around to his front and slipping it into the recycle unit. "Is brandy all right?"

"Anything, as long as it kicks."

She obviously felt the same way about this cursed cycle as he did. He got a clean glass and poured it half-way full, turning to hand it to her. She had moved closer, and he caught a whiff of her fresh scent. It wasn't perfume, or the cloying scented oils Jardonian women wore, just the fragrance of woman. He'd already become accustomed to, and greatly appreciative of, Celie's own natural scent—warm, musky, feminine. Her fragrance could almost banish the memory of the stench of Altair. Almost.

As she took the glass, he noticed her hair was down, flowing like waves over her chest. It gleamed in the pale light of the lounge. Raising the drink to her lips, Celie downed the contents in one gulp. She held out the glass. "More."

His brows arched, but he took the glass and poured another drink. "You might take that one a little slower," he advised.

"Only if it's enough to dull my senses." She took a healthy swallow but didn't down it all this time. She stood there a moment, then tossed her head back, staring at the ceiling, her lips compressed. "Damn. It didn't work."

He wished he could see her face more clearly. He suspected he'd see his own pain reflected there. "Would you like me to turn up the lights?" he asked.

She lowered her gaze and shook her head. "No. The darkness matches my mood."

"Fine." Since she made no move to sit, he rested his hip against the bar and crossed his arms on his chest. They remained in silence a few moments. Celie stared at her drink, seemingly lost in her own thoughts, and Rurick stared at her.

He'd never met a woman like this. In general, Riordan women were dainty and fragile and would never get their soft hands dirty. Most would have taken one look at the conditions on Altair and become hysterical. Not Celie. She and Raven charged into action, doing whatever needed to be done, without question or complaint. Images of her valor would be forever burned into his memory, two instances in particular: once when he had seen her holding a dying woman; then again when she'd held a sobbing mother whose baby had died.

He had never seen a person die. In all his thirty-three seasons, in all his travels, with the political and social visits to planets on behalf of his family and the Council, he had never seen death at close range. He'd been only six seasons of age when his mother died but had been kept from her chambers as she labored for her last breath.

Witnessing death today had shaken him to the core.

He didn't know if he could have held that dying woman the way Celie did. Didn't know if he could have found the soft, comforting words she murmured over and over. That horrible moment when the baby expired, he'd felt as if something had died inside himself.

Yet, tears streaming down her face, Celie had comforted the distraught mother, and then Raven. Then she'd pulled herself together and continued tending the ill. Even later, when she had to be totally exhausted, she'd found the energy to talk to the other settlers and offer them encouragement and hope. She was the most extraordinary woman he'd ever met.

"What in the blazing hells is going on in this sector?" she demanded suddenly, jolting him from his thoughts. "How could this be allowed to happen?"

Wearily, he shook his head. "I honestly don't know."

"That's a stupid answer." She glared at him. "Why aren't you and Max doing more? Why haven't you reported this to the Council?"

Why, indeed? he asked himself. If only he *could* go to the Council. He gestured toward the table. "Let's sit down. I'll tell you what I know."

"All right," she muttered, but she reached around him and grabbed the bottle before she marched stiffly to the table.

He pulled out a chair for her, then took the one to her left as she refilled her glass. "You might consider the need to be clearheaded tomorrow," he pointed out.

"Maybe I don't want to be."

She was refreshingly outspoken. Under other circumstances, he would have enjoyed verbally sparring with her—among other things. "Your choice," he replied.

He went on to detail how he and Max had been touring the quadrant but avoided any mention of his mother, or the fact that he'd been searching for her family. Any references to Queen Lisha might nick the armor

108

of his android disguise. He simply told how they made an unscheduled stop on Joba when their ship developed mechanical problems. Shocked at what they found there, they headed out of the sector, planning to make an immediate report to the Council. But they'd received a call for help from Altair and gone there first. The discovery that conditions there were similar—if not worse—than those on Joba had raised a red flag, and they visited several other settlements before leaving the sector. All had been poverty- and disease-stricken.

"The conditions were so widespread, Max and I realized someone had to know about them. To pull off such an effective cover-up, it would have to be someone in a position of power, most likely more than one," he explained to Celie. "Which is why we've been reluctant to go the Council. When we approached m—Max's father about the situation, he was shocked and adamant that such a thing could not be. We're afraid if we bring this matter before the Council, whoever is behind it will take steps to silence us. So we have people planted on Sarngin, checking out Council members and making discreet inquiries."

"Max has spies on Sarngin?" Celie seemed surprised by this. "I can't imagine such a thing in this quadrant."

"Pretty drastic," Rurick agreed. "But what else can we do?"

"I don't know." She took another long drink. "Spirit, I hate to hear this. But why am I surprised? Unfortunately, human nature has always had its dark side." She glanced at him. "Not something you would be familiar with."

"Most things have positives and negatives. I'm aware of human failings."

"Human failings. That's a good way to put it. It's not just human, though. Every species in existence seems to have a propensity for cruelty and ugliness, with the

109

possible exception of the Shens." Celie rose and paced behind her chair.

Intrigued, Rurick suspected that was how she dealt with excess energy when she couldn't take action. He often did the same thing. After a moment, she whirled and strode to the portal. She stared out at the stars a long time before she spoke again.

"Life in the other quadrant was a living Hades. The Abyss itself couldn't have been any worse. The Controllers were in charge, and they demanded complete and total submission. Anyone who didn't comply was tortured, then executed. The Controllers had others do their dirty work—either the Anteks, who were too stupid to resist, or the shadowers, who were too greedy for the gold to be had." She sighed and ran her hand through her hair.

Sensing she needed to talk, Rurick held his silence.

"There were places the Controllers didn't care about dominating, probably because they had nothing to offer," she continued. "Planets like Calt that became sanctuaries for the criminals of the quadrant. Hellholes like Joba."

"I guess every civilization has places like that."

"Yeah. I'm afraid so." She traced a finger along the plexishield. "There was an area of the quadrant, a sector that separated the planets under Controller command from the hellholes. Since it was a main link to other sectors, many ships had to traverse it. Some were on legitimate missions, others were not. Criminals traveled that corridor, either pirating ships or looking for a place to hide. That brought the bounty hunters in droves, as well as the Anteks. It was a dangerous and deadly place to be. Since I was a smuggler—" She paused and turned, noting his expression. "You didn't know that, did you?"

He was surprised and fascinated. "No. You've told me very little about yourself."

"My sister Moriah ran a smuggling operation. She risked her life on a daily basis, delivering prohibited goods across the quadrant in order to support our small settlement. When she took a mate and started a family, I took her place. I flew many unauthorized shipments through that sector."

A part of him was shocked, but he'd had a few crash courses on reality these past months. "I see," he replied neutrally.

"No, you don't. I don't think you can imagine life in that quadrant, what traveling through that sector was like. It was known as Shadow Crossing, an area so dark and corrupt it existed only in shadow, despite the brightness of the stars."

Her gaze locked with his, her eyes glistening. "I thought we had escaped from that. That by coming to another quadrant, we could live our lives away from darkness and depravity. I was wrong. I guess every place has a Shadow Crossing."

She shuddered, and he stood. He didn't know what to say. He couldn't refute her words, as much as he wanted to. "Celie—"

"I'm all right." She stared down at the empty glass still clutched in her hand. "Blazing hells, that's not true. Nothing is right anymore."

He stepped closer, placed his hand on her shoulder. "All is not lost. I'm not giving up. You don't strike me as a quitter."

"I'm not." She wiped at her eyes and sniffed. "I don't know why I'm telling you all this. You're a machine. Do you have any capability of understanding emotions?"

He hesitated, choosing his answer carefully. "Androids are programmed with information on the psychological processes of those they serve. They can also

111

analyze the pheromones that humans produce to determine their mental state. I can tell you're feeling emotional pain."

"You're right about that." She walked past him and refilled her glass. "It's odd, but I trust you, and I don't even know why. I've shared things with you that I've never told anyone. You seem amazingly human, more so than many real humans I know, like Max. I guess that's because he's so formal, which probably comes from growing up in royalty."

Rurick felt a sinking feeling in the pit of his gut. He didn't want Celie's unconditional trust. How was she going to feel if she ever learned the truth about him? She was bound to view his deliberate deception as a personal affront. He told himself she'd never find out. Once she got back to her ship, she'd be gone from his life—a thought he found most disturbing.

"Rurick, I don't want to die," she said abruptly.

What had brought that on? "Celie, you're not going to die." He reached her in one step and slid his hands along her arms. "You're young and healthy and should live many more seasons."

"Tell that to the baby who died today."

He stared at her, at a loss for an answer. "What do you want me to say?"

"There is nothing you can say. Don't you see? We don't have true control over our lives."

"We do have control," he argued. "We have free will, choices—"

"What choices do the people of Altair have?" she interjected vehemently. "Someone decided they're nonentities and don't even rate the most basic of care. Why couldn't that happen to me? To you?"

The logic of her statement stunned him. "I don't know," he said lamely. "But it won't. It can't."

"Oh, it most definitely can. Maybe it won't be an official decision from a Council member. Maybe it will be a ship crash instead, or illness, or any number of things that are out of our control. Today reminded me that one thing is certain—we're all going to die sooner or later, and we don't know when."

Her gaze skimmed him, coming to rest on his triton band. "Except for you, of course. Although I guess your circuits could eventually wear out."

"Let's not talk about me," Rurick urged, wanting them away from that topic. "Celie, the odds are very strong in your favor that you have many seasons left to live."

"But I can't be certain, can I? And I don't want to die without experiencing life to the fullest." Her eyes huge dark orbs in her face, Celie chewed her lower lip, a curiously vulnerable action. "I've realized something else tonight."

"What is that?"

"I want—" She drew a deep breath. "I want to experience mating." Her voice changed, deepening to a timbre that did serious things to Rurick's libido. "And I want you to be the one to show me."

Stunned again, he released her arms and took a hasty step back. That he hadn't had a clue where this was headed attested to his mental exhaustion. "That's not a good idea. Not at all."

Her eyes narrowed, and she stepped forward. The table behind him halted his retreat. "Listen, you wimpy android, you don't have to worry about dying. You're not alive." She punched her index finger into his chest. "Why are you so determined to avoid me? You've been trained for mating. You've probably serviced numerous women. What's wrong with me?"

Rurick felt a flash of utter panic. The gods spare him. He wondered how many times this issue was going to appear—and how long he would be able to resist. He reminded himself of the two reasons he could *not* do this: It would most likely blow his cover, and he couldn't take Celie's innocence. Not with deception between them, and not being able to give her what she deserved.

"Answer me!" she demanded.

"Nothing is wrong with you. You're beautiful and desirable." He paused, scrambling for the right words. "But I'm not in the habit of *servicing* women, as you so bluntly put it. Nor do I take advantage of them, especially when they've been drinking—which impairs good judgment, as I'm sure you know."

"I'm not drunk. Not even remotely close, unfortunately. In my line of work, I often have to drink with clients, most of them male. I've learned to imbibe quite a few alcoholic beverages and hold my own. A funny thing about men: they tend to judge other men by how much they can drink and by the size of their—"

"Don't," Rurick interrupted, before the conversation could go any further astray. "Don't pursue this, Celie. You need to wait for the right man. You'll be glad you did."

"I've already told you there will never be a man for me." She dropped her hand and stepped back.

"You think that now, but . . ." He froze, staring as she began unbelting her robe. "What are you doing? Don't do that." He reached out, grabbing her wrist to stop her.

She used his forward momentum against him, slipping one arm around his back and yanking him flush against her. "Celie," he warned, just as she slipped her other hand behind his head and held him still while she lifted her mouth to his. Dazed, all he could think was how perfectly their mouths fit together. She was so warm against him, so . . . alive. As was he.

Of their own accord, his lips opened to her questing

tongue. She tasted of brandy and the promise of desire. Heat and need roared through him, evaporating logical thought, and worse, disintegrating all self-control and good intentions.

Stars, but he no longer had the strength to resist.

She knew she'd won the minute he opened his mouth and thrust his tongue against hers. With a small sigh she slid her arms around his neck, pressing her breasts against his firm chest. Although she wanted to be an active participant, his superior experience in the matter of mating was so apparent, she relaxed into him and let him take the lead.

He kissed her the same way he did everything: confidently, with absolute, shattering competence. She'd never dreamed kissing could be so satisfying, yet at the same time so stimulating, so . . . erotic.

He appeared willing to linger over her lips, despite the obvious signs of his ability to proceed directly to the main event. She could feel his hardness pressing into her abdomen, yet he continued the drugging kisses, his tongue engaging hers in an elaborate dance, evoking startling images of the mating act.

When he finally moved from her lips, it was to continue with a trail of kisses down her face to her neck. Spirit, she'd never known her neck could be so sensitive. She sighed, tilting her head back to give him better access. He took full advantage, mapping her neck and the exposed part of her shoulder with his talented lips. Need, hot and urgent, uncoiled from deep within her, spreading like a desert wildfire through her veins.

"Rurick," she murmured, sliding her hand down to explore the alluring bulge in his flight suit. She cupped him, amazed at the hardness, at the size of him. Max had been right about the android being very well

115

endowed, she thought dreamily, stroking her fingers across that endowment.

He grabbed her wrist, pulling her hand away. "Don't do that," he gasped, his voice strained. He put her hand behind her back, holding it there.

"Why not?" She started to protest, but just then his free hand slipped open her robe and claimed her breast. It was her turn to gasp.

"You like that?" he murmured huskily, his fingers teasing the nipple.

"Oh . . . yes."

"Good." His lips traced a trail down her chest, burning a wake of anticipation and need. She arched back as his mouth closed over her nipple. The sensation was electrifying, and her legs buckled. He caught her, bracing himself against the table.

"This won't work," he said raggedly. "We need to lie down."

He tugged her down to the lush carpet, and she went willingly, pulling him against her, both of them tangling in her hair. He rolled enough to keep his weight off her, rising over her to stare down at her a moment before lowering his mouth to hers. She welcomed him, kissing him back. She was barely aware of him sliding her arms out of her robe, of the fabric falling away from her, spreading out around them like a makeshift blanket.

But she was fully aware of him running his hands along her skin, pressing heated kisses on her breasts and lower. "You are so beautiful," he told her. "Like a crystal fountain against a Jardonian sunset." He touched her breast, the lightest of caresses, then bent to worship it with his mouth.

It wasn't just his words that made her feel truly beautiful, but the look in his molten eyes, and the way he touched her with his hands and his mouth. She'd never before felt so desired . . . so cherished. She yearned to

116

touch him the same way, to feel the texture of his skin, to discover what he was really like beneath the flight suit. It didn't matter that he was an android. He was real to her at that moment, and she wanted to experience mating to the fullest. She began to slide open the seam to his top.

He trapped her hand against his chest. "No. Let me do this."

"I want to touch you," she argued, frustration mingling with desire. "I want to feel your skin against mine. Besides, you have to undress to mate with me."

"No," he said again. She was getting damned tired of that word and started to tell him so, but then his hand slid along her thigh. The sensation reverberated through every atom in her body, chasing off any rebuttals.

He swept his fingers up to the apex of her thighs, teased the golden curls there. "Open for me," he whispered against her ear. "Let me touch you, show you the pleasure."

She couldn't have resisted the indoctrinating seduction of his voice if her life depended on it. Nor could she resist the temptation of his touch as he nudged her legs apart and claimed her most intimate flesh. Heat and electricity arced through her as he stroked her. She gasped, all awareness fixated on the incredible sensations he was creating. His mouth returned to her breast, layering another staggeringly erotic surge over the first.

Her thoughts scattered as if shot through a rocket coil projector. She slid her hands through his hair, and held his head against her breast, trying desperately to ground herself in this sensual maelstrom of feelings. Then he slipped a finger inside her, and she couldn't think about anything else. She could focus only on the feel of his finger as it moved in and out, over and over. Then she felt the pressure of his thumb on an outside point that sent another lightning bolt through her. She tossed her head to the side, helpless in the throes of a building crescendo.

Rurick slid up and kissed her, then whispered, "Let go, Celie."

She felt totally defenseless in the undertow sucking her into a sensual black hole. "I don't know if I can," she gasped.

"Let go," he repeated, moving his finger faster. "You're safe with me."

Safe . . . She accepted the truth in his words. She knew on some deep level that she and Rurick weren't locked in a power struggle. They were simply sharing the most basic, elemental relationship a male and female could experience. As she relinquished her last hold on control, the wave crashed over her and she cried out, arcing upward against Rurick, slammed by incredible sensations that seemed to go on for an eternity. When they finally subsided, she went limp, letting her breath out in a sigh. She felt totally drained, exhaustion seeping through every pore. She didn't know if she was capable of moving.

Rurick gathered her close. "You all right?" he asked softly.

She found his embrace and his concern touching. For an android, he was amazingly sensitive. She was grateful he had given her this experience, yet she still felt thwarted and frustrated. Back to the proverbial caroba pie. She'd had a taste; now she wanted the whole thing. She felt cheated.

Twisting out of his arms, she sat up, pushing her hair out of her face, and looked down at him. "I'm fine. It was wonderful, as I'm sure you know."

He ran his finger over the top of her breast. "Your breasts are flushed. That's one sign . . . among other things."

Feeling the heat spreading to her face, she jerked the robe free and slid her arms into the sleeves. Then she caught herself and stopped, refusing to show embarrassment. "I'm sure you're very proud of yourself. But what we just did is not the real thing."

"I disagree. It was very real." He sat up and finished the job, gathering the folds of her robe together and tying the belt. "It's an accurate taste of what you'll feel during mating."

"But why not the actual act?" Celie stared pointedly at the telltale bulge still present beneath his flight suit. "You appear quite capable of performing."

His jaw tightened and he stood, offering his hand. She allowed him to pull her to her feet. He grasped her chin, forcing her to meet his gaze. "It's not a performance, Celie. There's much more to it than that. The *real thing,* as you call it, the full act of mating, is an expression of caring, and is not only physical but spiritual, when done with the right person."

"I'll never have that. Why can't you understand?"

He slid his hand up to cup her cheek. "I know you believe that right now. But I'm betting you're wrong."

For a moment she found herself mesmerized by his eyes, by the glow of shared intimacy she saw there. Disconcerted, she stepped back. "I guess there's nothing more to say."

"I'm sorry I can't give you what you want."

She knew he had no intention of ever mating with her, although she no longer believed it was because he found her undesirable. She'd probably never know the reasons behind his refusal. Now, with the return of relative normalcy, she suddenly felt very awkward. "Well, I'd better call it a night." She turned and headed for the entry.

"Good night, Celie."

She paused, chewed her lower lip. Android or not,

he'd treated her with respect and courtesy at every turn. She'd just experienced stunning intimacies with this android, gone to a level more personal than she'd ever been with any other being. She didn't want him to think her ungrateful.

"I . . ." She turned and saw that he hadn't moved. "I want to . . . thank you." She gestured lamely. "For tonight . . . for everything."

"It was my pleasure," he said quietly.

Again, she felt the heat rise to her face. She couldn't see how he'd gotten anything out of what had transpired, but Max had been right about the android's ability to give pleasure. She was still tingling from that incredible expertise.

"Good night," she said, turning back to the entry.

She suspected she would have a hard time sleeping. If she did sleep, she felt certain the nightmare would return. Yet she couldn't be sorry about tonight. At least she'd experienced a taste of what sexual fulfillment might be like in a normal romantic relationship.

No. That was a ludicrous assumption. An emotionally scarred woman who had committed a despicable crime, begging an android to mate with her? That was anything but normal.

Filled with an abject loneliness she knew would never abate, Celie returned to her cabin.

Chapter Eight

Chase McKnight arrived the next cycle in a ship almost as impressive as Rurick's cruiser. Celie and Raven were dealing with ill settlers, so Rurick and Max, along with Taman, went to greet their visitors. Dr. McKnight disembarked first, carrying two large black cases, followed by another man and two women.

"Dr. McKnight?" Max asked, offering his hand. "I am Max Rior, and we are most grateful you have come."

The doctor was a big man, a few inches taller than Max and with more mass, which appeared to be solid muscle. "Call me Chase." He shook Max's hand, then gestured to the people behind him. "This is my wife, Nessa, my partner Sabin san Travers, and his wife Moriah."

Moriah must be Celie's sister, Rurick realized. Except for the coloring, their resemblance was amazing. He stepped forward when Max introduced him and Taman. The newcomers eyed his armband, but he could tell they

121

were more interested in seeing their family members.

Nessa, a petite, fragile woman with beautiful dark eyes scanned the compound anxiously. "Where is my daughter Raven? I want to be sure she's all right."

"I'd like to see Celie," Moriah added. "It's been too long since I've heard from her."

"They are both well," Max assured them. "Ah, here comes young Raven now."

The girl came running across the compound, her long ebony hair flying out behind her. "Mother! Father!" She nearly knocked over her mother, hugging her tightly. She hugged her father just as tightly, then looked up at him beseechingly. "Father, you must come with me now. There's a little girl who's going to die if she doesn't get help right away."

"Of course I'll come immediately." Chase glanced at Max. "We'll talk later." Then he was gone, his long strides eating up the ground, his petite wife running alongside him.

Sabin, a dark-haired, intense man slightly smaller than Rurick, stepped forward. "Moriah and I aren't very skilled in medical matters, but we can assist in other areas. Just tell us what to do."

Moriah nodded. "We can see that the need is great. We'd like to help." Her voice had the same husky quality as Celie's.

"Thank you," Taman said, his voice deep with emotion.

Rurick looked around the group. "I suggest we get to it."

This was an amazing day, Rurick thought, many hours later. They had worked every bit as hard as they had the previous cycle, but without the sense of failure they'd felt then.

No more people had died, thanks to Chase Mc-

122

Knight's remarkable medical skills, along with assistance from Nessa and Raven. The man had most of the medicines needed, and those he didn't have were quickly compounded in his ship's laboratory. With all the patients stabilized, he turned his attention to the other settlers and gave them immunizations so they wouldn't contract the diseases that had killed so many of their fellow colonists. Altair's medical emergency had been effectively brought to an end. After the night cycle, Chase planned to treat the other, less-serious physical ailments of the community.

Sabin had also been a tireless worker, and with his help, repairs on the huts and outbuildings had been completed. He planned to begin repairing the run-down farming equipment tomorrow, with Max's assistance. He explained he'd had a lot of experience repairing old machinery, particularly a ship he'd used for many years.

Moriah turned out to be an agricultural expert, and had plans to search for underground aquifers to provide more water and facilitate crop irrigation. She wanted to help the colonists create a strategy for growing crops suitable for Altair's environment, and teach them natural rotation and fertilization techniques.

Most amazing was the fact that these people hadn't asked a single question. They'd stepped off the ship, seen the need, and gone to work. Rurick couldn't imagine others in the quadrant doing such a thing. He realized the visitors would expect explanations, but they had put the welfare of people in need before their own curiosity, then worked nonstop. He was incredibly impressed. But he shouldn't be surprised, not after knowing Celie and Raven.

Celie. He hadn't been able to stop thinking about her. The hard physical labors had done nothing to occupy his mind, giving him too much time to think, to remember last night. He remembered her taste and scent, the satiny texture of her skin, how warm and vibrant she'd felt, how she had come apart in his arms. He'd been in a state of low-level arousal ever since, and it didn't appear his condition would abate any time soon. Not unless he could forget about her, and that wasn't likely.

He knew he'd done the right thing by refusing to mate with her. It had taken all his control and self-discipline to hold back, but he'd maintained enough presence of mind to realize that giving in to his baser urges would be dishonorable. He refused to take advantage of Celie's naïvete and his false identity.

Yet a part of him longed to be the one to initiate her into lovemaking, to be the man to fully awaken the natural sensuality she possessed, to positively alter her perception of men in general. But that could never be. It always came back to the fact that he had responsibilities as the future king of Jardonia, and in dealing with the atrocities of the ninth sector. Duty, first and foremost. He couldn't offer Celie the commitment and permanence that she deserved. He couldn't even offer her the truth, something he suspected was very important to her.

He had done the right thing, Rurick told himself again, as he put away his tools and joined the others. They were sharing a simple evening meal with Taman and some of the settlers. Then they'd offer full explanations to Chase and his party.

In deference to Altair's customs, they gathered around Taman's fire for their meal. With an unspoken agreement they wouldn't discuss the grim sector-wide conditions during the meal, they settled into sociable conversation.

Celie sat next to her sister, who gave her a big hug. "I've missed you, 'rax," Moriah said affectionately.

"I've missed you, too." Celie hugged her back. "How is that adorable niece of mine?"

"Sometimes not so adorable. Now that she's two, she thinks everything should be her way," Moriah answered, the warmth and pride in her voice denying any real vexation with her daughter.

"There's no thinking about it," Sabin said. "Everything *is* Alyssa's way."

"Whose fault is that?" Moriah demanded of her husband. "You act like melted caroba every time you're around her. She's never heard the word 'no' from you."

Celie laughed. "I miss the little stinker. I can't wait to see her."

Rurick watched the two sisters together, again marveling at how closely they resembled one another, even though their coloring was very different. Moriah had hair a rich copper color and stunning golden eyes, presenting a strong contrast to Celie's golden blond hair and rich brown eyes. But their facial features and body structure were practically identical.

He admired the rapport they shared, the obvious warmth and affection. Jardonians were more formal in their family relations. Rurick had never shared such easy affections with his parents or his half sister, Kalina, although he had a strong bond with his half brother, Sev.

Raven appeared to share a close relationship with her parents as well. She was seated between them now, telling them about her adventures. Rurick had been surprised at how youthful Chase and Nessa were, particularly Nessa, who couldn't have seen her thirtieth season. Certainly too young to have a daughter Raven's age, but Celie explained that Chase and Nessa's five children were adopted, and Nessa was only ten seasons older than Raven.

"We have news from Shamara," Nessa said, her small face lighting up.

"What?" Raven shook her mother's arm. "Tell me!"

"Eirene is expecting a baby." Nessa smiled at Raven's squeal of delight and turned to Max. "She's the mate of Jarek san Ranul, the colony leader. You've probably met him at Council meetings."

"I have, indeed," Max replied, stepping into his charade of crown prince. "Please offer my congratulations upon your return."

"The birth of a child should be a happy event," Taman said, then sighed. "But here, it is simply another mouth to feed."

"That's exactly how it was for us in the old quadrant," Sabin said, his midnight eyes hard. "We can't allow such conditions here. Not while we have a choice."

"There doesn't appear to be much choice in the matter," Taman replied. The settlement leader looked far older than the fifty-six seasons Rurick knew him to be, his hair gray and his face lined with fatigue and the heavy yoke of responsibility. "It seems we've been effectively cut off from all assistance," Taman continued, then nodded to Max and Rurick. "With the exception of you two. I don't know how you managed to get back into the sector, much less bring supplies."

Everyone put their plates aside. The niceties over, it was time to discuss grim realities. "I would like to know how this happened," Chase said, gesturing at the huts scattered around them. "And why."

Rurick and Max alternated explaining how they had stumbled on first Joba, then Altair, and then searched out and found at least a dozen more settlements in the same dire need. They shared their theory that the checkpoint stations were preventing information from getting outside the sector, and assistance from getting in. They also explained that Max's royal status made him exempt from having to pass through the sector checkpoints.

"What about the other settlements in this sector? Have you been able to discuss this with them?" Sabin

126

asked Taman. "If you could join forces, you might be able to fight."

The leader shook his head. "As the seasons passed, our communications equipment became obsolete, as did our spacecraft. The flow of parts and new equipment from other sectors stopped completely ten, maybe fifteen, seasons ago. Now we cannot contact anyone, or go anywhere. It was only by the grace of the gods that Max picked up our weak distress signal and investigated."

"I noticed the only goods I was permitted to bring into the sector were food, medicine, and basic building supplies," Celie commented. "I thought it odd I couldn't transport any technological products, like telecommunication or spacecraft components, machinery, or any weapons. But I just assumed that other suppliers had exclusive contracts on those commodities. I never realized they weren't allowed in this sector at all."

"We believe that's part of the cover-up," Rurick said. "If the people of the ninth sector can't communicate with anyone else, or travel anywhere, then they're effectively isolated and helpless, and can be controlled."

Moriah leaned forward. "How could something like this be kept secret for so many seasons?"

"Only powerful members of the Council could achieve such a cover-up," Max replied. "Which is why we have been reluctant to go to the Council without knowing who is behind it."

"We'd send in more of our own ships with supplies, but we're afraid it would raise suspicions," Rurick said. "And we don't want our efforts to help stymied completely."

"We can get supplies in," Moriah said. "I guarantee it."

"But you'll have to go through the checkpoints," Rurick argued, both surprised and heartened by her offer

127

of help. "Once you do and exit the sector, my guess is you'll have no memory of what you've seen here."

"Not necessarily," Chase said thoughtfully. "I was able to protect myself from Controller psionic brain waves, and I might be able to do the same thing at the checkpoints, depending on what mind-bending techniques are being used. Nessa, Raven, and Sabin are Shielders. With their natural chemical shields, it's possible they might be immune to memory erasure too."

"Celie and Raven mentioned that," Max said. "It is a fascinating conjecture. I have done some research on Shielders and their genetic makeup, and I project there is a ninety-five-point-two-percent probability that—"

"Both Max and I are hoping that Shielders might be resistant to any mental bombardment given out at the checkpoints," Rurick interrupted, before Max could get too technical and sound suspiciously like the android he was. "If they are truly resistant, perhaps they'd be willing to help us."

"Of course they will. We're all going to help," Moriah said firmly. "I have complete faith in Chase's ability to protect us from memory erasure. Just as I know I can get supplies, including spacecraft and communication equipment, into this sector." She turned to Max. "Can you provide me with four star-class ships? I would have to make some modifications in their inner structure to create hidden storage compartments."

Rurick was amazed these people would so readily step forward to offer assistance. But he sensed Moriah's sincerity and felt he could trust her, could trust them all. Gratitude, and for the first time since he and Max had discovered the situation, a ray of hope, shot through him. When Max glanced at him for acceptance or rejection of Moriah's request, he nodded.

"I can provide you with the ships," Max answered. "I will contact the spaceport at Jardonia, and have them delivered wherever you wish. I believe I can also contribute some trusted personnel to help you with the modifications."

"I think Shamara would be the best place to work on the ships," Sabin said, and looked to his mate for confirmation. She nodded and he continued, "We can provide the know-how for hiding the goods in the ships and we can provide the pilots. But unfortunately, our settlement on Shamara is still struggling, and we have no extra funds or supplies to donate."

"We can take care of that as well," Max assured him.

"I'll be one of the pilots," Celie said. "But I want my own ship. It's fast, and I'm familiar with it." She looked pointedly at Max. "Get me to my ship, and I'll help you."

Because of the dire need in the sector, Rurick had been reluctant to take the time necessary to personally return Celie to her ship. Now that there was a solid plan of action and some relief coming for the settlers, he decided he would escort Celie to Joba. That way he could personally guarantee her safety. If he were totally honest with himself, he'd admit he wanted to spend those extra cycles with her too.

"Max," he said to his android, "we can take Celie to her ship."

Max frowned. "I do not believe that is a good idea. Since we were attacked at Joba—"

"I would recommend that you contact Jardonia," Rurick interjected, "and have them send two armed escort ships to meet us there. That should be ample protection. Then we can get Celie outside the sector without her having to pass through a station."

Max considered, then nodded. "That is acceptable. I will request the escort."

"I'll begin the preparations to protect Moriah and myself against the checkpoint memory erasure," Chase said. "But I'd like to let Nessa and Raven and Sabin go through the points without any preventive measures, to see how they do. Unfortunately, if we fail, we won't remember any of this."

"Then we'll remind you," Celie answered. "I'm sure I can convince anyone about this sector. Plus I'll have Max and Rurick to back me up."

Chase nodded. "All right. After I take everyone to Shamara, Nessa and I will return to visit the settlements in this sector and attend to their medical needs."

"I don't want to go back to Shamara!" Raven protested. "I want to stay with Celie."

"That's something we need to talk about, young lady," Chase said sternly. "How you sneaked off and had your mother and I worried—make that terrified—that something horrible had happened to you. We had no idea where you'd gone."

Raven had the grace to look ashamed. "I left you a holocording and told you I was going with Celie. I was afraid to ask your permission because I knew you'd say no. I am old enough to be on my own."

Chase opened his mouth, but Nessa laid a slender hand over his, and he paused to look at her. "It's getting late and we're tired," she said softly. "Why don't we finish this discussion later, in private?" She hugged Raven again. "We missed you, and we were concerned, sweetness. But we'll talk more in our cabin."

"All right," Raven conceded.

"I'm exhausted," Moriah admitted, standing and stretching, her graceful movements so much like Celie's.

Sabin remained seated, staring thoughtfully into the fire. "What are we going to do about the Council?" he asked. "How do we uncover the perpetrators of this crime? There has to be a way."

Rurick hadn't even considered the possibility these people would be willing to take on the Council and help

130

him ferret out whoever was behind the ninth-sector tragedy. He silently thanked the gods for sending this unexpected assistance.

"That's a good question," he answered. "I ha—I mean, Max has some of his people stationed on Sarngin, but so far we've discovered nothing."

"Whoever is behind this wouldn't discuss it openly. You'd have to have some way of listening in to their conversations, or . . ." Sabin's brows drew together. "I have an idea."

Moriah sat back down, watching him. "Are you thinking what I'm thinking?"

They looked at each other. "Enhancers," they both said at the same time.

Max snapped to attention. "Enhancers?" he inquired. "That is a very interesting suggestion. With their empathic and telepathic abilities, they might indeed be very useful."

"But they're not members of the Council," Rurick pointed out. "To the best of my knowledge, they've never expressed any interest in having representation on the Council, or participating in decisions made for the quadrant. I don't believe they've ever visited Sarngin."

"You're right," Sabin said. "They are reclusive, preferring to keep to themselves. They're peaceful and nonviolent and don't like involvement in political affairs. But there comes a time when we all have to be involved, when we have to fight for our rights and for freedom. Being too passive is every bit as dangerous as being too aggressive."

Rurick leaned forward, fascinated by political concepts to which he'd never given much thought. His family had always been an integral part of the Interstellar political system, but more for the power and the prestige than to ensure personal freedoms. But then, it had

131

always appeared that everyone in the quadrant had equality and basic rights. An appearance that was blatantly false. Sabin was right. Complacence could be a dangerous trap. "How can we convince the Enhancers to get involved?" he asked.

Nessa smiled. "We have an advantage. Not only do we share the same planet with the Enhancers, but our leader, Jarek, is married to one. Eirene is the woman who made it possible for the Shielders to escape to this quadrant. And Jarek is my brother. I know he and Eirene will listen to us."

Another amazing stroke of luck—or fate? "Do you think Eirene or any of her people might help us?" Rurick asked.

Sabin nodded. "I know Eirene will. And hopefully, she and Jarek will be able to convince the other Enhancers that they have to get involved. Their race was almost eradicated by the Controllers. Their involvement is the only way to ensure their continued existence. Moriah and I will speak with them when we get back to Shamara."

"That would be most appreciated," Max said.

"I think we've covered everything." Rurick stood and reminded himself that he couldn't show how stiff and sore he was. Everyone else rose, agreeing there wasn't any more to be done this cycle. Tomorrow they would tie up the few remaining details, then they'd go their separate ways.

Rurick would have Celie with him for only a few more cycles, then she'd be on her ship and gone from his life. He might see her from time to time as they brought supplies into the sector, but he would have to return to Jardonia, and then their contact would probably be permanently severed. He felt a jolt of sadness at the thought, but he knew it was for the best. Hopefully Celie would have positive memories of their sensual encounters. And if his luck held, she would never know about his deception.

Somehow Raven managed to convince her parents to let her stay with Celie, much to Celie's consternation. Celie couldn't understand it. She'd told both Chase and Nessa about Raven's enamored fascination with Max, but they hadn't seemed concerned. They researched Max and the Riordan royal family on the Universal Data Web, the UDW, and were impressed with what they found. They believed Max to be upstanding and honorable.

They also preferred that the two armed escort ships from Riordan see Raven and Celie safely out of the sector, especially after Max promised their daughter would not go planetside when the group retrieved Celie's ship. And Raven had insisted that she be allowed her independence. Celie suspected that Chase and Nessa didn't want to leave their oldest child behind but had decided Raven would rebel even more if they forced her to return with them.

Thus Celie was once again in the unwanted position of chaperone. It was proving to be quite a challenge, with Raven spending every moment she could with Max. Then there was Rurick. Celie's feelings about him were ambivalent, jumbled like debris in a meteor storm. She still felt the attraction, the startling electricity that arced between them whenever they were together, and with it, the rush of desire she could no longer seem to stem.

It was as if the floodgates to her physical yearnings had been thrown open and could never again be contained. Quite frankly, it was a major pain. She cursed her stupidity in thinking she could safely test dangerous waters and be satisfied. At least her runaway libido explained why she had this insane attraction to an android—*an android*—for Spirit's sake!

She would control it. She *would*. Rurick had made it very clear there would be no further intimacies between them, which was for the best. She'd gotten what she asked for—well, almost. With their time together drawing to an end, it was simpler to distance herself from him, best achieved by avoiding him as much as possible. Cowardly perhaps, but easier than being around him.

Celie leaned back in the pilot's seat and stared out the portal. She had cockpit duty until Max's ships arrived. Their own ship was one cycle out from Joba, and the escort ships had messaged that they'd be approaching within the hour. She told herself she'd be relieved when she was on her own ship and had Raven safely out of the sector.

She longed to be able to bury herself in her painting, to get back to the normal, calming routine she'd had for the past two seasons. Besides, she'd be doing deliveries to the ninth-sector colonies, to people who desperately needed the goods, while trying to circumvent the checkpoints. These new challenges would fill the void in her life and then her libido would settle down. She hoped.

"May I join you?" Rurick's voice jolted her from her reverie. He slipped into the co-pilot's chair. His muscular body filled the seat, a dominating presence in the compact cockpit.

The recessed lighting overhead reflected off his thick mane of hair, highlighting the rich shades of brown and gold. He was gorgeous; there was no other word for it. Celie quickly turned her gaze back to the location-verifier sensors.

"I understand we've heard from the escort ships," he said.

Obviously, he was settling in for a while. She felt the

familiar energy building between them and willed herself to ignore it. "Yes, we did. They'll reach us within the hour."

He nodded. "That's good."

She wondered why he'd bothered to come to the cockpit, given their stilted conversations of the past few cycles. She didn't want to sit there in discomfiting silence, his presence a painful reminder of her dysfunction and his nonhumanness, not to mention what had passed between them. She had told herself repeatedly that there was no need for embarrassment, since Rurick wasn't capable of real emotion, and he probably hadn't given the night in the lounge a second thought. But that didn't seem to change how she felt . . . and she now felt uncomfortable around him.

She pivoted her chair from the console. "Since you're here, if you don't mind, I think I'll take a short break."

She stood to leave, but he reached out and grabbed her hand. "You don't have to run away."

As always, his astuteness was disconcerting. "I'm not," she protested lamely. "I was just going to check on Rav—"

"She's in the galley with Max, learning how to replicate caroba." The corners of Rurick's perfect mouth turned up, and humor danced in his eyes. "You ladies certainly put a lot of stock in that stuff." His smile took her breath away. He was far too potent. How could an android be so charismatic? He tugged on her hand. "Raven is fine. Sit."

She chastised herself for her cowardice. She'd faced Anteks and pirates, entire ships of them; had handled the lowlifes on Calt, had navigated Shadow Crossing in the old quadrant more times than she cared to remember. There was no reason she couldn't deal with one sinfully handsome android. Even if she had been almost as intimate with him as a man and woman could be . . .

even if she had practically begged him to mate with her, and he had refused. No reason whatsoever to be uncomfortable. Once again, she reminded herself that he was *not* human, no matter how much he might appear to be.

"All right." She sank into her chair, meeting his challenging gaze. "Did you want to talk to me?"

"I did. It will get hectic once the escort ships arrive. Max's officers will board to give status reports on Jardonia and political happenings throughout the quadrant. Max and I will be occupied for a while. We'll need you to man the cockpit."

"Of course. I'll be glad to do that."

"As always, I imagine you'll handle the responsibility competently," he said. The warmth his eyes were so oddly able to project seemed to seep into her body. "There won't be much time after our escort arrives, so I thought this would be a good opportunity to talk."

Since there were limited topics to discuss, she thought she had a good idea where this conversation might be heading. She didn't want to go there. "I'm not sure there's anything else for us to discuss—"

He raised his hand to halt her rushed protest. "Please hear me out. First of all, I want to thank you—and Max does too—for everything you and Raven did on Altair. You were both amazing. And thank you for suggesting we contact Dr. McKnight. All of your people have been wonderful. We will always be grateful."

She didn't know what to say. Rurick's praise made her almost as uncomfortable as the topic she was hoping to avoid, that of their shared intimacies. "I didn't do that much. I couldn't have done anything else, not after seeing those people suffering. Chase is the amazing one, especially since he's been able to create a way to protect us from memory erasure."

"He is most impressive. His success in resisting the

checkpoint mind-altering procedures was more than we could have hoped for. Not to mention the discovery that Shielders appear to be immune to the process. With help from them, and hopefully the Enhancers, we might make some real progress on the ninth-sector conditions." He paused, as if considering his next words. "I know the situation on Altair was hard for you, especially the deaths."

"Don't," she whispered, battling the ever-present anguish from her mental images of the dying, pictures that bombarded both her waking and sleeping hours. She clenched her hands together in her lap. "I don't need to be reminded."

"I'm sorry," he said quietly. "It was not my intent to upset you. I'm well aware that you'll carry some bad memories with you when you leave this sector. I know we all will. But I'm hoping you'll carry some good ones as well."

There was no doubt which memories he was referring to, and no sense in refuting the fact that he'd awakened sexual yearnings she'd never experienced, had shown her planet-shattering pleasure. He'd certainly proven he'd been very well programmed in the giving of physical pleasure. Why deny it?

"I will take some very . . . special memories," Celie said. "I thank you for them."

His eyes darkened, and she felt as if she were falling into them. "Don't give up on love, Celie. You're beautiful, sensuous, and passionate. You have so much to offer some lucky man. I believe you can overcome your . . . doubts with the right man. It would be a waste to live your life alone."

An android with sensitivity training. The situation would be laughable, but his words touched her. He couldn't possibly understand how deep her mistrust of male-female relationships went. It would be too difficult, too traumatic for her to overcome those roots. Not to mention what she'd done six seasons ago. Her father . . . She shuddered at the memory but quickly walled it off as she always did. She had acted of her own free will, and she would have to live with her actions.

An alert on the console went off, advising of approaching ships. At the same moment the subspace transceiver beeped. Max's ships had arrived. "I'd better get to work," she muttered, relieved the conversation was over. She punched the comm to the kitchen. "Max, are you there?"

"Yes. I am watching this very small woman eat a very large plate of caroba."

Raven giggled in the background, and Celie found herself smiling. "Your ships are approaching. They're in visual range."

"Very good. I will be there in a moment."

She felt Rurick rise from his chair, but she kept her gaze on the monitor. "I'll leave you to maneuver the ship for docking," he told her. "I hope you'll think about what I said, Celie."

Then he was gone, and she didn't have any time to consider his words. She got to work, slowing the ship and contacting the captains of the other two craft to set up docking procedures.

Flanked by two other officers, a large gray-haired man stepped through the airlock. All three were dressed in blue uniforms, which were decorated with silver braid and various medals and multicolored bars that probably denoted rank. The man seemed to hesitate a quick moment, his glance flicking from Rurick to Max. Then he bowed deeply to Max, the two officers behind him doing the same. "Your Highness," he said, his voice a resonant baritone. "I am at your service."

Max nodded regally. "Commander, it is good to see you." He gestured toward Celie and Raven. "May I present Celie Cameron and Raven McKnight? They will be our guests until we retrieve Captain Cameron's ship from Joba. Ladies, this is Commander Benek Zane. He heads up my personal regiment."

"A pleasure to meet you." The commander, heavyset with vivid blue eyes, bowed to Celie and Raven, as did the others.

The formalities brought home the reality of Max's royal status, and Celie was impressed despite herself. She'd never met any royalty, since Controllers were the only ruling class in the old quadrant. She glanced at Raven, who glowed with excitement.

Commander Zane straightened and turned to Max, although he glanced at Rurick first. "I'm afraid I have bad news, Your Highness. Right before we docked, we received a communiqué from Jardonia. Your father has become ill again. The physicians are completely baffled by his condition."

Rurick stepped forward, a concerned expression on his face. "How serious is the king's illness?"

The commander inclined his head in an odd show of respect for the android. "They don't really know, Your—sir. The physicians have requested that the prince return home as quickly as possible, in case King Domek . . ." The older man drew a deep breath. "In case the king's condition worsens."

"Then we will go at once," Max said.

Celie could sense the seriousness of the situation, and she didn't want to be selfish, but she had to ask: "Is there any possibility that Joba is on your way? Could you take us to my ship without delaying your trip home for too long a time?"

Max seemed to be considering this, but Rurick stiffened, his expression suddenly wary. "No," he said.

"Joba is in the opposite direction. It would delay our trip two cycles to take you."

Bitter disappointment whipped through Celie, but she called on her self-discipline to not voice her unhappiness over the situation. This was Max's father who was quite possibly dying. "I see," she said.

"I'm not sure you do," Rurick replied. He turned to Max and the officers. "Set course for Jardonia immediately. Notify the two escort ships to do the same. I want continual updates on the king's condition."

They all nodded, and Max headed for the cockpit. Before Celie could absorb the fact that it was Rurick, not Max, who had given the orders, Rurick raised his right arm and fingered the triton band on it. He appeared deep in thought; then a resigned expression crossed his face.

"There's no sense hiding it any longer," he said to the officers. "They'll know when we reach Jardonia anyway. This way, they'll have some time to get used to it."

Commander Zane bowed. "As you wish, Your Highness."

Turning toward Celie, Rurick looked directly at her as he unhooked the triton band and removed it. He held both it and his arm up. She stared dumbly for a moment, not comprehending. There were no holes in the arm of his flight suit, no sockets or connectors of any kind. Then it dawned on her. She heard Raven gasp, so she assumed the girl had reached the same conclusion.

"What is this?" Celie demanded, incredulous.

"The band is a disguise," Rurick said, his gaze still locked with hers. "I'm not an android, Celie. Max is the android."

"I don't understand." Although she was beginning to—and as the shock wore off, the implications began to sink in.

Rurick walked slowly toward her. "I am Maximilian Rurickko Riordan, Crown Prince of Jardonia."

Chapter Nine

Celie placed her hand against the wall, reeling from the impact of Rurick's announcement. "You're not the crown prince," she whispered, stubbornly, desperately holding on to what she had believed all this time. "Max is."

Rurick shook his head. "No. Max is an android who impersonates me when we travel, as a protective measure. I disguise myself as the android and he presents himself as me."

She accepted that he was telling the truth. A surge of anger burst through her. "You bastard," she hissed.

Regret flashed in his eyes. "I'm sorry, Celie. I hated lying to you, but I had given my word I wouldn't reveal my identity to anyone. Not even to you."

Spirit, she wished the shock wasn't wearing off, because the sudden flash of clarity was brutal. How she'd thought him nonhuman and therefore safe; how she'd practically thrown herself at him, begged him to mate with her. How foolish and pathetic she must have looked to him; how he must have laughed at her behind her back, even as he touched her with shattering intimacy. Most of all she felt the pain of having trusted him, and his betrayal of that trust. Another betrayal from a man.

Fury blasted over her like a sonic wave. It burst into her head and she saw red. All she could feel was rage, fed by the anguish of Rurick's treachery. Balling her hand into a fist, she acted without thought. She closed the distance between them and hit him in the face with all her might.

He staggered back, pain and surprise reflected in his expression. There was a roaring in her ears, and vaguely she heard raised voices in the background. But all she could think was, *Good, I hurt him,* and she stepped in to hit him again. Then a blinding agony shot through her. And everything went black.

The pain was the first thing she felt. Her head pounded like a malfunctioning rocket coil. She heard a groan and was shocked to realize it was coming from her. She tried to open her eyes, but everything blurred. As she turned her head, a wave of nausea rushed over her. Groaning again, she rolled to her side, drawing up her legs as if that could stop the crippling agony.

A cool hand touched her cheek. "Oh, Celie, thank Spirit you're waking up." Raven's concerned voice sounded distorted, as if she were far away. What in the universe was going on?

Celie tried to lift her head, and another wave of nausea hit her. "I feel sick," she gasped, battling to keep her stomach from rebelling. "What happened?"

"Don't try to move." Raven pressed a damp cloth against Celie's forehead, and the nausea subsided to a controllable level. "You took a bad shock, but you're going to be fine."

"Blazing hells." Celie clenched her teeth together, inundated by another surge of pain. "I'm thinking I'd rather die right around now."

"It's just the aftereffects from the stun gun."

"What?" She forced her eyes open, waited until the room stopped spinning and the blurred figures before her came into focus. She was lying on a bunk, with Raven perched on the edge beside her. Max stood next to Raven, some sort of monitor in his hand. Rurick was behind them, with Commander . . . what was his name? Oh, Hades—whatever his name was, he was standing just to Rurick's left. Seeing those people, the worry etched on their faces and all of them staring at her, was too much for her shaky equilibrium, and she closed her eyes again.

"After you punched Rurick," Raven said slowly, anger reverberating in her soft voice, "one of Rurick's soldiers decided to do his macho protection routine and used his stun gun on you. The idiot didn't realize he had it set too high."

"He will be disciplined." Rurick's cold voice drew Celie's attention.

She opened her eyes just enough to look at him. He was stiff and grim, and appeared furious. *And he wasn't an android.* Despite her throbbing head, her mind was rapidly clearing, the memory of all that had transpired before she passed out rushing back with ruthless clarity. Damn, damn, damn!

"Max has extensive programming for medical emergencies," Rurick said. "He'll give you something for the pain and the nausea. We'll put some ice on your hand." He gestured to the *real* android, who moved around Raven, holding a filled hypochamber.

A part of Celie wanted to refuse the medicine, wanted

nothing to do with Rurick and his minions. But in view of her current incapacity and the grating pain, it would be foolish to turn down anything that offered relief. Besides, she'd already displayed unprecedented stupidity. No need to sink any lower.

"You're just as despicable as he is," she snapped at Max, although she allowed him to administer the medication.

"I am sorry for the deception," Max answered. "Although it was necessary."

"Spare me your excuses." She sighed as the throbbing in her head receded to a manageable level. She was able to relax enough to stretch out her legs and roll onto her back. Hovering like an anxious mother, Raven pulled a light blanket over her and wiped her face again with a cool cloth. Celie patted her hand weakly. "Thanks, sweetness," she whispered.

Rurick moved to the bunk. "I'm sorry this happened. As I said, Lieutenant Cartan will be disciplined for his mistake. I'll see to it personally."

His supreme arrogance and authority were so obvious, she couldn't understand why she hadn't noticed before now. The large bruise on his cheekbone, where she'd slammed her fist, gave her a glow of satisfaction. "You just do that, *Your Highness*."

He didn't react to her sarcasm. "Is there anything I can do for you?"

"Yes." She drew a deep breath, told herself she should ignore his deception, shouldn't allow him to see how badly it had shaken her. But the hurt and the bitterness weighed heavily, and she was too debilitated right now to contain her resentment. "You can leave me alone. I don't want to see you again."

His face hardening, he stepped back. "I think I can avoid offending you for the remainder of the trip to

144

Jardonia. However, I can make no guarantees once we're at the royal residence."

She didn't need that reminder. She didn't want to go anywhere with Rurick, much less leave her ship behind. "Wait," she gasped, trying to sit up, which was a mistake. The room began spinning again, and the pain returned with a vengeance.

"Lie still," Raven chided, pushing her back down. "You need to rest now."

But Celie's attention focused on Rurick. He turned toward her, his expression unreadable. "I'm waiting," he said coolly.

"There's no reason to drag Raven and me to Jardonia. Take us to my ship before you leave the sector."

"I've already told you, I can't do that. My father could be dying, and I must reach him as soon as possible. I've already given the orders to return to Jardonia. We're well underway."

"So your orders are always followed," she jeered, wishing she could wipe the determined look off his handsome face.

He stared at her, imperious royalty reflected in every millimeter of his tense body. "Always."

She sank down, inwardly seething but too weak to do anything about it. She would find a way to return to her ship, and soon. Then she would make certain she never again crossed paths with this lying, arrogant bastard.

Celie hated Jardonia—every single thing about it.

She hated the massive Riordan palace, the Paladais, with its vaulted, skylit ceilings and pink, crystal-paneled hallways. She hated the opulent bedchambers, with their padded, silk-covered walls; hated the soothing pastel shades and the white crystalline floors, some covered with carpets so lush that it felt like she was sinking

145

when she stepped onto them. And the beds—enormous, ornate, covered in satin and too many pillows to count.

Then there were the bathing rooms, almost as large as the bedchambers, with huge sunken tubs and more of the ever-present crystal walls and gold gilt. She felt uncomfortable around the numerous android servants, called androservers, with their pleasant faces and simple silk uniforms—again in soothing pastels—and the way they glided soundlessly across the floors.

As for the person responsible for bringing her to this disgusting, gilded wonderland, her feelings couldn't even be put into words. Nor could she begin to probe the depth of the pain she felt at Rurick's deception. She couldn't understand why she was so hurt. She'd only known Rurick a matter of cycles—thirteen, to be exact. There was no reason, even with the physical intimacies they'd shared, for her to be so upset.

Celie was not one to shy away from a problem, and she tended to analyze things, perhaps too much. She thought a lot about her reaction to Rurick and to the fact that he was human rather than android, and came to two realizations.

The first was the obvious one: Being attracted to Rurick opened up the old wounds from her father and Pax. And thoughts of her father led to memories that always brought a return of her nightmares, which only served to remind her that she could never be a candidate for a "normal" life—especially not one that included male-female relationships. Since she had no intention of undergoing lengthy and painful sessions with a spiritual healer, or turning herself in to authorities to pay for her crime, she'd have to deal with those nightmares on her own. Alone.

The second, and far more startling, was the realization that it wasn't the physical but rather the spiritual bonding that had occurred between her and Rurick that was the source of her internal conflict. He knew about her past—most of it—knew her deepest fears about men. He knew, with a perception that she found painfully embarrassing, why she had approached him and asked him to demonstrate the mating act.

Strangely, his knowledge left her feeling violated. It had been all right when she thought Rurick was just a machine and would make no judgments, but it was very disconcerting for Rurick *the man* to have seen so deeply into her psyche. It angered her that his deliberate deception had made her vulnerable to him in such a way.

A light rap on the panel joining her chamber with Raven's pulled Celie from her analysis. She strode to the well and opened it. Raven stood there, in a long, feminine dress that was a deep burgundy color. "Look at you," Celie said, taken aback.

Raven stepped through the door, her expression radiant. "What do you think?" She spun around to show off the dress, its gauzy layers swirling around her. "Isn't it beautiful?"

The bodice fit her small breasts too tightly, and the low-cut neckline was more revealing than Celie thought proper for a girl just reaching the bloom of adulthood. The burgundy shade set off Raven's dark hair and eyes to perfection. Her hair had been pinned up into elaborate coils and interwoven with glittering jewels. She looked older, more mature, and incredibly lovely.

"It is very nice," Celie agreed, none too happy.

"I feel like a princess!" Raven spun again, then stumbled against her, laughing.

"You're wearing makeup," Celie said, noting the mauve shadow on Raven's eyelids and the blush on her cheeks. "And perfume."

"I know." Raven smiled, her eyes glowing. "Jirca, my androserver, helped me put on the makeup. She did my

147

hair too." She placed her wrist to her nose and inhaled deeply. "I love this scent. I've never worn perfume before."

Celie didn't like this at all. Raven would have every male in the Paladais sniffing after her. "Listen, sweetness, I know we're both tired, and I'm certain a formal dinner will be quite boring. Why don't we eat here, where we can relax?"

"Oh, no! I want to go to the evening meal. I want to see Queen Amaris and Lady Kalina in their elegant dresses, and the men in their uniforms, and taste all the different foods. Jirca told me there will be at least fifteen courses. And she said there will be hundreds of flowers decorating the dining hall. There will be music, and sometimes they have dancing, and . . ." Raven threw up her hands dramatically. "So many wonderful things."

"You don't know how to dance," Celie said, envisioning young men falling all over themselves to woo the innocent Raven.

"It doesn't matter. I can always ask one of the men to show me. Besides . . ." Raven's face took on that calculating expression that always put Celie on guard. "Don't you want to see Rurick in his dress uniform? I'll bet he'll be gorgeous. Just think, Celie, you kissed a *prince!* How was it? It looked to me like Rurick really knew what he was doing."

"No, I don't want to see Rurick, and it's none of your business," Celie answered tartly, doing her best to ignore the sudden surge of carnal heat that always seemed to accompany thoughts of the man. "Besides, he probably won't be at dinner tonight. He's been with his father since we got here."

"Jirca said King Domek is doing better. I know Rurick has been terribly worried." Raven's expression reflected her innate empathy for others. "I'd be frantic if my father were very ill."

Celie didn't want to feel any sympathy for Rurick, but she wasn't a vengeful person, and she sincerely hoped the king recovered fully. But she also hoped Rurick remained by his side, so she wouldn't have to endure his presence.

"Anyway," Raven said, changing the subject, "this is the most fabulous place I've ever seen. I love the crystal and the gold and the furnishings. Being here is so . . . neat."

Being here was horrible. "I think we should stay in our rooms tonight and rest," Celie urged. "We haven't had much sleep since we were on Altair."

"You can stay, if you want," Raven said. "I know you're still tired from the stun gun."

How could she have known that? Celie had repeatedly stated she was all right, refusing to see the royal physician, although her muscles still ached with every movement. It was better than it had been on Rurick's ship, and she knew the symptoms would be gone in another cycle or so. "I'm fine," she insisted. "Although I wouldn't object to a quiet evening."

"Then stay here and rest," Raven urged. "I don't mind going by myself. It's a private family dinner tonight, so I'll know almost everyone there."

Celie had absolutely no intention of letting the girl go alone. "Well, maybe it would be interesting to go," she hedged. "But let's call it early, all right?"

Raven nodded eagerly. "Sure. Is that what you're wearing?"

"Yes." Celie looked down at her simple black dress. Apparently, Rurick had ordered clothing replicated for her and Raven, because they had each been provided with a generous assortment of dresses and accessories that fit amazingly well. The dress Celie wore was tighter than she liked, with a square neckline that offered decent coverage, although the back scooped quite low, but it was also the most conservative evening dress she'd found in the wardrobe. "Is anything wrong with it?"

"No." Raven looked her over. "It's just rather plain. You could dress it up with some jewelry. You could redo your hair, put on some makeup. Where's your androserver?"

"I sent her away. I didn't want an android hovering over me." Celie patted the simple, upswept twist of her hair. "I'll make do with this. I'm not much on makeup and jewelry. I'm willing to dress for dinner, but I'm not trying to impress these people."

The fact was, she found the clothing worn at the Paladais too ornate and ostentatious for her liking. She'd never been much for fashion, preferring a flight suit and boots to more feminine apparel any day. She felt guilty participating in such opulence, especially while the people of the ninth sector were starving. But Moriah had taught her to use good manners and to respect the customs of other people. So she would try to dress appropriately, but only to a certain point.

"I'm just not into fancy styles," she told Raven. "I like simpler clothes. But that dress looks great on you, Raven."

"Thank you." The girl smiled. "You look fine, Celie. With your coloring and your killer figure, it doesn't matter what you wear. The men will be all over you."

"Yeah, right." Celie looked at Raven's young face and felt a flash of guilt. She'd been so caught up in her anger at Rurick and at being forced to leave her ship and come to Jardonia that she hadn't given much thought to how Raven might be feeling about her own situation.

She took the girl's hand. "Sweetness, how are you doing with all this? Did it upset you to learn that Max was not a real man?" *It certainly couldn't have been as much of a shock as Celie learning she'd thrown herself*

*at the crown prince of Jardonia, begging him to mate
with her.*

"It was a surprise, I can tell you that." Raven pursed
her lips thoughtfully. "But I'm not too upset. I thought
Max was a really cool guy, and I even wondered how
he kissed." She grinned at Celie's expression. "Don't go
giving me that shocked, adult-disapproval look. I get it
all the time at home. I'm nineteen, and I happen to have
a normal, healthy interest in men."

"Just not too much, all right? I'm responsible for
you."

"No, you're not," Raven said gently. "I'm an adult,
and I'm responsible for my own actions. You worry too
much, Celie. Relax and have some fun."

This was going to be anything but. Especially since
she'd be dealing with Rurick. Celie sighed in resigna-
tion. "Shall we go, then?"

They stepped out into the wide, curving corridor and
looked in both directions. "Why do they have all these
loops and curves?" Celie groaned. "What's wrong with
neat, linear hallways?"

"I like it," Raven said. "It's pretty, and it keeps the
energies flowing continuously, without disruption."

"I'm not worried about the 'energies,' whatever that
means. You could go in circles in this place and never
get anywhere. We need a map to navigate it. I can probably print one off the computer in my chamber."

"A map to get around a residence?" Raven shook her
head, laughing. "What a thought. I think I know where
the private dining chamber is. Jirca told me how to get
there."

"I'm glad one of us knows. Lead on." Celie fell in step
with Raven, still put off by the overwhelming grandeur.
No one family should own this much.

They passed several chamber panels and two corridors curving off from the one they were in. Raven paused and looked around.

"Are you sure you know where you're going?" Celie asked.

"I think we go to the end of this corridor, then turn down another hallway."

"Good luck finding the end," Celie muttered.

They started forward and had gone a few steps when a familiar voice came from behind them. "Good evening, ladies."

They turned and saw Rurick, who must have come from a side corridor. He was wearing a dark uniform similar to that of his officers, only it was more a royal blue and almost iridescent, reflecting purple tones. Heavily decorated with interwoven silver and gold, it fit him perfectly, accentuating his broad shoulders and narrow hips. He looked cool and totally self-possessed.

Celie had only seen him briefly since the stun gun incident, when they had landed at Jardonia and disembarked earlier in the cycle. He had gone straight to his father's chambers, leaving Max and Commander Zane to make the introductions to the royal family. Seeing him now, she experienced an unwelcome rush of emotions—agitation and renewed anger at his betrayal, underscored by a surge of adrenaline—and the ensuing excitement.

Damn him for keeping her so stirred up. Why, of all the men in the universe, did this one have to have such an effect on her? She didn't want to feel anything for him. Yet, at the same time, a part of her welcomed the adrenaline rush and the challenge of dealing with him. Not a good thing. She would get her runaway emotions under control, by the Spirit. *She would.*

"Hello, Rurick, er, I mean, Your Highness," Raven said.

He turned his charismatic attention on her. "Ah,

152

Raven, there is no need for formalities. We are good friends, I hope."

She smiled. "Of course."

"Then please call me Rurick, as all my friends do. By the way, you look beautiful." He took her hand and bowed slightly as he brought it to his lips.

Her face radiated delight. "Thank you, Rurick. And thank you for letting us stay here, and for the beautiful clothes."

"You're very welcome."

"How is your father doing?" she asked.

"Better. He's weak, but he's improving. The doctors still don't know what caused his illness." Rurick released her hand. "Would you mind if I have a moment alone with Celie?"

Raven might not mind, but Celie did. Anger simmered so close to the surface she didn't know if she could rationally deal with Rurick right now. With the way she was feeling, the more distance she could keep between them, the better.

"That's not necessary," she said. "We have nothing to discuss. Come on, Raven." She started to walk past Rurick, then thought better of it and spun back around. "No, on second thought I do want to talk to you."

Raven looked from Rurick to her. "I think I'll go on to the dining chamber. It's down that last corridor, isn't it?"

The prince nodded. "Yes. Go to the final hallway in the circle, turn left, then follow it to the end. If you get lost, request directions aloud. The computers will guide you." He watched until Raven located the correct corridor before returning his attention to Celie. "You look tired," he said quietly. For a moment Celie found herself caught in his mesmerizing gaze, and in the concern reflected there.

153

She shook herself out of it. "I'm fine. I want to talk to you about—"

"You didn't go to see the physician. Why?"

Irritation at his persistence edged in. "I told you, I'm all right."

"You don't look it. You need to take care of yourself. You endured a dangerously high stun charge, for which I blame myself. Don't refuse to see the physician just because I requested it."

"I assure you, I don't care enough to base my actions on your requests. If you want to take the blame for anything, take it for bringing me here instead of returning me to my ship. All I need, and all I'm asking for, is to be taken to my ship."

"I have every intention of returning you to your ship, but I want to escort you personally to guarantee your safety. I can't leave Jardonia until my father is well on the way to recovery."

His insistence on personally escorting her, and the ensuing delay, frustrated her beyond good sense. "Has it occurred to you that maybe I don't want to go anywhere with you?" she snapped.

Anger flashed in his eyes. "Has it occurred to *you* that you're being unreasonable?"

"This from a man who lied repeatedly to me about his true identity, and who took advantage of his masquerade to humiliate me."

"So, we get to the heart of the matter," he murmured. "You claim you don't care, yet your reaction would indicate you have a higher emotional stake in what happened between us than you're willing to admit."

His perceptiveness slashed through her emotional armor. She stepped back, feeling as if she'd been cut. Spirit, he was right, and she just didn't have the means to deal with the reality. "Go to Hades!" She spun on her heel and stalked away. She heard his footsteps behind her and speeded up.

"Celie—"

"Your Highness, your father is asking for you."

She slowed, glancing over her shoulder to see one of Rurick's officers striding toward him. "I'll be right there." Rurick looked back at her. "We'll finish this discussion later."

"We have nothing further to discuss." She whirled and marched away, grateful for the interruption.

The realization that Rurick could affect her as no one else ever had, that he could stir up such a maelstrom of emotions, convinced her she had to get away from him. She had no intention of allowing him to escort her to Joba. She'd get there on her own. Just as soon she hijacked a Jardonian ship.

Raven turned into a wide hallway. She walked slowly, entranced by the crystal walls and the shimmering starbursts of light suspended high above her head. Every few meters there were niches in the walls, some with crystal benches, some with trees shaped like animals, and, best of all, some with holos of past and current royal family members.

To her delight, Raven discovered that if she touched the surface of a holo, it immediately coalesced into a three-dimensional holographic projection of the person pictured. It then showed a holovideo of that person's life, presenting various highlights, with one scene flowing into the next.

She watched one of an older man, whom she guessed was King Domek. Not only did he share a strong resemblance with Rurick, but his coronation ceremony was shown. She found the pomp and circumstance fascinating. When the HV was over, she went eagerly to the next holo. It was that of a striking young man of about

155

twenty seasons of age, who also bore a strong resemblance to both King Domek and Rurick.

He had the same exotically shaded hair, only it was shorter, and his eyes were the same intriguing gold Raven had learned was an inherited trait among the royal family, obviously a dominant gene. His face was more rounded and youthful than Rurick's, his full mouth disdainful and his stance arrogant.

Raven studied him, intrigued. She had only met Rurick's stepmother and half sister when they arrived on Jardonia, so she hadn't been introduced to this young man. She touched the holo and watched the flowing scenes, depicting first a plump, laughing baby, then a little boy surrounded by numerous toys, then an older boy astride an unfamiliar large animal, which was harnessed with a special seat and gold and silver trappings. The scene flowed to one of a young man, fighting expertly with an unusual saber.

"I trust you find that interesting," came a masculine voice from behind her. "Although I've been told I'm far more handsome in person."

Raven turned, surprised to see the young man from the holovideo before her. He wore a dark uniform similar to Rurick's, the same royal blue with iridescent purple tones, and decorated with silver and gold. He was almost as tall as Rurick, but not as muscular. He stood there expectantly, as if awaiting homage from her. An unusual spark of irritation flared in her. He was very handsome, but as far as she was concerned, his obvious conceit marred his good looks.

"You're all right, I guess," she retorted, refusing to feed his ego.

The young man's tawny brows raised. "You obviously do not realize who I am."

She was fairly certain of his identity now, and her

dislike of this pompous young man escalated rapidly. "It wouldn't matter to me."

His golden eyes narrowed. "I am Prince Sevilen Domek Riordan. You may show your respect by bowing to me. I will allow your impertinence this once because I know you are a visitor to Jardonia and not aware of our ways."

Her impertinence? Oh! His arrogance was maddening. Raven had been raised to believe that all beings were created equal in the eyes of Spirit, and that no individual should be placed above another. She had no intention of taking a subservient role to this young braggart.

"I don't think so," she said sweetly. "I'm not a Riordan citizen, and therefore not one of your subjects. I don't bow to anyone."

"Your manners are appalling. We have many visitors to Jardonia, and all bow to members of the royal family."

"Well, I'm not going to. So what are you going to do, throw me in some crystal prison?"

She found the flush that spread over his face amusing. She knew she should be ashamed for baiting Rurick's half brother, especially since she and Celie were enjoying Riordan hospitality, but this young man was obnoxious and she would not defer to him.

"I can see to it that your requests to our family are refused," he said.

"I'm not asking for anything from your family," Raven snapped, thoroughly disgusted. "As a matter of fact, I'm here because your brother brought me. And you are a pompous, strutting echobird."

She pushed past the gaping prince with a swirl of her skirts and made her way toward the dining hall, passing several more corridors. She saw the entrance up ahead but was too upset to enter just yet. She went to sit on a bench in an alcove and compose herself. Looking back up the corridor, she saw Prince Sevilen was nowhere to be found. Good.

Closing her eyes, she forced herself to breathe slowly. She couldn't stop thinking about the obnoxious young man. What a conceited Kerani's ass! She told herself to forget about him.

"Raven? What are you doing?"

She opened her eyes and saw Celie standing before her. She looked as upset as Raven felt. "Celie! What's wrong?"

"Nothing." Celie straightened her skirt with a sharp jerk and blew out her breath. She glanced over her shoulder, and her mouth set into a resolute line. "Absolutely nothing."

She was practically crackling with emotion, most likely anger at Rurick. That was good, Raven decided. Strong emotions, even negative ones like hatred and anger, were close relatives to other strong emotions—such as love. She smiled to herself. Where Celie and Rurick were concerned, things were going very well. Very well indeed.

An identical pair of male androservers stood at the huge door panels leading to the family's private dining hall. They wore triton armbands, as did most androservers at the Paladais. Celie had learned the bands had many sophisticated functions, one of them communication. Of course, Rurick had worn his band only to perpetuate his deception.

The two androservers were dressed in elaborate uniforms colored gold on one side and silver on the other. One server stared intently at Celie's eyes, while the other did the same with Raven. Celie decided they must be doing retinal scans—an unobtrusive way to identify and screen anyone entering the dining chamber. She and Raven had both submitted to retinal mapping when they exited the spaceport earlier, so she assumed the scanner would identify them.

After a moment, both servers moved back and bowed, then ushered Celie and Raven into the chamber, one stepping forward and announcing: "Captain Celie Cameron and Lady Raven McKnight, honored guests of the crown prince."

Like the rest of the Paladais, the royal family's private dining chamber was ornate. A massive, curving table with intricately carved crystal legs stood in the center of the room. Three crystal chandeliers descending over the table bathed the chamber in brilliant light.

The table was covered in a heavy gold damask fabric, and Celie saw that Raven's android had been right about the flowers. Masses of them adorned the center of the table, and more spilled from huge crystal urns that lined the glittering walls. Their scent, a light, sweet fragrance reminiscent of the balmy, perfumed breezes of Elysia, permeated the room. Gold and crystal bird cages hung over each urn of flowers, and were occupied by various birds with stunning jewel-tone feathers.

A group of people stood near the entry, and all looked toward Celie and Raven when the androservers announced them. Queen Amaris, in a flowing silver dress that accentuated her fair skin and pale blond hair, swept forward as they approached.

"There you are," she said, waving a hand adorned with jewels. "I'm glad you could join us for the evening meal. Raven, you look lovely, like an exotic flower to grace our table."

"Thank you, Your Highness," Raven replied demurely.

"Captain Cameron." The queen turned to Celie. "It's nice to see you."

"We appreciate your hospitality." Celie stared down

at the dainty woman, feeling like a giant. Every female she'd seen thus far in Jardonia had been small, and she towered over them.

"My stepson tells me you assisted him in a difficult situation," Amaris said. "But he wouldn't go into any detail. I can't imagine what trouble he could have encountered. The Riordan name is known and respected throughout the quadrant." Turning gracefully, she gestured to the woman beside her. "I presume you remember my daughter, Princess Kalina."

"Yes," Celie inclined her head. "Princess."

Kalina wore a vivid red dress that had a single strap over the left shoulder, leaving the right shoulder and a generous expanse of tawny skin bare. Her silvery blond hair was piled on her head and interwoven with glittering gold chains. Jewels sparkled in her ears and around her neck and arms.

She stared at Celie somewhat contemptuously, scanning her from head to toe. "Oh, dear, Captain," she said with feigned concern. "Did you find your androserver lacking in grooming programming? I will be sure it is reprimanded and has a diagnostic check."

Celie had never worried about others' approval, but she suddenly felt out of place here, beside these glamorous women. She didn't care, she told herself fiercely. Their clothing and jewels were only a glittering, false surface over what appeared to be very shallow interiors. She didn't appreciate Kalina's rudeness, but she also didn't want any android to be unfairly punished.

"I prefer to dress conservatively," she told Kalina, keeping her temper in check. "I'm not used to servants, so I dismissed Jemmi."

"I see." Kalina's voice was haughty. "I suppose we can't fault you for having simple tastes."

Celie clenched her fists, reminding herself she was a guest here and far from the world she knew. An overwhelming longing for her own ship and for her painting flooded her: They were her anchors, her stability in a life that had been volatile and perilous, at best. She had Moriah, she reminded herself, along with a large extended family that included the women from Risa, and the Shielders.

Yet she had always walked a solitary path. She'd chosen a risky vocation, first because the survival of the Risa colony depended upon it; later because the adrenaline rushes from risky encounters with pirates and Controller agents were the only things that made her feel truly alive. Until she'd met Rurick.

"You look very nice, dear," Queen Amaris broke in with a reproving glance at her daughter. "Black is becoming to you. Why don't I introduce you to some of the other family members?"

"Of course," Celie said stiffly, turning her back on Kalina.

She and Raven were introduced to a number of aunts and uncles and cousins, all dressed in glitzy, ornate clothing, and all who stared at Celie as if she were a dead bird dragged in by a lanrax. Raven, on the other hand, was accepted quickly into the group, her gracious manner and sweet nature easily winning over the stuffy Riordans.

Moments later beautiful tones chimed, reverberating through the large chamber, and the conversations ceased. Everyone turned expectantly toward the double gold-paneled entry, and Celie and Raven followed suit. Rurick and a younger man stood there, the two androservers flanking them. Max and Commander Zane stood behind Rurick. One server stepped forward and proclaimed, "Now entering—Crown Prince Maximilian Rurickko Riordan!"

Rurick smiled and moved into the hall. Celie rolled her eyes at this elaborate ceremonial display. And this was just a private family meal. She'd hate to see the pomp at a formal event. The chimes reverberated again. "Now entering—Prince Sevilen Domek Riordan!" proclaimed the second androserver, and the young man stepped forward.

Feeling Raven stiffen beside her, Celie turned and saw the girl staring at Prince Sevilen with an irate expression. Curious, she turned back to study the prince. He looked similar to Rurick, with the same tawny-streaked hair and golden eyes, but his face was fuller, his features not as sharply honed. He was almost as tall as Rurick, but thinner, his muscles not as well-delineated. "Do you know him?" she asked Raven.

"I met him briefly, and I don't like him," the girl answered. "He's conceited and obnoxious."

Interesting. Good-natured Raven rarely disliked anyone. Since the girl was unhappy with Prince Sevilen's presence, Celie hoped her wish to get through the evening quickly might be granted. She noticed Rurick staring at her, and her heart stuttered. She was relieved when family members surrounded him, several talking at once. Although he kept glancing in her direction, he was forced to converse.

"Come on," she told Raven. "Lets go to the other side of the hall. That way, you won't have to talk with Prince Sevilen." *And I won't have to deal with Rurick.*

"Fine with me." Raven sniffed.

They worked their way across the room, making small talk with quite a few people. The Riordans were surprisingly curious, and had many questions about life in the old quadrant and the new colony on Shamara. Snaring a glass of wine off a silver tray an androserver was carrying, Celie sipped it and politely answered their questions. She felt a sense of relief now that she had a plan of action. All she needed was a ship—easy enough to come by with her particular skills. Very soon, she and Raven would be gone from here. And Rurick would be out of her life forever.

Chapter Ten

Only half-listening to Kalina's chatter, Rurick watched Celie, who sat halfway down the long table. With her height and stunning figure, the woman stood out vividly from the others, despite their fancy dresses and sparkling jewels. He didn't think she was having a good time; she looked like she'd rather be anywhere else. While some of her discontent probably extended to being on Jardonia, he suspected his presence unsettled her too.

She'd managed to avoid him so far, but he'd have plenty of opportunity to remedy that, even if not tonight. Returning to Jardonia under the alarming circumstance of his father's near death had driven home a crucial point, one Celie herself had explained. Life was unpredictable, and it was short.

Rurick had decided there was no reason he shouldn't go after what he wanted, as long as it didn't interfere with his royal duties. And he wanted Celie Cameron.

He hadn't fully explored the depth of his feelings for her, but he knew he wanted to spend time with her and see what developed. In the short while they'd been separated on Jardonia, he'd missed her, missed her light-speed intelligence and wit, the way she spoke her mind. And he'd missed the way she tasted, the feel of her lithe body pressed against his. Since there was no longer any secret about his true identity, he could pursue her without guilt.

It didn't matter that Celie wasn't Riordan. His own mother had been from a different society. Although Amaris and Kalina liked to point out that Queen Lisha, who died when Rurick was six, had been lax about the importance of protocol, and had let things at the Paladais become far too casual, the truth was that the Jardonian people had loved and respected his mother.

"Rurick, does that *android* have to be at the table with us?" Kalina's petulant voice caught his attention. She was staring pointedly at Max, who was seated next to Raven.

The myriad conversations around the table came to a halt, and everyone watched Rurick, awaiting his response. Celie looked angry, her dark eyes narrowed, her gaze fixed on Kalina. Raven looked distressed. Max wiggled his brows at Kalina and smirked. She huffed and turned away from him.

Rurick was weary of Kalina's snobbery and her rudeness. Yet he was aware of his position as the crown prince, and the need to be diplomatic. "Max is a member of my personal regiment and has saved my life more than once," he said calmly. "He's also acquainted with Captain Cameron and Lady Raven, and I thought they might appreciate sharing the meal with someone they know."

Kalina's finely arched brows raised, and she shook her head as if dealing with a child. "He's an *android*, not an acquaintance. And I don't think it's proper that any of your regiment be present at a private dinner." Her cold gaze moved to Commander Zane, who sat on the other side of Celie. "Your officers are not members of the upper class."

"I'm far more interested in people's loyalty and how they perform their duties than I am their class," Rurick said calmly, although he was furious inside. "Both Max and Commander Zane have been exemplary in those areas. They dine with me at my request. I would expect you honor that."

Kalina flushed, and her eyes narrowed into a scathing glare. But she inclined her head and murmured, "Of course, *brother*." Despite her verbal compliance, she managed to convey her loathing of him with a sneer.

Not wanting to challenge her in a public forum, and certainly not on his first evening home, Rurick chose to let her insolence go. He'd speak to her privately.

She wouldn't change, though. Kalina believed that, as a member of the Riordan royal family, she was superior, above everyone else. She'd even managed to pass on much of that attitude to her brother Sevilen. Sev, however, possessed a good heart and could be reasoned with; Rurick couldn't say the same for Kalina. When he was tired, as he was tonight, her attitude and her airs grated unbearably.

Conversation around the table started back up, and Rurick leaned back in his chair. He sent Raven a reassuring smile, and she smiled back. She was a sweetheart, and he'd grown very fond of her. His gaze shifted to Celie, who quickly focused on her food. She was obviously determined to ignore him. Tomorrow, he decided. Tomorrow they would talk. With his father starting to recover, he'd be able to take Celie and Raven back to their ship. Though he planned to delay that as long as possible.

166

Queen Amaris tapped his arm. "You need to be sure you speak with everyone here before you leave tonight. It wouldn't do for word to get out that we snubbed any member of any clan."

Rurick nodded stiffly, not allowing his irritation to show. He'd always hated these affairs, always wondered why everything had to be so stilted and formal. He felt like an outsider here, had felt that way since his father remarried when he was eight. His sense of isolation had increased with each passing season, as his half siblings, Kalina, and then Sev, were born. He'd had to fight for his father's attention; any he received seemed hard won and due only to the fact that he was the crown prince.

Out of respect for his father, and for the crown, he endured the pomp and formality of court life. It was the Riordan tradition, as his stepmother reminded him repeatedly during his youth. But his real mother hadn't been so fixated on external trappings. He'd been told by many of the elders that she had been a breath of fresh air in the staid Riordan court.

When Rurick was twenty, he'd decided to find out more about his mother. He'd learned that Queen Lisha had come from Valera, a settlement on the planet Mangon, in the ninth sector. But his duties had prevented him from pursing it further.

It had been twelve more seasons before he was actually able to travel there to search for that part of his heritage, arriving too late. Rurick's fingers tightened around his glass, and he lost his appetite. He stared at the abundance of food being served by the androservers, at the rare and expensive delicacies imported from all over the quadrant. He thought of the starving colonists on Altair, and the emaciated baby who had died in Celie's arms, and he cursed his inability to do much more than sneak supplies to the desperate ninth-sector inhabitants. But he intended to have answers soon, and to act on those answers.

Just as he intended to pursue Captain Celie Cameron.

"You told me my flight suit would be cleaned overnight and returned to me this morning." Celie stared at her androserver. "I planned to wear it today."

"I know, Captain Cameron," Jemmi answered, her eyes downcast. She was a pretty little thing, with skin as white and smooth as Elysian moon glass, and light brown hair and large blue eyes. "Our laundry operates all night to provide clean clothing for those in the Paladais. But your flight suit is gone."

"I don't understand."

"Princess Kalina told the cleaners to destroy it. She said it was inappropriate apparel for the Paladais."

Anger spiked through Celie. "Kalina is more conniving than a Controller," she muttered, ignoring the fact that Jemmi could be recording every word. "Now what? I have to wear something." While Raven was touring the Paladais with Max, Celie planned to stake out the spaceport and target a ship she could steal. It would have been much easier, and much more comfortable, in a flight suit.

"Yes, Captain." Jemmi whizzed over to a double wall panel and pushed a button. The panels opened to reveal a huge closet. "I'm sure we can find something suitable."

At least, suitable to Kalina, Celie thought, fuming. She was tempted to walk through the Paladais in the sleeping gown that had been provided, just to spite the princess. But since the gown was pretty sheer, she herself would probably be as mortified as Kalina.

"Blazing hells," she snapped, thoroughly disgusted. "Don't worry about it, Jemmi. I'll pick out something."

A few moments later, she emerged from the closet

with a sleeveless emerald dress. Its vivid color would draw unwanted attention, but everything else had been worse—backless or too low cut, too heavy, too full, too ornate. Spirit, did the Riordans ever wear anything simple? Stepping into the dress, Celie let Jemmi fasten the crystal clasps at the back. And what was wrong with self-sealing seams?

She stared at the mirror, not at all pleased. Like the black dress she'd worn last night, this one was snug with a dipping neckline. The bodice hugged her breasts, pushing them upward and creating an unnecessary amount of cleavage. It was almost as bad as the silk rhaphas she and Moriah had worn as a disguise in the old quadrant. *Well, at least I can walk,* she thought sourly.

Dismissing Jemmi, she left her chamber and headed for the main entrance. Once she got outside the Paladais, she felt confident any androserver could direct her to the spaceport—assuming she could find the main entrance. She stared down the long corridor, with myriad other corridors splitting off it. They didn't run at straight angles. The Riordans loved curves, so many hallways ran in circular patterns, making it even more difficult to navigate the place.

"Damn pretentious labyrinth," she muttered, thoroughly frustrated.

"Are you casting aspersions on the Paladais?"

There was no mistaking that voice, or the rush of sensation through her body the millisecond she heard it. Tension thrummed in its wake, kicking up the anger that had been simmering ever since she'd learned about Rurick's deception. Hands clenched, Celie turned to face him.

He was dressed casually, in soft brown meroni-skin pants and shirt. The shirt had loose, flowing sleeves, and the neck was open, revealing an enticing view of

169

golden skin. Dark brown boots completed the outfit. He radiated the confidence of a man used to having his orders obeyed and to getting exactly what he wanted.

"What are you doing here?" she demanded.

He shrugged, his nonchalance irritating her even more. "I live here. You?"

She didn't want to deal with him. "I'm really not in the mood to exchange pleasantries."

He ignored her, his gaze sweeping down her body. "You look good. That color is perfect for you, and the fit is . . . very nice."

"I'm not wearing this dress for your benefit, or to impress anyone, for that matter," she snapped, willing her traitorous body's reaction to calm. "I wouldn't be wearing it at all if your sister hadn't confiscated my flight suit."

His brows lifted in surprise. "Kalina took your suit?"

"Not personally. I don't think she'd ever touch such a lowly garment. She had the cleaners destroy it, so I wouldn't be 'unsuitably clothed.' "

"I see." He cleared his throat, and it sounded suspiciously like he was trying to stifle a laugh. "She has some definite ideas about protocol."

Celie had some definite ideas about Kalina, but she didn't voice them. "You can go back to your royal proceedings now." She turned and strode toward what she hoped was the main entrance.

The prince fell into step beside her. "Your boots provide an interesting contrast to the dress."

She glanced down at the chunky, scarred boots kicking out from beneath the dress hem. "I'll have to make sure Kalina doesn't get them."

He did laugh then, and her heart did a little dance. Why did he have to be so charming and appealing? He was a liar, she reminded herself. Just like any other man—not to be trusted.

"Look, I'd rather be alone, if you don't mind," she said. "I'm sure you have a lot of business to catch up on."

"Not really. I have advisers and assistants and officers, and their assistants, to handle the business. My father's health is improving, and that was one of my main concerns. I can finally afford to devote some time to my guests."

"First off, I am *not* your guest. A glorified prisoner is a more accurate description. Secondly, why aren't you working on plans to help the people in the ninth sector?"

"I *am* working on it. The four ships I promised Moriah are being readied and will leave tomorrow for Shamara. Supplies to stock the ships have been purchased. I've dispatched a contingent of my most trusted advisers to Sarngin to see if they can learn anything more about the cover-up."

"And then?" she demanded, not willing to admit he seemed to be doing all he could.

He blew out his breath and considered. She should have noticed the rise and fall of his chest before now. How could she have believed this living, breathing man was an android? Her hormones had dominated her good sense, that was how. Never again.

"As soon as the ships are on their way to Moriah and my father is on his feet, I'll return you to your craft and escort you from the sector. I can arrange a rendezvous point for you to pick up supplies if you want to help in the sector."

"I do want to help." But in her own way, without contact with Rurick. She wanted to put as much distance between them as possible. His deception, and the ugly memories it resurrected, still burned in her soul. Just as upsetting, however, was her inexplicable reac-

171

tion to him. She'd never responded to any man like this before, and she didn't like it.

"I can make my own contribution," she told him. "As soon as I have my ship back. Now, please excuse me." She turned and headed down the corridor.

He walked with her. "Where are you going?"

She stopped, sighing. Why wouldn't he go away? Surely he had better things to do than bother her. "I want to visit the spaceport. I'd like to inspect the ships you're sending Moriah, perhaps make some suggestions on modifications."

"That's an excellent idea. You know a great deal about smuggling, while we know nothing. Your input would be greatly appreciated."

And she'd be willing to give it—while she was picking out the ship she would be stealing. "I'll be glad to help."

"Good," he said. "I'll go with you."

"That's not necessary."

"I insist. I'd prefer you have an escort to ensure you don't get lost, and I'm available."

He was determined to accompany her, and there wasn't anything she could do about it. She'd just have to find a way to study the spaceport without revealing her true objective. Piece of caroba pie. She'd executed many complex schemes during her smuggling career. She'd be polite to Rurick even if it killed her, and silently endure his presence. And she'd succeed at her objective. "Fine," she said through gritted teeth.

He led the way—not the direction she'd been headed—and within moments they were stepping through ornately carved panels, into the most stunning gardens Celie had ever seen.

Masses of brightly colored flowers followed the curve of crystal paths, which wound through sculpted shrubbery and miniature trees. Brilliant green expanses of lush, thick grass blanketed out from the flower beds and paths. Fountains and small ponds dotted the landscape, and strategically placed benches beckoned invitingly. The soothing sounds of flowing water and wind chimes drifted across the fragrant air.

"Oh, my." Celie gaped at the scene before her. She'd never seen anything so beautiful, not even on Elysia.

"You like it?" Rurick asked, pride reverberating in his voice. "Our gardens are renowned throughout the quadrant. I thought you might enjoy seeing them. These are the family's private gardens. The public ones are much larger."

"It's amazing," she breathed.

"Believe it or not, Kalina is part of the genius behind these. She's an expert botanist and cultivated many of the flower species here."

Celie was surprised. She couldn't imagine the snooty, pristine Kalina ever getting her hands dirty. Nor could she help drawing an unwilling comparison between Kalina and her own sister. Moriah had wrought miracles on Risa, turning it from barren desolation into a virtual oasis. But she would never judge others based on appearance or birthright, as Kalina seemed to do.

"Come." Rurick took Celie's hand. "Walk with me."

She was too entranced to object, or to retrieve her hand. She strolled along a crystal path beside him, trying to take in everything. Miniature drones whirled through the flowers, dipping down and extending metallic sensors into the ground, probably to check moisture and nutrient levels. Other tiny drones moved from flower to flower, and Celie wondered if they were performing some sort of artificial pollination. Even more fascinating were the butterflies. They were twice as big as her fist and flitted majestically through the air or landed on blooms. There were also numerous birds with exotic, vividly colored plumage.

173

She would love to examine the various flowers and plants and see if dyes could be extracted from them. And she would enjoy painting the enchanting scenery, to attempt to capture the vivid blooms and the slow-moving butterflies in two-dimensional form.

Thinking of her paints and artwork sent a twinge of concern through her. She hoped she would find her ship intact. She knew there was a possibility it had been ransacked or destroyed; had known it from the beginning. Yet she had to keep her focus on returning to her ship because she couldn't bear to consider the alternative.

Rurick halted and indicated a bench. "Care to sit down?"

She took a closer look and noticed the bench had no visible support but hung in midair, levitated by some unseen force. As she and Rurick stood there, it shifted upward and downward. "I've never seen anything like this."

"All the benches adjust automatically to your height, so your feet can comfortably touch the ground. Would you like to sit for a while?"

"I don't think so," she answered, still scanning the lush landscape. She saw long strips of what appeared to be plexishield panels inset into the ground, stretching as far as she could see into the horizon. They were flanked by overflowing flower beds and brilliantly colored blooming vines stretched along the frames on either side of the panels.

"What are those panels in the ground?" she asked.

"You'll see when we go to the spaceport." Rurick turned her down another path. They walked in silence. He seemed lost in his own thoughts, and Celie was grateful she didn't have to keep up a conversation. He stopped by an exquisite fountain.

"I wanted to show you this." He dipped his fingers in the water. "It's one of my favorite spots."

The fountain was made from sheer blue crystal, and its lip came almost to Celie's waist. A deeper blue carving sat in the middle of the fountain, a long sweep of moons, planets, and stars: a glorious depiction of space. At the very top was a sun, with myriad multicolored crystal beams shooting off it. Water poured from the sun and cascaded down the starry sweep, taking on the color of the crystal as it flowed over it.

The real sun was not fully overhead yet, hanging like a backdrop behind the fountain. Its light reflected off the crystal, and the fountain sparkled like a thousand suns. Celie's breath caught at the beauty of it. Suddenly, she thought of Rurick's words to her that night in the lounge, when she'd bared more than her soul to him: *"You are so beautiful . . . like a crystal fountain against a Jardonian sunset."*

Surely he hadn't meant those words. Yet he'd spoken them with a quiet, fervent sincerity. She didn't want to think about that night. It was over and done. Time to move forward, and retrieve her ship from Joba.

"Can we go now?" she asked. "The gardens are lovely, but I'm anxious to see the ships for Moriah. We can't forget the need in the ninth sector." She deliberately used the one argument she knew he wouldn't refute.

"You're right, of course. This way." He directed her out of the gardens and to a covered walkway. It led to a lift that took them beneath the ground. They entered a tunnel and took a fast, silent tram to the spaceport. Light poured in from large skylights above them, making it seem like they weren't below ground at all. Celie realized those skylights were the panels she'd seen from the garden, an ingenious use of natural light.

As they sped toward the spaceport, she considered the wonders she'd observed on Jardonia. She'd researched the Riordans and knew they had the most ad-

175

vanced technology in the quadrant, with the possible exception of the Enhancers. The difference was that the Enhancers refused to use their understanding of technology, preferring a spiritual, nonmaterial existence.

Riordan tech, however, was used extensively throughout the quadrant, and was Jardonia's main source of revenue. That, and the fabulous crystals and stones they harvested from the plentiful mines that lay beneath the planet's surface.

Celie and Rurick got off the tram and took a lift up to the spaceport. They passed through retinal scanners as they entered: the first security measure, she noted. Although not very large, the spaceport was impressive. It was composed of a circular hub encased entirely in a crystal dome. Three sizable bays radiated out from the center like spokes on a wheel. As with the Paladais and the gardens, everything was immaculately maintained.

"One bay contains the Jardonian fleet," Rurick explained. "The second is designated for incoming and departing craft. The third houses visiting ships."

Through the sparkling clear dome, Celie saw ships taking off and landing, all in well-organized patterns that Rurick explained were directed by an ultramodern operations and control station occupying the center of the hub. A surprising number of personnel and technicians bustled about, mingling with arriving visitors.

Jardonia was a relatively small municipality, but it received a fair amount of visitors—some to ply the wealthy royal family for financial assistance in business ventures, others to study the amazing Riordan technology or enjoy the gardens. Hospitality androids greeted the arrivals and directed them to the underground trams. Celie was impressed with the efficiency and smoothness of the modest operation.

"Let's go this way." Rurick directed her toward the

rear left bay. "This is what houses the Jardonian fleet," he explained as they entered the spoke.

Celie studied the gleaming ships, all marked with the swirling gold Riordan crest. They were some of the finest craft she'd ever seen. She'd love to test-fly a few of them. Rurick directed her to the rear of the bay, where technicians worked over the four ships designated for Moriah. They were beauties—sleek, fast, with highly advanced equipment.

"We're working on stealth technology," Rurick explained. "Unfortunately, it's not yet perfected, so Moriah's pilots won't be able to use it to circumvent the checkpoints. Before now, we never saw the need to have stealth on our ships." He shook his head. "Never thought it necessary."

Despite the fact that he'd lied about his identity, Celie could never accuse him of lacking compassion and concern. He obviously cared about what went on in his quadrant and intended to take an active role in shaping events. Irritated with the slight softening she felt toward him, she forced her attention back to his ships.

"These are great. However, we'll need to build false floors and walls in their bays, to store food and medicine. It's possible the checkpoint stations might start searching ships if anyone discovers we're bringing aid to the people in the ninth sector."

"Moriah mentioned that and said her people could do it, but I've got the materials and both android and human power, so I've ordered my technicians to install the false structures."

"That's a good idea," Celie said. "It will speed things up."

"Your Highness?" A technician approached, removing a dust mask and gloves. "I'm glad you're here. I have a few questions about your instructions."

"Please excuse me a moment," Rurick said to Celie, then turned to talk with the man.

Celie took advantage of his distraction to slip away, hoping to get a closer look at the spaceport. She headed toward the main hub, studying the Riordan ships as she went. Her gaze was drawn to a sleek, compact private cruiser, and she studied it. Although relatively small, it was star-class and should be fast enough to travel to Joba in a few cycles. It was perfect for her purposes.

Her conscience twinged, but she reminded herself that the royal family was wealthy beyond comprehension. The small cruiser was nothing to them, easily replaced. And Rurick was the one who'd forced her to flee this way. Of course, she hadn't gotten away yet. She had to confiscate the ship and reach outer space before the Riordan security force could take action to stop her.

Rurick wouldn't come after her, she felt certain. He had too many other concerns weighing him down to worry about the loss of a single ship. And he wouldn't concern himself with a woman so pitiful that she had practically begged him for sexual enlightenment. Remembering her actions, Celie felt another rush of heated embarrassment. No, Rurick would be relieved she was gone.

Regardless, security was something she needed to check. She continued on to the hub and took a good look around. Observing a few guards pacing the hub's perimeter, she saw with closer scrutiny that holocorders were also mounted at set intervals around the dome. Ultrathin and virtually transparent, they almost blended with the plexishield. Very clever. Even so, Riordan security, while sufficient for a government that had never been threatened by overthrow or warfare, appeared lax enough for her to gain access to a cruiser and fly it off the planet.

She might need weapons, though: stun guns in case she had an encounter with guards, and blasters for more solid protection while she was navigating the ninth sector. If she could determine where the weapons were stored, the seeming laxity in security should allow her to appropriate whatever she needed.

Where would weapons be kept? Celie speculated some would be stored at the spaceport, probably close to the operations center. She saw a young man standing guard near the entry to the control station. He might be able to provide the information she needed. She strolled over to him, well aware he was staring at her. She thrust her chest out, exaggerated the sway of her hips, and his eyes widened. As she got closer she realized he was just a youth, barely over the threshold of adulthood. He had a light smattering of freckles across his young face.

"Hello," she said. "I'm a visitor to Jardonia. My name is Celie."

He inclined his head politely, shifted nervously. "Lady."

She stepped closer. He wasn't wearing a triton band and didn't have the remote expression common to the androservers, so she didn't think he was an android . . . but she wanted to be sure. She could outwit a human easier than she could a machine. "Are you an android? The technology here is so amazing, I can't tell."

He cleared his throat. "No, ma'am. I'm the real thing."

"I'll say." She smiled flirtatiously. "Are all the Jardonian men as handsome as you are?"

He swallowed hard, his gaze flashing to her chest. "I . . . I don't know."

She allowed her own gaze to sweep over him. "You're wearing a weapon!" she said in mock surprise. "Why would you need one?"

His gaze brushed her chest again, and a slight flush

179

spread over his cheeks. He straightened proudly. "This is just a stun gun, in case anyone steps out of line or threatens a member of the royal family."

"But that doesn't happen *here,* does it?"

He shook his head. "I've never had to use my stunner."

"Well, that's good." Celie pretended to be relieved. She ran her fingers playfully up his arm. "So, you wouldn't have other weapons around."

He took a step back, his body ramrod stiff. "Actually, we do." His voice squeaked a little.

"Really?" She took a step forward, brushing against him, and leaned close to his ear. "I don't suppose you could show me the weapons vault?" she whispered. She stepped back to watch him, her hand lingering on his chest. "I find weapons"—she dropped her voice to a seductive pitch—"and the men who use them, very stimulating, if you know what I mean." She might be inexperienced when it came to mating, but she'd long ago learned to use her looks and her voice to her advantage.

The guard's heart pounded beneath her fingers, and his face flushed even brighter. "I . . . I don't think I can do that," he stammered, his gaze cutting to an inconspicuous panel a few meters away. "It's against regulations."

"I won't tell." She made a mental note of the panel, then moved in again, her breasts brushing his chest, her lips hovering close to his quivering mouth. "Why don't you show me?"

"I don't know—"

"What's going on here?" a voice boomed behind her.

Great. Gritting her teeth in frustration, Celie stepped back and turned. Rurick stood there, his jaw rigid, his eyes flashing.

His angry gaze slashed the young man. "Ensign Karvas, you're on duty. You know the regulations. No conversations with civilians." He stepped forward, radiating fury and intimidation. "I repeat, what's going on here?"

"Sir!" Ensign Karvas squeaked, then cleared his throat. "The lady was asking some questions, Your Highness, and I was just trying to answer them."

"Really?" Rurick's piercing gaze cut to Celie. "And what was she asking?"

"I was inquiring about security," Celie spoke up, before Karvas could implicate her and raise Rurick's suspicions. Truth was always the best strategy when spun correctly. "I wondered what weapons and security measures are necessary on Jardonia. I still find it hard to believe there's virtually no crime here, or in the quadrant."

Rurick considered, then returned his burning perusal to Karvas. "That true, Ensign?"

The young man swallowed, nodded. "Yes, sir."

"Return to duty, Ensign." Rurick took Celie's arm before she could evade him. "A word with you, Captain Cameron." His voice was cold, his grip merciless. He practically dragged her to the back side of the control station, maneuvering her into an alcove.

"What in Hades were you doing?" he demanded, his expression stormy.

She yanked her arm free and stepped away. "I already told you. I'm interested in Riordan military procedures."

His eyes narrowed. "What is your game, Celie? I know for a fact you're not one to flirt with men."

He was jealous! The sudden insight shot an odd rush of satisfaction through her. It spurred her to vent the anger and hurt churning inside her. "As far I know, there's no law against enjoying a handsome young man's company," she said. "Besides, Ensign Karvas appears very capable of demonstrating mating, which I have an interest in exploring, as you're well aware. Not that it should matter to you, since you're obviously not man enough to demonstrate it."

"Oh, I'm man enough," he said softly, dangerously. "But you don't want to mate with a human, do you? Too risky."

Another lightning bolt of unwelcome perception. And with it, a brutal reminder of the reasons for her solitary existence. "Go jump in the Abyss!" She whirled to leave.

He moved like a laser burst, grabbing her arm and spinning her around. How dare he handle her like that? Her fury boiled over and she swung at him. He caught her fist in his hand and twisted it behind her back, bringing her flush against him.

"Let go of me!" Furious, she struggled against him, stymied by his strength. "You son of an Antek! You sorry, lying bas—"

He silenced her with his mouth, taking possession of her lips with startling heat. The spark was instantaneous, a fierce rush of desire sweeping like wildfire through her body. Stunned, she couldn't fight him, couldn't have stopped her response if her life depended upon it.

When he demanded entrance to her mouth, she gave it. When he pulled her closer to his body, against the obvious proof of his ability to mate, she offered no resistance. He released her hand, and she grabbed his shoulder. All she could do was hold on, rocked by the kiss and her body's tumultuous reaction.

He tasted rich, sweet, better than caroba. She could feel the heat radiating off him, smell the clean, woodsy scent of him. Could feel the hardness, the tension, the passion. An answering desire welled up inside her, an overwhelming need to get even closer to him, as if that were possible. A small moan escaped the back of her throat.

He ended the kiss suddenly, releasing her and stepping back. He stared at her, his chest heaving. Feeling strangely bereft, she battled to regain her own breath and calm her reeling senses.

"Make no mistake," he said harshly. "I'm very capable of mating with you. The only reason I didn't was because I don't like being used just to satisfy someone's curiosity. And because you thought I was something I wasn't."

Rational thought returned, and with it the need to distance herself. "How very honorable of you," she sneered.

"Stars!" He raked his fingers through his hair. "Celie, I wanted to mate with you. So badly, I ached with it. You don't know how difficult it was to turn away."

She didn't want to hear that. Didn't want to hear anything that exonerated him. Damn him—for being human, and for tearing down her belief that he wasn't attracted to her. And damn her own rebellious body. She felt panicked, almost suffocated by the thoughts and feelings bombarding her. Needing to make a clean break, here and now, she chose to take the offensive.

"We'll never have to worry about it, will we?" she said, forcing air into her constricted lungs. "Because the experiment, dismal failure that it was, is over." She retreated before he could respond, pivoting and heading toward the trams. She'd learned what she needed to know. By this time tomorrow, she and Raven would be long gone from Jardonia. And she'd never have to think about Rurick—or the effect he had on her—again.

Chapter Eleven

Raven was having a grand time. She loved the opulent formality of the Riordan court; adored the beautiful dresses and jewels, and the exquisitely ornate decor of the Paladais, the elaborate meals, and all the attention she was getting.

She'd forged a close friendship with Max, and he was going to great lengths to ensure she enjoyed her visit on Jardonia. They had explored the Paladais and the private gardens this morning, and now he was teaching her how to dance.

"Left foot over, move back, step forward, right foot over, turn—no, the other direction," he corrected patiently.

Gripping his ever-steady hand, Raven concentrated on the movements. As with everything else, Riordan dancing was intricate and complicated, but she was coordinated and a quick learner. However, this was a particularly complex sequence. She stumbled and teetered, off balance, then burst out laughing as Max deftly deflected her fall and set her back on her feet.

"Laughter is not a component of this dance," he chided. "You must remain very serious. It would not do to have too much fun at a Riordan event."

"Oh, Max, you are so wicked," she gasped, trying to stop giggling. "You're right, though. The Riordans are rather stuffy, aren't they?"

"They are overly serious." His lopsided grin appeared. "They cannot tell when I am mocking them. They do not think me capable of humor."

"I love your humor. I'm so excited about this evening." Raven sighed dreamily. "I've never been to a dance in my entire life. I can hardly wait to whirl around the floor tonight. I intend to flirt with all the young men there." She thought of a certain pompous male and amended, "With the exception of one."

"That would be Prince Sevilen," Max guessed. Raven had told him about their encounter.

She sniffed disdainfully. "He's a Kerani's ass."

"I assume you mean the rear part of the animal." Max considered. "Now there is a visual image."

Raven dissolved into giggles again, and Max's crooked grin widened. He was obviously quite pleased with himself. Sobering, she hugged him tightly. "Sometimes I wish you were human," she whispered. "We have so much in common, you and I."

"I am an android; you a human. We are not very much alike."

"Well, let's see." She ticked off on her fingers. "You have a great sense of humor. You are programmed to feel emotions, and you have sexual functions."

"True. I am—how did you put it—an incredible stud," he said smugly.

She shook her head, grinning. "Too bad I'm not into gratuitous sex. I think Celie is afraid I'm going to mate with every handsome male who comes along. I must admit, it's fun keeping her stirred up. However, I'm not as frivolous as she thinks. I intend to wait for the right man."

"As well you should," Max said sternly.

"Now look who's stuffy," she teased, then grew serious. "Max, will you ever have a mate? Can androids form bonds between themselves?"

"I have not thought very much about it. My duties and responsibilities keep me occupied ninety-three-point-eight-percent of the time. I shut down for diagnostics and circuit checks the balance of each cycle."

"Rurick won't live forever," she reminded him gently. "What will you do when he's gone?"

His expression turned contemplative. "I do not know. I . . ." He froze momentarily, something he did when an internal program was activated or he received a message. "It is now twelve hundred hours. I must report to the spaceport. I am to meet with the technicians who are preparing the spacecraft for Moriah san Travers."

"That sounds like work." Raven kissed his smooth cheek. "Will you give me the first dance tonight?"

"I would be honored." Max's grin was practically sideways. "Princess Kalina will be horrified."

"I'm assuming taunting the princess isn't the only reason you've agreed to dance with me."

"Of course not. Will you be all right on your own?"

"Absolutely," Raven assured him. "I'm going to look at the gardens again. They're incredible."

"That is an acceptable pastime," he agreed. "I will see you tonight." He strode off, his posture perfect, as always.

Smiling fondly, Raven headed for the private gardens. She'd quickly learned her way around the Paladais, discovering there was a decipherable pattern to the circling interior corridors. She planned to do the same with the grounds.

She stepped into the fragrant gardens, savoring the scents. She chose a specific crystal path, hoping to find the site she'd seen earlier that day. The path curved past masses of flowers and carefully pruned miniature trees. The sun was shining, the air sparkling. It was a stunning day.

Filled with elation, she couldn't resist spinning around, simply to feel the soft flow of her skirt against her legs. She loved the dress she was wearing, a deep sapphire-colored garment that hugged her upper body like a lover's caress, then flowed out from her hips and teased the tops of her matching satin slippers. The Riordans certainly knew how to dress.

She thought of the suffering in the ninth sector and felt a twinge of guilt. Yet, a practical spiritualist, Raven knew Riordan abundance—or abundance anywhere else, for that matter—had little bearing on the conditions in the ninth sector. Free will, and the ugly side of humankind, had created those conditions, and now the events that would change them had been put into motion. She couldn't feel guilty for being here. She would contribute where and when she could.

She continued along the path, and knew she'd chosen the right one when she saw the fountain ahead. It was oval-shaped, carved from a solid piece of rose crystal and rimmed with a ledge that was low and wide enough for sitting. The bowl of the fountain was set into the ground, so it was deeper than it appeared at first glance.

The centerpiece was a carving of a woman with flowing hair and graceful lines. Most interestingly, she was nude, which seemed odd, considering the conservative bent of the Riordans. Raven thought the woman beautiful. She sat on the ledge and trailed her fingers through the cool water. Closing her eyes, she inhaled deeply and simply enjoyed being.

"How can you see anything with your eyes closed?"

The voice jolted her from her idyllic reverie. She opened her eyes and decided the cycle had just taken a downhill turn. Prince Sevilen stood three meters away. He was dressed all in black, his shirt loose with flowing sleeves and open at the top, the pants snug over solid thighs, then slipping down into gleaming black boots. He wore black leather gloves and carried a sword. Sunlight glinted off his thick hair, reflecting rich shades of brown and gold. His stance was arrogant, his full mouth petulant, his eyes dispassionate.

The same dislike she'd felt the previous cycle swelled inside her, assuring her that she hadn't changed her opinion of him. She remained seated, refusing to show him any sign of honor. "Whether or not the eyes are closed has nothing to do with true vision," she countered. "Sometimes blind people can see better than those with perfect physical sight."

"You talk in riddles." He raised his sword, gestured toward her. "You're still disrespectful, I see."

"Respect is not an automatic privilege. It must be earned."

He scowled. "Good manners dictate respect be shown in certain political situations."

"So you consider me rude?" Raven discovered her dislike of the prince was rapidly transforming to loathing. "Well, I suppose that's better than insolent, egotistical, and obtuse."

"You're calling me stupid?" He stabbed his sword into the ground, and a tuft of dirt and grass shot upward.

At least he had a grasp of vocabulary. "Don't forget insolent and egotistical," she retorted.

"You're mistaking pride for arrogance." He took a

step forward as he jerked off his gloves. "I *am* very proud, but with good reason. The Riordans have more power on the Interstellar Council than the majority of principalities represented. We have the most superior technology in the quadrant." He swung his gloves in a broad arc. "And our gardens are galaxy-famous."

He acted as if he were solely responsible for the Riordans' lofty position in the quadrant's political hierarchy. But Raven would bet gold miterons he'd never worked a day in his life.

"What exactly have you to do with any of these remarkable accomplishments?" she challenged.

He looked taken aback, but only for a millisecond. "I am a member of the Riordan royal family. That is sufficient to link me to our success."

"It means nothing, you pompous fool," she snapped.

Sevilen's eyes narrowed, and his body stiffened. He yanked his sword up and turned to leave. Raven regretted her words. She *was* being rude. Sevilen was a product of his environment, and his obnoxious behavior wasn't totally his fault. She wondered how Rurick had managed to grow up so unaffected. He appeared light years more empathetic and grounded than the rest of the royal family.

"Wait!" she called. Sevilen halted but didn't turn. "I'm sorry." She rose from the ledge and walked over to him. "I don't agree with your opinions, but that's no reason for me to be rude. I apologize for my hurtful words."

He was silent, tension and anger radiating from him. She placed her hand on his arm. "Perhaps we can call a truce. You'll only have to endure my company another few cycles anyway."

"I am a prince. I can be magnanimous," he finally said grudgingly. "I guess I can overlook your behavior."

She still wanted to slug him, but she told herself she

could be tolerant the short time they would be on Jardonia. "Truce, then." She took a deep breath. "Your gardens are truly beautiful."

He lowered the sword until the point nicked the ground. "As we've already established, they are the finest in the quadrant."

"Why don't you show me your favorite areas?" she invited, hoping that would smooth things out between them.

"If you wish." He strode to the fountain and leaned the sword against it, then rested his hand on the lip. "*This* is probably my favorite place in the gardens."

"This fountain?" Raven asked, following him. He nodded. Her gaze skimmed over the pink crystal. "I like it too. I especially like the lady of the water."

"Even though she's nude?"

Feeling a surprising rush of heat in her cheeks, she kept her gaze firmly on the statue. "That's what I like best about her. Her nudity is so un-Riordan, don't you think?"

"It most definitely is," he agreed. "Which is why I like her, as well. It's better than trying to sneak into adult sites on the UDW."

Shocked, she flashed her gaze to the prince. Laughter twinkled in his eyes. "You have a sense of humor!" she accused.

He smiled, showing strong white teeth. "I'm afraid not even royalty is perfect."

An answering smile tilted her lips. "You're definitely different than I originally thought."

"I'll take that as a compliment." He eased down on the edge of the fountain and let his fingers drift in the water.

Amused, Raven also slid onto the edge, leaving a meter between them. Sevilen leaned sideways over the water, his gaze on the bottom of the fountain. "What's this?" he demanded.

She looked into the water. "What?"

"There's dirt in there. This is the second time in five cycles. It's unacceptable." He rose and yanked on his gloves. "There is no excuse for such negligence, especially since I've reported this once already. I'll have the android responsible for this area disciplined."

"Why would you do such a thing?" Raven asked, appalled. "It's just a little dirt, easily cleaned up."

"Errors are unacceptable."

"It's not even an error," she argued. "That dirt could have blown in there right before we arrived."

"Then it should have been corrected. I will assign a new android to this section."

"And the old one?" she asked, already suspecting the answer.

"Will be deactivated and disassembled."

"Disassembled?" Raven rose, her heart racing. "Just like that?"

He shrugged. "They are machines, nothing more."

"No," Raven murmured, thinking of Max. "That's not true." To her, Max was a real person, or at least a genuine personality. He had independent thought processes, emotional reactions, and humor. He was a sentient being as far as she was concerned. She was also beginning to feel that way about her androserver, Jirca.

"Prince Sevilen, do you not have any attachments to the androservers who take care of you, cycle after cycle?"

"No. Why should I?"

She felt sick inside. How could he not recognize the personality that resided in each android? Memories of her twelfth season, of the six horrible months she had spent as a slave, reared in her mind. She generally managed to keep the memories corralled, but they were always with her, just below the surface.

Now they were unleashed, with a ferocity that shook her to the core. This discussion served as a horrific reminder of what happened when one group of beings considered another group inferior. Bad enough Sevilen thought androids were nonentities; she wondered if his attitude extended to nonandroids.

"Do you feel the same way about humans?" she asked.

"People like my family? I cherish them, of course."

"What about the people who serve you, who pilot your ships and oversee the mines? What about them?"

"There are humans in our society who are inferior and must be designated a lower class. They do have some value, though."

"Some value?" She took two steps that placed her millimeters from him, tilting her head to meet his gaze. "That's nice of you to admit. What happens if you determine a person has *no* value? Is he or she terminated, like the androids?"

"We don't condone terminating humans," he snapped. "All humans have worth. Even the lower classes can contribute to our society, if only as servers or manual laborers."

He simply didn't understand. But that didn't temper Raven's rising anger, fueled by the painful memories of her experiences as a slave. Ignorance and arrogance were deadly, especially in the hands of someone with authority. In her mind, she saw the rows of slaves lined up in Slaver's Square on Elysia; saw the filthy, huddled beings shuffling along, bound by chains and by the cruelty of others, punished with painful electrolyzer rods if they slowed or stumbled. Her fury swelled, but she couldn't strike out at the slavers. They were out of her reach.

The overbearing, condescending Prince Sevilen wasn't, though. In a rare burst of violence, Raven placed her hands against his broad chest and shoved hard. The lip of the fountain was low, and her offensive unexpected. He went into the water.

She didn't wait around to savor the satisfying image of a soaked prince who, at the moment, resembled a lanrax caught in a Saron rainstorm. Instead, she made a run for it, her heart pounding and her soul reeling with pain.

She ran blindly, tears blurring her vision, then saw the entrance to the lift ahead. She knew it went to the underground tram tunnels, and she didn't want to go there. She swerved to go around it and slammed into a solid obstacle.

"Raven?" The sound of Max's flat voice was wonderfully welcome.

She threw her arms around him. "Oh, Max!"

"Raven, what is wrong?"

What wasn't wrong? She laughed, a touch of hysteria ending on a sob. "You might have to hide me," she managed to get out. "In case it's illegal to drown a Riordan prince."

That evening the royal family celebrated King Domek's continuing recovery. They opened the largest ballroom in the Paladais to guests and high-ranking Riordans. It was an opulent affair, with fabulous food delicacies, flowing alcoholic drinks, and a wonderful Jart orchestra providing music. Celie wouldn't have been there if it wasn't for Raven, who insisted on attending. So Celie steeled herself and came along, ignoring the girl's protests about her wearing the black dress again. The other outfits were simply too revealing or flashy.

She was dismayed at the number of people present and the fact that Rurick's attention appeared focused on her. Determined to avoid him, she pointedly ignored his imperious stare and kept a safe distance between them, weaving through the crowd whenever he tried to approach. His expression was none too happy and, even as numerous people stopped and talked to him, his irate gaze tracked her around the cavernous room. She knew it was rude, but she simply couldn't deal with him tonight.

She was exhausted, emotionally and physically frayed, from the stress of Altair, the overwhelming opulence and political maneuverings of Jardonia, and, most of all, from thoughts of Rurick. For whatever reasons, his presence, and the inexplicable attraction between them, managed to keep her in turmoil. She yearned for the sanctuary of her ship, her routine, and the serenity therein. She was actually looking forward to being lonely and bored. It had to be better than feeling spiritually battered—or trying to deal with a raging desire she could never satisfy.

She could put most of the blame for her emotional turbulence on one troublesome android-turned-prince. Forget that he was breathtaking in his official iridescent uniform, that the lights reflecting off his hair highlighted rich caroba and sunshine hues. Forget that his golden eyes reminded her of the huge Calandan birds that had soared high above Risa. Or that her heart also soared whenever she fell into his intense gaze.

Rurick was a major threat to her well-being. The situation was ridiculous, and she was a fool for ever thinking she could experiment with sexual matters. She was too damaged. Far worse, she was a murderer, something she lived with every waking moment. The stain on her soul had left her too tainted to offer anything to any man. Dark memories rose: the brutality of her childhood and her adolescent years; the final act of violence, the blood, the open, shocked eyes staring at her. . . .

She felt chilled to the core, despite the heated press of bodies around her. Her hand shaking, Celie took a healthy gulp of her second—and last—drink of the evening. She needed to keep a clear head for what she had planned. She forced her attention to the dance floor, where Raven and Max were dancing. Several young men were watching Raven, who was ethereally beautiful in a silver dress with crystal, glitter-studded straps.

Celie glanced back to see Rurick moving toward her, and slipped away from the dance floor. It was childish and cowardly, but she had decided bravery was overrated, except in battle. Rurick speeded up, and so did she, bumping into Kalina.

"I'm sorry," she began, then saw that the princess was glaring at Max guiding Raven through an intricate turn.

"That's disgusting!" the young royal snapped. "An android cavorting with a human. It makes me sick."

Anger flared through Celie, and she couldn't resist leaning close and commenting, "Max is a magnificent dancer, don't you think? He and Raven make a lovely couple."

"Oh, what would you know?" Kalma hissed. She swept Celie with a spiteful perusal, her eyes widening as she took in the re-worn plain black dress. "You're as unacceptable as he is."

"I'll take that as a compliment, coming from you," Celie retorted, then continued her evasive maneuvers through the crowd.

She saw Prince Sevilen sitting on a velvet-covered chair near the dance floor, a drink in one hand. His mouth was drawn into a pout and his expression was as disgruntled as Rurick's. He was flanked by two beautiful women, but his attention was on the dancers—specifically on Raven and Max.

Celie realized she had no idea what was going on with Sevilen and Raven, although she knew the prince had raised an uproar around midcycle, and Raven had somehow been involved. From the few details she'd gathered, Max and Rurick had stepped in and settled the situation quickly. Sevilen had stormed off to his apartments, and Raven secluded herself in her chamber for several hours. Celie couldn't get anyone, including Raven, to tell her what had happened, so she'd finally given up. She had other things to worry about, like confiscating weapons and hijacking spaceships.

Raven had apparently gotten over whatever upset her. She was in her element tonight, her eyes glowing as the first dance ended and she turned from Max to talk to a group of eager young men vying for her attention. For once Celie was grateful for Max's presence. After Raven went into the next dance with a new partner, the android remained nearby, apparently keeping a watchful eye on the girl. Celie was developing a genuine affection for him. The fact that Kalina seemed to hate him, and that he appeared to take great pleasure in baiting the princess, endeared him to her further.

Celie sighed, watching Raven twirl and laugh. The girl loved the luxury of the Paladais, loved the ritual and the clothing and everything about Riordan life. Celie knew she might have to use very strong persuasion to get Raven to go with her, but she had no intention of leaving her behind. And she wasn't going to stay on Jardonia, or anywhere near Rurick, any longer than necessary.

In fact, they were leaving tonight.

Celie slipped into Raven's sleeping chamber. Faint sleep-shift lights glowed, and she paused by the panel a moment to let her eyes adjust to the dimness. A quick glance assured her Jirca was propped in a corner of the chamber, inactive. The small mound on the massive bed that was Raven, and the girl's soft, even breathing, told her she was asleep.

Celie steeled herself for what she had to do. Raven was not going to like this, and would most probably balk at leaving Jardonia, especially after the evening of dancing and flirting with its young men. It might even be necessary to use a stun gun.

Celie had one, because she had returned to the spaceport late that afternoon and investigated the unmarked panel Ensign Karvas had glanced at during their conversation. Sure enough, it was the weapons vault, with a simple lock that was easily decoded. No one paid her any attention, and she had slipped inside and taken a stunner and two laser guns, cramming them into the tops of her boots. For once, she was grateful for her long dress, which hid her acquisitions. Now, in the heart of sleep shift, she was ready to make her move.

She went to the bed and shook Raven gently. "Raven! Raven, wake up!"

The girl stirred and muttered, then pulled the covers higher. Celie shook her again. "Wake up. We're leaving."

Dark eyes blinked sleepily. "What?"

"We're leaving," Celie repeated. "Now."

Raven sat up, pushing her long hair from her face. "Why?"

"I'm not going to wait until Rurick is ready to take us back. I need to return to my ship before something happens to it."

Raven yawned. "What's the hurry? It may already be too late."

Cold dread squeezed Celie's heart. She was afraid Raven was right, but she wanted to know for certain. She was honest enough to admit, at least to herself, that Rurick's unsettling presence added urgency to the need to leave. "We're going *now*."

197

"Ohhhh," Raven whined, throwing herself down and covering her eyes with her arm. "I don't want to go. This place is so fabulous, and I'm having a great time. Rurick will take us in a few more cycles." She peeked out from beneath her arm, clarity obviously beginning to seep in. "Rurick doesn't know about this, does he? Where are you getting a ship?"

"I'm stealing one."

Raven bolted upright. "How could you do that? Rurick and Max saved our lives, and offered us their hospitality. This is ridiculous, rude . . . and illegal!"

"I don't care. I don't want to stay here any longer. Besides, I've done many illegal things in my life. I can't see how one more can make any difference."

"This is Rurick you're stealing from. He's a friend, not an enemy."

"I have to do this," Celie insisted.

Raven regarded her with a knowing look. "It's him, isn't it? Rurick."

"It's my ship, damn it. I need to get back. I'm leaving tonight and you're going with me. I won't leave you behind. Please cooperate." Celie felt for the charged stun gun in her boot. "I don't want to use force."

Raven stared at her a long moment. "You would, wouldn't you?"

Spirit, she hated this. Celie nodded, her throat tight. "I'm sorry."

"Well, blazing hells," Raven muttered, shocking Celie, who had never heard the girl utter a single curse word. She threw back the covers and swung her slender legs over the edge of the bed. "All right, I'm coming. But you owe me big time. I'm giving up a lot of life experiences for you."

"Thank you," Celie said sincerely. Still, knowing how tricky Raven could be, and just in case they met with resistance, she palmed the stun gun.

198

Moments later, Raven was dressed and they slipped into the quiet corridor. No one was in sight, not even an androserver. Moving quickly, they made their way to the gardens. From there, they went to the lift and took an underground tram to the spaceport. Within the hour, they were on a stolen Riordan cruiser, clear of Jardonia airspace and on their way to Joba.

Rurick stood in the bay, staring at the empty pad where Sev's private cruiser had rested until a short while earlier. Two of his security men were injured, one from a stun charge and one from a kick to the solar plexus. One android had also taken a stun, which had scrambled some circuits and sent him stumbling around the spaceport, spouting gibberish.

The injuries and damage weren't serious. Neither was the loss of the ship. The men would recover fully, the android was repairable, and the ship could be replaced. Yet Rurick's pride and ego had taken a hit. He was galled that Riordan security was lax enough to allow a single woman to take out two soldiers and an android, then steal a spacecraft. Never mind there had never been a need for heightened security; this shouldn't have happened. He clenched his hands and scowled.

He knew who was responsible, would have known even without the holocordings or retinal-scan records, the soldiers' reports, or the conspicuous absence of a certain two female guests from the Paladais. He suspected Raven was an unwilling participant, coerced into hijacking a ship and fleeing. But oh, yes, he knew who was responsible.

Captain Celie Cameron. Fascinating, captivating, oddly vulnerable at times, but also a smuggler and a thief. And an unknowing seductress. His eyes narrowed and his heart rate increased. She might think she'd gotten away from him, but she was in for a surprise. He wasn't through with her, not by a long shot.

Riordan pride demanded he show her the folly of stealing a ship from him. Ego, and more personal male pride, fueled by a healthy dose of testosterone, demanded he show her that she couldn't run away from him. He wanted to teach her she couldn't hide from her own sensual nature. Desire entwined with erotic memories of Celie in his arms made him ache to claim her in the most primal way a man could claim a woman.

She'd bared both her soul and her body to him. They had formed an inexplicable bond that continued to draw them together, despite her resistance. She wanted to repress the demons haunting her; he wanted her to face them. She wanted to avoid the emotional entanglements that accompanied healthy heterosexual relationships; he wanted her—wanted *them*—to experience and explore every nuance of spiritual and physical bonding.

Quite simply, he wanted her.

No, he wasn't through with her. Duty and responsibility could be set aside for now. His father was almost recovered from the strange malady that had beset him so suddenly, and ships laden with food and medicine were headed to the ninth sector. Rurick could take some personal time. He had a score to settle with Celie Cameron. And he knew exactly where she was going.

Fortunately, he'd just sent two scout ships to cruise the perimeter of the ninth sector and make sure Moriah's ships got in safely, as well as to watch for any other craft entering and leaving. Those scout ships had departed this morning and should reach the ninth sector well ahead of any ships leaving Jardonia this evening. He'd contact them once he was underway.

He turned sharply on his heel. "Max! Ready my personal cruiser. Arrange for two armed ships to escort us. We're departing immediately for Joba."

Chapter Twelve

Celie approached the ninth sector, grateful the Riordan royal crest on her ship would allow her to skirt the checkpoints without being challenged. However, she was concerned about getting through the stations on the trip out in her own ship. She was somewhat optimistic, though, because she'd contacted Chase, and he had transmitted the auto-hypnotic program he used to resist mind control. She didn't have the chemicals to temporarily scramble her brain's neurotransmitters, so the program would have to do. If it wasn't sufficient, then Raven could refresh her memory once they were free of the checkpoints. Thank Spirit the Shielders appeared to be unaffected by the memory erasure procedure used at these stations.

Celie wasn't worried about Rurick catching up with her. She honestly didn't believe he would bother to pursue her. Why would he care, except for the loss of his ship, which was nothing to him? If he did follow, however, she had enough of a head start to land on Joba, get her ship, and be out before he could intercept her.

This was a piece-of-caroba operation—if her ship was still intact. But she refused to let herself dwell on the possibility that it might not be. She'd come this far; her ship had to be all right. It was her life, everything she'd acquired and created for herself, a safe haven from the universe. Her ship would be fine, she told herself firmly. As soon as she retrieved it and left the sector, she'd rendezvous with Moriah, stock it with supplies, and head back to the ninth sector. She looked forward to the challenge of joining the others in smuggling goods into the sector.

The clamor of alarms jolted her from her strategic planning and back to the cockpit. "What's that?" Raven asked from the co-pilot's seat, where she'd been immersed in the computer, scanning the Universal Data Web.

"I don't know." Celie leaned forward to study the readouts. She looked at the radar monitors and saw two blips on the screen. Where had they come from?

"Blazing hells." She hit some switches, trying to get a readout on the blips. "It looks like we have company."

"Really?" Raven became alert. "Pirates, maybe? Will we have a battle?"

"Pirates aren't very likely in this quadrant, and certainly not in this sector. What's there to steal?" Celie turned and entered a request in the main computer for weapon specs on the cruiser. "Damn. This ship doesn't have any weapons, unless you count meteor deflectors, which are strictly close range. Who on Shamara travels in ships without weapons?"

"Everyone in this quadrant?" Raven supplied helpfully.

The blips on the screen were much larger now—definitely ships, and only a thousand meters away. Celie started evasive maneuvers, just as her subspace transceiver beeped on a universal frequency. Great. Whomever it was, they wanted to chat.

"Want me to respond?" Raven asked.

"No. Let me handle it." Celie steered her craft one hundred and eighty degrees from the two approaching ships and fired her thrusters before hitting the comm link. "Who is this?"

"This is Commander Nelek, of the Riordan Space Squadron. You are in a stolen Riordan craft. Surrender immediately."

"Or what?" she challenged, refusing to slow her ship. "We're friends of Prince Rurick. This ship is not stolen. It's on loan." All right, so maybe that was a slight exaggeration. But Celie knew Rurick wouldn't want Raven or herself blown up. "You wouldn't fire on us," she continued.

"I repeat, surrender immediately."

She was alarmed to see how rapidly the two ships were closing the distance, obviously much faster than her cruiser. She nosed the ship at a perpendicular angle to the pursuing craft, opened to full throttle. The ship shuddered, jolting them with a bone-crunching intensity. What the—? Celie shook her head to clear it and studied the scanner. Oh, no. They were caught by a magnetic grappler and being reeled in like a fish on a hook!

"Do not resist," Commander Nelek intoned, "and you will not be harmed. I repeat, do not resist."

Celie threw herself back in her seat, frustration a bitter bile in her throat. "I wonder if they'll board this ship;" she muttered, "or just tow us in. If they board . . . we have two laser guns—not much help, since I don't want to seriously injure any of them. We just have one stun gun. Damn!"

"We are not going to attack them when they board," Raven declared. "I won't help you, Celie. I won't. Besides, they're sure to have stunners. And what if they have them set high, like they did before?"

She was right. Celie ran her fingers through her hair, resisting the urge to scream. There was no way of knowing how many soldiers would be on each of those ships, or what kind of weapons they had. Besides, they'd probably be expecting resistance and would have their weapons ready. There was nothing to do but surrender—and be dragged back to Jardonia.

"I told you it was wrong to steal a ship from Rurick," Raven said.

Celie didn't want to think about Rurick. She'd be forced to face him soon enough. She wondered how things could get any worse.

Commander Nelek and his three men had activated stunners ready when they boarded the ship. Celie and Raven were hustled aboard the commander's craft and her weapons confiscated. An armed guard was assigned to Celie, yet Raven had free rein of the ship—a sure sign that Rurick had given the orders. While Raven chatted with the commander over tea and caroba he'd replicated especially for her, Celie was herded to the ship's council chamber and asked to remain there. Her guard was polite but firm. Chafing beneath his scrutiny, she paced the chamber.

She didn't know how much time had passed when she heard the entry panel open. Whirling, she almost groaned when Rurick entered. And she'd thought things couldn't get any worse. No cool-down time before they faced each other, either. She envisioned a nuclear explosion.

Yet, if Rurick was angry, he didn't show it. His expression impassive, his eyes cool, he nodded to the guard. "I'd like to speak to Captain Cameron alone. Please wait outside."

The guard bowed and left the chamber. Blowing out her breath, Celie wiped her palms on her pants. Rurick stared at her a long moment, and she met his gaze steadily, although her heart was trying to pound its way out of her chest. She resisted the urge to move to the other side of the conference table.

"Captain Cameron." His deep voice was as smooth as Sarnai silk, again offering no indication of his inner feelings. "Good to see you again. I'm sure you didn't expect our paths to cross so quickly."

Watching him warily, she didn't respond to his obvious taunt.

"I believe it's safe to say you insulted my hospitality." He took a step toward her.

She stepped back, thinking it best to remain out of reach until she could determine his intentions.

"You injured two of my men, damaged an android." His expression hardened, and he moved forward again. "You stole one of my ships."

So far, all true. She revised her plan and moved to the far side of the table. His eyebrows raised at that. "Not afraid, are you, Captain? What do you think I'm going to do to you?"

A lot of things came to mind, although she didn't believe Riordans tortured prisoners like the Controllers did. She also knew better than to show fear to an adversary. She angled her chin defiantly. "I have no idea. You tell me."

"Which option? What I'd really like to do to you, or what I'm held to by civilized constraints?"

She forced air into her constricted lungs and went for bravado. "I'm not interested in your fantasies."

"Oh, I have a lot of fantasies." He moved stealthily around the table. "I'm well aware that you do too."

Celie felt a rush of heat to her face—and to other, more intimate places. The man did not play fair. She

205

forced herself to remain still as he stopped within mere millimeters of her. "Let's focus on the matter at hand," she suggested.

His glittering gaze seemed to bore right through her. "Yes, let's do." He gestured to a chair. "Sit down."

"All right." She started to back away, toward a chair at the end of the table.

He grabbed her arm, halting her retreat. "No, you'll sit right here." He moved her over enough to pull out the chair by her hip and pushed her into it. "And I"—he pulled out the chair beside him and folded his large body into it—"will sit here."

He rolled forward, encasing her legs with his and leaning over to grasp the arms of her chair, effectively trapping and surrounding her. He was so close, she could feel the warmth from his body, smell his clean, masculine scent. She could also sense his anger and some other emotion she couldn't quite define. She felt crowded, threatened. He was trying to intimidate her. She narrowed her eyes in irritation and shoved her boots against the floor, trying to scoot away.

"Oh, no you don't." He retained his grip on the chair arms, dragged her back. "You're going to sit here and listen to what I have to say."

Definitely intimidation tactics. She clenched her hands so tight, they ached. "Then talk."

"Let's start with the fact that you stole a ship from me."

So this would be the topic of discussion. Celie rolled her eyes. "You've already pointed that out. But I didn't steal the ship. I just borrowed it."

"Although rare in this quadrant, theft is still a crime," he continued, as though she hadn't spoken. "And is punishable under interstellar law."

Insidious cold knotted in her chest. Surely he didn't intend to turn her over to the Council for trial and possible incarceration. "Why are you doing this?" she asked. "I fought beside you when we were attacked on Joba. I helped repair your ship. Raven and I did all we could for those people on Altair."

"True, you did. In turn, I got you safely off Joba and took you to Jardonia, where you were offered luxurious quarters and every amenity imaginable."

"Oh, yes, you did that," Celie snapped, anger evaporating good sense. "After you lied to me about your identity. After you let me assume . . . let me make a . . ." She broke off, still mortified at the memory of how she'd thrown herself at him.

"Oh, I don't think you made a fool of yourself," he said, then tightened his thighs against her legs when she tried to kick him. "Until you stole my ship."

"Oooh," she seethed. "You sorry son of an Antek. Let me up!"

"I also offered to take you to your craft," he reminded her. "How do you think you're going to get to it now?"

That took the fight out of her, and she sagged back in her chair. Spirit, how *could* she get back to her ship? It was her heart and soul, her haven, her comfort in a life marked by dark memories and abject loneliness.

"I don't know," she replied tiredly. "Although I'm sure I won't receive any assistance from you."

"Actually, I could still be persuaded to offer you a safe escort to your ship."

She ran her fingers through her hair and studied him. She could tell nothing from his calm expression. What game was he playing now? "What type of persuasion did you have in mind?" she asked cautiously.

"I want you to mate with me."

"What?" Shock pounded through her, and if Rurick hadn't had her hemmed in, she might have slid out of the chair. "What did you say?" She gasped, her voice rising sharply.

207

He watched her, his expression still bland, as if he hadn't just stunned all sense out of her. "It's simple enough. I want you. In my bed. Or here." He waved his hand at the table. "Or in the cockpit of my ship." He shrugged. "It doesn't matter where."

Great Spirit in the heavens. Celie closed her eyes, trying desperately to regain her equilibrium. "You're just saying this to get back at me."

"No, I'm not. I've wanted you from the moment I saw you in that wretched bar on Joba."

The memory of his rejection burned inside her. "I find that hard to believe. You certainly didn't act like you had any desire for me when we were in the ninth sector."

"Believe me, I did. But it wasn't the right thing to do, not with you thinking I was an android."

"And this is?" She glared at him, outraged. "Threatening me, using my ship as a lure so I'll mate with you? Now, that's honorable. You're a hypocritical lowlife."

"I'm a man, Celie. And I want you. It's that simple."

She ignored the heat snaking through her body. There were many reasons she'd never mate with Rurick, or any man, but she focused on the moral ones. "What you're asking is prostitution."

"Really?" Cool amusement colored his voice.

"Yes." She wouldn't give in. No matter how much appeal his request might have. "You know it is. You're asking me to give my body to you in return for something I want. That's prostitution in every society I've been in."

"I don't think of it that way. I think of it as sex between consenting adults. Hot, uninhibited, and very . . . climactic."

His words set her heart racing and heat pooling in her lower body. Damn, why couldn't she get her libido under control? But even with her raging hormones, she knew she couldn't do what Rurick wanted. It would do nothing to alleviate her demons, might even create more. She couldn't give him that kind of power over her, especially knowing he was a real, flesh-and-blood man. Nor could she ignore the ethical issue.

"I can't do that," she finally said. "I won't."

"Not even to get your ship back?"

He really was a bastard. She felt as if a part of her were being ripped out, as if she'd just lost her best friend. And perhaps she had, if she couldn't get to her ship. No; she had to believe she'd find another way to get to Joba. She was smart and resourceful. She would *not* mate with this man for any reason. "I won't do it. Not even for my ship."

"All right." He paused, and she waited for him to tell her he was turning her over to the Council. Instead, he took her hand, his touch surprisingly gentle. "If you won't mate with me, then give me an opportunity to change your mind about me."

"What?" She knew she sounded like a broken disc recording, but he had her shaken up. She felt like she was in the middle of a Supernova, being blasted to dust.

"We got off to a bad start. I want a chance to make it up to you. To court you properly."

He wanted to *court* her? What in Hades did that mean? She shook her head, trying to clear it. "I don't know," she hedged, reeling from this latest twist. "I don't have any experience in this kind of thing." She took a deep breath, went for brutal honesty. "Rurick, I wouldn't be any good in a relationship. It won't . . . it can't work."

"I think you underestimate yourself," he said, compassion softening his gaze.

His sudden change in attitude threw her off-kilter. How could he be such a jerk one moment, then so sympathetic the next? Were all males like this? Confusion diluted her shock. "I don't understand what you want from me."

"It's very simple. After we retrieve your ship, I have to go to Sarngin, to see if I can get to the bottom of this ninth-sector cover-up. I want you to accompany me. We'll get to know one another better; then we can decide if we want to pursue anything more serious."

"This is crazy." *He* was crazy. She freed her hand from his grasp. "It will never work."

"Do you want your ship or not?"

He was back to being a jerk again. She gritted her teeth, shot him a killing look. "You know I do."

"Then you'll agree to accompany me to Sarngin?"

Things had gotten a lot worse than she could ever have envisioned. She thought of her ship, considered her other options for retrieving it. What were they? She twisted her hands together, poised on a mental brink, then sighed. "All right. I'll go with you."

"Good. I only ask one other thing."

"Ask? I think you've *demanded* enough."

"This is important. I want honesty between us. I already know about your past and your feelings about men. It's out in the open, so now we can deal with it. No more secrets."

He didn't know *everything*. Despair welled inside her. What would he think if she told him she'd murdered her father? No. She could never tell him, or anyone. Not even Moriah knew. But she wouldn't lie about it. She just wouldn't talk about it.

"I'll go with you to Sarngin," she conceded, hating the dark secret that would follow her to the grave. "And I'll be as honest as I can. But there will never be anything between us."

"A chance is all I ask." He finally moved away from her, relaxing back into his chair. His eyes gleamed triumphantly, and a small smile flirted around his lips.

Suspicion slid though Celie as she considered him. She had the distinct feeling she'd just been neatly maneuvered to exactly where Prince Maximilian Rurickko Rior wanted her.

"You tricked me, didn't you?" she hissed, her eyes narrowing. "You manipulated me to get me to agree to this."

He shrugged nonchalantly. "A deal is a deal. Are you reneging?"

Righteous indignation fired through her. "You didn't really expect me to mate with you, did you? That was just a ploy!"

His eyes flared, and he leaned forward, invading her space again. "I wouldn't bet on it. Would you like to put your theory to the test? We can go back to my original request, if you wish. I'm ready whenever you are. Shall we go to my cabin?"

Her breath caught at the desire she saw in his eyes. At the promise of sensual pleasures, similar to what he'd already demonstrated, only better. A melting sensation spread through her body, and she battled for control.

She dug her heels into the carpet and shoved forcefully, rolling back from him. "I don't know why you're playing this game," she snapped. "I have no intentions of mating with you—ever. But I always honor my word, so I won't renege on our deal. I'll go to Sarngin with you . . . in my own ship. But that's all. You hear me? *That's all.*"

He sat back in his chair, regal, indolent, and a satisfied smirk on his face. "I hear you, Celie." His heated gaze swept over her. "Actions, however, usually speak louder than words. We'll see which bear out, after we reach Sarngin."

What could she say to that? To any of this? She chose

211

a different tack. "Am I a prisoner until then?" she demanded icily.

"Not at all. You may have free rein of the ship."

She stood and walked with as much dignity as she could to the entry, acutely aware of him watching her. Even as she moved to put as much distance as possible between them, she knew it would do little good. What had she gotten herself in to?

Rurick frowned at Commander Zane's image on the viewscreen. "Then the ship is completely destroyed?"

"Not totally, sir. The hull is intact. But the hatch has been blown off, and the interior has been looted and ravaged."

Rurick had feared they would find just this scenario, but he had promised Celie he would bring her to Joba to retrieve her craft. He suspected the ship meant a tremendous amount to her, since she'd been willing to make a pact with the gods of darkness—the way she obviously viewed her agreement with him—to get back to it. Now he had to tell her it had been demolished.

"Order your men to retrieve anything that can be salvaged," he told the commander.

"Yes, Your Highness. Anything else?"

"No. We'll contact you as soon as I decide whether we'll be landing." Rurick signed off and contacted the cockpit. "Max, tell Captain Cameron I want to see her as quickly as possible."

He sat back, staring blindly at the computer screen set into the conference table in his council chamber. He felt terrible about Celie's ship, and he dreaded telling her the news. Guilt twinged through him. It was his fault that she'd come to Joba in the first place; his fault they'd been attacked, forcing her to leave her ship behind. And it was his fault they hadn't returned sooner, although her ship might have been ransacked that very first day. There was no way to know. Regardless, he was responsible. He vowed he'd make it up to her.

The panel slid open and Celie entered, stopping inside the entry. Rurick rose from his seat. She inclined her head. "Your Highness."

He shoved back his irritation. Since his forced victory over her accompanying him to Sarngin, she had been cool and distant. She refused to call him by his name, referred to him instead by his title. If he didn't know better, he might have thought she was expressing her resentment; however, he suspected her behavior was more a protective mechanism. She intended to keep her distance from him. He intended quite the opposite.

"Captain." He strode around the table.

She looked fatigued. Raven had told him Celie wasn't sleeping well. He felt another flash of guilt, this one for mentally shaking her up after she stole his ship, for forcing her to go to Sarngin with him. Yet it was the only way he knew to keep her close until he could find a way to get past the emotional barriers she had erected.

She'd been right about his deception. He would have been stunned if she'd agreed to his first proposition. Not that he wouldn't have taken her to bed, and quickly, as soon as he recovered from the shock of her acquiescence. But she had reacted just as he expected, falling neatly into his snare. He'd had no intention of letting her get away from him. He was confident he could overcome her fears. She *would* share his bed. It was only a matter of time.

She tilted her head, her gaze searching. "Have they checked the landing bay yet?"

"Commander Zane and his men have secured the bay and inspected your ship."

Her dark eyes locked with his. "And?"

He took a deep breath. "It's pretty much destroyed."

Pain flashed through her eyes, and she staggered

back. He reached for her, but she quickly regained her balance. She must have realized there was a chance her ship would be ransacked, but reality was always more horrific than simple probability.

"I'm sorry," he said quietly.

"I want to see it."

"I don't think that's a good idea. It will only upset you further."

"I *have* to see it," she insisted, her expression a mixture of panic and denial. "Please."

He sighed inwardly. "All right." He moved around to the comm and hit the pad. "Max, are you there?"

"Yes, sir."

"Take the ship down. Let Commander Zane know we're coming, and make certain the landing bay and the surrounding area is secured."

"Yes, Your Highness."

Rurick looked at Celie, standing there mutely. She gripped the back of a chair, her knuckles white. "Come," he said gently. "We need to strap in for landing."

The ship looked almost normal, except for the blackened, gaping hole that had been the hatch—until they got close and saw where the explosives had blown huge cracks in the hull. Celie stared at the remains of her ship for a long moment, her slender body rigid.

"Oh, Spirit," she whispered, reaching out to touch the ripped metal. Her anguished words twisted Rurick's heart. He went to stand beside her, offering the comfort of his presence. There was damn little else he could do.

She stepped inside, moving with a stiff, automatic gait. He followed, allowing her space but determined to be with her. Remaining by the entry, he watched as she walked through the ruined ship, sifting through debris. He saw nothing salvageable. Utterly silent, Celie went

214

into every cabin. Finally coming out of the last chamber, she stood at the far end of the corridor, her face expressionless. "There's nothing left," she whispered.

He walked to her, stepping over the piles of debris. "My men have already retrieved whatever they could."

"Nothing left," she said again, her voice flat and dull.

"Maybe they found some things." Taking her icy hand, he pulled her toward the entry.

"My reading disks, my paintings . . . gone. My plants, my dyes, my custom-made paints. All gone." She kept scanning the interior, as if her prized possessions might suddenly materialize.

"Come on." He lifted her off her feet and hauled her outside the ship. She tried to turn back toward the entry, but he stepped between her and the craft and gripped her shoulders. "Celie, look at me."

She looked past him toward the ship, and he grasped her head in both hands, forcing her to face him. She was pale, alarmingly so, and her skin abnormally cool—from shock, perhaps. Her pupils were fully dilated, making her eyes appear black, an appropriate background for the stark pain and despair he saw there.

"I'm sorry," he murmured. "I wish there was something—"

"Don't!" She twisted free, tensing when she saw the Riordan soldiers ringing the bay. "What are they doing here? I don't want them here." Her voice rose, a hysterical edge to it, and she tried to jerk away when Rurick took her arm. "Leave me alone!"

"I'm not going to do that." He pulled her against him, holding her tightly despite her resistance. "Shhh. Be still."

He looked toward Max and Zane and motioned for the men to leave the bay. "All of you out," he ordered. Max hesitated, clearly not pleased. "It's fine," Rurick insisted. "Keep the outside perimeter secured." He waited until the men filed out, then lowered his head next to Celie's. "It's all right, sweetheart. I sent everyone else away. You and I are the only ones here. Hold on to me. Just hold on."

She did, clutching the front of his uniform, her fingers digging into the silk and into him. She didn't cry, but he felt her shaking, sensed her battle to keep control. He tightened his left arm around her and raised his right hand to stroke her hair. He felt a renewed surge of guilt. Celie didn't deserve to lose her ship, which had probably served as both her livelihood and her home. That meant she had basically lost everything.

"I'll get you another ship," he promised.

"No!" Her body stiffened, and he could feel the rage pulsing through her. "I don't want another ship." She drew back, and he let her, a tactical error in hindsight. Her fist pounded his chest. He stumbled, stunned by surprise and pain.

"I don't want another ship!" she screamed, advancing on him and pounding him again, this time with both fists.

"Celie!" He lunged, grabbing her wrists and holding them immobile. "Stop this! It's not doing any good."

He shook her, and she froze, the wildness in her eyes fading to shocked realization. "Oh, Spirit," she whispered. "I can't believe I just did that. I'm sorry."

"It's all right," he gasped, struggling to catch his breath. "I'll recover." He started to release her, but then he felt her trembling, saw the tears glittering in her eyes. Remorse stabbed through him. "Ah, Celie. Come here."

He cradled her against him and held her while she cried.

Chapter Thirteen

Celie sat in the co-pilot's seat, watching Rurick's strong, lean hands as they moved over the console. Like everything else he did, he piloted with total competence and a quiet confidence that she might find assuring under different circumstances. In her old life, perhaps.

But that was light-years in the past. She stared blindly at the controls, grief slashing through her, more agonizing than anything she had ever experienced. Her entire existence was gone. Rurick's men had found a few items in the shell of her ship: three paintings, some scratched reading disks, two plants with broken stems, a few containers of dye, a few personal toiletries. That was it—a pitiful representation for a lifetime.

She was grateful Rurick had insisted they be the only two passengers on his private cruiser as they traveled to Sarngin, trailed by the two escort ships. Somehow he had known she needed to be alone, that she didn't want Raven hovering over her, didn't want to be the object of curious—even pitying—stares from his officers; didn't want Max's precise and proper condolences.

Of course, Rurick was with her, so she wasn't completely alone. Yet she found his calm presence oddly comforting. He didn't try to maintain conversation; he simply let her break the silence when she wanted to say something.

She didn't know why he had been so solicitous of her, considering she had attacked him in the landing bay. Embarrassment flooded her as she remembered how she had then proceeded to cry all over him. She had been too incapacitated with pain and grief to contain the tears, much less resist Rurick's arms closing around her. Facing him afterward had been awful, although he'd been understanding and reassuring, which had only made her feel worse.

In fact, she'd displayed a disconcerting lack of control around him on a number of occasions, something she was not proud of, especially considering the fact that he seemed to have magnasteel control. She sighed, leaning back in her chair. "I've hit you twice now," she said. "I regret my actions. Well, at least the second time. You deserved it the first."

"Maybe I did." He glanced at her. "Both occasions had understandable motivations. No need to apologize."

"I'm normally not violent like that."

He looked at her again. "It's all right."

"Fine." She crossed her arms, feeling at a loss. She was out of sorts, her emotions fluctuating between regret and grief. For some reason, his agreeableness irritated her. She was tired of everyone being so careful with her. Right now, she'd prefer a fight to conciliatory words. "That's just fine," she muttered.

"All right, Celie." He swung around, his gaze probing. "What's the matter?"

That was another thing: He was too damned percep-tive. She swiveled her seat to face him. "It bothers me that you're being so nice to me."

His eyebrows raised at that. "You would prefer rougher treatment?" He cocked his head toward her, pure devilry in his eyes. "A little force, perhaps?"

She ignored the increased pace of her heart, telling herself there was no innuendo in his response. "No, of course not." She gritted her teeth in frustration. Her comment sounded absurd, even to her. "I just don't want to be treated with meroni gloves. I'm not fragile. I won't break."

"I see." He considered a moment, then turned back and shifted the controls to auto. Very deliberately, he rose from his chair and stepped to hers.

She watched him with a heart-pounding, breathless feeling that accompanied the realization that she had somehow provoked something, and didn't know what. Adrenaline sang through her blood as he leaned down, slipped his hands beneath her elbows, and propelled her to her feet in one smooth motion. He slid his hands down her sides, resting them lightly, possessively, on her hips. Acutely aware of his fingers curving over her rear, she suddenly had trouble catching her breath.

"I'm glad to hear that you won't break, Captain," he murmured, his eyes heating to molten gold. "Because what I have in mind is not for the frail or weak."

His fingers pressed into her rear, bringing her flush against him. She knew she should protest, should push away, but her body felt heavy, weighed down with a strange lethargy. Her senses were another thing, how-ever, honed to a keen edge by adrenaline and by the energy radiating between her and Rurick.

He slid one hand up her back, slowly, sensuously, his fingers impressing a tantalizing, heated trail through the fabric of her flight suit. His hand reached the nape of her neck, the sensation of his touch even more electrifying against her bare skin. Then he cradled the back of her head, those long, sure fingers sliding through her hair and applying just enough pressure to hold her still. Sudden awareness of his intent jolted her out of her lethargy.

"Your Highness," she gasped, trying to muster up a protest, to put mental distance between them by using his title. She raised her arms to push him away.

"There's no prince here." He splayed his other hand against her rear, pulling her even closer, letting her feel the hard evidence of his intentions and making it impossible for her to wedge her hands between them. "Only a man."

He lowered his face toward hers and panic evaporated any remaining languor. The man was far more threatening than the prince. She squirmed in his grip. "I don't think—"

His lips halted her protest. He molded his mouth to hers, applied pressure for a moment. Then he pulled back just enough to whisper, "No thinking, Celie. It's time to trust your feelings."

Her feelings? Spirit, her feelings were a riotous mess, her defenses wrecked, and— His mouth came back down on hers, and the breath whooshed from her lungs. Then his tongue slid between her lips, and her legs suffered operational failure. She wrapped her arms around his neck in a desperate bid for balance.

He kissed her as he had on the ship in the ninth sector, and again on Jardonia, with that same staggering absorption and expertise. She made the heady discovery that she liked it even more this time; that it sent her heart racing and dispersed a sultry, needy heat through her body. Her skin tingled and her breasts ached. She craved Rurick's touch, *needed* it. She pressed against him, wanting more contact.

220

He responded with a low groan, rotating his pelvis against hers, leaving no doubt about his state of arousal. The aggressive action yanked her from a desire-induced fog. Mental alarms blared in the back of her mind, bringing her back to reality.

She tore her mouth away. "No," she gasped, finally managing to get her hands between them, and shoving hard against his chest. "No!"

He let her go and she staggered back against her chair. Her chest heaving, she grabbed the headrest for support. "Rurick . . . Your Highness . . . I can't—It's not—" She realized she was babbling and clamped her mouth shut.

At least she had the satisfaction of knowing Rurick was also affected by the kiss. His breathing was ragged and there was an impressive bulge in his uniform. Realizing where her gaze fixated, she jerked her head up and eased around the chair.

His brows arched. "It's not . . . what? Not rough enough?"

Her eyes narrowing, she slapped the back of the chair and sent it spinning. "I don't want rough!" she snapped. "I don't want anything from you."

"Oh, I think you do." He stepped back, a satisfied gleam in his eyes. "Consider this a warm-up for when we mate. And we will. You can count on it."

She clenched her hands to keep from throttling him and ending up in a wrestling match she couldn't win. Damn him—for kissing her, for shaking her up, both emotionally and physically, and for indirectly reminding her about that cursed agreement to accompany him to Sarngin. With the shock of losing her ship she hadn't given much thought to their agreement, or to Rurick's bold proclamation that he wanted her. Men had been interested in her since she was seventeen; she was used

221

to it. So why was she having so much trouble dealing with this situation? With him?

She forced her breathing to calm and tried to act nonchalant, as if she hadn't been devastated by his kiss. "We won't be doing any more of this," she said coolly. "I have better things to do with my time."

"Really?" Amusement gleamed in his eyes. "We'll see about that. Now, since you don't want to be treated with meroni gloves and your color looks more robust, why don't you clean the galley?"

She gritted her teeth and told herself she would *not* hit him again, no matter how much he deserved to have pain inflicted upon him. "Fine!" she snapped. "I'd prefer solitude in the galley to putting up with your arrogance, *Your Highness.*"

She marched from the cockpit, seething. It occurred to her that she was the one always storming off—or running away, if she were to be honest. Fortunately, she wasn't overly prideful. She'd long ago learned too much pride was dangerous, and not every battle could be won outright. Sometimes strategic retreat was necessary. It was proving to be imperative where Rurick was concerned.

Rurick settled back at the controls. He was torn between amusement at Celie's indignant outrage and his body's savage need for release. He wasn't above employing heavy-duty sensual prodding to bring her around. Still, he had to wait until she willingly came to him. Damn, it was hard. He shifted his body and glanced down wryly at his raging need. *Very hard.* He envied Max's ability to inflate and deflate certain body parts at will.

Shaking that thought away, he scanned the monitors. Everything appeared in order. He sat back in his chair, drummed his fingers on the console, fiddled with some displays, leaned back in his chair again. Out of curiosity and boredom, he requested written information on the nearest planets. The navigation pod printed a report that he didn't bother to read.

It was too quiet, too dull, without Celie in the cockpit. On a whim, he flipped on the comm to the galley. A loud crash burst over the speaker. Celie muttered something unintelligible, and the sound of another crash erupted from the speaker. Wincing, Rurick turned off the comm. After thinking about it a moment, he grinned. She *was* affected by him, despite her denials.

A loud clanging sounded in the cockpit, and he checked the comm. It took a moment to realize it wasn't Celie venting her wrath in the galley. Red lights began flashing on the console, and the audio warning system kicked in.

"Alert, alert!" the computer intoned. "External ventilation valves are open. Oxygen levels are dropping."

What? Rurick stared at the environmental readouts, trying to tune out the strident alarms and computer warnings. What would cause the ship's systems to vent oxygen while they were in deep space? Surely it was a sensor malfunction. But the readings showed rapidly decreasing oxygen levels. "Computer, close the external vents," he ordered.

But the alarms continued blaring and the levels continued to drop. He typed in the command, real concern tightening his chest when nothing happened. He punched the comm to the galley. He had to shout over the cacophony. "Celie, are you there?"

"I'm on my way to the cockpit. What's with the alarms?"

"We may have a major malfunction. The life support sensors indicate that we're losing oxygen."

"How could that happen?"

"I don't know. I'm hoping it's a sensor malfunction,

but I can't get the system to respond. Get to the airlock and suit up."

"What about you? How fast are the levels dropping?"

"Don't worry about me. I have portable oxygen. Go to the airlock immediately. Then get back to the cockpit as soon as you're suited up."

"All right. I'll bring you a suit."

Rurick turned from the comm just as the environmental panel went blank. He punched in the command to go to backup, but nothing happened. Panic swept through him. Stars! Was it his imagination, or was he starting to feel lightheaded? He reached up and released the small panel above him. An oxygen mask dropped down, and he slipped it on. The oxygen was stale and warm, but immediately he felt more clear-headed.

The lights in the cockpit flickered, once, twice, then went out. Red emergency lights glowed dimly, giving the cockpit a surreal appearance. Another alarm sounded, increasing the noise level. "Main power down," the computer warned. "Must shut down for maintenance."

"What? No! Computer, do not shut down!" Rurick ordered. The alarms cut off abruptly, the silence startling after the deafening blare. The entire main console went blank, then let out a high-pitched whine, as if the computer had flatlined. As if it were . . . dead. Then that sound ceased. Total silence blanketed the cockpit.

"Go to auxiliary power!" he yelled, frantically typing the command. Nothing.

Incredulous, he forced himself to remain calm. He punched the subspace transceiver pad to contact his escort ships. He'd already sent them on their way, but they would be the closest ships. Again, nothing. No lights on the communications monitor. He checked the engines, the propulsion systems. All dead.

"What's going on?" Celie slipped into the cockpit,

carrying a spacesuit. Her voice, coming through the external speaker in the helmet, sounded slightly distorted. "The regular lights are off throughout the ship."

"Damned if I know. All our systems appear to be down. Environmental, communications, engineering, propulsion." Rurick stood and took the suit from her.

"What about the backup systems?" She moved around him, took the pilot's seat, and punched some pads.

He stepped into the suit. "Everything is down."

"Did you contact the other ships?" She hit the subspace comm, stared at the blank console.

"I tried. Communication is also down." He closed the seams, pulled the oxygen mask off his face, and put on the helmet. They were speaking through their headsets now.

"Blazing hells," she muttered. "There must be something we can do."

"We still have manual overrides. I've never used them, though."

"I have." She turned to look up at him, her face barely visible through the plexishield in the dim light. "I've flown enough junkers to have experienced system failures several times. But we don't want to use our manual thrusters unless we have to. They burn a lot of fuel, and we have a finite amount."

"True." He sank into the co-pilot's chair. "Stars."

"We can drift until Max or Commander Zane realizes we've fallen behind and comes back."

Rurick cursed himself. "That's not likely. I sent them on. Max is taking Raven to Shamara, and Zane is returning to Jardonia to keep watch on my father." He sighed. "Since this ship has defense weapons, I felt confident we could travel safely to Sarngin."

Celie sat frozen, like a statue in one of the Jardonian

225

gardens. "How long does the oxygen last in these suits?" she asked finally.

He hadn't even considered. He'd never been faced with malfunctioning equipment before. Riordan technology, along with a fanatical emphasis on flawless maintenance and upkeep, had meant no equipment failures. Until now. "We have four hours of oxygen," he answered. "Plus we have an additional oxygen pack for each suit."

"A total of eight hours," she murmured. "In that case, we need to locate a habitable planet and land."

"Good idea, but easier said than done without the navigation pod. Wait!" Rurick leaned forward, grabbing the printout on the nav console. "I printed this out before the systems went down. It's a listing of planets in our general vicinity."

"Thank Spirit." Celie leaned toward him. "Let's see what we have."

There was only one planet anywhere close to their position. It had been tagged *Toba/08/995.624/ 100.556*—"Toba" being the temporary name assigned, "08" representing the sector in which the planet was located, and the remaining numbers coordinates. Although quadrant-mapping teams had not yet explored the planet, probes had been sent out and determined the atmosphere contained oxygen. Not that it mattered. Toba was their only hope.

"I don't think we have any choice," Rurick said. "We have to head there."

"Agreed." Celie rose from the pilot's chair. "You may take the controls, Your Highness."

"No, Captain. I defer to your superior experience in these matters. You take the controls. Please."

"All right." She blew out her breath, sank back into the seat. "I'll do my best to land this ship."

"I have the utmost confidence in you. And Celie, if

you call me Your Highness one more time, there will be hell to pay when we're on terra firma again."

She looked at him, her eyes dark orbs behind the plexishield. He wished he could kiss her again. With that denied him, he settled for grabbing her helmet between his hands and pressing his plexishield against hers. "Get us out of this, Captain," he said lightly. "So we can make mad, passionate love."

"How about I just get us out of this and we'll leave it at that?" she retorted. She pulled back, began manually setting the coordinates. "And I suggest we both start praying."

They needed more than prayer, Celie thought as they flew downward through thin gray clouds. There was enough light outside the portal to indicate it was daytime on this side of the planet, which was in their favor. She glanced at the chronometer. They had fifteen minutes of oxygen left. They had slightly less time on the battery backup powering the manual flight instrumentation, according to the readouts.

She studied the dials, so different from the computerized panels she was used to. Four thousand meters above Toba, and she couldn't risk speeding up their descent. Their fuel was almost gone, and she would need the manual thrusters for landing. Gravity and the ship's mass would have to bring them down. A megasized miracle was needed now.

She glanced at Rurick. His breathing was steady and he seemed calmer than she felt. He'd kept her grounded with his quiet confidence and his able assistance with the ship. She couldn't imagine a better co-pilot in an extreme situation such as this. Or a better person to die with. She thought of Moriah, of little Alyssa, and Janaye, and the other women on Risa. Of the Shielders who were like family. Resolutely, she pushed away those thoughts. She had to focus all her energy on surviving.

They came out of the clouds at fifteen hundred meters, over a gray landscape punctuated with barren mountains. Great. Landing in mountains without hoverlifts gave them a zero percent chance of success. "Nowhere to land," she murmured, keeping her voice calm.

"Then we'll go a little farther." Rurick took her hand and squeezed it. "It's been a pleasure flying with you, Captain."

Her throat tightened and she squeezed his hand back, wishing that things had been different between them. Wishing that her past hadn't made it impossible for her to have a relationship with this man, or any man. "The pleasure has been mine . . . Rurick."

Releasing his hand, she concentrated on the instruments. She brought the ship down, leveled out at four hundred meters. Without comment, Rurick lowered the wheels. They worked well together, she thought, studying the terrain. Snow capped the mountains, and more swirls of snow hampered visibility.

She glanced at the horizon and wing-position indicators just as they winked off. Her manual flight instruments were gone. She was on her own. Another glance at the chronometer. Five minutes of oxygen left. She focused on the horizon, held the ship steady. Drawing a deep breath, she realized her oxygen was almost gone. There was no way of knowing if Toba's atmosphere had enough oxygen to sustain them, and she couldn't risk passing out.

"Hold on!" she said, mounting panic releasing a familiar rush of adrenaline. "We'll have to touch down soon."

"Flaps are fully extended," Rurick reported. "Go for it, Captain."

She pushed the yoke down and retarded the throttles. The ship descended as it sped over the rocky landscape, while she desperately searched for any sort of opening. There! A clearing!

"I'm going to put it down." She slowed the craft, locking her gaze on a point midway in the clearing and adjusting the flight path accordingly. They dropped like a massive meteor, then she pulled back on the yoke as the ground rushed up to meet them. She shut down the thrusters. They hit the ground with a shattering impact, and she braked hard. Hurtling, hurtling forward . . .

White blanketed everything. Then darkness.

Chapter Fourteen

She couldn't breathe. Celie clawed at the plexishield, finally locating the release, and snapped the plate up. Cold air drifted over her face and she inhaled deeply. Her head throbbed and she ached all over. Something hard and unyielding cut into her chest. Disoriented, she opened her eyes. Murkiness swirled around her, dust and bits of debris floating in the faint streams of light coming from above.

She shook her head to clear it, and pain and dizziness reeled through her. It took a moment for the spinning to stop; then she was able to focus her eyes. The wreckage jolted her to awareness. The ship! They had landed . . . or crash landed, as appeared to be case. Rurick! She glanced over, but the co-pilot's seat was no longer to her right.

"Rurick? Where are you?" She looked around, able to see only vague shapes in the semidarkness. Her eyes adjusted to the dimness as she struggled with her harness. The ship had split into two parts upon impact, almost exactly down the middle. At least they were right side up. Most of the light was coming from the huge fissure in the top of the ship. Snow and bitterly cold air were also drifting in.

"Rurick?" she called, finally wrestling her harness loose. She shoved away the remainders of the crash bags that had encased her chair on impact and hefted herself out. She was sore and shaky, and her head throbbed like Hades, but she appeared to be in one piece.

Sloshing through chunks of foam that had filled the inflating crash bags, she picked her way around equipment. She saw Rurick, strapped in his chair and on his back, with part of the console collapsed over his legs. "Rurick!" She stumbled over more debris, coming down to her knees beside him. "Are you all right?"

He didn't appear to be breathing, and she realized the oxygen in his suit must have run out. She opened the shield on his helmet, but he didn't move. She touched his cheek. His skin was cold. Panic raced through her. "Rurick, wake up." She shook his face. "Rurick!" She felt the sudden rise and fall of his chest as he drew a breath, and his eyes fluttered open. They were dulled with pain and shock and nonrecognition. He closed them again and lay still, but he was breathing.

She had to get the console off his legs. She rose and stumbled around the destroyed cockpit, locating a loose magnasteel beam. She pried it free and dragged it to the console. It took a long time to raise the console: first shoving a large piece of equipment beneath the beam to brace it; putting all her weight on the beam to raise the console a few millimeters at a time; forcing more chunks of metal beneath the beam so it couldn't fall back down, then repeating the process.

Finally she had the console jacked up high enough.

She dragged Rurick from beneath it millimeter by millimeter. He was heavy, plus she had the added weight of the chair to deal with. Sweat dripped inside her flight suit, despite the bitter cold of the cockpit, and she was gasping for breath by the time he was free.

She checked him anxiously, relieved to find he was still breathing. His legs didn't appear crushed, but she couldn't tell the extent of the damage. She decided to leave the harness on him until she could find medical supplies, so he couldn't thrash around and injure himself further.

She was weak and lethargy pulled at her, but she knew she had a lot to do before she could rest. She headed for the rear of the ship, a hazardous process with rifts in the hull and twisted fixtures and equipment at every turn. The wreckage looked eerie in the dim glow of the emergency lighting.

The extensive damage to the ship made it impossible for her to get below-deck from the upper level. She was able to open the jammed hatch after kicking it several times. A blast of frigid air and swirling snow greeted her when she swung it open. As an added precaution, she armed herself before going outside, snapping two blasters, a stun gun, and an extra power pack on her belt. No telling what life-forms might exist on Toba. She lowered the ladder manually and climbed down, on the alert for anything.

At the bottom of the ship she took a good look around. She saw nothing but rocks and snow; an uneven stone surface beneath her feet, huge boulders partially ringing the area; and, farther away, towering bare mountains. The snow fell at a rapid rate, propelled by the relentless wind. No sign of life, either plant or animal. Looking at the treacherous terrain, she realized it was nothing short of a miracle they had managed to find a clearing, much less survive the crash landing.

The lower level of the ship was badly damaged and the bays had split open, scattering crates and equipment across the expanse of rocks. Moving toward the closest bay, Celie could tell the planet's gravity was lower and the air thinner than she was used to. She'd have to pace herself, at the same time circumstances demanded she push herself. With Rurick out of commission, everything depended on her.

First she located medical supplies and a generator. She had to use a rope to haul both to the upper level. Next came the solar lanterns, which could be powered by the generator in the absence of sunlight. When she rolled the generator into the cockpit, she saw that Rurick was awake. He was struggling with his flight harness.

"Hey! What are you doing?" she demanded, going to him.

"I'm trying to get out of this stupid contraption," he gasped, sweat beading his face. "Where have you been? I was scared witless when I came to and you were gone."

"Be still." She moved his hands from the harness. "You're not going anywhere. You legs might be broken. Sorry I frightened you, but I was trying to get the supplies we need before dark."

He shifted, groaned. "My legs hurt like Hades," he agreed.

"Stop moving around. I don't know the extent of your injuries yet."

"But I need to get up and see what—"

"No! Listen hotshot, you're not going anywhere. Not until I check you over." She unpacked the medical supplies and located a medipad and a handheld monitor. She laid the pad over Rurick's chest and ran the monitor over the rest of him.

"At least tell me about ship damage," he persisted.

"Would you be quiet? I'm trying to figure out this

233

darned medical equipment. You have to be a rocket scientist to read it. I'll fill you in after I take care of your injuries."

She determined he had two broken legs—no surprise there—and some minimal internal bleeding, along with a lot of bruises. His pulse was a little fast and his blood pressure a little low. Fortunately, there was no injury to the neck or spine. The well-designed flight chairs and harnesses, along with the crash bags, had kept them both alive. She could treat everything but the internal bleeding—which was the thing that worried her the most.

Rising, she rolled the generator closer and programmed it to provide both heat and a power charge. Then she located a medi-vial containing a narcotic and snapped it into a hypochamber. "I'm going to give you something for the pain before I put the portamedics on your legs," she told Rurick.

"I don't want anything," he protested. "It will make me groggy, and then I won't be able to help you."

"Tough. As if you're not already helpless with two broken legs. Just be grateful this stuff is pre-measured so I don't overdose you accidentally—or intentionally. Here, let's get this helmet off." She lifted his head and removed the helmet. She smoothed his lush hair, savoring the feel of it.

"Ah, that feels good." He lay quietly while she stroked his hair. She took the opportunity to press the hypochamber against his neck and hit the release. "Hey, that hurt!" He grasped her arm with both hands. "You wouldn't be treating me like this if I weren't flat on my back and stuck in this harness."

"Don't flatter yourself," she retorted. "I'll treat you far worse when you're on your feet again."

That got a wan smile. "I'm looking forward to it."

Even with the narcotic in his system, he gritted his

teeth as she undid the harness and carefully slid him off the chair. It probably hurt even worse when she moved each of his legs into the portamedic units, hampered by the tight quarters. He didn't make a sound, but the sheen on his ashen face, along with the tight lines around his mouth, indicated he was in tremendous pain.

The units immediately encircled his legs, inflating and shaping to their contours. They began a steady pressure, along with a rocking motion that would gently force the bones back into proper alignment. They would also inject pain meds at regular intervals and disperse electrical currents to stimulate bone and muscle healing. She hoped there were enough power packs to keep both the generator and the portamedics going.

"How are you feeling?" she asked after Rurick was settled and covered with a thermal blanket.

"Never felt better," he murmured, his gaze unfocused. "What about the ship?"

"I'll tell you about it later."

"Sure . . ." He closed his eyes, exhaled a sigh.

She ignored the traitorous softening of her heart, resisting the urge to run her fingers through his hair again. "I'll be back in a little while. Don't try to move." She doubted he heard her.

She went outside to gather more supplies. The sky was darkening, and snow continued falling. The temperature had dropped. Her spacesuit was insulated, but she'd removed her helmet to see better. She was chilled by the time she'd lugged in five more crates, leaving them in the passenger cabin. Her last load included bottled water and packaged food.

She went back outside to throw tarps over the remaining crates scattered across the rocky plateau upon which the ship rested. When she finally trudged into the cockpit, Rurick was dozing, apparently free of pain. The

235

generator was producing enough heat to cut the chill, and she stood next to it as she stripped off her spacesuit. Although the insulated suit offered extra warmth, it was difficult to move around in, much less take care of basic human functions. She had her regular flight suit on, and she could use a thermal blanket for extra warmth.

She discovered the lav just off the passenger cabin was still functional, although she had to use the manual foot controls. Returning to the cockpit, she set up an electrical screen just inside the main fissure line in the ship's hull, effectively walling them off in the largest half of the cockpit and keeping the heat in.

She was too exhausted to eat and figured Rurick needed rest more than food. Shaking out a thermal blanket, she collapsed on the floor next to him. She placed her weapons beside her and wrapped herself in the blanket. Resting her head on her hands, she said a prayer of thanks to Spirit. She didn't remember a thing after that.

"Celie. Celie!"

"Hmmm." She burrowed into the blanket. Tired . . . she was so tired.

"Celie! Wake up. *Now!*"

Something in Rurick's tone, an urgency, dragged her to the edge of consciousness. She reluctantly forced her eyes open. A gray mist drifted just above her line of vision. Her gaze shifted upward. It wasn't a mist, but a gray orb hovering about twenty-five centimeters from her face. A gray, furry orb.

Her eyes widening, she scrambled back from it, rolled to a sitting position. It moved closer. Slowly, she reached for one of the blasters she'd left nearby. "What is this thing?" she asked in a low voice, her fingers curling around her weapon.

"I have no idea. But you'd better slide me a blaster while you're at it."

"What?" She allowed her gaze to dart to Rurick. He had pulled himself up and now leaned against the upturned console, his portamedic-encased legs stretched out before him.

"Look behind you," he said.

She glanced over her shoulder and saw six more orbs hovering in midair. "By the Spirit!" She raised her blaster while leaning forward to slide the second toward Rurick. He picked it up. All seven furry orbs zipped away, then continued hovering on the other side of the console. "They don't seem overly aggressive," she commented, shoving her hair from her face.

"No," he agreed.

An odd, high-pitched beeping echoed in the cockpit. "What's that?" She looked around the wrecked equipment. It didn't appear to be a low-battery alert.

"I think it's coming from those things."

"I think you're right." She studied the orbs. "Since they're covered with fur, I would guess they're creatures rather than machines."

"That makes sense." Rurick lowered his blaster, and the orbs drifted closer, the beeps lowering in pitch. He raised it, and they immediately moved back, their beeps faster and higher. "They appear to be fairly intelligent as well."

Celie looked up at the widest fissure in the hull above them. Dull light filtered in, along with snow. It was daylight already, which meant Toba had relatively short cycles. These little creatures must not be nocturnal, unless they had been here during the night. They had probably squeezed through the smaller cracks in the hull, as the force field she'd set up was on this side of the large split.

"Now what?" she asked, still aiming the blaster in the general direction of the creatures.

"I have no idea." Rurick also kept his blaster raised. "Unless we want to destroy them outright."

"We can't do that," she protested. "They might be benign."

"Then we need to determine their intentions, don't we?" He lowered his blaster. "Let's see what they do."

Reluctantly, Celie lowered her weapon. She didn't want to shoot the odd creatures, but she didn't want to take any chances, either. They could be vicious, could have poisonous barbs or bites. She tensed when they immediately closed in, clenching her blaster, ready to use it at the slightest sign of threat. But they kept a reasonable distance, beeping softly. After a moment, four of them zipped away at lightning speed, buzzing around the ruined main computer and the navigation pod, their beeps again rising in pitch.

"They look like they're inspecting the equipment," Celie said. "That can't be possible . . . can it?"

"It appears that way," Rurick agreed. "Look at the one closest to you, on your left. Is it holding something?"

Sure enough, the creature on Celie's left had something white clutched beneath its body. Cautiously, she held out her hand, palm up. The creature edged forward, and Rurick raised his blaster. It skittered backward with a loud beep.

"They know these are weapons," Celie said, "and seem to understand the danger. Rurick, put your blaster down. I want to see what it's holding."

"All right, but if it makes a wrong move, I'm shooting."

"I don't think they mean us any harm." Celie held out her hand again. "If they'd wanted to hurt us, they could have done so while we were sleeping."

The creature eased forward over her hand, its beeps lowering to more of a chirp. It released the white object, which drifted down to rest in her palm. "It's a leaf of some sort," she said in surprise. "It's almost clear and very thin."

"Do you recognize it?"

"No." She scooted back, then started to get to her feet.

"What are you doing?"

"I want to see what this is." She rose and turned off the electrical screen, then backed toward the passenger cabin. All seven orbs reacted to her movement, retreating in the opposite direction. They didn't seem at all aggressive. Reaching the crates, Celie dug around for a diagnostic scanner. She ran it over the leaf and studied the readouts.

"Amazing," she said, stepping back inside the cockpit. "This leaf is not only completely edible but it's packed with protein, carbohydrates, and a small amount of fat. It's food." Astonished, she looked at Rurick. "They brought us food."

Celie and Rurick decided to call the little creatures Tobals, after the planet. The Tobals seemed basically harmless. They also appeared very intelligent, and utterly fascinated with every piece of equipment on the ship. They quickly learned when the electric shield was off and began exploring the rest of the ship, zipping around so rapidly it was difficult to track their movements.

More Tobals came in through the myriad cracks in the ship's hull, until there were at least two dozen of them exploring the ship. They wouldn't let Celie or Rurick touch them, but they would settle onto nearby surfaces. About sixteen centimeters in diameter and covered with a soft-looking gray fur tinged with white, they had no visible features such as eyes, ears, nose, or mouth. They had odd, flipperlike appendages that appeared to work like wings, as well as four-toed feet that were very dexterous. They brought more of the leaves—a lot more. Pretty soon the crate Celie put the food in was half full.

After a while, she and Rurick pretty much ignored the Tobals and went about their business. She helped him stand, and he moved slowly around the cockpit. The portamedic readouts indicated that the bones had properly set, and the units also acted as casts and would not flex, so he walked with his legs locked.

"It feels good to be up and moving," he said.

"You're walking so stiffly, you really do resemble an android," she teased, unwilling to admit how relieved she was that he was all right.

"Riordan androids move fluidly," he said with mock irritation.

He followed slowly as she explored the upper level, looking for a place where they might be more comfortable. They discovered one of the private cabins was habitable, although they had to force open the entry panel, and the cracks in the hull extended here, as they did everywhere. Rurick watched, complaining about his inability to help, as Celie cleared the mess in the cabin, then rolled the generator inside. She dragged in some crates with supplies, then set up the force field in the ruined entry after they were inside. A group of Tobals zipped around the room, inspecting the control panels and investigating the lav.

Celie looked around the cabin, satisfied. "This will be a lot better than the cockpit. We have more room, and it will be easier for you to rest on the bunk than on the floor."

"It's pretty tough getting up and down when I can't bend my legs," Rurick agreed. "Would you help me out of this spacesuit? It's cumbersome, and I don't need it in here."

"Pretty helpless, aren't you?" She went to him and started to unhook the clasps of the suit.

"Care to test that theory?" He slid his arms around her and pulled her close. His golden gaze swept her face with a look that was unmistakably possessive and suggestive. "I assure you, my legs are the *only* things that aren't fully functional."

He was over six feet of pure, rugged male, and she had no doubt of his capabilities. No denying her heated response to him, either, but she reminded herself firmly that she could control her reactions. "Behave," she said, shoving him back. "I don't want to have to hurt you."

He grinned and released her. She unsnapped the shoulder clasps to his suit and tugged it off his arms and down his body until she reached the portamedics. He eased down on the bunk so she could remove them as well. "How do your legs feel?" she asked after the units were off.

He leaned forward and rubbed his shins. "Much better. There's no pain at all, not even when I put weight on them. I'd been told the portamedics were miracle workers, but seeing it firsthand is pretty amazing."

"Riordan technology is very advanced," Celie agreed. She tugged the spacesuit off Rurick's legs, then put the portamedics back on over his regular flight suit.

She located some foam soap, and they each visited the lav to take care of necessities and rinse off some of the grime. Then they settled on the bunk and ate some of their packaged food.

Rurick leaned against the wall and drank bottled water. He looked pale, and she knew he was still suffering from the trauma of the crash. It was by the grace of Spirit that she'd escaped basically unscathed, although

241

she was sore all over, as if she'd been tossed around inside a rocket projector.

"Tell me about the damage to the ship," he said.

"It would be easier for me to tell you what's not damaged." Celie rested her arms on her upraised knees. "The lower level is badly crushed, which is why I had to use the upper hatch, then enter the lower bays from outside. Other than supplies and a few pieces of equipment, not much is salvageable."

She gave a little laugh. "It looks like I'm bad luck where ships are concerned." She was trying to be light-hearted, but renewed pain at the loss of her own ship washed over her.

"Hey." Rurick reached over and took her clenched hand, smoothing it open and wrapping his long fingers around it. "I consider having you on board when the systems failed the luckiest cycle of my life. I've never flown with a better pilot. And your survival skills are pretty impressive."

Warmed by a surprising flush of pleasure, she shifted her gaze away. "Thank you."

"The computer systems were sabotaged." His voice took on a hard edge. "Since it was my private cruiser, which I use whenever I travel, I'm assuming whoever did it was after me."

She looked at him. His mouth was set in a grim line and his eyes blazed with fury. "Yes," she agreed. "I've been thinking about it. There's no way every system, including the backups, could go down like that. The failures had to be programmed. Do you think this is related to the ninth sector?"

"I can't think of any other reason someone would want me dead. My father is still the king of Jardonia, and I have no real power, other than the threat of exposing the conditions in the ninth sector and finding out who's behind it. I'm getting too close to the truth."

"Unfortunately, I think you're right."

"As soon as we reach Sarngin, I intend to force the issue," he said.

"We have to be rescued first," she pointed out, unwilling to voice her fears.

"We will." Rurick's eyes softened, and he squeezed her hand. "All Riordan ships are equipped with emergency beacons that automatically activate if systems fail or the ship crashes. I checked our beacon earlier, and it's working."

The low-power tone on the generator sounded. Celie got up to change the power pack. She could feel the increased chill in the cabin and looked upward. Snow was filtering in through the cracks at a rapid rate. Outside, the wind howled over the hull.

She counted the power packs. There were three remaining.

Chapter Fifteen

The weather had worsened, elevating to a full blizzard. Celie stuffed flight suits and blankets into the largest cracks in the ceiling. It kept the snow from coming in, but it couldn't keep out the biting cold. The ship was normally very well insulated, but with both hulls riddled with numerous cracks and crevices, the cold seeped through like an insidious, invisible assassin.

They had stopped using the electric screen because its power packs were depleted, and recharging them would strain the generator. Celie tacked a thermal blanket over the entry to keep in as much heat as possible. The portamedic packs were also depleted, so the units now served solely as splints to protect Rurick's legs. The solar lanterns had a little power left and were used only when necessary. All the packs were imbedded with solar chips, which would allow the sun to recharge them, but no sunlight was even remotely visible at the moment.

The weather didn't seem to bother the Tobals, nor did the murky dimness of the ship. They popped in and out, sometimes with more leaves, which they presented with their odd, high-pitched beeps. Then they'd resume their investigation of the equipment in the cabin and elsewhere. They never seemed to tire of it.

Celie was accustomed to them now. She put another power pack in the generator and scooped up the newest leaf offering, adding it to those already in the crate. "Where are these leaves coming from?" she wondered. "They can't be growing out there."

"No color in them, so I'd guess they don't grow in sunlight," Rurick answered. "Caves, perhaps?" He was resting on the bunk, his back propped against the wall. He'd gotten up at regular intervals to test the strength of his legs, survey the damage, and help in the futile attempt to keep out the cold. He was considerably better today.

"I'll bet you're right." Celie cocked her head at him. Even in the semidarkness, she could see the powerful lines of his shoulders, the outline of his aristocratic face. "You're smarter than I thought."

"Absolutely." He sounded affronted. "I'll have you know Riordan royal children receive an extensive education."

She smiled halfheartedly at his indignant tone, but her frown quickly returned as she felt the chill nipping at her. She glanced at the remaining power packs, wishing there were more.

"Hey, Captain." Rurick held out his hand. "Come here."

She walked over, growing concern gnawing at her. She took his hand and he tugged her down on the bunk. "Take a break and sit with me."

She settled next to him, leaned her head against the

245

wall. "We only have two power packs left, and the temperatures outside are subzero."

"I know." Shifting, he slid his arm behind her and pulled her against him. It didn't occur to her to protest, especially when he spread a thermal blanket over them, blocking out the chill. "The emergency beacon is still broadcasting," he reminded her. "Max and Zane have our projected flight coordinates. Since they haven't been able to contact us, and we're not at Sarngin, I'm certain they're looking for us."

They might get a fix on the beacon, but there was no possibility of landing in such treacherous terrain in a blizzard—a storm that showed no sign of abating. If the generator ran out of power, things would get rough.

"The weather—" she started, but he placed his fingers against her lips.

"Hush. It does no good to worry about things that are out of our control." He slid down and rested his head against hers, staring at the nearby crate heaped with Tobal leaf offerings. "At least we're not in danger of starving."

She laughed, in spite of the situation. Spirit, she was glad Rurick was here with her. It amazed her how much comfort his solid strength offered, how relaxed she felt with him, especially since he'd ceased his annoying I-want-you alpha-male routine.

Actually, it hadn't really been so annoying; rather, it had been surprisingly provocative. The realization that he could evoke such strong physical and emotional responses within her, despite her determined resistance, had sent her seeking shelter behind the protective barriers she'd spent a lifetime building.

Now another emotion twisted inside her—regret. Regret that the events in her life had scarred her so deeply she could never fully give herself to a man; regret that

Rurick deserved so much more than she could ever offer.

"You find that amusing, do you?" He turned toward her. "I love the way you laugh. It has a stimulating effect on me."

The husky edge to his voice was unmistakable, the timbre of desire mesmerizing. She could only watch as he leaned toward her. He nuzzled her cheek, as gentle as a whisper. Then his lips brushed hers with the lightest of touches, nibbling, teasing. He slipped into the kiss so subtly, so skillfully, she wasn't even alarmed. Not even when his tongue entered her mouth to stroke and taste, sending tiny shock waves through her body.

Spirit, but the man knew how to kiss. She found herself sinking into the pure enjoyment of kissing him. Maybe it was her fatigue or her shaken mental state, but she didn't fully comprehend his true intent until he slid one hand behind her head, fingers tangling in her hair as he deepened the intensity of the kiss, stroking in, out, in, out, a blatant, breathless reminder of how his finger had moved inside her; and until his other hand covered her breast. *That* jolted her into full awareness. She pulled back and he followed, leaning into her, his lips hovering an atom-breadth from hers.

"Mate with me, Celie." He covered her mouth again before she could protest.

She grabbed his head and forcibly pushed him back. "Rurick, we've been through this. I don't want a relationship, not with you, not with any man."

He rubbed his fingers over the peak of her breast. "On Altair, you told me you didn't want to die without experiencing life to the fullest. You asked me to show you the act of mating."

The sensations his fingers were sparking from her breast to other parts of her body didn't slow her mortification over what had happened on Altair. She didn't appreciate being reminded what a fool she'd been. She grabbed his wrist and tugged his hand to her lap, where she kept a firm grip on it.

"That was a mistake, and I don't want to talk about it. Besides, we're not going to die." She angled her chin in challenge. Yet she knew she was trying to convince herself as much as she was him. "Are we?"

"If we get a vote, then mine is no." His voice was calm, but she heard the same concern she was trying desperately to ignore in herself. "What you said on Altair was right, Celie. Life is too short not to be experienced to the fullest." His free hand cupped her face. "I want you."

She took hold of that hand as well, holding tightly to both his wrists. "We might be in a precarious position, but there's no reason to behave any differently," she argued, searching for a way to make him understand why they—why *she*—couldn't do this. Yet, she wasn't even sure of the reasons herself, only that the demons lurking in the depths of her soul would be resurrected if she gave in to her desire.

"I don't agree. Life has too many uncertainties. Remember what else you said that night on Altair?"

Did the man have to have a holographic memory on top of everything else? "I don't want to talk about Altair. That's behind us." She released his hands and tried to scoot away, but he gripped her upper arms, stopping her. His intense gaze bored into her.

"You said that only one thing in life is certain: That we're all going to die sooner or later and we don't know when. When we left Joba, we had no way of knowing our computer system had been sabotaged, or that we would crash on an uninhabited planet. We have no way of knowing what will happen here, or when we leave here, the gods willing. We could be hit by a meteorite; I could be assassinated—"

"Don't say that!" She punched him on the shoulder. "Don't even think it." The thought of him being killed shook her far more than she cared to admit.

He moved faster than a striking Oderian serpent, dragging her onto his lap and wrapping his arms around her. The blanket slid off them, but she hardly noticed. "So you do care." His mouth unerringly found hers, even with her attempts to dodge him. He seemed to have a built-in radar where her mouth was concerned.

She turned her face away. "No! Well, yes . . . I mean . . . Blazing hells, Rurick. Stop twisting my words and throwing them back at me. You know I care. As obnoxious, overbearing, and demanding as you are, I do care. But I can't do this, and you know the reasons why."

"Those are your fears speaking, Celie. They can be faced and overcome. Let me show you."

His pull was too persistent, far too potent. She felt the lure of the ever-present attraction between them, the flow of molten heat through her blood, followed by the familiar panic encroaching intimacy always evoked. "This will never work. Your legs are broken, for Spirit's sake. And I'm no good at this, and I can't—"

"Stop it," he said firmly. "I'm not going to let you come up with a hundred reasons why we shouldn't make love. There's only one thing that will halt this, Celie."

His hand moved up, capturing her face and turning it toward him. Even in the dim light she could see the glint in his eyes, feel his gaze probing the depths of her soul . . . and delivering a staggering blow to the demons there.

"Tell me you don't want me," he said huskily. "Look at me and tell me you don't want me and I'll stop."

He was already seducing her, she realized. With his eyes and his voice; with his touch and his words. The sizzling chemistry intensified the effect, as did the surprising bonds of trust and camaraderie she and Rurick had forged. They all worked in tandem, weaving a powerful net of need and desire. She *did* want him. While her mind frantically searched for a way to distance herself, her body was melting into his. Her heart pounded; her lungs struggled for air; heat pooled in her abdomen, and lower. Spirit help her, she couldn't lie to him.

"I can't tell you that," she whispered.

His eyes glittered, full of sensual promises. "Then you're mine. Here. Now."

He didn't give her an opportunity to protest further, launching into a sensual assault that sent her reeling. One arm around her shoulders pressed her sideways against him, while his other hand splayed across her cheek, pinning her head against his shoulder and tilting her face up. He held her still for deep, probing kisses that fanned the flames already stirred.

She clenched her hands, raising them. She should shove him away, should get off the bunk and move to the other side of the cabin. She should—His tongue stroked hers and his fingers slid down to tease the seam of her flight suit. By the Fires! Of their own accord, her hands unclenched and flattened against his chest. Instead of pushing him away, they curled against him.

She kissed him back, with a growing sense of inevitability that somehow dissolved every fear, every reason why she couldn't mate with him. How she could have gone from the certainty she would never mate with a man one moment to the total crumbling of her resolve the next was beyond her.

She only knew her desire was stronger than her resistance, that Rurick fostered a sense of trust and safety she'd never expected to find with any man. That the sudden freedom from her self-imposed constraints was a heady elixir. She felt no inhibitions or shyness as he stripped her top away. He'd already seen all of her, already touched her on Altair, as he touched her now, filling his hands with her breasts, stroking, teasing.

Because she knew what to expect now, anticipation thrummed through her, spurred by the erratic beat of her heart. She arched back as his lips traced a path down her neck and the slope of her breast, cried out when his mouth closed over her nipple. He sucked gently, and she felt the pull all the way down to her feminine core.

"Rurick," she gasped, fisting her hands in his hair.

"Celie," he whispered against her breast, "open to me."

His free hand slid between her thighs, nudged them apart, stroked her through the flight suit. Potent sparks of sensation shot through her body. She gasped again, and he pressed harder, rubbing the fabric against her, creating an excruciating friction. Need swept through her with terrifying intensity.

She clutched his arms, all equilibrium gone. "Rurick . . . slow down."

"Now why"—he slid up until his mouth hovered over hers—"would you want me to do that?" He kissed her, his tongue a merciless invasion. At the same time his hand smoothed upward over her abdomen, those clever fingers feathered beneath the waistband of her pants—sliding lower, lower over her quivering muscles, until he reached her female flesh. One finger stroked, circled, over and over, hurtling her toward a sensual explosion. Her breath caught, her body poised on the brink . . .

He withdrew his hand. "Take off your pants."

She felt as if the breath had been knocked out of her. For a moment she couldn't think straight. "What?"

"Take off your pants. They're in the way of what I have in mind."

"You were doing just fine with them on," she blurted, frustration eroding her dignity.

He laughed, and her ardor cooled a notch. She tried to push away, but he hauled her against him and held her tightly. "Ah, Celie, Celie. You are an amazing woman. A beautiful woman." He leaned down and nuzzled her ear. "An incredibly sexy woman. Sweetheart, in a perfect universe I could do this right. I could ply you with wine and flamelight and dancing. I could undress you slowly, lay you on the softest satin bed, kiss and taste every inch of you at my leisure. I could show you any number of mating positions. All without being hampered by two broken legs. Unfortunately, under the circumstances it's very difficult for me to do those things."

He nipped at her lips then soothed them with his tongue. "For now, the best I have to offer is one position, on a hard bunk in a wrecked ship, with a blizzard raging outside. But if you'll take off the rest of your clothing, and help me take off mine . . ." His hand covered her breast, teased her nipple. "I can promise you pleasure."

The sincerity and the hunger in his voice melted her annoyance and stoked her desire. "I'm holding you to that," she murmured, doing some nibbling of her own along his jaw. Then, because she herself had found it so pleasurable, she swirled her tongue in his ear, felt his surprised reaction. Lowering her hand between them, she cupped him. Now *there* was a reaction. He gasped and jerked, growing impossibly large and hard beneath her stroking fingers. "You're not going to stop me from touching you this time," she told him.

"No." His voice was definitely strained. "Matter of fact, I was going to insist on it."

"Then don't move," she whispered.

She slid off his lap. Kneeling beside him, she continued to stroke him with one hand while she slipped the fingers of her other hand beneath the seam of his shirt and slid it open. She ran her fingers along his chest. Despite the chill, he was incredibly warm, his nipples beaded into tight nubs. She might be totally inexperienced when it came to mating, but she figured what felt good to her would also feel good to him. She could gauge his reactions for guidance. Leaning forward, she swirled her tongue over his nipple, and he groaned. Oh, yes, he liked it. And she liked being able to affect him this way.

She pressed kisses along the muscular swells of his chest, continuing to caress and massage the straining hardness between his legs. The feel of him had the oddest effect on her, sending her pulse and breathing racing, heat tingling through every sensitive nerve in her body.

"Enough." He grabbed her wrists, moved her hands from his body. "Take off your pants. Now."

He sounded as breathless as she felt. She scooted to the edge of the bunk and removed her boots. Then she stood and faced him. He'd pulled off his shirt, and his magnificent chest was heaving. His eyes darkened to burnished gold, his heated gaze branding her as she slid her pants down and kicked them away.

"Stars, but you're beautiful," he murmured. He pressed his shoulders against the wall, arching his hips off the bed as he tried unsuccessfully to get his pants off. He collapsed back with a frustrated sigh. "Damned legs," he muttered. "Please help me out of this flight suit before I explode."

She did, waiting until he levered himself up on his arms and she could yank the pants down over his hips. He sprang free, and she stared, having never seen a naked man before. He was all sinew and muscle, breathtaking masculinity.

253

He lowered his rear to the bunk and leaned forward, jerking the fabric to the tops of the portamedics. Her mouth dry, Celie started to unfasten the units, but he stopped her.

"No," he bit out. "Come here." She knelt on the bunk and he lifted her over him, positioning her so that she straddled him. "Where were we?" he murmured, trailing his fingers up the inside of her thigh. "Ah, yes. Now I remember."

He remembered very well. He found the heart of her need, touched and stroked, until all she could think about was the building tension, the urgent need for what he'd given her on Altair. She trembled, on the verge of release, and he suddenly withdrew his fingers. She groaned, then gasped as he shifted beneath her, and she felt a much different hardness pressing against her. Pleasure gave way to a burning, tearing sensation.

"Oh." She tensed, gripping his arms. She'd forgotten that mating was usually painful the first time.

"Sorry, sweetheart." He pressed kisses along the corner of her mouth. "I know it hurts. Try to relax."

"Easy for you to say," she muttered, but forced air into her lungs. He slid deeper, and she automatically clenched around him.

He groaned, resting his forehead against hers. "Stars, you're so tight. I hope I don't embarrass myself in about thirty seconds."

"You'd better not." She wiggled slightly, her breath catching as he filled her even more.

"Almost there." He raised her chin. "Kiss me."

She did, taking his face between her hands and giving back to him everything he'd taught her. He grasped her hips and lifted her, then slowly lowered her down on him. He filled her completely now, stretching her with a fullness that bordered on real pain. She rested her forehead against his.

"Are you all right?" he asked against her hair.

She took a few deep breaths, nodded.

"It will get better. Much better," he promised. He lifted and lowered her again. It still hurt, but not as much. He continued to guide her slowly, and she started using her legs to move herself.

Pain faded to sharpening pleasure. Blindly, she again sought his mouth, letting out a small moan as his tongue duplicated the mating pattern. He slid one hand between them and stroked right above where they were joined. Electricity jolted through every cell in Celie's body. Oh . . . Spirit. She tore her mouth away and dropped her head back, totally focused on the sensation of him filling her, the glorious friction as she moved on him. Up, down . . . more . . . more . . . oh, Spirit!

She climaxed with an explosion of light and color, the sound of Rurick's hoarse cry reverberating through her. The aftershocks seemed to go on and on. Finally, his grip on her hip relaxed and she collapsed bonelessly against him. He stroked her back as the sound of their labored breathing slowed, and the throbbing sensations in her body diminished to a warm, satiated glow. If she was going to die, she thought, this wasn't a bad way to go.

Sitting on the edge of the bunk, Rurick watched Celie put another power pack in the generator. There was one left, and no sign of the storm outside abating. Three Tobals hovered over the generator, inspecting the new pack and emitting a rapid series of beeps. Two of the creatures were fluttering above his portamedic units. They didn't seem to care that the units had no more power.

The situation was grim, but not impossible. They had two more cycles of generator heat; then they could use the insulated space suits. They had enough food and water to last at least ten more cycles, and Toba's oxygen, while thin, was sufficient. All they needed was a break in the weather so Riordan rescue ships could land. Rurick had no doubt Max and Zane were looking for him and Celie. Loyal to the core, neither android nor human would rest until they found him. It was a good feeling to be so revered.

If only a certain stubborn female would do a little revering.

He knew better than to declare his growing feelings for Celie. She would run like a startled elderdeer if he moved too fast. She might try to convince herself she was only interested in experimenting with mating, but she was fooling herself. She might have mated with an android without emotional ties, but not with a human male. Once she learned Rurick wasn't an android, she'd steadily resisted the compelling chemistry between them. For her to come to him, for them to make love, could only mean she had developed feelings for him—whether or not she was willing to admit it. Those emotions, while exactly what he wanted from her, were also what terrified her.

He fully intended to capitalize on those feelings, as well as on their current predicament. Their situation wasn't ideal, but it had proved a major opportunity to woo and seduce Celie. He held her close each night—the necessity of sharing body heat another crystal opportunity—they talked, each sharing bits of their souls, weaving invisible bonds. He'd convinced her to mate with him, which she had done with breathtaking sensuality and abandon, claiming his heart in the process.

It was a start . . . but he realized the battle had just begun. Already, she was again distancing herself, rebuilding emotional barriers. She hadn't been in the bunk when he awoke this morning, and their conversation had been formal and stilted. He'd just have to keep tearing down the barriers. He was a patient and methodical man, used to having his way. No reason to believe any differently where Celie was concerned.

He watched her standing in the center of the chamber, her arms wrapped around herself. "Captain, you look cold." He patted the edge of the bunk. "Come share my warmth."

She hesitated. "I'm not that cold," she hedged.

"Then at least sit down for a while. We both tire easily in this atmosphere. There's nothing that needs to be done right now." He patted the bunk again, and she slowly walked over, easing down beside him. He reached out and touched her face. "You *are* cold. Come here." He hitched himself back on the bunk, swinging his legs onto the pad. "Come."

She followed rather reluctantly, and he settled her against his side, tugging the blanket over them. They lay there quietly, the combined heat of their bodies mingling. He stroked her hair, felt the increase in her heart rate. His matched it, as the chemistry between them flared.

"Yesterday was very special," he said softly. "I will always cherish the memory."

He felt her tension escalate—whether from embarrassment or reluctance to think about mating with him, he didn't know. But she'd better get used to thinking about it; he was determined it wouldn't be a one-time event. "How do you feel?" he asked.

"Fine," she murmured, trying to shift away.

He tightened his arm around her. "Are you sore?"

She hesitated, then he felt the barely perceptible shake of her head. "Not really."

"Good." He brought his hand down and cupped her breast. Her chest heaved with her indrawn breath, and erotic energy surged around them.

"Rurick—"

He halted her protest with a kiss. He ran his hands over her, his touch both possessive and gentle, telling her without words how much pleasure she gave him. He felt the increasing tension and heat in her body, rejoiced when her tongue dueled with his. He pulled away, whispered, "Give over to me, Celie." Sensing her indecision, he lowered his forehead to rest against hers. "I want you so much it hurts."

Her hand crept up between them, stroked his chest, lingered over his pounding heart. "I don't think this is a good idea." Her voice was deeper, huskier.

"The only way to know is to give it a try." He stroked her breast, pressed kisses against her neck.

With a little moan, she arched against his hand and pulled his face up to hers. She kissed him, tasting of passion and need. Thanking the gods for this gift, he sank onto the bunk with her, immersing himself in the taste and texture and satiny curves of Captain Celie Cameron.

They rested quietly together on the bunk. They had been two cycles without heat or power of any kind. The spacesuits they wore were well insulated, but without oxygen packs they couldn't close the face shields completely. If they opened the shields fully, bitter cold seeped in. If they closed them too much, the plexishield fogged and the quality of the air they breathed was poor. The suits were lightweight and flexible, but they weren't designed to be lived in. Rurick couldn't feel Celie's warmth against him, although he could still hold her.

Outside, the storm raged. Inside, almost total darkness blanketed the ship, except for a few patches of hazy light penetrating the cracks in the hull. The Tobals continued to buzz around the cabin, sometimes hovering over Celie and Rurick, their beeps rising and falling in an odd cadence. Their leaf offerings littered the bunk.

There wasn't much Celie and Rurick could do, so they spent most of their time on the bunk, their heads together as they talked. Rurick shared the details of his life: his childhood punctuated with learning to become a king and the royal duties entailed; his mother dying when he was six, his father remarrying when he was eight, and the births of Kalina and Sev. He glossed over the animosity his stepmother and Kalina had displayed toward him, and the hurtful ways they had insulted his mother's memory over the seasons. Nor did he talk about his own restlessness, his concern that once he was tied to the throne, its duties and demands would suffocate him. He took his obligations very seriously, though, and would do what was necessary to uphold the honor of the royal family.

Celie shared information on some of her life, with very obvious omissions about her father and the time spent with the Shadower who had won Celie and her sister Moriah in a game of chance. She talked mostly about Moriah and the community on Risa, which had been carved from a barren terrain and turned into a lush, thriving landscape. She also shared a little about her smuggling activities.

Neither of them was quite ready to bare the most painful aspects of their lives, but it was a start. Someday, Rurick thought, Celie would trust him enough to tell him everything, and he would do the same. In the meantime, they discovered they still had much to talk about.

They must have dozed off. Rurick awoke with a start, a blinding light in his eyes leaving him momentarily disoriented. Raising his hand to block the light, he felt Celie stirring beside him.

"Your Highness," came Commander Zane's excited voice. "You're alive!"

Thank the gods. "Shine that light elsewhere." Rurick sat up. "We've been in the dark several cycles now, and our eyes will have to adjust."

The light was immediately averted, and Rurick stood, waiting for his legs to steady. He offered Celie his hand and helped her to her feet, supporting her as she found her balance. They were both weaker than he had realized. He looked toward Zane's familiar figure and the others standing behind him, silhouetted in their deflected lights. "Commander, you don't know how glad we are to see you—all of you."

They were on the *Riordan Spirit,* the flagship used when the entire royal family traveled. It had been chosen by Max and Zane because it had the most comprehensive medical bay, and they had feared the worst. Yet outside of his broken legs, Rurick's injuries weren't serious—mild frostbite on his face, a little dehydration, cuts, and bruises. His condition were readily treated, and ultra-flex casts placed on both legs. He was finally able to bend his knees again. Daily treatments would see the casts off completely by the time they reached Sarngin.

Celie had been treated for mild frostbite and dehydration, then taken to a private cabin. Reassured that she was fine, Rurick ignored the physicians' urging to rest, stopping only long enough to shower and put on a clean flight suit. Feeling halfway human again, he called a meeting with Max and Zane. Within moments, they were gathered around the conference table in Rurick's large cabin.

"You're looking much better, Your Highness," Zane said. "It's good to have you back."

"It's good to be here. Thank you for coming to our aid. What happened to the Tobals that slipped onto the shuttle?"

"We finally captured all five of them," Max replied,

"although it took a concerted effort. They fly quite fast, considering the ratio of their flipperspan to their girth, and they were highly agitated. However, they are now in containers in the science lab."

"Keep me updated on their condition and the staff findings."

"Yes, sir." Max cocked his head, a surprisingly human gesture. "I am curious as to what happened to your ship, and how you ended up on Toba."

Renewed anger washed over Rurick as he thought about the treachery that had caused his ship to crash. "The computer system on my cruiser was sabotaged."

"Sabotaged?" Zane looked appalled. "Why do you think that?"

"There's no other way every system on the ship could have failed. Even the backup went down."

"Theoretically, that should be impossible," Max mused. "Yet if that is what happened, then you are correct about subversion. Only a very advanced program could cause total system failure. It would have to be quite complex and geared specifically for your systems. Which means whoever implemented it had inside information about the ship's computer specifications."

"Why in the universe would anyone do that to your ship?" Zane demanded.

"That's a very good question," Rurick answered. "And I intend to find out. Max, have my orders been followed?"

"Yes, sir. The computers were removed from your cruiser before we departed Toba and are in Bay One. I will personally analyze them to determine what happened, and possibly be able to ascertain who did this."

"I want a complete report as soon as you know anything." Rurick sat back, fatigue pulling at him. "Is there anything pressing that occurred while Celie and I were stranded on Toba?"

Max and Zane exchanged glances, and Zane frowned. "Your Highness, I'm sorry to tell you that your father had another relapse. His condition is much worse this time, and the physicians don't know what's wrong. They've never seen symptoms like his before."

Rurick's gut clenched. Despite the differences between them, he loved and respected his father. "Then we need to set course for Jardonia."

"You might wish to reconsider, until you hear the rest," Max said.

There was more? Cursing the events that had put him out of commission seven cycles, Rurick met Max's cool gaze. "Tell me."

"Regarding your father, I took it upon myself to contact Dr. Chase McKnight and ask him to travel to Jardonia to examine the king. After analyzing all available data on Dr. McKnight, as well as my personal observations, I determined there is a ninety-eight-point-six-percent probability that he is more knowledgeable and skilled in healing than are the Riordan physicians."

After witnessing McKnight's amazing abilities firsthand, and the way the man saved the dying colonists on Altair, Rurick felt his apprehension ease. "I agree. Dr. McKnight is possibly the most competent physician in the quadrant. Good decision."

Max inclined his head. "I am hoping that you will now consider going directly to Sarngin. I believe it to be urgent that you do so."

Rurick's inner alarms went off. "Why do you say that?"

"If I may?" Zane looked at Max, who nodded. The commander shifted his gaze to Rurick. "Your Highness, in your absence, Princess Kalina and Prince Sevilen traveled to Sarngin. The Council has already been called into session."

262

"What? Session isn't scheduled for five more cycles. Why was this done?"

Zane rubbed the back of his neck, looking as frustrated as Rurick felt. "We haven't been able to find out. But Princess Kalina arrived in time for the opening. And she . . ." He paused, his eyes narrowing with outrage. "The princess told the Council that your father was too ill to represent the Riordan government."

"I don't believe it. How could she have done that?"

"You weren't available for consultation," Zane pointed out. "When you weren't present at the opening of the session, Princess Kalina told the Council it was believed you had perished in a ship crash. In view of your father's illness and your absence, the Council appointed her the new Riordan representative."

Shock ricocheted through Rurick. None of this made any sense, but ominous suspicions nagged at him. Something was very wrong. He turned to the android. "You're right, Max. I want to go directly to Sarngin."

Max nodded. "I thought you might agree. We are already headed there."

Chapter Sixteen

Celie had hardly seen Rurick since they'd come aboard the *Riordan Spirit*; most of the time, he was in meetings with Max and Commander Zane. She hated meetings. Hated official mumbo jumbo and fitting into a rigid mold and expectations, which was why she'd felt so uncomfortable on Jardonia. Too much fuss for her tastes. Give her a fast ship and open space any cycle.

With nothing to fill her time, she explored the ship. To her delight, she discovered an atrium located in the aft part of the lower level. It was a miniature replica of the Jardonian gardens. A rose quartz fountain occupied the center, the domed ceiling had been painted like a sky, and skillfully hidden lighting imitated sunlight. There were even some giant butterflies drifting through the scented air.

A little bit of Haven, Celie thought, sinking onto a bench facing the fountain. The sudden longing for a sketch pad so she could draw this scene struck a painful chord. She'd had very little time to think about the loss of her ship and her artwork until now. Grief burned in her throat. She told herself she would not dwell on something she couldn't change. She willed her thoughts elsewhere, and they automatically shifted to Rurick.

Another subject she'd be smart to avoid, considering the way her body reacted at the mere thought of him. Not good. She sighed, knowing her innate honesty wouldn't allow her to gloss over her feelings for the crown prince. She had developed a strong attachment to him, cared deeply for him. Love? Surely not. She didn't dare consider the possibility. She could never love any man. She was emotionally crippled when it came to men, especially after what had happened with her father. The memory of that cycle rushed back at her, every horrifying detail as vivid as if it were happening again now.

A bone-deep cold chilled her, more harsh than the blizzards on Toba. No . . . no! She leaped from the bench and paced around the fountain, rubbing her arms and willing her breath to slow. That was all over, in the past. She couldn't undo it, even if she wanted to—and she wasn't sure she did. Faced with the same events and the same choices, she would do it again. Yet the events of that cycle had tainted her for the rest of her life. She would never be worthy to be any man's mate, much less the mate of a future king, assuming Rurick even wanted her. She had no idea of his true feelings, outside of obvious lust.

Another rush of memories sent a flood of heat through her body. She'd discovered a wanton side to her nature. She'd come alive with Rurick's kisses and caresses, reveled in their lovemaking, shed all inhibitions and joined her body with his in a wild abandon that shocked her. Now she craved his touch, yearned to experience every exquisite sensation again.

Blazing hells. Celie paced some more. She had to cut her losses quickly. She needed to help Moriah carry supplies to the destitute people in the ninth sector. It was selfish and futile to entertain unrealistic thoughts about Rurick when there was so much suffering she could help alleviate. She didn't deserve such happiness, and the ninth-sector colonists didn't deserve disease and starvation. She could do something about the latter.

"I thought I might find you here."

Rurick's voice behind her sparked an instant physical response—one she could not acknowledge. She turned slowly and drank in the sight of him. He filled out his gold flight suit beautifully, and the color enhanced his streaked hair and amber eyes. He looked tired, with hollows in his cheeks and circles beneath his eyes. She resisted the urge to go to him and smooth away the lines of fatigue and worry.

"This is beautiful," she said, gesturing around the atrium.

"It's my favorite place on this ship." He walked over and slid his arm around her. Intent glowing in his eyes, he leaned down. She tensed, turning her face; his lips grazed her cheek instead of her mouth. His arm dropped away and he straightened.

Avoiding his piercing gaze, she stepped back, rubbing her arms again. "You're walking much better in those ultraflex casts," she said quickly. "When will they be removed?"

"In two cycles." He moved forward and grasped her shoulder, halting her retreat. "What's wrong? Are you cold?"

She dropped her arms to her sides. "No. Just a nervous habit."

He raised her chin with his other hand, forcing her to look at him. "Why would you be nervous?"

His intensity and perceptiveness always unnerved

her. "I'm not. I'm . . . I guess I'm still recovering from our adventure."

That golden gaze pierced her. "Is that why you won't kiss me?"

Blazing hells. Time to end it now, before she was even more enmeshed. "No, it's not. Rurick, what happened between us on Toba was a mistake. It can't go any further."

His hand slid up to cup her face, his touch searing her skin. "You think mating with me was a mistake?"

She closed her eyes, struggled to find words. Blowing out her breath, she opened her eyes and met his gaze. "I only know we can't have a relationship. It's not possible, for too many reasons, some of which you already know."

"So, we start again," he murmured. "Like chipping away a layer of shale in the mines, only to find another, then another, yet knowing the precious crystal is there, beneath the layers."

She didn't like the sound of that, even if she wasn't certain of his meaning, so she took the offensive. "I don't think I should accompany you to Sarngin."

The color of his eyes cooled to a pale gold. "So, you're reneging on our agreement. I thought you were a person who honored her word."

"I am," she retorted, stung. "But consider the gist of the agreement. You wanted to mate with me, and you wanted us to spend time together. I think both objectives have been met."

"Is that how you define what we shared on Toba—meeting damned objectives?" Quiet anger filled his voice.

"I would like to think what happened on Toba was much more than that. Even so, there is nothing—*absolutely nothing*—to be gained from further association."

His eyes narrowed. "My answer is no," he said, a dangerous edge to his voice. "I will not release you from our agreement. You will accompany me to Sarngin. I command it."

His arrogant words sparked her own anger, yet she knew they had reached an impasse. Realizing heated words would only make the situation worse, she forced herself to answer calmly. "Since I have no choice, I'll go to Sarngin. But I'm not going to mate with you again." She held up her hand as he started to speak. "Please don't say anything else. It will only make matters worse. I'm not the woman you think I am. You deserve better. I'm sorry."

She turned and walked quickly from the atrium. As she slowed in the outside corridor and placed her hand against the wall for support, myriad emotions assailed her: regret, a sense of loss, aching loneliness. At this point, she wasn't sure if she was fleeing from Rurick or herself.

He had *ordered* her to accompany him. *Ordered!* She grew angry every time she thought about it. On some level, she knew her anger was a protective mechanism, but she held on to it. She needed every available weapon to extricate herself from this emotional web in which she was caught.

Looking down at the large sketch pad in her lap, Celie realized she'd ruined her drawing. Cursing, she tore the sheet from the pad, balled it up, and hurled it across the atrium. It went into the fountain, but she didn't bother to retrieve it.

Why did Rurick have to be so stubborn? Worse, why did he have to turn right around and do something nice, like having the paintings that had been salvaged from her ship mounted on the walls of her cabin? Or sending her paper and drawing implements?

Why had he touched her with such incredible tenderness and passion on Toba, ensuring that her first mating was a beautiful experience she would always cherish? And why couldn't she stop thinking about him? By the Abyss! She stared at the blank paper, holding her drawing implement in a death grip.

"I do not believe the fountain is a designated refuse receptacle."

She almost came off the bench. "Max! You startled me."

"I am sorry. That was not my intention." Humor gleamed in the android's eyes as he held out the dripping wad of paper. "I believe you will find a receptacle for this right outside the atrium entry."

Celie took the paper and dropped it on the growing pile beside the bench. "Sorry. Were you looking for me?"

"Yes. May I join you?"

"Of course." She scooted over and made room for him. He looked so much like Rurick that she still found it disconcerting. However, his eyes didn't contain the sensual warmth, and his facial features weren't quite as expressive. His voice didn't have quite the same deep, rich timbre. And he wasn't as arrogant.

He settled next to her. "We will arrive at Sarngin in approximately ten hours. His Highness thinks, and I concur, that it would be wise to brief you on what to expect."

"I've been to Sarngin before. What will be different?"

"To begin with, if you agree, you will be registered as the prince's envoy. You would only be cleared for General Council meetings and would not have voting privileges."

"Why would Rurick want me to be an envoy?"

"So that you may observe the Council members."

Celie's interest stirred. "Looking for information on the ninth-sector cover-up?"

"Exactly," Max said. "Also, you might like to know that the Enhancers have sent a contingent from Shamara, asking for representation on the Council."

"That's interesting. I didn't think they would get involved."

"Apparently, Shielder colonies have convinced them of the necessity. We have been informed that Jarek san Ranul and his mate, Eirene, are also attending the session. Raven is there as well."

"Raven is on Sarngin? Where are Chase and Nessa?"

"Dr. McKnight is on Jardonia, treating King Domek, and his mate is assisting him."

"What's wrong with the king? Why is Chase treating him?"

"King Domek has had a relapse," Max explained. "The Riordan physicians cannot determine the problem. The king is gravely ill and growing worse. I felt it wise to summon Dr. McKnight, as he has superior healing skills to our own physicians."

"That was a good decision. Chase is the best there is." Celie felt a twinge of concern for Rurick. She knew he loved his father. "Please tell Rurick I'm sorry about the king."

"I will do that."

"Is there anything else?" she asked.

"Not at this time. We will keep you informed on future developments, if you agree to be an envoy."

"All right. I'd like to help any way I can." Even if it meant she had to work closely with Rurick.

A low beep came from Max's arm. He pushed back his sleeve to reveal a built-in comm. "Max here."

"Where are you?" Rurick's voice came over the unit.

"I am in the atrium, with Celie."

270

"I want both of you to report to the science lab immediately."

"Yes, sir." Max switched off the comm, and he and Celie headed for the lab.

"What do you think is going on?" she asked as they walked along a gleaming corridor.

"It probably has something to do with the Tobals," Max surmised.

He was right. The science lab was large and busy, with a dizzying array of humming equipment. But the focus of the technicians and Rurick was on the Tobals. Three of them were inside a large glass cage, lunging blindly against the glass and emitting high, panicked chirps. Hitting the side would knock them to the bottom of the cage, but they'd shoot back up and charge the glass again and again.

The other two Tobals were in a smaller glass warming unit. They lay on a white pad, barely fluttering. Two technicians, their arms inserted through attached, heavy-duty medical sleeves, were examining the creatures.

"We've had to keep them sedated to prevent this behavior," the head technician, whose badge identified him as Brader, explained. "But as soon as the medication wears off, they start this again. We're afraid to give them much more sedative, as it might kill them." He gestured toward the two prone creatures. "I'm afraid it's too late for these."

Horror and pity welled inside Celie. "Spirit, the poor things." She watched the three frantic Tobals battering the glass. "It will certainly kill them if they keep smashing into the sides like that. Rurick, we have to do something."

"We've lost this one," a female tech announced, her protective glove resting on a still form in the warming unit.

271

"Oh, no," Celie murmured, her throat tightening.

"Interesting," Max mused. "It appears the Tobals cannot tolerate captivity. Being enclosed in a foreign environment incites a state of panic that ultimately kills them."

"Release them immediately," Rurick ordered.

Brader hesitated. "Your Highness, we don't know anything about these creatures. They could be dangerous."

"They're not," Rurick said. "Release them now. They're to have free range of the lab until we can decide what to do with them."

Brader opened the cage door, and the three Tobals streaked out and began zooming in frantic patterns over the equipment. The female tech opened the warmer and lifted out the live Tobal, setting it on a nearby console. It wobbled unsteadily, emitting a low chirp.

Celie moved to the warmer and gently touched the dead Tobal. She stroked its soft gray fur, tears filling her eyes. Poor little thing. It hadn't deserved for its life to end like this, in captivity and absolutely terrified. Saddened, she started to turn away but felt the faintest of movements. She froze, not daring to believe it was anything. Yet there it was again, a flutter against her palm. The Tobal stirred, let out a weak chirp. "It's alive." Celie scooped the creature into her hands and turned carefully. "Oh, Rurick, it's still alive!"

He reached down and stroked its fur, his large hand almost covering it. It beeped again. "It is alive," he said, his relief evident.

"Lay it back in the warmer," Brader instructed. "We'll keep it warm, but we won't close it in again."

Her mood much lighter now that she knew the Tobal might survive, Celie did as he directed. She stood back, watching as the furry creature struggled to its feet. Fear of captivity, the panic of being trapped and suffocated by a lack of freedom, had nearly killed it. She could definitely relate.

Rurick strode down the wide, arched corridor toward the massive double panels at the end. His boots made no sound on the thick white carpet. The walls were a pale gold, inlaid with exquisite holotiles and jewels from all over the quadrant. They did a good job here on Sarngin of camouflaging the monitors and sensors reading his every move. Around him, the air shimmered with power. For power was definitely wielded here, in this high-security section of the Collassium, where the Interstellar Council conducted business in exclusive meetings.

Only twenty-one members sat on the Council, which was headed by Regent Mandek Comar and Vice Regent Verene Tasia. The regent and vice regent held the most power, and were elected by the members of the General Council. They served a ten-season term, which could be extended by re-election. Both Comar and Tasia were nearing the end of their second terms. To ensure equality and fairness, the remaining nineteen members of the Council were chosen by a lottery system for a term of three seasons. They could serve more than one term, but not consecutively.

King Domek preferred to stay out of the interstellar political arena, so Rurick had been the Jardonian representative to Sarngin since he was twenty-two. He had served two full terms on the Council, the last ending a year ago. Currently, he was merely a voting representative. That made it more difficult to gain access to the inner workings of the Council to see who might be involved in the ninth-sector cover-up.

Gods, he wasn't even a voting member of the General Council at this point! The thought of Kalina holding that position for Jardonia was infuriating. She didn't have the experience to deal with the power games of the Council. He didn't know what she was playing at, but she would have to step down. He was very much alive and fully intended to resume his rightful place on the General Council. He stopped before the double panels, which were framed by intricate wood carving trimmed in gold gilt, and stared into the retinal scanner.

"Greetings, Crown Prince Maximilian Rurickko Riordan of Jardonia," a melodic, female computer voice intoned. "How may I serve you?"

"I wish an audience with Regents Comar and Tasia. It is a matter of grave importance."

"One moment, please."

Rurick waited impatiently, a growing sense of wrongness weighing heavily inside him. He could see how the Council might have granted Kalina the status of Jardonia's voting envoy, in light of his being missing in a ship crash and King Domek being incapacitated, especially with session starting. But he would expect the situation to be reversed immediately when he turned up alive and well.

The computer's voice whirred back on. "I apologize profusely for the wait, Prince Riordan. Regents Comar and Tasia will be able to see you at fourteen hundred hours, on the eighth cycle."

"But that's four cycles away!" Rurick protested. "Session will be over by then."

"I am sorry, Your Highness. The regents are very busy at this time, and have graciously agreed to work you into their schedule at fourteen hundred hour—"

"Then I wish to see Emissary Karon immediately." Jade Karon was the next most powerful member of the Council, having served four full terms, and also a term as the world president of Jartan, a huge planet with several billion inhabitants. Rurick had known the emissary since his youth. He trusted her.

"One moment, please."

As he waited, Rurick pondered the issue of trust. True, he had always trusted Emissary Karon, but the past season had clearly shown that many things were not what they appeared to be. He'd have to be cautious, even with her.

"Again, I apologize most profusely for the wait, Prince Riordan. The High Council is meeting right now, so Emissary Karon is unavailable. She will be delighted to converse with Your Royal Highness at oh ten hundred hours tomorrow."

Rurick hadn't really expected either of the regents or Emissary Karon to leave a High Council session. He would have to be satisfied with a meeting in the morning. In light of the precautions he was being forced to take, he decided he'd ask Eirene san Ranul or one of the other Enhancers visiting Sarngin, to visit Jade Karon with him. "I will be there. Please tell the emissary that I will be escorted by several advisers."

He turned and strode away, not waiting to hear the computer's convoluted closing comments. Suspicious events were occurring at a dizzying rate, and he had to unravel them quickly. His thoughts flashed to Celie. Unfortunately, he'd had no time to deal with her reluctance regarding him, or her fear of relationships, no doubt fueled by the scars of her youth. He'd decided that perhaps it was best to give her some time; but only so much. Hopefully, she would miss him as badly as he missed her. When this political mess was straightened out, he intended to stake a claim—a permanent one.

His next step was to attend the fourth cycle of the general session, which was beginning within the hour, and issue his challenge in a public forum. If the High Council would not hear his case, then he would present it before the General Council.

He stepped through the security points leading in and

out of the Council chambers. Max and Zane and three soldiers awaited him. "I did not expect you back so quickly," Max said as Rurick approached the group.

"I didn't either. I was denied an audience with the regents for at least four cycles."

Surprise flashed across Max's face. "That is strange."

"Yes, it is. Something is way off kilter here, but we don't have time to analyze it. Come on." Rurick turned toward the stately hallway that led into the massive meeting hall of the General Council. "We're going into the general session."

Max and Zane and the soldiers kept pace with Rurick's rapid stride. As they approached the first of four checkpoints into the hall, Zane and his men dropped back, where they would wait.

Rurick turned to Max. "I want you to run full holocordings of the entire session."

"Yes, Your Highness."

Taking a deep breath, Rurick entered the checkpoint, Max right behind him. The first battle was beginning.

Celie found the chaos of the General Council hall overwhelming. Granted, it was a controlled bedlam, with representatives and their envoys and escorts entering through pre-assigned entryways. All seating was reserved, each government assigned an enclosed box with multiple seats. The more important and influential the representative, the larger the box, and the closer to the lower level.

The Riordan box was on the bottom, and held ten plush, gold-gilded seats. Each chair had controls in the armrests, and a wraparound surface containing a computer and more controls. Headsets plugged into one arm, ensuring that the session could be heard, and in the language selected. Seven other people were currently in the Riordan box, and still there was ample room to move around.

Celie stared up the steeply rising levels of box seating, too many to count. She could barely see the top of the huge circular hall, and looking up gave her a feeling of vertigo. She turned her attention to the white marble platform in the center of the lower level. Twenty-one thronelike chairs were arranged in four semicircular rows, two in the front, the rest split as evenly as possible. Massive viewscreens hung in the center of the hall, facing six different directions to ensure that even those in the highest levels could see the proceedings. She'd never seen anything like it, nor so many people in one enclosed space. Not even the Elysian marketplaces could compare.

"What do you think, Captain?"

She started at the sound of Rurick's voice and turned to face him. Even though there were other people in the box, he was staring straight at her. Her mouth went dry at the sight of him, tall and handsome, resplendent in a purple dress uniform, a gold and silver sash across his broad chest. She'd thought she had her reactions to him under control, especially since they'd hardly seen each other the past few cycles. But her traitorous body refused to be corralled, with her heart speeding up and a rush of desire slamming through her. She glanced at Eirene and the other two Enhancers. Blazing hells. No way they could have missed her emotional maelstrom.

"Rurick!" With a little squeal, Raven launched herself at him, wrapping her arms around his waist. "I was so worried when Max told me your ship's communications had gone down, and you hadn't arrived at Sarngin." She grinned up at him mischievously. "Later, you'll have to tell me all about being stranded on an uninhabited planet with Celie. She refuses to talk about it."

"Does she, now?" Rurick squeezed Raven's shoulders, but his gaze locked with Celie's. A wealth of sensual memories glowed in his eyes. The Enhancers were probably getting quite a mental picture.

"Really! Such a display is very . . . plebeian," Kalina sniffed.

Rurick turned toward his half sister, his expression hardening. "Kalina."

"*Brother*," she answered, spitting out the word as if it were something despicable. "I see you survived the ship crash. How fortunate."

Rurick's eyes narrowed. "Very fortunate indeed."

Celie's chest tightened in anger. Max had told her about Kalina's actions when the news came that Rurick was missing. The princess hadn't even waited for the communication to fade away before she'd rushed to Sarngin and declared herself the Riordan representative.

"Rurick, how is your father?" Celie asked, trying to move the topic to hopefully safer ground.

Rurick stared at Kalina a moment longer before turning to Celie. "Much improved. I spoke with Dr. McKnight this morning, and he reported that the king's condition has stabilized. He's still running tests to determine the cause of the illness."

"I'm glad to hear that." It seemed strange talking to Rurick about his family, as if nothing had happened on Toba; as if she weren't desperately trying to wall off her feelings for him. She turned toward the others in the box. "I'd like to present Commander Jarek san Ranul, the leader of the Shamara colony, and his mate Eirene."

"I've met the commander." Rurick shook Jarek's hand and nodded at Eirene. "It is an honor to meet you, Lady Eirene. This is my chief adviser, Max."

Eirene, ethereal and beautiful with her flowing black hair and sky-blue eyes, and glowing from the new life growing inside her, smiled serenely. "My pleasure, Your Highness; Max." She gestured toward the other two Enhancers. "This is Elder Skell Morven and Lady Sarine Noura. They have applied for representation of the Enhancer settlement near Shamara."

Enhancers did not touch casually because they were such sensitive empaths. They only used physical contact when they were healing or channeling. Rurick appeared to know this, as he merely nodded at Elder Morven and Lady Sarine. "An honor to meet you. I'm glad you've decided to have a voice in governing the quadrant."

"While we would prefer to distance ourselves from the machinations of the physical world, we realize that is not always possible," Elder Morven, a middle-aged man with a shock of midnight hair and the typical blue Enhancer eyes, replied. "We will strive to stay informed of events in the quadrant."

Sevilen, who had risen from his chair, gave Rurick a stiff hug that was unusually demonstrative for the reserved Riordans. "I'm glad to see you, brother. Thank the gods you're safe."

Rurick clasped Sevilen's shoulders, genuine warmth and affection in his expression. "I'm glad too. I'll fill you in later." He turned back to the visitors. "The session should be starting very soon."

Raven quietly stepped away from Rurick and Sevilen, moving to the chair on the other side of Celie. She did it so unobtrusively, only Celie suspected it was to avoid the younger prince. The animosity that simmered between Raven and Sevilen, as well as that between Rurick and Kalina, had to be stressful for the Enhancers. Even though they were adept at shielding themselves, it would be hard to completely avoid emotional bombardment from all directions.

"Thank you for letting us use your box to observe the session," Jarek was saying to Rurick. "This is much nicer than the Shielder box, which is at the very top."

"You'll get better seating as you gain seniority." Rurick gestured to the chairs. "Shall we sit down? You might need a few moments to learn how to operate the controls." He looked meaningfully at Jarek. "We'll discuss details of other matters in my private chambers."

Three loud gongs reverberated through the Collassium, announcing the opening of the session. Rurick slid into the unoccupied chair on Celie's right. "Do you have any questions, Captain?" he asked softly.

Trying the ignore the effect his voice had on her, she shook her head. "No, I think I know how all these controls work."

The gongs sounded again, drawing her attention back to the center of the arena. The regent and vice regent, dressed in flowing white robes, strode onto the marble platform, followed by the blue-robed Council emissaries. The regents and emissaries took their seats, then Regent Comar announced the session was open.

A lengthy list of business matters, running the spectrum from zoning and beautification edicts to major trade regulations and legal actions against transgressors, was brought up for discussion. Various representatives were recognized, in order of seniority, to state their views on whatever topic was currently being debated. The dialogues were transmitted through the headphones, while huge viewscreens pictured the current speaker.

Once, when Celie removed her headset, she heard thousands of keypads clicking as the GC representatives transmitted their votes to the console on the marble platform. Max had explained that, as a rule, the Council honored the votes on most issues but had the power to override with a majority vote of the regents and emissaries. The system was weighted, with the regents' votes counting for a higher percentage.

Oddly enough, neither Rurick nor Sevilen could vote. Only one voting representative was allowed per acknowledged government, and Kalina was now the designated Jardonian. However, appointed envoys could bring up new business. Celie felt certain Rurick must be angry and frustrated with the turn of events, yet he appeared calm and collected as he entered his request to speak and waited for his turn.

When it finally came, he rose and addressed the huge gathering. "Regent Comar, Vice Regent Tasia, Emissaries, esteemed members of the General Council. Most of you know me, as I have served two terms on the Council and have been a voting representative on the General Council over the last ten seasons. My father, King Domek, has always been Jardonia's designated alternate representative if I could not attend a session.

"Due to an unfortunate series of events, neither my father nor I were able to be here when this session opened. Princess Kalina graciously stepped forward, and the Council appointed her the Jardonian voting representative in my stead. But now I am here, quite capable of serving. I respectfully request that Jardonian representation be reverted to me."

"No!" Kalina protested, coming to her feet. "I object. Representation should not be returned to him."

"Princess Kalina, do you have grounds for your protest?" Regent Comar asked.

She lifted her chin haughtily. "I do indeed. Rurick is not the rightful heir to the Riordan throne. I am."

At this pronouncement, thousands of voices buzzed through the great hall. Rurick looked at Kalina as if she had suddenly gone mad. Celie wondered what the princess could possibly hope to accomplish with such an accusation.

Standing tall and upright at the special podium on the platform, Regent Comar seemed unaffected by Kalina's shocking pronouncement, or the uproar. He raised his hands and requested silence before continuing. "On what basis?" he asked in his sonorous voice.

"On the basis of the Orior laws, Your Lordship."

"What?" Rurick's voice boomed out. "The Orior laws are obsolete. They haven't been in force in over a hundred seasons."

Kalina flashed him a triumphant smirk. "They've never been removed, or declared void. Therefore, they're still in effect."

"That has no bearing here," Rurick answered. "Regent Comar, I again ask that I be reinstated as the Jardonian Council representative."

"You have no right," Kalina sneered. "The Orior laws are based on maternal succession. They state quite clearly that Jardonian citizenship and the Riordan royal line is determined through its women. A person must be born to a Jardonian woman to be a legal citizen, and to a female of the Riordan line to be eligible to ascend to the throne."

She flashed Rurick a triumphant smirk. "Your mother was a commoner, not even born in Jardonia. Which means you're not a Jardonian citizen. She wasn't Riordan; therefore, neither are you. You can't ascend to the throne, much less be a Jardonian representative. I am the firstborn daughter of King Domek and Queen Amaris, and she is both a Jardonian citizen and from the Riordan line. *I* am the heir to the throne."

The roar of voices immediately started again, while Celie simply sat there, too shocked to react. Rurick appeared stunned as well; he stared at Kalina with a look of utter amazement. She cocked a brow at him, smiling openly now. Fury replaced Celie's shock. Rurick had more honor in his little finger than Kalina had in her entire body.

Sevilen had leaped to his feet at Kalina's shocking

announcement. In two strides, he reached his sister and glared at her, his hands clenching. "You go too far!" he growled.

Kalina's mouth compressed into a hard line. "Watch it, brother. I'll soon be your queen."

"Silence!" Regent Comar demanded. "Silence now, or I'll end this session."

Rurick waited until the commotion settled to a dull roar. "Regent Comar, the Orior laws haven't been observed in Jardonia for over a hundred seasons. They're invalid, and therefore Princess Kalina's claim is immaterial."

"I do not know that I agree with you," Regent Comar replied. "This is an unfortunate situation, one with many ramifications. I think the Council should discuss it and return a ruling at tomorrow's session."

His body ramrod stiff, Rurick reached out and gripped the banister circling the Riordan box. "I must protest, Regent Comar. It is not the Council's place to interpret the laws of individual governments."

"As a general rule, that is correct." The regent drew himself up, his narrow face resolute. "But the issue of representation *is* Council business, and we must be certain that only legitimate representatives are voting on issues that are crucial to every being in the quadrant. The Council will consider arguments from all parties involved. Submit your holostatements by twenty-two hundred hours this evening. We'll offer our ruling tomorrow."

It appeared Rurick was going to argue further, but after a moment's hesitation he nodded. He turned and left the box.

Celie sat there, still in shock. It occurred to her that the well-ordered, omnipotent government of the Verante constellation had just gone to Hades.

Chapter Seventeen

Raven left the Council session feeling ill. The long, tedious hours of the session and the tension in the Riordan box had left her with a headache. She begged off visiting with Celie and the others, agreeing to meet them for a late dinner in a few hours. Instead of returning to her room at the Sarnonian, she headed for the gardens flanking the Collassium. Hopefully some fresh air would clear her head. She walked through the entrance, drawing a deep breath of fragrant air. At this time of the cycle, the Collassium was basically empty, so the gardens were quiet.

They weren't nearly as spectacular as the ones on Jardonia, Raven thought, strolling down a winding path. The flowering blooms weren't as profuse and vivid, and although there were quite a few full-sized trees, there were no miniature ones. No wind chimes or any huge butterflies, either. The benches and fountains were marble instead of soothing crystal.

There were, however, charming gazebos scattered across the grounds, with circular marble walls halfway up and intricate gold latticework from there to the shimmering metal domes on top.

Intrigued, Raven took the path to her right, eager to explore a gazebo at the end, beneath an ancient Talipo tree. As she approached, she realized the gazebo was larger than she'd thought, with arched entryways on both sides. She mounted the marble steps, entering and discovering a cylindrical room with two opposing benches and . . . Sevilen Domek Riordan.

He sat on one of the benches, hunched forward dejectedly, his forearms resting on his muscular thighs as he stared at the intricately tiled floor. At Raven's involuntary gasp, he jolted upright. He looked as surprised and dismayed as she felt.

"Oh," she said, taking a step back. "You."

"You," he returned accusingly, as if she were a blight to be avoided at all costs.

She felt exactly the same way about him. "Excuse me," she said stiffly. "I have no intention of interrupting. I'll leave you to your self-absorption."

"Good idea." Then the rest of her words must have sunk in, because his eyes narrowed. "Still rude, I see."

"Still obnoxious, I see," Raven retorted. She flounced out of the gazebo and started away, but slowed her steps. Something about Sevilen's expression, the despair she'd seen in his eyes before he'd recognized her, roused her compassion. She halted on the path, her mind urging her to leave the arrogant prince to his solitary musings; her heart telling her that he was in pain. She hated to see anyone suffer.

Shaking her head at her own softheartedness, she turned and walked back to the gazebo. She mounted the steps quietly. Sevilen had resumed his pose, only his

285

hands were clasped now, and he was staring at the wall. "Prince Sevilen," she said softly.

He turned his head, his expression wary. "What do you want?"

He *was* in pain. His eyes clearly reflected a soul-deep misery. Drawn like debris to a black hole, she slipped inside, taking the opposite bench. "Are you all right?" she asked.

"Why aren't you gone?" he shot back. "I thought you were leaving me to my own selfishness."

"I shouldn't have said that." She leaned forward, lightly touched his forearm. "I'm sorry about the conflict between Rurick and Kalina. It must be difficult for you."

He sat up, rubbing the bridge of his nose. "It's hard to believe Kalina would do this, and with our father so ill."

"But he's better, isn't he?"

"Yes." The young prince nodded, his expression pensive. "Dr. McKnight told Rurick that Father would recover. I hope he's right."

"If Dr. McKnight said that, then you have nothing to worry about. He's a wonderful physician, the best there is," Raven said. "I should know—he's my father."

Surprise flashed across Sevilen's face. "That's interesting. I wondered how Rurick knew him."

"Trust me. If anyone can cure King Domek, my father can."

"That's good to know. I wish he could cure the situation on Sarngin. I certainly haven't been able to help." Sevilen sighed. "I tried to get an audience with Regent Comar, or anyone on the Council who would talk to me, but no one would see me."

He looked utterly dejected. Raven moved to sit on the bench beside him. "Don't feel badly. I don't think this is a situation you can fix. I'm not sure anyone can."

He leaned against the wall, stared up at the interior dome. "You're probably right. I feel so helpless sometimes, like I'm so far down the line that what I think or say has no influence on anyone. I'm just an irritating interruption." He glanced at her. "You seem to think so."

She had implied as much to him, and now she regretted her hurtful words and actions. "I'm sorry I pushed you into the fountain. It was childish of me. I was distraught when I did it."

"I don't even know what I said to provoke you."

She felt that she owed him an explanation, although she wasn't sure he would ever understand the fundamental differences in their philosophies regarding civil rights. "It wasn't what you said as much as your attitude toward other sentient beings, which I believe includes androids."

He threw up his hands in frustration. "They're machines."

"We could argue whether or not artificial intelligence is a viable life-form all night and never resolve that issue," Raven replied. "But that's not what upset me so badly on Jardonia. It was your attitude toward *humans*—those who serve you and your family in various capacities. How did you put it . . . something about inferior humans in your society who must be designated to a lower class, although you did admit they had 'some value'."

Sevilen looked genuinely perplexed. "What's wrong with that? I do believe they have value, and I certainly don't condone terminating human life."

She suspected his attitude was more ignorance than true indifference or a lack of compassion. How could she make him understand? She placed her hand on his arm. "Sevilen—"

"Call me Sev. Most people do." He turned toward

287

her, sliding her fingers from his arm and into his own large hand. "Continue."

His flesh was warm, distracting. She forced herself to concentrate on what she was trying to say. "When people or societies begin to think that others are inferior, it starts a dangerous precedent."

"What sort of precedent?" He watched her, his golden gaze intent. She'd never realized how nice his eyes were, or noticed the burning intelligence in them. Maybe she could make him understand.

"Oppression, subjugation . . . slavery," she said bluntly.

"I do not condone any of those things!" He sounded shocked. "Nor does anyone on Jardonia. Where did you come up with the idea of slavery? That doesn't exist anymore."

Her chest constricted and she battled to breathe. "Yes, it does."

"No, it doesn't. I've traveled throughout most of the quadrant and never seen even a hint of it."

She'd be willing to bet he hadn't been in the ninth sector. "Slavery does exist," she insisted. "Not in the Verante constellation, perhaps, but definitely in the quadrant where I used to live."

"I find that impossible to believe."

"Believe it. I know, because"—she closed her eyes, gripped his hand—"I was a slave for almost a year."

"Tell me you're joking."

"No," she whispered. "I wish I were."

The darkness of her past, never far away, rushed back to her with overwhelming intensity. To her dismay, hot tears flooded her eyes. Mortified, she swiped at them with her free hand. "I'm sorry to get so emotional," she gasped, a sob slipping out.

"It's all right." He patted her shoulder awkwardly, an

utterly endearing gesture despite her marauding memories.

With another sob, she hurled herself against him, burrowing into his chest. She sensed his surprise, felt his hesitation; then his arms closed around her, surrounding her with strength and warmth. The tears overflowed and streaked down her face, and several hiccuping sobs escaped before she had them under control.

"What . . . what can I do?" he asked, and she could hear the panic in his voice. Raven smiled despite herself. Like most men, a woman's tears apparently unnerved him.

"You're doing just fine." Reluctantly, she moved away from him with a shaky laugh. "That was a great hug, exactly what I needed. I'm sorry about crying all over you."

"Don't worry about it." He cleared his throat. "You're all right now?"

She nodded, wiping her eyes. "I've pretty much dealt with what happened to me, but every once in a while it gets the better of me."

He finally looked directly at her again. The concern in his eyes both surprised and warmed her. "I can well imagine. It's still unbelievable. I'd like to hear about it sometime."

"I'd like to tell you about it. Just not right now. There are too many other stressful things happening."

"That's true enough."

She leaned back against the marble wall, staring up at the domed roof and the tiny twinkling lights imbedded within it. Dusk must have activated them. Sev leaned back beside her.

"The lights are pretty," he commented.

"Yes, they are."

An awkward silence settled between them, as there

289

appeared to be nothing further to discuss. Raven was very aware of the young man next to her, of his heat and woodsy, masculine scent, of the robust energy he exuded. She was attracted to him, she realized. Maybe the tension between them was more than that of two essential strangers trying to make stilted conversation—an alarming thought. It might be a good idea to leave now. She rose. "I'd better be going. Celie and the others are expecting me."

"No," he protested, grabbing her hand. "Stay." As if realizing how imperious he sounded, he added, "Please."

As she stared at him, bemused by his adamant request, he flushed and said, "I don't feel so alone with you here."

"Really?" she asked, inordinately pleased that he wanted her to stay. He gazed into her eyes, and she found herself free-falling into their depths.

He tugged her closer. "Really."

"I can stay for a little while," she breathed, leaning closer. She'd never realized how appealing his lips were, that they looked extremely capable of kissing a woman senseless.

She wasn't quite sure how it happened, but a second later she was experiencing the feel of those lips against her own. And yes, Prince Sevilen Domek Riordan was quite capable in the kissing department. She sank nearer, savored the taste of him; the strength of his arm around her; the perfect way his other hand cradled her head as he kissed her with far more finesse than any of the young men on Shamara ever had.

She gloried in the reaction of his body against hers, the hard proof that he was as affected as she. At the same time, she realized they had to stop. As much as she wanted to continue enjoying his marvelous kisses, she had always prided herself on not being a tease. She had no intention of taking this any further, so she reluctantly pulled back. He followed, grasping her face in both hands, his mouth seeking hers again.

She pressed both hands against his chest. "We have to stop."

He looked at her, his gaze slightly out of focus. "Why?"

"I have to go." She shoved against him, but he didn't release her. She pushed again. "I *really* have to go."

He dropped his hands, and she scrambled to her feet. "I—" What did one say in a situation like this? *Thanks for the planet-shattering kisses. I'm now a quivering, senseless mass?* "I . . . It was . . ."

"Incredible." He took her hand, pressed it against his lips, and Raven's legs went weak. "Meet me here tomorrow."

"I don't know," she hedged.

"Little coward." Challenge glittered in his eyes.

She could handle him. *She* wanted *to handle him.* That thought shocked her, but she was unwilling to back away. "Tomorrow, then. Before session?" Daylight would be safer. Wouldn't it?

He nodded. "Twelve hundred hours, straight up?"

"All right. I'll see you then. Good night." She turned and left before she lost her nerve and changed her mind.

All the way back to the Sarnonian she tried to tell herself there was nothing between her and Sev. Tomorrow they would just talk, and she'd attempt to change his attitude about working-class citizens and androids. That was it. Absolutely.

Emissary Jade Karon, former world president of the largest planet in the Verante constellation, third most powerful person in the quadrant, sat behind her massive, ornately carved desk of rare Chelah wood. She was a striking woman with a strong, square face, high cheek-

291

bones, and intense black eyes. Her skin was firm, with virtually no lines. Her solid white hair was the only indication of her true age—and her lack of vanity.

Rurick sat opposite her, flanked by Eirene on one side and Elder Morven on the other. Eirene and Morven's hands rested lightly on the desk. Their touch there would amplify Jade Karon's emotions and thoughts, making it easier for the two Enhancers to read them. Jarek was seated on the other side of Eirene, and Max stood behind Rurick.

Jade shook her head. "This is a fine mess you're in, Rurick."

"At least we agree on that."

Sighing, she steepled her hands and pressed them against her chin. "I don't know if I can get you reinstated this session. Regents Comar and Tasia are set on investigating the Orior laws further, and they have a majority vote."

His gut clenched. "So they're going to rule in favor of Kalina."

She nodded, her expression unhappy. "For now. I think they are setting a horrific precedent. It's not the Council's job to arbitrate internal political disputes in a governing body unless the rights of the citizens are being violated. It's also my belief that archaic laws that are no longer observed should not be resurrected to further misplaced political ambitions. I have no idea why the Council would even consider Princess Kalina's claim. They should have sent both of you back to Jardonia to settle matters between yourselves."

Rurick couldn't have agreed more, though there wasn't time to fight Kalina over this. He leaned forward. "Emissary Karon, I must be reinstated on the Council *now*. I need to present some urgent matters, and I'd carry more weight as a representative."

"I'm sorry, but that's not going to happen." She

sighed, then leaned back in her chair. "For what it's worth, I think you'll get your position on the Council back, just not this session. Can you discuss these urgent matters with me? Perhaps I can present them to the Council on your behalf."

He considered for a moment, torn between challenging Kalina and the situation in the ninth sector. Urgency, along with a self-reminder of why the Enhancers had accompanied him to this meeting, won out. "What do you know about the ninth sector?"

She stared at him, seemingly confused. "Is something wrong in it?"

"You're not aware of any irregularities there?"

"No. The inhabitants in that sector want nothing to do with interstellar government and have refused to send representatives to Council for almost twenty seasons now. Surely you're aware of their isolationism. What's going on in the ninth sector?"

Rurick glanced at Eirene. She gave him the pre-arranged signal of smoothing her hand over her visitor badge. Elder Morven did the same. Their findings were negative. Jade apparently had no idea what was happening in the ninth sector. Rurick's own instincts concurred.

Drawing a deep breath and sending a quick prayer to the gods, he took the plunge and told Jade about his discoveries. He showed her videoholos Max had taken with his internal cameras—actual footage from Joba and Altair, and recorded testimony from Celie and Raven. Then Max gave his own testimony. Eirene and Morven kept their gazes on Jade's face the entire time, guaging the emissary's thoughts. Rurick knew they would signal him if they sensed anything amiss. Neither Enhancer gave any indication that Jade's thoughts were incriminating.

In fact, the emissary's reactions included incredulity,

shock, and anger, if her facial expressions were any indication. She held her silence, however, until Rurick finished speaking.

"My Creator," she said, pressing the fingertips of one hand against her forehead. "How can this be? And why?"

Rurick had spent a great deal of time wondering the same things. "I can only speculate. I believe it might be some sort of racial or ethnic discrimination, that peoples who have been labeled undesirables are being held virtual prisoners in their sector."

Jade paled. "Segregation of the weak from the strong, the propagation of a supreme race? But by whom? And how?"

Rurick shook his head. "I honestly don't know."

She leaned forward, her steely gaze probing his. "Are you, Max, Celie Cameron, and Raven McKnight prepared to testify before the Council?"

"Absolutely. However, I believe there may be another problem."

"And that is?"

"The fact that this has been successfully covered up for so long is very disturbing. I have to believe that some of the Council members are behind the situation."

All remaining color drained from Jade's face. "That is unthinkable."

"I agree, it is incomprehensible. But how else could something of this magnitude stay hidden for so long?" Rurick argued. "It would take someone very powerful to control the checkpoints in and out of the sector, to endorse mind tampering—and there's no other way to describe erasing someone's memory. Someone with the power to ensure that ship and communication components didn't get in, so that the people trapped there couldn't get out or communicate to anyone in another sector."

"Unthinkable," Jade said again. She rose and paced to the window behind her desk, her blue robe swirling around her. She stared out the window, seemingly deep in thought. "How else, indeed. As much as I hate—no, utterly *despise* the possibility—I have to admit you might be right."

She whirled, her eyes glittering with determination. "I've devoted most of my life to ensuring that the Verante constellation is a safe and equitable place for all. I'm not going to let some power-hungry supremacists ruin what the vast majority of Council members have worked so hard to achieve."

She strode back to her desk, tapped her finger on the wood. "How do we go about uncovering the perpetrators?"

Rurick glanced at Eirene, then Morven. Both nodded and stroked their badges. Jade was completely sincere in her response.

"I have a plan, Emissary Karon," he said. "What do you know about Enhancers?"

Jade looked toward Eirene, her brow raised. "I know that they can manipulate both natural and artificial energy, that they are somewhat empathic . . ." She paused, her gaze shifting between Morven and Eirene, then settling on Rurick. Her eyes narrowed and her mouth thinned. "You brought them here to spy on me."

He met her accusatory gaze steadily. "Let's say they're here to ascertain your loyalties. It was unethical, perhaps, but I had to be sure of you."

"It is also illegal, Prince Riordan," she said coldly. "Secretly tapping and recording events in any chamber in the Council wing is a crime. Enhancers might not be recording devices, but their ability to read minds puts them in the same category."

"Desperate times call for desperate measures," he replied. "Would it be illegal if you gave Lady Eirene and

295

Elder Morven permission to be present when you meet with the other Council members, and to read the members' responses?"

"Perhaps not, but it would be unconscionable."

"Not any more so than what's happening in the ninth sector."

Jade whirled and strode back to her window. She stared out, her body tense.

"Emissary Karon, may I speak?" Jarek asked. When the woman turned and nodded, he continued.

"My people fled from a quadrant rife with immorality, greed, and a darkness greater than I pray you'll ever know. In that quadrant all the power is held by a very small group, and I believe that was largely responsible for the heinous conditions there. The only way to ensure freedom is to have complete openness, and to allow everyone to share the power. Don't underestimate the dark side of human nature, and don't ever stop your vigilance. You must consider every avenue to bring an end to this situation, and quickly."

Jade clasped her hands together. "I'm afraid you're right." She turned to Eirene. "You are willing to use your powers to help us?"

"Yes, Your Ladyship," Eirene replied quietly. "Spirit gave me these gifts, and I believe I should use them to aid others whenever possible."

Jade looked at Elder Morven, and he nodded. "I will help. We cannot allow these atrocities to continue."

She released a heavy sigh. "I will allow this only because of the situation—and only this once." She turned a stern gaze on Rurick. "The Enhancers, or others like them, are never to be used in this way again unless the Council gives full consent. We can't allow this to become a precedent. It goes against every principle of morality the Council has worked for."

He nodded. "I agree completely."

"All right, then. I'll set up a meeting with the Council. And may Creator be with us."

Sarngin's two orange suns hovered overhead as Raven stood before the gazebo. She drew a deep breath and wiped her hands down her red silk dress, telling herself she'd chosen the form-fitting garment because she was attending session in two hours and *not* to impress Prince Sevilen Domek Riordan. She mounted the steps slowly. She was *not* nervous about seeing him again. They were going to talk, that was all—

Two strong hands grabbed her and dragged her inside the gazebo. She saw a flash of dark brown hair streaked with blond and amber eyes as two hard arms wrapped around her. She tried to speak, but was quickly silenced by Sev's mouth taking complete possession of hers.

No! She flattened her palms against his chest to push him away. But, oh, he tasted wonderful. . . . *No.* This was going way too fast. Oh, my . . . The man definitely knew how to use his tongue. A heady thrill ran through her. Who the heck wanted to talk, anyway? She slid her hands up to his shoulders.

He widened his stance, pulling her against his hips, and gave the kiss his full and talented attention. Where had the self-conscious young man from last night gone? Did he think she had come here for the purpose of satisfying his lust?

That thought brought back enough sanity for her to end the kiss and push away from him. "I'm glad to see you too—I think," she managed to get out. Why was she gasping like that? It was embarrassing.

He grinned and framed her face with his hands. "I thought about you all last night." He nipped her lips, exuding utter male confidence, then tried to claim her mouth again. She stepped away, and he frowned—but not before she saw the hurt flash across his face. So, he wasn't as confident as he appeared.

"I'm sorry if I put you off," he said stiffly.

Raven reached out and took his hand. "You didn't. It's just moving a little fast for me. I really am glad to see you." She tugged him toward the bench. "Could we sit and enjoy each other's company for a while?"

He relaxed a little, and a small smile flirted with his lips. Spirit, what a great mouth. Actually, the whole package was pretty impressive. "All right," he said. "As long as I can kiss you later."

"I'll insist upon it," she said. His smile broadened.

They settled on the bench. He slipped his arm around her, and she rested her head on his chest. It felt so right being here with him it was downright scary. It occurred to her that she might be falling in love with him, and her heart stuttered.

"What do you want to talk about?" he asked.

Up until this moment she'd hoped to continue their discussion about civil rights and Kalina's surprising claims. But now all she could think about was his kisses, and the fact that it was very likely he was too sexually advanced to be interested in an innocent like her.

"You probably have a lot of experience with women," she blurted, then wanted to kick herself.

He gave her an odd look. "I've been around many women, from all over the quadrant. I've escorted quite a few to various functions. I don't know if that constitutes a lot of experience."

She'd gone this far . . . might as well finish. Raven took a deep breath, then said, "I meant *sexual* experience."

Sev's brows drew together and his look was disapproving. "That question is highly inappropriate."

She relaxed, pleased that he wasn't the sort to boast about his sexual conquests, and also enjoying the fact that she'd managed to rile him. "Good. I'd hate to be stuffy or boring."

He laughed. "Raven, you're not stuffy, and certainly never boring, I promise you that."

"You didn't answer my question. Do you have a lot of sexual experience?" She held up her hand before he could put her off. "I'm serious, Sev. It's important to me."

He considered her a long moment. "I don't have any sexual experience in a personal relationship," he said finally. "Female androids and human courtesans are available at the Paladais to meet any needs I might have. I can assure you, I have a healthy, normal sex drive. Does that answer your question?"

So he'd never shared sexual intimacy with anyone, which pleased Raven, although she wasn't ready to probe her motives for asking. She smiled. "Yes, thank you."

"All right, then. I think turnaround is fair. What about you?"

She shook her head, too honest to play silly games. "No. I've never been intimate with a man . . . or an android."

His expression turned speculative. "Ah. Virgin territory, so to speak."

Her eyes narrowed. "Don't go taking that as a challenge."

"I wouldn't dream of it. I respect your self-control."

"Who says it's control?" she retorted. "Maybe men don't find me attractive. Maybe I'm just not interested in them."

He shook his head. "I'm not buying that. You're far too attractive for men not to notice you. As for not being interested in men, I don't think so. You have too much fire and passion burning inside you. Besides, you kiss too well." He lowered his face toward hers.

"I may not be sexually experienced, but . . ." She placed her hand on his chest and shoved him back. "I've been kissed." Pride dictated that he didn't think she was totally untouched.

"Have you, now?" Humor laced his voice.

"Yes. A lot."

"That's very intriguing." He nuzzled her hair, circled his tongue around the rim of her ear, sending pleasurable chills through her body. "Why don't you show me some of the techniques you've been practicing *a lot?*"

She really wanted to, but she had no intention of things progressing too far, and had to be honest with him.

"Sev." She pulled his face around and looked into his beautiful eyes. "I'd love to explore kissing techniques with you, but I intend to keep my virgin status a while longer, until I know I've found the right man. I don't want to lead you on."

He cupped her cheek, a tender warmth turning his eyes molten. "I appreciate your honesty. And I respect you, Raven. I won't try to do anything you don't want to do. Right now, I'm very much hoping that you'll let me kiss you again."

She had to will her heart not to melt. "Well, what are you waiting for?"

"You," he whispered, lowering his mouth to hers. Instantly the magic was back, and she wrapped her arms around his neck with a little moan. They kissed until her body pulsed with need she'd never experienced. He didn't try to touch her any other way, and that told her more than anything that he was honorable. She knew, in that moment of insight, that she could fall in love with him.

She pulled back, pressed kisses over his face. "Sev?"

"Hmmm?" He lowered his lips to her neck, and she sighed.

"Would it be a . . . hardship . . ." It already was hard, from what she could feel. "Um, would it be very difficult for you if we did a little more but didn't actually mate?"

"What?" He raised his head, his passion-glazed eyes searching hers.

"I don't want to be a tease, but . . ." She felt selfish and embarrassed now. "Could we do a little more than just kissing?"

He smiled, only a little strain showing. "Sweetheart, I'm a big boy. I can handle it. We'll do whatever you want, no more."

Oh, Spirit, she couldn't fall in love with him; she *was* in love with him. She took his hand, placed it on her breast. "Would you touch me?" she whispered.

His gaze holding hers, he stroked his fingers across her nipple. "Gladly," he murmured.

Trusting him implicitly, Raven allowed herself to sink into an incredible realm of pleasure as he caressed her through the silk. She moaned when he opened her dress and touched her bare skin. And when he lowered his mouth to her breast, she arched upward with a little cry. She curled her fingers into his thick hair, amazed at his generous, giving nature and the stunning sensations his mouth was producing. Her whole body was on fire, and she wanted him with a frightening intensity.

It took a few moments for the nearby voices to intrude into the erotic fog in which she was drifting. The words "Crown Prince Riordan" nudged her to a more alert state. She opened her eyes, listening. "He'll be attending this afternoon's session. We'll get him then," came a man's voice.

Startled, Raven jerked on Sev's hair.

"Ouch! What the—"

She pressed her hand against his mouth. "Shhh. Listen."

He raised his head, and they both listened intently.

301

The voices drifted through the latticework circling the upper half of the gazebo. The speakers were standing under the nearby Talipo tree. "You don't want to do it very close to the Collassium. Too many people." This voice was different from the first one Raven had heard. It was familiar, but pitched too low for her to recognize.

A third voice said, "We're going to get Riordan outside his ship, when he leaves to go to session. We'll get his android too. They're always together. There won't be any other guards, and there shouldn't be any other people in that part of the landing bay."

What about Rurick's personal guards? Raven thought. Unless . . . these *were* his guards! Horrified, she looked at Sev. Holding his finger to his mouth to indicate continued silence, he slipped closer to the entryway.

"A good plan," said the second voice. "What kind of weapons are you using?"

A third voice spoke up. "Laser rifles. Riordan will never know what hit him. The android will be destroyed."

"What if anyone sees you?" the second voice asked.

"There won't be any witnesses," said the first voice. "We'll also make sure Emissary Karon is taken care of before she can attend the session. We have men stationed around her quarters."

A chill shot through Raven. She stared at Sev. His face grim, he motioned her to get beneath the bench. It took a moment for it to register that they might be discovered in the gazebo. Her heart racing and adrenaline making her movements stiff and jerky, she quickly fastened her dress, then got down on her knees and then onto her stomach.

"This whole situation is getting out of control. Riordan and his android were supposed to be out of the

302

picture before he could approach the Council," the second, hauntingly familiar voice said. "We have to finish this now."

"Yes, sir," said the third voice. "What about the kid prince? What if he knows something?"

"Him?" The second voice laughed. "He's no threat. He's so full of himself and his weapons that he never pays any attention to politics or what goes on at the Paladais. He'll be easy to control."

Raven's gaze flew to Sev, who was working his large body beneath the bench across from her. His face was stony and pale. She slid under her bench and squeezed herself all the way over.

"Look at the time," the second voice said. "You'd better get into position. Rior should be leaving soon."

"Don't worry," said the first voice. "We're headed there now. We won't fail."

"You did check that gazebo when you got here, didn't you?"

"Well, no, sir—"

"Imbecile! Check it now, and make sure there are no witnesses to any of this. Are we clear?"

"Yes, sir."

Footsteps headed away from the gazebo. Raven lay there frozen, her heart pounding so hard, it felt like the blood was rushing inside her ears. She sensed the presence of the two men, saw their shadows fall across the marble floor. She glanced across at Sev, crammed under the opposite bench. They stared at each other for a terrifying eternity.

"Nothing here," one man said. "I knew there wouldn't be. No one comes here when the Council is in session."

"Let's go," said the second man. "We have a job to do."

Their footsteps faded. Sev pushed his way out from

beneath the bench and strode to the entry to look out. Raven struggled out and joined him.

"Damn! I couldn't tell anything from their backs," he said. Anger glinted in his eyes. "They had on helmets and . . . Riordan uniforms." She didn't have time for the shock to sink in as Sev grabbed her arm and pulled her outside. "Come on! We've got to warn Rurick and Emissary Karon. Gods! I wish I had a comm unit."

They ran up the pathway. "You warn Rurick," Raven suggested, "and I'll get to a guard station and tell them what's going on. They'll send soldiers to the landing bay, and to Emissary Karon's quarters."

"All right. Go . . . go!" he shouted, and sprinted away.

Hiking up her dress, Raven raced in the other direction, toward the Collassium. Her heart had yet to slow its pounding, and she felt nauseous from fear and adrenaline. She forced herself to focus on getting help to Rurick and Jade Karon.

Please don't be too late, she prayed. *Oh, Spirit, please don't let either of us be too late.*

Chapter Eighteen

Celie strode through the immaculate landing bay, headed for the Riordan flagship at the far end. She was amazed at the quietness of the massive bay, but then most visitors to Sarngin stayed in its various guest lodges. Rurick preferred to remain on his ship. With the Council in session, and the Riordan scandal causing more excitement than had been seen in many seasons, no attendees were leaving early. Thus, no activity in the bay.

Celie wasn't sure what she would say to Rurick, or if seeing him was even a good idea. Yet she hadn't been able to stop thinking about him, or forget the stricken look on his face when he left the council hall yesterday. Word was out that the Council had ruled in favor of Kalina, although the official announcement hadn't yet been made. *Unbelievable*.

She knew Rurick must be upset, and added to that would be his concern about his father and the ninth sector. He didn't deserve what Kalina and the Council had done to him. Celie wouldn't be much of a friend if she didn't offer her support.

They *were* friends—a startling but true realization. She and Rurick could never have a romantic relationship, but they had been through a lot together. She'd never forget how he'd held and comforted her when she'd seen her destroyed ship; or his sensual lovemaking. Despite her desperate need to keep a safe distance between them, she wasn't going to turn her back on him in a time of crisis. She wanted to help if she could.

Ahead lay the concourse leading to the *Riordan Spirit*. As Celie approached it, two guards passed along the concourse, going in the same direction in which she was headed. Since they wore Riordan uniforms, she assumed their destination was also Rurick's ship. They didn't appear to see her, and she turned left onto the concourse, following about eight meters behind them. Odd, but they had on helmets and carried rifles. She'd never seen Rurick's personal guard carry anything other than stunners or low-charge blasters; nor did they usually wear helmets. She wondered if the strange political atmosphere here on Sarngin warranted additional security.

Motion up ahead caught her attention, and she saw Rurick and Max walking toward the guards. Rurick, looking somewhat perplexed, said something to them, but she couldn't hear what. Then, to her stunned amazement, both guards halted and raised their weapons. Celie froze one second before instinct and training kicked in, then she hurtled forward.

"Rurick!" yelled a male voice from behind her. "Rurick, they're going to kill you. Run!"

The guards faltered momentarily, distracted by the voice, which continued yelling. They quickly re-aimed their weapons.

"No!" Celie screamed, leaping forward and knocking down one. His rifle discharged as he slammed into the other guard, sending both men to the ground. Horrified, Celie watched Rurick crumple, a red stain spreading across his chest.

One guard scrambled back up and aimed again. Celie grabbed his arm and jerked, at the same time kicking his legs out from under him. He pulled her down with him. They rolled, grappling, as she struggled to keep him down. She saw the other guard had regained his footing and was aiming at Max, who was charging him at superhuman speed.

"No!" she screamed again, managing to kick out despite the armlock she was in. The second guard went down, but not before Max took two blasts, one in the chest and one in the head. He faltered and fell, almost in slow motion.

"Bitch," the guard pinning her said, raising his fist. She tried to twist away, but there was an explosion of pain as his fist slammed into her cheek. Celie's head snapped back, and for a moment the light faded in and out. By sheer will, she forced herself to stay conscious. *Rurick*. She had to get to Rurick. "You're dead," the guard snarled, fumbling for his weapon.

A renewed surge of adrenaline gave her the clarity and strength to slam her knee up. She missed his groin but managed to hit his abdomen. He grunted and rolled onto his feet with his rifle in his hand. She scrambled for her own footing. Before she could rise, a weapon blast filled the air, and the guard collapsed, a startled look on his face.

"Halt right there!" an authoritative voice rang out. "Surrender your weapons."

Celie looked around. Sarngin's interstellar troops surrounded her. She pushed to her feet, holding out her hands to show she had no weapon as they subdued the conscious guard and put shackles on him.

"Gods!" came Sevilen's anguished voice. "Get medical help here. *Now!*"

"It's on the way, Your Highness," said one soldier, apparently the commanding officer.

Rurick! Oh, Spirit, let him be all right. Celie tried to push past the press of military bodies. "Let me by," she demanded. "I have to get to Rurick."

"Halt!" demanded the officer. "You're not going anywhere." He gestured toward a soldier. "You there. Shackle her."

"No!" she protested, panic descending. "I have to see Rurick!"

The soldier reached for her and she jerked away. "Do not resist," the CO ordered. "You risk being injured if you do."

"Let her go!" Raven's tearful voice cried from beyond the circle of soldiers. "She was trying to help Rurick and Max. I need her over here. Sev! Tell them!"

"Release her," Sevilen said, his voice none too steady.

Celie wasted no time shoving her way through the soldiers and running to Rurick's inert body. Raven was kneeling beside him, her hands pressed over his chest, which was soaked in blood. He was unmoving, pale as death. Sevilen, his face twisted with grief, knelt on the other side.

"Rurick!" Celie dropped beside Sevilen, fear clawing at her. There was so much blood, and Rurick was too still. It reminded her, way too closely, of the time Jarek san Ranul had almost died on Saron. She whipped around, ordered, "Get the Enhancers here. They can help him better than your healers can."

She turned back, leaning over Rurick and taking his face between her hands. "Rurick!" She shook him, slapped his face. Spirit, he was so cold. "Rurick! Stay

with me. *Stay with me.* Don't you dare leave me. Do
you hear me? Rurick . . . Rurick!"

She lowered her face beside his, grief wracking her
soul. He couldn't leave her. Not like this. She'd planned
on saying good-bye and walking away one cold cycle in
the very near future. *But not like this.* She didn't know
if she could bear living if he wasn't somewhere in the
physical universe. The warm moisture of her tears
tracked down her face, onto his.

"Rurick," she whispered, "Don't leave me like this.
Please. *I love you.* If you leave me, I'll never forgive
you." She held him to her, oblivious of the blood, although she was careful to keep clear of Raven's minis-
trations. She knew she had to make him hang on. "I
love you," she whispered again. "You can't leave."

"Celie." Strong hands grasped her shoulders and
pulled her back.

"No!" she cried, trying to hold on to Rurick.

"We're here to help," said a male voice, which she
belatedly recognized as Jarek's. "Let Eirene and the others work on him."

Comprehension set in and she reluctantly moved
back, her gaze locked on Rurick's face. He had absolutely no color now. *Please don't let it be too late,* she
prayed as Jarek helped her to her feet and moved her
out of the way.

Immediately, Elder Morven and Lady Sarine sank
down beside Rurick, one on each side. They placed their
hands over him and began channeling healing energy
into his body. Eirene knelt by Sarine, touching her to
ground the energy. Meanwhile, a Sarngin medical team
went to work, unpacking equipment and running scanners over him.

Celie couldn't stop the tears, or the awful trembling,
or the terrible certainty she'd lost Rurick. Jarek drew
her against him and held her tightly, lending her his

strength. "Oh, Jarek," she murmured against his shoulder. "I can't bear to lose him."

"It will be all right." His calm voice washed over her. "The best healers in the universe are working on him. I should know."

She stared at Rurick, willing him to live. Eirene had been able to save Jarek from a fatal wound, but she'd been right there when he was injured. Celie was afraid too much time had elapsed between Rurick's injury and this aid.

If he died—and he might already be gone—the sun in her universe would be extinguished.

Rurick lay in a floatation bed, drifting in and out of wakefulness. He knew where he was; Sarngin's galaxy-renowned Novaturn Interstellar Medical Center. And he knew he'd been mortally wounded in an assassination attempt, and that the Enhancers had wrought a miracle, healing him with universal energy. He knew only because the physicians had shared this information. His memory of what had happened was very blurry.

He did have a collage of vague images, although he didn't know what was real and what was possibly induced by his near-death experience. Had Celie really been there, leaning over him and calling to him as his life-force drained away? Or had he imagined her husky, grief-stricken voice murmuring, "I love you"? He'd pay dearly to know if that had been real.

He should be focusing on who had tried to assassinate him instead of thinking about Celie, but he couldn't shake the feeling her voice had kept him grounded within his dying physical body, his soul unwilling to leave her for the spirit world. As soon as he got out of this medical facility, he intended to get to the heart of the matter.

And he wanted out quickly, having endured visits from both Sev and Kalina. While he was always glad to see Sev, Kalina was another matter. He wasn't sure why his half sister had visited him; most likely to gloat over his helplessness. Or to give the appearance of a proper, grieving relative. He'd been relieved when she left.

A panel whisked open, drawing his attention. Commander Zane, one of the few non-family members authorized to enter Rurick's chamber, stepped inside. "Zane." Rurick managed a weak smile for his commanding officer. "Good to see you."

"Good to see you, Your Highness." Zane stepped forward, looking careworn. He clasped Rurick's forearm, one hand over the other and pressed it, an unusual gesture for him. "I thought we had lost you."

"It was close, from what I hear." Rurick shook away a sudden wave of dizziness. "I hate lying here like this, as weak as an infant."

Zane managed a strained smile. "You would, sir. Just listen to your doctors and you'll be out of here in no time."

Fatigue pulled at Rurick, but he forced himself to stay alert. "What have you learned about the assassination attempt?"

The commander's face hardened. "The two men were from Kalina's personal guard. They told your men that they had been sent as replacements."

"Kalina's guards?" Shock swirled through Rurick, along with the dizziness he couldn't seem to shake. "I can't believe she would go this far. I know she wants to be queen, but . . ." He paused as another thought occurred to him. What if this wasn't completely about the Riordan throne? What if Kalina was involved in the ninth-sector cover-up?

"Poison," Zane was saying.

311

Rurick tried to clear his rapidly clouding thoughts. "What?"

"We've learned your father was being poisoned. By a plant compound found in Kalina's laboratory."

It couldn't be. Surely Kalina wouldn't try to kill their father. Insidious cold seeped through Rurick's body and he struggled to breathe. Not possible . . .

"Your Highness?" Zane's worried face loomed over him.

He tried to speak, but a gray mist descended; then there was nothing but darkness.

"Prince Riordan. Rurick."

He struggled upward from a deep, dark void. He felt his body grow heavier as a male voice commanded him to consciousness. "Prince Riordan, can you hear me? If you can, open your eyes."

Another struggle, but he managed to raise his lids, squinting against the glaring lights.

"Good. He's back with us," said the voice. A blurred face looked down at him.

Rurick blinked, his vision sharpening, clouding, then finally clearing enough that he could see the man watching him so intently. The man looked familiar. Rurick shook his head, trying to clear his confusion and disorientation. "Where am I?" he asked, surprised at the hoarseness of his voice. "Do I know you?"

"We've met before. I'm Chase McKnight. You're still in the Novaturn facility. And alive, thank the Creator."

Why wouldn't he be alive? The last thing he remembered was . . . talking to . . . Zane. Yes, that was it. He'd been shot and Zane had come to see him. "What's going on?" Rurick asked, wondering why his body ached and felt so weak.

"Give me a moment and I'll explain." McKnight ran

a scanner over Rurick's head and chest, nodding a little as he checked the readings.

Rurick's mind began clearing more, and other details crystallized. "What are you doing here? How's my father?"

Dr. McKnight handed the scanner to a woman behind him. Rurick realized there where two others in the room, a man and a woman, both wearing tunics with healer insignias. "These are acceptable readings," McKnight told the others. "I'd like a few moments alone with the prince. Would you feed these into the main computer and integrate them with his other medical data? I want a full readout." He waited until they were gone before turning back to Rurick.

"What is going on?" Rurick demanded, still confused and very concerned at the fact that McKnight was here instead of on Jardonia. "My father?"

"Is fine. He's here, on Sarngin." McKnight placed a hand on the headboard. "When he heard about Princess Kalina's claims to the Riordan throne and the Council's decision in her favor, he was very upset and insisted on coming to Sarngin. Since he was still weak, I accompanied him."

A vague detail stirred at the edge of Rurick's memory. "Poison," he murmured.

McKnight's tawny brows arched. "Yes, you were poisoned. How did you know that?"

"*I* was poisoned?"

"Yes. After we landed on Sarngin, King Domek asked that I check on you. I arrived here to find you comatose. Someone had placed a poison patch on your arm." McKnight pressed his index finger against Rurick's left forearm. "Right here. If I hadn't treated the king for the identical poison and already compounded the antidote, you would have died. You must have heard me talking

313

about the poison as I worked on you. It's amazing what unconscious patients can still perceive."

"My father was also poisoned . . ." Rurick said slowly, trying to remember. "I was referring to him when I brought up poison . . . I think."

"Not possible," McKnight said bluntly. "Although you're right: poison was causing the king's so-called illness. But there's no way you could have known that, because I didn't tell anyone except King Domek and Queen Amaris, and, of course, my mate, Nessa. I wanted to be absolutely certain of the facts before I made such an accusation. I asked them to keep silent until I was sure, as I planned to report directly to you."

Rurick rubbed his throbbing forehead, certain he'd known his father had been poisoned. But if not from McKnight, then how? "You're saying that first my father, then I received the identical poison."

"That's correct. One I'd never seen before. I've analyzed it, and it's from a plant that grows in abundance on Jardonia. It was very hard to detect because it breaks down in the human body very quickly and causes symptoms that mimic a multitude of other medical conditions. I was lucky to find it at all.

"There is one difference," McKnight added thoughtfully. "King Domek didn't receive a large enough dose to kill him, only enough to incapacitate him. You, however, received a dose that would have been fatal had I arrived an hour later than I did."

"Kalina . . ." Rurick narrowed his eyes, tried to focus. His half sister was a botanist and had a laboratory where she formulated natural fertilizers and insecticides. *"A plant compound found in Kalina's laboratory."* Where had he heard that?

"What about Princess Kalina?" McKnight prompted.

Her personal guards had been the ones trying to assassinate him. Was that right? It seemed someone had told him that as well. "She came to see me after they brought me here," Rurick finally said, utterly frustrated that he couldn't remember anything. Had Kalina poisoned the king and tried to have Rurick killed, resorting again to poison when the assassination attempt failed?

"Why is my memory so bad?" he demanded.

"It's a combination of your chest injury, the poison working its way out of your system, and the meds we gave you. You'll see a dramatic improvement over the next cycle."

Not soon enough. "Is there a comm in here?"

"Yes. Let me activate it for you." McKnight punched a pad on the wall beside a flotation unit, and Rurick heard a beep.

"Novaturn central dispatch," came an automated unisex voice.

Rurick rolled toward the speaker, cursing his weakness. "This is Crown Prince Rurick Riordan. Locate my head of security, Commander Zane, and send him to me immediately."

"Yes, Your Highness."

Rurick sank back, sickened inside. Kalina. He felt tired and emotionally drained as he considered the implications of her actions.

Moments later, the panel hummed open. Commander Zane stood there, staring at Rurick as if he saw a ghost. "You're a-alive," he stammered. "I thought . . . I heard you'd had a relapse and weren't expected to survive."

Zane's burly presence stirred something inside Rurick, another memory, elusive but there, on the fringe of his mind. What was it?

"We've learned your father was being poisoned." The memory clarified, bringing with it Zane's voice as he'd uttered those words in this very room.

Rurick stared at the man who had been a trusted adviser and friend for over twenty seasons, utter shock rendering him immobile for several moments. Then he reached over and punched the comm again. "This is Prince Riordan and I need Sarngin security here immediately."

He didn't dare call for his own soldiers because he no longer knew whom he could trust.

Celie stuffed a flight suit into her duffel bag. Chase and Nessa were departing for Shamara early in the morning and she was going with them. She would hook up with Moriah and Sabin and equip a ship to fly supplies into the ninth-sector. Somehow, she couldn't get excited about it, not even about seeing her sister and her brother-in-law, or her adorable niece, Alyssa; much less delivering a shipment that was desperately needed. Spirit, what was wrong with her?

Stupid question. She knew very well that a certain Riordan prince, and the reality of her situation, were the root of her problem. She should have told Rurick good-bye in person, but that would have been too difficult. She hadn't spoken with him at all since he'd almost died—and twice, at that.

She'd slipped into his Novaturn chamber soon after he'd been taken there, while he was still unconscious, to see for herself that he was really alive. She'd watched the rise and fall of his chest and touched his face, savoring the warmth of his life-force. Then, after he'd been poisoned, she'd relied on reports from Chase and Sevilen for assurance that he was all right.

Her overwhelming feelings of grief and love when he'd been shot in the landing bay had proven how dangerous it was to be around him. Better if she left without seeing him, without the tangible reminder of what could never be. The nightmare, which had returned with a vengeance, only served to emphasize what she already knew: A Riordan prince could not marry a murderer.

Rurick, along with Emissary Karon, King Domek, and the Enhancers, was in the process of unraveling multiple situations. And there were quite a few: the ninth-sector cover-up, Kalina's actions, the sabotaging of Rurick's ship and the assassination attempt, as well as the poisoning of King Domek and Rurick.

Emissary Karon had recovered from the attempt on her life, having sustained only a shoulder wound, thanks to intercession from Sarngin troops. Kalina and Commander Zane had been taken into custody and were being questioned on the attempts to kill Rurick and the poisoning of King Domek. Zane's apparent involvement had been the biggest shock to all concerned.

Hopefully, all the issues would soon be resolved, and the cover-up in the ninth sector exposed and actions taken to correct the conditions there. King Domek had said he would revoke the Orior laws, so Rurick would eventually assume his rightful place on the Riordan throne, and life would go on. There was nothing Celie could contribute to his universe. It was time to go where she could be useful.

She'd decided a holocording would be the best way to tell Rurick good-bye. She would transmit it from Chase's ship after they left Sarngin. That settled, she'd showered and packed her few belongings. All she could do now was try to get some sleep before she met Chase and Nessa at the spaceport.

She looked around her chamber at the Sarnonian, finding it barren and lonely despite its opulence. She was glad she'd opted to stay here, rather than on the *Riordan Spirit* where she'd have been in far too close proximity to Rurick. Her paintings were still on his ship, and she intended to leave them, hoping he might enjoy them. That part of her life was over.

Resolute, she sat cross-legged on her bunk and absently ran her brush through her hair. The panel tone sounded. She wasn't expecting anyone, but Eirene often came by in the evening to chat for a while. Raven's visits, on the other hand, had grown scarcer, and Celie suspected a second Riordan prince might have something to do with that. The charm of Riordan males could be irresistible, as she well knew.

Belting her robe more tightly around her, she padded to the panel and activated the viewscreen. She gasped when Rurick's face shimmered onto the screen. What was he doing here? His gaze locked onto her, and he smiled. She realized belatedly that she had the viewscreen set for two-way interaction. There was no way she could pretend she wasn't in.

"May I enter?" he asked.

Panic skittered through her. What could she say to him? She knew it would be difficult to maintain her hard-fought emotional distance if she saw him. Blazing hells. "I don't know if now is a good time," she hedged, hating her cowardice but clinging to it as if it were a lifeline. "I'm getting ready for bed."

His smile widened. "I have no objection to that."

Her knees developed a sudden weakness. Spirit help her. She tried to rally her defenses against his allure. "Rurick—"

"Don't shut me out, Celie. I need to see you."

The sincerity in his voice undid her. *She'd almost lost him.* How could she turn him away? Telling herself this was her opportunity to buck up and tell him good-bye in person, which he deserved, she opened the panel.

He walked in, and her senses soared at his nearness. Spirit, but he looked good. A little pale, a little tired; but then, his survival and subsequent recovery had been nothing short of miraculous. He took her hand, raised it to his lips, lingering over it, and her heart began an erratic beat. Stepping closer, he slid his other hand beneath her hair and pressed it against her face. "How is your cheek? You took a nasty blow."

The bruise from where the guard had punched her was gone, but the awful memory of Rurick being shot would stay with her forever. She took a deep breath. "It's healed. Any word on Max?"

Distress clouded his gaze. "Nothing new. The technicians fear they won't be able to repair him. The damage was extensive."

She felt sadness and regret that she hadn't been able to stop the guards from shooting Rurick or Max. "I'm sorry. I'd grown quite fond of him. I know Raven is terribly upset."

"I miss him, even though he was a pain at times." Rurick paused, his gaze roaming possessively over her face. "And I've missed you."

She felt his tenderness seeping into her, vibrating through every cell; felt his warmth, inhaled his intoxicating, masculine scent. She didn't need this. She stepped back—another one of those tactical retreats. "I'm glad you're better," she said. "You had us worried there for a while."

"So you were concerned for me."

Terrified. Devastated. She blew out a breath. "Yes."

"That's a start." He glanced toward the control panel. "Computer, play music program one."

Melodious Jart music flowed into the room. "Program one?" Celie asked. She hadn't created any personalized music programs.

"Nice, isn't it?" He strode to the autocooler and took out a bottle of wine.

She eyed the bottle suspiciously. "I don't remember that being in there earlier."

He raised his brows roguishly and set the wine on a small table. He gave a twist of the ceramic-topped cork and pulled it out of the bottle. Then he got two glasses from the dining area console and filled them, leaving them on the table. He reached back inside the console and pulled out a stunning, intricately carved gold firestand. Setting it on the table, he clapped his hands, and flames leaped into the circling bowls.

"Lights off," he commanded, and the chamber winked into semidarkness, lit only by the glow of the firestand.

Celie's mouth went dry. This was not a good sign for a clean break and a quick good-bye. "Tonight isn't good for socializing," she said, striding to the table. "I need to get some rest—"

"Is that what you consider this? A social call?" He turned and handed her a glass. "I don't think so." He clinked his glass against hers. "Here's to a beautiful, courageous woman, a woman who saved my life." His eyes never leaving hers, he drank.

Reluctantly, she raised the wine to her lips. She resisted the nervous urge to gulp it down and grab the bottle. It was Prylian wine and tasted wonderful, melting on her tongue with a heady flavor and flowing down so smoothly, it was nearly impossible to discern the substantial alcoholic kick for which Prylian spirits were renowned.

Lowering the glass, she chewed her lower lip, stopping when she realized his gaze had fixed there. "I'm truly glad you appear to be recovered from your injuries, but—"

"Oh, I am." He took the glass from her hand and set it, along with his, on the table. Before she could read his intent, he slipped his arm around her and drew her flush against him. *"Fully* recovered."

And fully aroused. She flattened her palms against his chest, tried to push him back. "Rurick, please release me."

"When we were on Toba, I believe I promised you

flamelight and dancing," he murmured, not budging a millimeter. He pried her hand from his chest, wrapped his fingers around it, and swung them around, his body still imprinted against hers.

"I don't know how to dance," she protested. What was wrong with her? A simple *no* would end this dangerous game. She needed to shove him away, to ask him to leave. *Now.*

"Just follow my lead." He moved her smoothly through a series of steps that only made her more aware of his powerful body molded so intimately to hers.

Honesty, she told herself. They'd shared so much; the least she could do was be honest with him. She dug in, freeing her hand and gripping his arms to stop him. "Rurick, we can't do this."

"Why not?" He halted, stared down at her. "I watched the landing bay security holocording of the shooting. All of it."

Celie's insides clenched. She'd also watched the holo, so she knew exactly what he had seen. The holocording unit had documented the entire drama, from her fighting two armed guards in a desperate attempt to deflect their weapon-fire from Rurick through the amazing healing the Enhancers had performed.

It had also been active afterward when, once it was certain Rurick would live, Raven had collapsed over a decimated Max, sobbing her heart out. More interesting and very revealing had been Prince Sevilen going to Raven and gathering her into his arms, holding her as if she were a precious treasure.

All well and good, except for the section of the holo that was personally damning for Celie—that of her crouched over Rurick, tears streaming down her face as she pleaded, demanded, that he not leave her. Worst of all, the highly sensitive recording unit had picked up her whispered declarations of love. Words she couldn't very well refute.

"I watched the holocording several times, as a matter of fact," Rurick said softly. "I was most interested in the part right after I was wounded and you knelt beside me—"

"Damn it, Rurick." She wrenched away and moved around the table, keeping it between them, at the same time belting her robe more securely. It was patently unfair that she'd been forced to bare her soul like that, in front of numerous witnesses, most especially Rurick. "I can't be held accountable for anything I did or said under the stress of seeing you shot down. People often say things they don't mean under dire circumstances."

"On the contrary." He dealt with the table by moving it aside, and advanced on her with unmistakable intent in his eyes. "People are more likely to say *exactly* what they mean under such circumstances."

With the console behind her, she couldn't retreat any farther—and by Spirit, she was tired of being a coward. She held her ground, determined to put an end to his obvious expectations. She had to. She started to speak, but he cut her off, his mouth taking possession of hers and sparking intense, immediate need. She couldn't help herself, she kissed him back, tasting, savoring, clinging to this one last memory to take with her.

He ended the kiss, gathered her close. "I love you too."

Panic raced through her, quickly disintegrating desire. "Don't say that." She pressed her fingers against his lips. "For Spirit's sake, Rurick, don't say another word. We can't take this any further."

"So you keep telling me," he murmured, sliding his hands to her waist. "But you've given me no good reason not to."

Because I am a murderer, a fact she had vowed she

would never reveal to anyone, not even Moriah. And it was just one of many reasons. "We can't have a future together," she began, then sucked in her breath as he parted her now untied robe and slid his hand inside it.

"We can do anything we want," he breathed against her neck, his hand claiming her breast. "I believe we've covered wine, flamelight, and dancing. Now I plan to lay you on the bed over there and taste every inch of you."

He'd remembered everything he'd said on Toba, words she'd never forgotten. Her body responded to the memory of their awkward lovemaking on a cramped bunk in a wrecked ship, with his portamedic-encased legs hampering their movements but his touch tender and sure.

She tried to tell herself to forget Toba, to pull away now, so the break would be easier. Yet she wanted this, wanted to mate with Rurick one more time. As if sensing her indecision, he slid her robe off her shoulders, baring her breasts. He bent her backward over his arm and lowered his head, his mouth closing over her nipple.

Any resistance she'd been struggling to raise washed away on a flood of desire. Instead of pushing him away, her fingers tangled in his hair. *Spirit, just one more time.*

Straightening, he stripped off her robe and carried her to the bed. The feel of the cool satin against her bare skin was incredibly erotic, as was the way his heated gaze swept over her, followed by his caresses. She grabbed the front of his flight suit and yanked him down on top of her. She opened the seam of his shirt as his lips claimed hers again.

She managed to get his shirt off and ran her hands over his back. Their kiss became wild and rough, a deep, drugging tangling of tongues that left her boneless. The feel of his hands on her breasts, of his heated skin and the muscles bunching beneath her fingers, was far more potent than the Prylian wine.

He slid his hand between them and found her wet and ready. He penetrated her with his finger, stroking in and out. Stunned by the intensity of her need, Celie didn't realize how much she'd craved his touch since Toba. Gasping, she rose up against him, spurred by the desperation to have him inside her.

"Soon, my love," he promised, slipping from her grasp. He slid down her body like Sarnai silk, igniting sparks of sensation with his lips. He kissed her belly, his hair trailing sensuously across her skin, then dipped his tongue into her belly button. He slid lower, coming close to the dark blond curls but detouring to nip and lave her thighs as he parted them, then settled between them, slipping his arms beneath.

"Rurick," Celie murmured, startled. "What are you doing?"

"Tasting you." He flashed her a wicked grin, then lowered his face between her legs and kissed her *there*. She almost came off the bed, but he had her thighs pinned. Ignoring her stunned resistance, he pushed her legs wider to give him better access. He stroked his tongue against her, then dipped it inside, and she was lost.

She should be shocked, but she no longer cared. Twisting helplessly as his mouth worked its magic, she was caught up in a rising tide so powerful, nothing could stop the headlong rush into the throes of sensation. The explosion surged through her and she cried out, swirling colors blinding her to everything but the pleasure.

She sagged against the satin, dazed and disoriented—but not so bewildered that she couldn't enjoy the sight of Rurick rising from the bed and stripping off his boots and pants. He was a work of art, a perfect male form of muscle and taut skin. He sank onto the bed beside her, rolling her into his arms.

She kissed his chest, swirling her tongue over his nipples and savoring his groan of pleasure. She traced the pattern of muscles down his abdomen, running her fingers through the fine line of hair. She heard his sharp intake of breath when she closed her hand around his erection. She'd never realized the feel of a man, hard and pulsing, could be so incredibly sexual, yet seem so natural and so right. She stroked him and suddenly found herself on her back, with him settling between her legs.

He leaned down and kissed her. "I wanted to take it slower," he whispered. "But, gods help me, I can't wait any longer. Next time, I promise." He eased inside her carefully, and this time there was no pain. Her internal muscles gripped him and he groaned again. "I'm afraid there won't be anything leisurely about this."

Celie didn't care. She only wanted him. "I say we go for it," she whispered.

"Do you, now?" He gave her a breathtaking smile, and love for him flooded her being.

"Absolutely," she said.

He came over her, lacing his fingers with hers. Then he moved against her, rocking her in an ageless mating pattern. She moved with him, unable to look away from his mesmerizing eyes; the love and passion reflected there binding her to him, physically and spiritually. The crescendo built again, rapid and powerful. Then the wave crashed over them, sweeping them both away.

Celie slipped from the rumpled bed, her body sore and satiated. Collapsed on his stomach, Rurick lay in an exhausted slumber. With his mussed hair, his golden skin, and his beautifully delineated muscles, he looked like a god. They'd made love a second time, slowly and thoroughly, a feast of the senses; of savoring, with lingering touches and kisses, and of murmured endearments.

"Heart of my heart," he had whispered to her as he moved inside her with exquisite, excruciating slowness, his powerful shoulders blocking out the flamelight. Yet even in the dimness, she'd been able to see the possessive glow in his eyes.

She would never forget his tenderness, his passion, or the shared explosion of incredible pleasure. Nor would she forget the words he uttered afterward, as they lay tangled together, heartbeat to heartbeat, his lips moving along her jaw and into her hair: "I love you."

She couldn't bring herself to say the words back, words that would only bind her heart further, a futile and foolish thing to allow. She'd kissed him instead, immersing herself in the taste of him, the feel of his hair entwined in her fingers.

And now she was leaving him.

She moved silently, dressing and stuffing a few more items into her duffel. Then she stared down at him a long moment, drinking in the sight of him, hoping it would be enough to last a lifetime. "Good-bye, Rurick," she whispered. *I love you.*

She left the chamber and headed for the spaceport.

Chapter Nineteen

Jade Karon stared at the computer screen, where Lady Eirene, Elder Morven, and Lady Sarine's reports were displayed. The three Enhancers had been willing to put their findings into writing.

Jade sighed. "I hate this. Both Regent Comar and Vice Regent Tasia are behind the ninth-sector cover-up, which is the only explanation that makes any sense. They're the only ones with enough power, and who have held their positions long enough, to pull off something like this."

She had taken the three Enhancers into a Council meeting with her, and they had "listened" empathically to the reactions when she began speaking about the ninth sector. The regent and vice regent weren't the only ones involved; five more Council members and numerous General Council representatives had been active participants in a secret society dedicated to segregating several races considered inferior from the rest of the quadrant. They were also shipping prisoners to the sector in great numbers and leaving them in appalling conditions.

Although Emissary Karon wanted to go to the ninth sector immediately, she had opted to confront the Council while all the representatives were on Sarngin for the current session. She was meeting with King Domek, Rurick, and the Enhancers in the *Riordan Spirit*'s conference chamber, away from the prying eyes and ears of other Council members, as they planned their strategy.

Jade looked at Domek, regret in her eyes. "When Comar and Tasia suggested the new penal colony be placed in the ninth sector, I voted for it. I never suspected conditions would be so inhumane, or that they would secretly move the worst criminals from the other colonies there."

"You couldn't possibly know, Jade. Even now, it's hard to imagine this could happen," Domek told her.

"Complacency is very dangerous," she said. "We start to think we have all the answers, that we're infallible. We forget there's a dark side to most living beings." She looked across the conference table at Eirene, Morven, and Sarine. "You are willing to testify before the General Council?"

"We are, Your Ladyship," Morven replied.

The emissary leaned back in her chair. "We'll do it tomorrow in session. Comar and Tasia have no idea I'm on to them. I'll have the holovideos on the chamber screens before anyone can stop me, and when I tell the thousands of members and envoys what's going on, there won't be any way the Council can deny it. The GC will order an investigation into the matter, and we'll go from there. What do you think, Domek?"

"I think it's the smartest way to do it," Rurick's father

answered. "That way, Comar and Tasia can't block an inquiry."

"Then that much is settled. Now we need to discuss Kalina," Jade said gently. Out of deference to years of friendship and respect, she had allowed the king to question his daughter, trusting him to see justice done.

"I know." Domek sighed heavily. He was a big man, an older version of Rurick and Sev, but he'd lost weight since he'd been poisoned, and gray was beginning to streak his hair. The events of the past cycles had aged him beyond his years. "Kalina told us everything. She even agreed to submit to truth serum, which verified her statement. I will turn over the holovideo to you."

"I don't think that will be necessary," Jade replied. "Your word is enough, if you're willing to share what you learned."

"There's not much to say. Kalina was . . ." Domek stopped, agonizing over the child he and Amaris had borne, and still loved, despite her crimes. Jade placed her hand on his arm.

Feeling an overwhelming sense of incredulity and shock over Kalina's actions himself, Rurick stepped in and continued where his father left off. "Kalina confessed she'd been poisoning Father but insists she was only giving him enough to make him sick. She wanted him out of commission so he'd be forced to abdicate the throne. Then she planned to use the Orior laws to strip me of ascension rights. She wanted to be queen."

"There's no evidence she was part of the assassination plot against us?" Jade asked.

Rurick shook his head. "No. She didn't know anything about that, even though her guards were involved. Zane had been bribing and controlling them for a long time. He ordered them to do the killings, hoping Kalina would be implicated."

The pain of Zane's betrayal stabbed through Rurick

even more sharply than that of Kalina's actions. He'd trusted Zane implicitly, had considered him a second father. He was still shocked.

"I've been wondering why Comar and Tasia were so insistent on supporting Kalina's claim to the throne," Jade said. "Is there any indication she was involved in the ninth-sector cover-up?"

"None," Domek replied. "I've given that a lot of thought as well. I believe Comar figured Kalina would be easier to control than Rurick or me." He sighed again. "It appears Kalina's only goal was to be queen, by whatever means were at her disposal."

"I know this is difficult for you." Jade patted his arm, her gaze compassionate. "What will happen to Kalina now?"

"She has been banished indefinitely to one of our palaces near Jardonia's border." Domek set his shoulders, his face now composed, although his eyes reflected his sorrow. "She will live there under heavy guard, very likely for the rest of her life."

"I'm sorry for all of you," Jade murmured. "Kalina's plot certainly muddied the waters with regard to the ninth sector, since it drew attention from Commander Zane and his secret alliance with Comar and Tasia. No one ever suspected."

"So Commander Zane was behind the attempts on your life?" Elder Morven asked Rurick.

"Yes. We've learned Zane is a member of a fanatical group that believes in the propagation of supreme races. He also liked lining his pockets with gold, so he was all too willing to work with Comar and Tasia. When I got too close to the truth, he orchestrated the attack on Joba. After that failed, he sabotaged my ship's computers when we returned to Joba a second time."

"Then he set up the assassination attempt on both of

us," Jade added, her eyes hard, "implicating Kalina in the process."

"Yes," Rurick said, with a sense of abject sadness. He'd lost an adviser and friend, and along with that his ability to readily trust again.

"But young Prince Sevilen, along with Raven, saved the day." Jade smiled. "I think Sev will make a fine Council representative one of these seasons."

"I do too." Domek finally smiled. He was very proud of Sev, and so was Rurick. His half brother had matured a lot these past cycles. There was no doubt Raven was a catalyst for some of these changes. She and Sev had been inseparable since the attack.

"How did Zane get the poison?" Lady Eirene asked. "Do you think Kalina gave it to him, since she wanted you out of the running for the throne?"

"No," Rurick answered. "Zane figured out what Kalina was doing and took the poison from her lab. When the assassination attempt failed, he used it on me. Emissary Karon might have been next, had she not been so heavily guarded."

Morven shook his head. "Zane and Kalina will pay a high price for their actions. If not in this life, then the next."

"There are others who must also pay for their actions. I think I've heard enough here." Jade rose, and everyone followed suit. "I must prepare for the session tomorrow. It should be very eventful." Her eyes glittered. "Especially since Comar and Tasia have no idea what's coming."

She leaned forward and kissed Domek on both cheeks. "Don't be a stranger to Council. Give my regards to Amaris."

He returned the gesture. "The gods be with you tomorrow."

331

"We'll be there to back you up," Rurick told Jade, then opened the panel for her.

Immediately, two Tobals whirred in. They headed for the Enhancers, chirping loudly. Jade's private guards followed, watching the creatures suspiciously. The emissary turned with a bemused expression. "What are these things?"

"We call them Tobals," Rurick explained. "Celie and I discovered them when we crashed on Toba. Some of them sneaked onto the ship that rescued us and traveled to Sarngin with us. They appear to be harmless."

"And very intelligent," Elder Morven said.

"How can you tell?" Rurick asked.

"They're telepathic," Eirene explained. She cocked her head as one Tobal fluttered around her, beeping rapidly. "It's communicating with me mentally. Telling me about the silver ship that crashed on Toba and all the wonderful equipment that was on it."

"Fascinating," Jade murmured. She turned to Rurick. "You're sure these creatures are benign?"

"As far as we can tell. We spent over six cycles with them, and they never displayed any aggressive tendencies. They even brought us food."

"Very interesting. I'd like a full report on these Tobals after we put the issue of the ninth sector to rest."

"Of course." He took her hand and bowed over it. "Thank you, Emissary Karon."

"I should be thanking you. Your efforts will bring help to the inhabitants of the ninth sector. That's an amazing accomplishment." She smiled at him. "I will see you tomorrow." She swept from the chamber, her guards close behind.

Rurick turned to see the Enhancers "listening" to the Tobals, who were chirping rapidly. Another amazing development. It seemed events were finally falling into place, with everything working out for the benefit of all.

He felt as if a huge weight had been lifted from his shoulders. The ninth sector would begin receiving the full-scale aid it so desperately needed. Just a few more things to clear up, and then he could go after Celie. He couldn't believe she had left him, not after the night they'd spent together.

He summoned Jael, Max's android replacement— although no other android could ever be Max—and told him to record everything the Enhancers learned from the Tobals. Then he bid his father good night and went to his cabin. He poured a glass of Maran brandy and settled at his console, flipping on the holocording loaded into his system. He'd watched the holo so many times, he knew it verbatim. Celie's image flashed onto the screen.

"This is good-bye, Rurick. I know I should have told you in person, but . . . Well, the opportunity never presented itself." She flushed, and he felt a flash of pure masculine satisfaction, entwined with the memory of an incredible night of lovemaking that had pretty much taken conversation out of the equation. Also a bad thing, because if he'd given her a chance to talk, he might have been able to head off her flight.

He frowned and sipped his drink as the holo continued. "Our time together has been turbulent in some respects and wonderful in others. But no matter my feelings for you, or yours for me, we don't have a future. You will be king of Jardonia, and I can't live the lifestyle of royalty. It's far too opulent for me."

She stared into the holocorder, her gaze earnest and intent. "I'm a restless spirit, Rurick. I can't be tied down. I need to be free, to roam and explore. If I were trapped on Jardonia, I'd eventually wither away inside and die. I'd be like a little Tobal, locked in a glass chamber in the lab, my spirit crushed by captivity, gasping for my last breath. And then there's . . ." She froze, her expression so tormented, Rurick found himself leaning forward, even though it was just a holocording. "There's no way it can work," she finished, a slight tremor in her voice.

Here was the heart of the matter, he thought in abject frustration, the key to her refusal to stay with him. Whatever it was, she wasn't going to tell him. "We have to go our separate ways," she said, regaining her composure. "You have an investigation of the ninth-sector cover-up to lead and a planet to rule. I have deliveries to make and a quadrant to explore. I'm sorry it can't work out. Good-bye, Rurick."

The holocording flipped off, and he sat back in his chair. She might think this was the end, but she was seriously mistaken. He was a prince, used to giving orders, not taking them. He had no intention of letting her get away. He would get to the heart of her resistance and deal with it. Thoughtfully, he drummed his fingers on the console. Coming to a decision, he punched the comm and requested an open line to make a subspace transmission.

She had a sleek, fast craft, with a luxurious personal cabin, three sizable cargo bays, and two android crew members, who were currently in inactive mode. She had canvas, paints in hundreds of exotic colors, and dozens of containers of flower petals from the Jardonian gardens to make into more paints. All these things were compliments of a grateful Riordan king.

She had, for the first time since she'd relocated on the Verante constellation, truly crucial deliveries, which should make her feel useful and needed. She had played a part in righting a terrible wrong and was now actively participating in restoration of the ninth sector. She had so much for which to be grateful.

She was miserable.

Since leaving Sarngin, she'd been irritable and restless. She couldn't paint, couldn't eat, couldn't sleep. When she did drift off into a fitful slumber, she was plagued by that damnable nightmare. She was also plagued by memories of Rurick, of their last night together. Blazing hells. She knew she'd done the right thing in leaving him, and yet . . . nothing was right.

She kept telling herself to get over it, kept pushing to make deliveries, but it was as if all the joy had gone out of her life. It was like grief, she decided. She was mourning the loss of her relationship with Rurick; and for being forced to forge a reluctant acceptance of the path she had to take. Surely the pain would fade in time, and she would find fulfillment in her life. But right now it felt as if her heart had shattered.

Today, like most cycles, she sat in the pilot's seat and stared at the controls, which were on auto and didn't require her attention. She should try to paint, but her creativity was lifeless, hopefully a temporary dormancy. She couldn't even seem to get upset over that.

Rapid, strident tones, warning of an approaching ship, shook her out of her lethargy. She leaned forward, studied the screens. Two ships, rapidly closing the distance. She felt a momentary flare of alarm but told herself it was unwarranted.

Since Emissary Karon had exposed the ninth-sector cover-up to the entire Interstellar General Counsel, a full investigation had been launched. Every member government of the Council had sent ships to patrol the ninth sector, and the checkpoints had been converted from mind-altering facilities to central warehousing, where supplies were delivered and systematically disbursed to the settlements. The entire quadrant was safer than ever.

Her transceiver beeped to indicate an incoming hail from one of the advancing ships. She punched the receiver pad. "This is Captain Celie Cameron. Identify yourself."

A shatteringly familiar face flashed on the view-screen. "Captain Cameron."

"Rurick," she gasped, stunned.

"Good to see you again." His deep voice seemed to fill the cockpit, to seep into her pores, to set her heart racing. "I want to talk to you. Requesting permission to board."

That would be wonderful. To have him on her ship, his arms around her; to taste his tongue tangled with hers, feel him deep inside her. Just like that, she felt vital, alive. No! Spirit, what was the matter with her? It was partly adrenaline, she told herself, as she felt that familiar rush as well. All the more reason to keep her distance. How could a wound heal if it kept being re-opened? Self preservation, she reminded herself, first and foremost.

"Boarding denied, Your Highness," she replied. "I'm on a very tight schedule and not allowing visitors at this time. Please state your business over the comm."

His brows drew together. "Boarding *denied,* Captain?" he asked softly, dangerously.

She clenched her hands on the console. "Denied," she repeated firmly. "I'm carrying vital supplies to the ninth sector and time is of the essence. We can communicate through the comm or by messaging. Your choice."

"You will slow for docking." Steel flashed in his eyes and edged his voice. "Or be boarded by force."

What could they possibly have to discuss? Her own weakness where he was concerned shot a bolt of panic through her; at the same time, his arrogance sparked her anger. "Damn it, Rurick, you have no business giving me orders and commandeering my ship. This is free space and I've done nothing wrong."

"We can do this easy or we can do this hard, Captain.

336

One way or another, I am boarding your ship. Shall I order my men to employ the grappler?"

She knew she couldn't outrun Riordan escort ships, and even if she could, Rurick would only send more after her. "Son of an Antek," she muttered.

"Excuse me?"

"I'm slowing the ship. Go ahead and board." She punched off the comm and shut down the thrusters. Blazing hells. What now?

She tried to think but couldn't come up with any reason why Rurick would approach her now. He hadn't attempted to contact her since she'd left Sarngin over thirty cycles earlier. She'd assumed he'd accepted her decision and gone on with his life. Besides, the trials of Regents Comar and Tasia, along with five other Council members, were underway on Sarngin. Why was Rurick here?

She paced the corridor, bracing herself against the wall when her ship jolted from the docking. Drawing a deep breath, she strode toward the airlock. The light flashed on, and the connecting panel slid open. Rurick stepped from his airlock into hers. They stared at each other as the panel behind him closed, sealed. Then the inner panel whispered open and he stepped into the corridor.

He looked wonderful. Her heart sped up and her spirit soared, despite her resolve. She steeled herself against the devastating effect he always had on her.

His gaze swept over her. "You look awful."

"It's good to see you too," she retorted, then indicated the second cabin. "We can talk in here."

He followed her into the cabin, which she used as storage space for her art supplies. He glanced around the chamber, his gaze resting briefly on barely started and empty canvases, then back to her. "You've lost weight," he said. "And you look tired. Are you ill?"

337

"I'm fine." She moved to a small table and indicated a chair. "Please sit down, Your Highness."

He scowled. "I think we've already discussed what would happen if you persisted in using my title."

She remembered very well the discussion right before they crashed on Toba. "Hell to pay, I believe you said. Been there, done that, I'm afraid."

He took a step closer, ignoring the chair, and she found herself locked in his gaze. "I know about your father."

She would have fallen if the table hadn't been there. Her knees buckled, forcing her to grab the edge to keep from going down. Then Rurick was there, gripping her upper arms and keeping her upright. "Here." He maneuvered her to the chair. "Sit down."

She sank into the chair. He couldn't know about her father. *No one* knew, not even Moriah. "I don't know what you're talking about," she said, her heart pounding against her chest.

Rurick squatted by her chair, rested his hands on her shoulders. "Gods, you're pale. Take a deep breath," he ordered. "That's it. Take another."

He watched as she finally managed a few full breaths, her thoughts whirling. Her father! How could Rurick know? He must be talking about her father's abuse, how he'd gambled them away to Pax Blacklock, the shadower who had raped Moriah repeatedly until they'd managed to escape him. That information wasn't a secret, but the other—

"Did you kill your father, Celie?"

Oh, Spirit! He knew. *He knew.* How? She gripped the chair arms, shaking violently. "Is this why you insisted on boarding my ship? To tell me you think I'm a murderer?"

"Look at me." He crowded against her, turning her

face toward him. "I don't think you're a murderer. But I believe you killed your father."

Staggering shock clouded her thoughts, but she managed to gasp, "How could you know that?"

"You *did* kill him, didn't you?"

What was the sense in lying? She nodded, shock giving way to an odd numbness.

"That's good to know," he said matter-of-factly, scooping her up and settling into the chair with her cradled against him.

She pushed away to look up at him. "How can you say that? There's nothing good about that. I'm a murderer, Rurick. A *murderer!*"

"Perhaps 'good' is the wrong term, but I can't be sorry that a monster such as your father is gone. Now I know what's keeping us apart, and we can deal with it."

"We can't be together," Celie insisted, trying to form a coherent thought process. "How did you learn about my father?"

"I had my suspicions. On Toba, you had nightmares and talked in your sleep. After you left Sarngin, I contacted your sister, and she confirmed my hunch."

Celie started trembling again. "That's not possible. Moriah knows nothing about this."

Rurick's arms tightened around her. "You might be surprised what Moriah knows. You had nightmares and talked in your sleep around her as well. She and Sabin did some investigating and learned that shadower Lothar Cameron had been found dead from a blaster wound to his heart in a lodging chamber on Elysia. The day before, that same chamber had been rented by Cenda Carlen, who disappeared after that. Since that was an alias you often used, and you were picking up a shipment on Elysia right around then, Moriah drew the logical conclusion."

Celie felt sick. She'd always known deep inside that someday her heinous crime would catch up with her. Yet it was still a shock that others knew, especially Moriah and Rurick. "So now you've learned the truth," she said dully. "I murdered my own father. There's no way a Riordan crown prince can consort with a murderer."

"You're right," he agreed. "But I know you, Celie. You're brave and noble and compassionate—not a cold-blooded murderer."

"I am," she insisted. "I could have used a stunner on him, but I used a blaster instead. Shot him in the heart." *The blood. There had been so much blood. Her father's eyes had been open, shock and horror reflected in them. . . .*

She struggled to get free, was brought firmly back against Rurick. "Tell me what happened," he said.

She sagged against him. "I don't want to talk about it."

He slid one hand through her hair, pressing her head against his chest. "Tell me. Please."

He already knew the basic truth. He'd hate her after he heard the whole story, but they didn't have a future anyway. She'd carried the burden alone for so long. She took a deep breath, and the words tumbled out.

"I was eighteen, doing one of my first solo pickups. I was on Elysia, had just finished loading goods on my ship. I was tired but decided to stop for a drink before I turned in."

She found herself gripping Rurick's shirt as the memories crystallized, replayed as clearly as a holo. "He was there, at the bar. I recognized him instantly, although it had been eight seasons since I'd seen the bastard. Eight long seasons since he'd backhanded me, then turned Moriah and me over to Pax Blacklock. He was heavier, grayer, but just the same."

Her voice shook, and Rurick's hand slid to her shoulder. She drew another deep breath, plunged on. "I was too young and inexperienced to mask my reaction. He noticed and took a closer look, then figured out who I was. Told me I'd grown up into a real beauty and to come over and give my old father a kiss. I threw my drink in his face and left. I was so upset, it never occurred to me that he would follow me. But he was a shadower, trained in stealth, and he tracked me to my lodge.

"He broke into my chamber, punched me a few times. I was trained to fight, but he caught me by surprise, and he was much larger and stronger. He pinned me against the wall, tore my flight suit, put his hand over my breast. . . ." She battled rising nausea.

"Gods, Celie. You don't have to go on."

She ignored him, the need to finish riding her. "I fumbled for a weapon. I still had on my utility belt and carried both a stunner and a blaster. Moriah always said a stunner was better, because we didn't want to kill anyone if we could avoid it. I knew that. But I drew the blaster instead. Placed it against the bastard's heart and pushed the discharge. The blood . . . it was everywhere. The look on his face . . ." She stopped, shuddering.

"It was self-defense, Celie. You did what you had to do."

"It was murder. I felt the stunner beneath my hand, moved on to the blaster. I could have stunned him; instead, I killed him. What does that say about me?" Hot tears filled her eyes and a sob escaped between her clenched teeth.

Rurick pulled her tightly against him, rocking her as if she were a child. "You were young, frightened, and defending yourself. There wasn't any time to think things through. The man was a bounty hunter. If you had merely stunned him, he would have tracked you down, finding Moriah in the process."

341

She shook her head wearily. "I don't know."

"I do. Have you ever killed anyone else?"

"No. If I was fighting against Antek ships, I just disabled them, using Radd's schematics. If I had to fight face-to-face, I used a stunner, or a low-charge laser. I never *had* to kill anyone, not even my father."

"Would you have killed if there had been no other choice? To defend Moriah, or your colony?"

She nodded slowly, knowing she'd do anything to assure the safety of her loved ones. "Yes, I would have, if necessary."

"This was necessary. You had to do it. If you could go back, you might choose the stunner, but then your father would have tracked you to the ends of the quadrant and he might have killed *you*. I think your god was guiding your hand that cycle, using you as an instrument to rid the universe of a monster. You've never killed anyone before or since, and you've helped countless people. If you hadn't been on Joba when we were attacked, if you and Raven hadn't summoned Dr. McKnight, then gone with us to Altair, I hate to think how many people would have died. I have to believe you were meant to survive the encounter on Elysia and your father was not."

"I just don't know." Exhausted, Celie closed her eyes. She still felt sick inside, but strangely, her heart was lighter. Maybe Rurick was right. One thing was certain: She couldn't change the past. "You still can't consort with a killer," she murmured.

"I can do whatever I damn well please. And you please me, Celie. More than anything in the Universe. I love you."

The tears returned, and she blinked them back. "You still don't understand. I explained it all in the holo—"

"I'm not the crown prince anymore."

That brought her fully upright to stare at him. "What?"

"I'm not the crown prince now. Sevilen is."

"I don't understand."

"I've always disliked the pomp and circumstance of the Riordan court," Rurick explained. "Only my sense of duty and honor held me there. That, plus the fact that I couldn't see Kalina as queen. But now she's been exiled to the Riordan border to live out her life there. That puts Sevilen in line to the throne after me. He's much more suited to royal life than I am. So I'm stepping down, and he'll be king after our father relinquishes the throne."

Perhaps it was exhaustion or stress, but Celie was having trouble comprehending. "You won't be king?"

"No, I won't."

She struggled to absorb the implications. "What will you do?"

"I want to continue to serve on the Council. I also want to travel. Explore the universe, have grand adventures, deliver supplies to the needy. With you."

"With me?"

He framed her face between his hands, forced her to look at him. "Yes, with you. I'm not letting you get away."

Panic stirred inside her. Everything she'd ever believed, about the universe, about herself, was being systematically decimated. It was frightening—terrifying, actually—to have her belief system gone. "I don't know what to say."

He smiled, his eyes glowing. "I have a proposition for you, Captain Cameron."

Despite her trepidation, heat began snaking through her body. "What is that?"

"I believe you're a little leery of men and commitment. So I'm proposing that we give our relationship a

343

trial run. We'll travel the quadrant together and see what happens."

He knew her far too well, perhaps better than she knew herself. He knew about her father, had her thinking that maybe she could seek forgiveness for her crime, that maybe Spirit understood. His offer was tempting, oh, so tempting. . . .

He lowered his face, his mouth hovering mere millimeters from hers. His hand slid down to rest lightly on her breast. "No obligations, only a chance to make it work. What do you say?"

She was having trouble thinking clearly, especially with his thumb brushing her nipple. "Do I have much choice in the matter?" she murmured.

He molded his lips to hers, nibbled, licked. "Not really."

Spirit, what should she do? Her heart knew what it wanted, but her mind, which had dominated her for most of her life, tried to think of all the reasons a relationship with Rurick wouldn't work. Good thing her thoughts were so muddled right now. Her heart, with her body coming in a close second, won out.

She grasped Rurick's head, looked into his beautiful eyes. "I say we go for it."

His smile was brighter than a sun going nova. "Do you, now?"

"I love you," she whispered.

"And I love you." He tumbled them both to the floor, onto the plush carpet. They rolled together, laughing, until Celie took matters in hand.

She slipped on top of Rurick, straddling him, and kissed him soundly. Ripping his top open, she ran her hands over the swells of his magnificent chest. "Don't try to resist," she warned him. "It won't do you any good."

His large hands slid up to cup her hips. "I wouldn't dream of resisting, Captain."

"Smart man." Thanking Spirit for this chance, she luxuriated in the taste and feel of Prince Maximilian Rurickko Riordan. She might not be able to give him the commitment he wanted, but she intended to give him the love in her heart. Rather than telling him again how she felt, she decided to show him instead.

And she proceeded to do just that.

Epilogue

Jardonia, one season later

The Riordan grand ballroom glowed from the light of a hundred, crystal-drenched chandeliers. Thousands of vividly hued flowers overflowed the vases lining the massive hall, lending their glorious fragrances to the air. Women in glittering gowns and jewelry mingled with men in dazzling dress uniforms, all enjoying exotic delicacies and fine liquor proffered by androservers. Voices were hushed, because most of the guests were watching the ornate dance floor, where Crown Prince Sevilen Domek Riordan led his new bride through the intricate steps of a traditional Jardonian marriage dance.

Her heart filled with pride and happiness for Raven and Sev, Celie slipped her hand into Rurick's and watched the couple whirl by. Raven was a stunning bride, in a white chiffon creation that sparkled with hundreds of crystal beads. Her ebony hair had been swept up and artfully woven with diamond and crystal strands. Sevilen, in a formal white satin suit, his gold-streaked hair brushing his broad shoulders, was strikingly handsome. Blissfully happy, the couple gazed into each other's eyes, oblivious to the presence of a mere thousand guests.

Standing on Celie's other side, Nessa wiped the tears from her face. "They make a beautiful couple. I can't believe Raven is all grown up and married—to a prince, no less! I feel old."

Chase snuggled his petite wife against him. "You are *not* old, my love. As a matter of fact, you grow younger and more beautiful with every passing cycle."

Smiling, Celie scanned the ballroom, locating her sister and Sabin about ten meters away. As always, Moriah was gorgeous in a shimmering bronze dress that hugged her voluptuous figure and accentuated her glorious copper hair. Sabin, darkly handsome in his customary black, rested a possessive hand on the small of his mate's back. He and Moriah were chatting with Jade Karon, now regent of the Council, since Comar and Tasia were gone. Most likely, Jade was discussing the efficient ninth-sector delivery system that Moriah had developed and continued to supervise.

On the opposite side of the huge hall, Jarek and Eirene conversed with King Domek, while Queen Amaris stood nearby, dabbing at her eyes as she watched her youngest child and his new wife. Eirene, as slender as ever, despite the fact that she now had a son more than half a season old, turned from Domek and Jarek and placed a gentle hand on the queen's arm. The two women had taken to one another immediately—not surprising, since the serene, soft-spoken Eirene charmed everyone she met.

Celie felt a deep glow of contentment. With family and friends around, the celebration of such a special occasion, and Rurick by her side, life didn't get much better. Activity on the dance floor caught her attention and she tugged at his hand. "There's Max."

In a royal-blue dress uniform, Max looked his usual cocky self as he took Raven from Sev and whirled her away. She threw back her head, laughing at something he said. Celie was glad the andro specialists had been able to restore him thanks to newly developed Jardonian technology.

"That's our Max, all right," Rurick said affectionately. "I'm glad he's back. I really missed the old guy, although I'd never tell him that."

"I know." Celie leaned into him, enjoying the feel of his body. "They certainly didn't tone down his 'obnoxiousness program' when they repaired him. He's worse than before he was damaged."

"True," Rurick agreed. "I heard he was trying to romance one of the new female androservers, claiming he had to be sure his 'instrument' was still fully functional."

Celie laughed. "Some things never change."

"Rurick, you're looking as handsome as ever." Jade Karon swept up beside them, elegant in silver satin. She smiled at Celie. "It's good to see you, my dear. I understand congratulations are in order."

"I'm not sure what you mean," Celie said, taken aback. She and Rurick hadn't told anyone their news yet. They'd decided to keep it quiet for a while, not wanting to upstage Raven and Sev's marriage. However, someone was bound to notice sooner or later.

"You're way too modest." Jade shook a disapproving finger. "Moriah told me all about it. How exciting!"

Rurick and Celie exchanged glances. "Uh, yes," she said cautiously, wondering how Moriah could possibly have known.

"Your own art showing at Alantra Galaxy Arts on

Sarngin!" Jade enthused. "That's the most elite and respected gallery in the quadrant. I didn't even know you were an artist."

"Oh, that," Celie murmured, relief sweeping through her.

"Celie is very talented, Regent Karon," Rurick said, his pride evident. "She compounds her own paints from plant dyes, and also uses different types of colored sand. She employs some very unique techniques to create her paintings."

Very unusual, all right. Celie thought of the bursts of creativity she often experienced after making love with Rurick. Desire snaked through her, along with a staggering punch of pure need. It never ceased to amaze her how much she needed him, how she craved his smile, his touch, the total joy of being with him. The jolt that went through her every time she saw him hadn't begun to dull, even after a full season.

"Be sure and let me know when the opening is," Jade said. "I want to attend."

"I will," Celie replied. "It would be an honor to have you."

"Have you visited the ninth sector lately?" Jade asked. "The conditions are greatly improved. Who would have thought those little Tobals would be such a find?"

The furry creatures were indeed remarkable. Their telepathic links with the Enhancers had shown them to be highly intelligent. Better yet, the odd leaves they'd showered on Celie and Rurick had been further analyzed. Not only did they contain an amazing spectrum of nutrients; the leaves didn't spoil and were easy to transport. They could be boiled, baked, or ground into a meal, were readily digested, and quite tasty. The plants sporting these leaves grew in caves below Toba's surface. They produced rapidly and required little water and no sunlight.

The Tobals had been delighted to trade these valuable leaves for technology. They now owned small spaceships designed just for them, along with computers and every kind of machinery. And the ninth sector had an abundant, cheap, and nutritious food supply.

"It turns out our crash landing on Toba was a blessing in disguise," Rurick told Jade. "We've been to the ninth sector quite a few times. You and your committee have done a phenomenal job, Regent Karon."

She shook her head. "I can't take the credit. That goes to you, for bringing the situation to light, almost at the cost of your life."

"I only did what was necessary. A very special lady helped me realize we can never relax our vigilance against the darkness." Rurick's amber gaze warmed Celie. "She taught me that we all face a Shadow Crossing at some point in our lives."

"Shadow Crossing? What is that?"

His gaze returned to Jade. "It represents the embodiment of the darkest side of human nature. Both good and evil reside in each of us, along with free will to decide which we'll choose."

"You're a very wise man, Prince Rurick. I expect you to go for a seat on the Council next term." Jade patted his arm, then leaned in to give Celie a quick hug. "Creator bless you both. Now, I'd better go congratulate Prince Sevilen and his beautiful bride. Please excuse me." She moved away, the bright lights reflecting off her white, elegantly coiffed hair.

Celie blew out her breath. "She threw me with her congratulations. I thought she was talking about Mangon."

Two lunar cycles ago, she and Rurick had traveled to the planet Mangon in the ninth sector for the ceremony. They had performed it in Valera, where Rurick's mother had grown up, and where she and King Domek had met and fallen in love. Rurick even located some of his

350

mother's family, who shared stories about Queen Lisha and also witnessed the ceremony between Celie and Rurick. It had meant a lot to him to explore his family roots.

"I thought we were caught for sure," he said, laughter in his eyes. He linked his fingers with hers and raised their entwined hands to his lips. "We can't hide it indefinitely."

Sliding his fingers free, he turned her palm up and pressed a kiss to the inside of her wrist, right over the Riordan marriage crest, which had been tattooed there as a part of the Jardonian wedding vows they had exchanged in Valera. It matched the one on his wrist.

Celie felt the old, momentary flare of panic, but it was occurring less frequently and growing easier to ignore. Rurick watched her knowingly. "Regrets?" he asked softly.

The crest on her wrist was just a formality; he had commandeered her heart long before the binding ceremony. She'd only needed time to work through her fears, and he had given her that and so much more. Their time together had been wonderful.

They'd traveled to every sector of the quadrant, from the ice lands of Toba to the tropical rain forests on Perma to the mountains of Maran. They'd made deliveries to the ninth sector, witnessing the amazing turnaround there. They'd spent hours exploring the museums and art galleries on Sarngin, when they were there for Council sessions. Every cycle of their time together, she'd grown to love Rurick more.

That love had brought her happiness beyond her wildest dreams. The permanent mating ceremony had simply been a natural and logical progression of their relationship.

She shook her head, smiling. "No regrets." She stretched up to kiss her husband. "No regrets now, or ever."

Shamara
Catherine
Spangler

In a universe of darkness and depravity, the Shielders battle to stay one step ahead of the vengeful Controllers, who seek the destruction of their race. Survival depends upon the quest of one man. Jarek san Ranul has found evidence of a wormhole, a vortex to another galaxy; an escape. But when his search produces the most intriguing woman he's ever met, he finds he wants something more than duty and honor.

On the run from a mighty warlord, Eirene Kane has to protect her identity as an Enhancer, one of a genetic few with a powerful gift. Then her flight hurls her into the arms of Jarek, a man who steals her heart and uncovers her perilous secret—and though she knows she should flee, Eirene finds herself yearning for both the man and the one thing he claims will free them forever.

___52452-X $5.50 US/$6.50 CAN